DIVISIBLE MAN™
TWELFTH KNIGHT

by

Howard Seaborne

ALSO BY HOWARD SEABORNE

DIVISIBLE MAN
A Novel – September 2017
DIVISIBLE MAN - THE SIXTH PAWN
A Novel – June 2018
DIVISIBLE MAN - THE SECOND GHOST
ANGEL FLIGHT
A Novel & Story – September 2018
DIVISIBLE MAN - THE SEVENTH STAR
A Novel – June 2019
DIVISIBLE MAN - TEN MAN CREW
A Novel – November 2019
DIVISIBLE MAN - THE THIRD LIE
A Novel – May 2020
DIVISIBLE MAN - THREE NINES FINE
A Novel – November 2020
DIVISIBLE MAN - EIGHT BALL
A Novel – September 2021
DIVISIBLE MAN - ENGINE OUT
AND OTHER SHORT FLIGHTS
A Story Collection – June 2022
DIVISIBLE MAN - NINE LIVES LOST
A Novel – June 2022
DIVISIBLE MAN - TEN KEYS WEST
A Novel – May 2023
DIVISIBLE MAN - THE ELEVENTH HOURGLASS
A Novel – October 2023
DIVISIBLE MAN - TWELFTH KNIGHT
A Novel – September 2024
DIVISIBLE MAN - THIRTEEN MOONS
A Novel – Coming 2025

REVIEWS

DIVISIBLE MAN – TWELFTH KNIGHT [DM12]
A *BookLife from Publishers Weekly* Editor's Pick - "A book of outstanding quality."

"A swift vigorous action thriller in a series that continues to soar." — *BookLife*

DIVISIBLE MAN - THE ELEVENTH HOURGLASS [DM11]
A *BookLife from Publishers Weekly* Editor's Pick - "A book of outstanding quality."

"Five Stars! A brilliant, action-packed thriller..." — *Readers' Favorite*

"A lean, fast-paced, and unpredictable story...An accomplished supernatural thriller from a series that keeps on delivering...Will Stewart is one of the most believable unbelievable characters currently running in fiction."
— *Kirkus Reviews*

"...thrilling...an effervescent pace...littered with slabs of wicket humor...relentless action...full of fun...truly compelling." — *The BookLife Prize from Publishers Weekly*

DIVISIBLE MAN - TEN KEYS WEST [DM10]
"The best possible combination of the Odd Thomas novels of Dean Koontz and the Jack Reacher novels of Lee Child."
— *Kirkus Reviews*

"Five Stars! A gripping read...the outstanding writing had me hooked..."
— *Readers' Favorite*

"The soaring 10th entry in this thriller series is as exciting as the first... Seaborne keeps the chatter fun, the pacing fleet, and the tension urgent. His secret weapon is a tight focus on Will and Andy, a married couple whose love—and bantering dialogue—proves as buoyant as ever."
— *BookLife*

"The author effectively fleshes out even minor walk-on characters, and his portrayal of the loving relationship between his two heroes continues to be the most satisfying aspect of the series, the kind of three-dimensional adult relationship remarkably rare in thrillers like this one. The author's skill at pacing is razor-sharp—the book is a compulsive page-turner…"
— *Kirkus Reviews*

DIVISIBLE MAN - NINE LIVES LOST [DM9]

"Five Stars! A blend of action, mystery, and love of flying and airplanes…this is a highly recommended read." — *Readers' Favorite*

"Seaborne's latest series entry packs a good deal of mystery. Everything Will stumbles on, it seems, dredges up more questions…All this shady stuff in Montana and unrest in Wisconsin make for a tense narrative…Will's periodic sarcasm is welcome, as it's good-natured and never overwhelming…A smart, diverting tale of an audacious aviator with an extraordinary ability."
— *Kirkus Reviews*

DIVISIBLE MAN - ENGINE OUT & OTHER SHORT FLIGHTS
"This engaging compendium will surely pique new readers' interest in earlier series installments. A captivating, altruistic hero and appealing cast propel this enjoyable collection…"
— *Kirkus Reviews*

DIVISIBLE MAN - EIGHT BALL [DM8]

"Five Stars! An exhilarating thriller filled with suspense and unexpected twists…another captivating and memorable read highlighting the series' consistent ability to deliver engaging and through-provoking thrillers." — *Readers' Favorite*

"Any reader of this series knows that they're in good hands with Seaborne, who's a natural storyteller. His descriptions and dialogue are crisp, and his characters deftly sketched…The book keeps readers tied into its complex and exciting thriller plot with lucid and graceful exposition, laying out clues with cleverness and subtlety…and the protagonist is always a relatable character with plenty of humanity and humor…Another riveting, taut, and timely adventure with engaging characters and a great premise."

“Seaborne…continues his winning streak in this series, offering another page-turner. By having Will’s knowledge of and control over his powers continue to expand while the questions over how he should best deploy his abilities grow, Seaborne keeps the concept fresh and readers guessing…The conspiracy is highly dramatic yet not implausible given today’s political events, and the action sequences are excitingly cinematic…Another compelling and hugely fun adventure that delivers a thrill ride.”
—*Kirkus Reviews*

DIVISIBLE MAN - THE SEVENTH STAR [DM4]

“Five Stars! A gripping, suspenseful read that was difficult to put down.”
— *Readers’ Favorite*

“Seaborne…proves he’s a natural born storyteller, serving up an exciting, well-written thriller. He makes even minor moments in the story memorable with his sharp, evocative prose…Will’s smart, humane and humorous narrative voice is appealing, as is his sincere appreciation for Andy—not just for her considerable beauty, but also for her dedication and intelligence. An intensely satisfying thriller—another winner from Seaborne.”
—*Kirkus Reviews*

DIVISIBLE MAN - THE SECOND GHOST [DM3]

“Five Stars! A suspenseful ride...difficult to put down…I was captivated by the plot’s thrilling twists and turns from beginning to end…This story was masterfully crafted and will stay with me for a while.” — *Readers’ Favorite*

“Seaborne…delivers a solid, well-written tale that taps into the near-universal dream of personal flight. Will’s narrative voice is engaging and crisp, clearly explaining technical matters while never losing sight of humane, emotional concerns. Another intelligent and exciting superpowered thriller.”
—*Kirkus Reviews*

DIVISIBLE MAN - THE SIXTH PAWN [DM2]

“Five Stars! Fast paced and action-packed...This page-turner had me on the edge of my seat…a nail-biting book…difficult to put down." — *Readers' Favorite*

A *Booklife from Publishers Weekly* Editor's Pick: **"A book of outstanding quality."**

"Seaborne…once again gives readers a crisply written thriller. Self-powered flight is a potent fantasy, and Seaborne explores its joys and difficulties engagingly. Will's narrative voice is amusing, intelligent and humane; he draws readers in with his wit, appreciation for his wife, and his flight-drunk joy…Even more entertaining than its predecessor—a great read."
—*Kirkus Reviews*

DIVISIBLE MAN [DM1]

"Five Stars! Seaborne has knack for tension in crafting this thrilling journey…the ensemble of dynamic characters around Will had me eagerly turning pages to see who we would meet next...a must-read for fans of suspenseful thrillers…" — *Readers' Favorite*

"Seaborne's crisp prose, playful dialogue, and mastery of technical details of flight distinguish the story…this is a striking and original start to a series, buoyed by fresh and vivid depictions of extra-human powers and a clutch of memorably drawn characters…"
—*BookLife*

"This book is a strong start to a series…Well-written and engaging, with memorable characters and an intriguing hero."
—*Kirkus Reviews*

"Even more than flight, (Will's relationship with Andy)—and that crack prose—powers this thriller to a satisfying climax that sets up more to come."
—*BookLife*

THE SERIES

While each DIVISIBLE MAN ^{TM} novel tells its own tale and can be read on its own, many elements carry forward. **The novels are best enjoyed in sequence**. The pivotal short story "Angel Flight" bridges the third and fourth novels and is included with the third novel, *DIVISIBLE MAN - THE SECOND GHOST*. "Angel Flight" is also published in the *ENGINE OUT* short story collection with eleven other stories offering additional insights into the cadre of characters residing in Essex County.

Publisher's Note: DIVISIBLE MAN novels contain harsh language and are intended for mature readers. An edited PG-13 version is available for younger or more sensitive readers in the **Large Print Edition**.

SUPPORT YOUR LOCAL BOOKSELLER

The entire DIVISIBLE MAN ^{TM} series is available from major online retailers as well as the many local independent booksellers who offer online ordering for in-store pickup or home delivery.

Search: "DIVISIBLE MAN Howard Seaborne"

For advance notice of new releases and exclusive material available only to Email Members, join the DIVISIBLE MAN ^{TM} Email List at **HowardSeaborne.com**.

Sign up today and get a FREE DOWNLOAD.

ACKNOWLEDGMENTS

Thank you, John, William, Matthew, Samuel, John, Robert, Elbridge, Stephen, William, Roger, Samuel, William, Oliver, William, Philip, Francis, Lewis, Josiah, Richard, John, Francis, John, Abraham, Robert, Benjamin, Benjamin, John, George, James, George, James, George, Caesar, George, Thomas, Samuel, William, Thomas, Charles, George, Thomas, Richard, Benjamin, Thomas, Francis, Carter, William, Joseph, John, Thomas, Edward, Thomas, Arthur, Button, Lyman, and George.

For signing your own death warrant while seeing the future brightly.

For the truth.

"O Fortune, Like the moon you are changeable, ever waxing and waning. Hateful life, first oppresses, and then soothes as fancy takes it; poverty, and power it melts them like ice. Fate—monstrous and empty, you whirling wheel, you are malevolent, well-being is in vain and always fades to nothing, shadowed and veiled you plague me too; now through the game I bring my bare back to your villainy. Fate is against me in health and virtue, driven on and weighted down, always enslaved.

"So, at this hour without delay pluck the vibrating strings;
since Fate strikes down the strong man,
everyone weep with me!"

"O Fortuna" from Carmina Burana

PREFACE

THE OTHER THING

It's like this: I wake up nearly every morning in the bed I share with my wife. After devoting a religious moment to appreciating the stunning, loving woman beside me, I ease off the mattress and pick my way across the minefield of creaks and groans in the old farmhouse's wooden floor. I slip into the hall and head for the guest bathroom two doors down—the one with the quietest toilet flush. I take care of essential business, then pull up to the mirror. The face offers no surprises. I give it a moment, then picture a set of levers in my head—part of the throttle-prop-mixture quadrant on a twin-engine Piper Navajo. The levers I imagine are to the right of the standard controls, a fourth set not found on any airplane, topped with classic round balls. I see them fully retracted, pulled toward me, the pilot. My eyes are open—it makes no difference—I can see the levers either way. I close my hand over them. I push. They move smoothly and swiftly to the forward stops. Balls to the wall.

For a split second I wonder, as I did the day before, and the day before that, if this trick will work again. Then—

Fwooomp!

—I hear it. A deep and breathy sound—like the air being sucked out of a room. I've learned that the sound is audible only in my head.

A cool sensation flashes over my skin. The first dip in a farm pond after a hot, dusty day. The shift of an evening breeze after sunset.

I vanish.

Bleary eyes and tossed hair wink out of the mirror and the shower curtain behind me—the one with the frogs on it—fills in where my head had been. The instant I see those frogs, my feet leave the cold tile floor. My body remains solid, but gravity and I are no longer on speaking terms. A stiff breeze will send me on my way if I don't hang on to something.

The routine never varies. I've tested it nearly every morning since I piloted an air charter flight down the RNAV 31 Approach to Essex County Airport—but the flight never made the field. The airplane wound up in pieces and I wound up sitting on the pilot's seat in a marsh. I have no memory of the crash. The running theory is that I collided with something— something I recently found under a crush of broken trees in a winter forest. I believe that object—whatever it was—saved me and left me this way. I may never know how or why. The object is long gone. As time passes, the memory of its discovery plays like a dream.

Since the night of the crash, whenever I picture that set of levers in my mind and I push them fully forward, I vanish. Pull them back, and I reappear. It applies to things I wear, things I hold, and even other people in my grasp.

A gimmick? A party trick? A useful tool for espionage—assuming I knew anything about espionage? I don't know.

There's one aspect of this *thing* that I may never understand. On a fogbound Christmas Eve I held a dying child in my arms and made us both vanish. I found out later that the child stopped dying. That when this *thing* envelops a child fighting cancer sometimes—often—it leaves the child whole and healthy.

This *thing*—what I call *the other thing*—allows me to disappear. It defies gravity. It cures where there is no cure. It saved me.

It may kill me.

That doesn't scare me.

Far darker things greet the dawn every day.

PART I

1

Strobing LED lights mounted on the Essex Police Department SUV paled against the stark urgency illuminating Andy's face behind the wheel. The vehicle heaved to a stop on the airport ramp. My wife swung her long legs out and hit the ground running. Phone to her ear and still at a distance, she uttered words I could not hear. She darted into the open Education Foundation aircraft hangar.

I shoved back the chair at the old desk I use in the hangar. I jumped to my feet.

"Where's Pidge?" she demanded.

I knew better than to ask why. Nothing about Andy's demeanor advertised patience for dumb questions.

"No idea."

She buried her free hand in the thick curls and waves of auburn hair that flowed back from her light caramel colored forehead and cascaded over her shoulders. When she left for work less than two hours ago, her locks had been captive in a tight professional bun. I've seen this before; she unconsciously tugs her hair free in moments of high stress.

She snapped words into her phone—words I could not distinguish.

She reversed course.

Andy broke into a run toward the Essex County Air Service fixed base operation building bordering the opposite side of the wide asphalt ramp. She moved fast for a woman who just last night lifted her nightgown to show off the early second trimester baby bump peeking from her previously flat abdomen. She sprinted across the airport ramp at a pace I'd last seen when she wanted to bruise my ego by beating me to the house in the days when she drafted me to join her morning run—days before I learned to milk a healing pelvic break to avoid such predawn torture sessions.

I launched after her. My western-style boots are not made for the hundred-yard dash and my said pelvic injury grumbled, but I made a decent show of chasing my wife. I reached the glass entry to the ECAS office before the door closed in her wake. Andy disappeared into Rosemary II's office.

The Goddess of the Schedule attempted to greet her.

"Hi, An—"

"Where's Pidge? Is she here?"

I hurried around the counter and filled the door frame behind Andy. A startled Rosemary II looked up at Andy, then me.

"Pidge. Where is she?"

Rosemary II blinked her dark brown eyes. Close in age to me, the woman is everyone's mother at the air charter operation, yet she is decades older than all of us unruly children if measured solely by parental instinct. Rosemary II is rarely caught off guard and never slow to grasp rapidly evolving events. Quick assessment of Andy's tension sharpened her focus on the whereabouts of the charter service's best pilot.

"Charter flight. Mason City. Wheels up twenty-five minutes ago."

"Who's the client?"

"Private. One off. They called yesterday for a quote, then booked the flight on the spot. Out and back with six to eight hours down time. Andrea, what's—?"

Andy raised a flat hand to cut her off. She tucked her chin and pressed her phone to her ear. "Gone. Twenty-five minutes ago. She's still in the air." Andy snapped a glance in my direction for verification. I nodded. Mason City is an hour and change in the charter service's Piper Mojave. Andy listened to her phone, then spoke.

"No...Right...Agreed...I'll get that." She added, "Will's here." Her brow furrowed. "Seriously? Okay, I'll tell him." She turned to me. "It's Leslie. How quickly can you get in the air?"

"Five minutes plus the time to answer that question."

"Go."

"Dee, wh—?"

"Go!"

I took off. Instead of circumnavigating the front counter, I planted both hands on the Formica surface and swept my legs up and over, a muscle memory remnant of high school gymnastics.

Dashing to the door I shouted over my shoulder.

"I'll call on twenty-two point nine five!" If Andy didn't know what that meant, Rosemary II did.

What the hell?

2

———————

I keep the Christine and Paulette Paulesky Education Foundation hangar spotless. It's an obsession. Except for the old wooden desk at the back corner, the white acrylic floor could be a kitchen countertop. The shovels, mops, and brooms necessary for maintenance and snow removal reside in a side cabinet that stores oil, boot cleaners, flotation gear, flashlights, and the assorted tools that support flight. The usual debris found in hangars—cartons of flight magazines, old airplane parts, bits of aluminum, junked lawnmowers, and rusted snowplow blades—are banned from my domain. Seen from behind the glass wall that separates the hangar from the former corporate flight office and lounge, the hangar could be an advertisement for the sleek Piper Navajo that I fly for the Foundation. The cabinet, the Aero Tow electric tug parked along one wall, and a floor polisher that looks like a miniature Zamboni are the airplane's sole companions. On slender legs, the Navajo points her aerodynamic nose at the door, always poised for flight.

Running back to the hangar, I knew that what I was about to do qualified for the *Dangerous and Stupid* category, yet I'd game-planned the concept before. A degree of my obsession for a clutter-free hangar anticipated that one day I would execute the crazy maneuver forming in my mind.

I tossed a glance at Arun Dewar's open office door. The twenty-something boy genius behind the Foundation's finances and day-to-day operations labored inside, no doubt nose deep in his laptop. Arun applies deft practical magic to manage the Foundation's funds and distribute grants to public schools across the country. Indian by genetics, British by birth, Arun treads a narrow path in all things. He does not paint outside the lines.

He's going to have a heart attack. A flicker of perverse amusement intruded on the seriousness of the moment.

I've seen silly movies in which a cluster of deadly characters board an executive jet inside a hangar and the next thing you hear on the soundtrack is a jet engine starting up. It's absurd. Nobody starts and taxis a jet inside a hangar. The blast would blow down a wall, to say nothing of igniting a hurricane of swirling debris that would damage the aircraft.

Dangerous and Stupid.

I cut a tight corner at the Navajo's wingtip and jumped up the airstair into the airplane. I reached back and yanked up the door and latched it, then crouched my way into the pilot's seat.

Really Stupid.

Firing up the Navajo indoors would unleash a blast of propwash. If not for my obsession with having nothing—not so much as a waste basket—loose in the hangar, this would never work.

I ignored the checklist laminated against the back of a clipboard used for notes and ATC clearances. My hands flew to the switches and controls.

Master.

Mixture.

Throttles.

Prime.

Hit it.

I cranked the starter on the left engine. The props marched through less than half a turn before ignition brought the six-cylinder beast to life. The engine tried to surge but I pulled the throttle back to a rough idle. The motor bubbled and burped as if not all the cylinders had joined the cause. The oil pressure needle staggered into the green. Normally, startup is performed with both feet firmly on the brakes. Not this time. The instant the prop gripped the air the aircraft rolled.

I stole a fast look at the back of the hangar. Despite my obsession with cleanliness, a swirl of dust rolled up in the tornado generated by the prop. I looked for but did not see anything airborne and capable of damaging aircraft skin.

The wall of the hangar moved in reverse.

My attention shifted to the open hangar door. Tossing prop blast against the big overhead panels might strain the cables and pulleys. Causing the door to crash down on me would ruin my day.

The huge panels wiggled but held.

I carefully centered the nosewheel and double-checked both sides. The wingtips cleared the door frame by the same abundant margin as always. It felt closer.

The big twin-engine airplane rolled past Andy's still-flashing police SUV and into warm July sunshine. The door did not crash down behind me.

A smile tugged at the corners of my lips. I thought of Arun, blown out of fiduciary concentration by an engine startup inside the building. He would have run to the commotion and arrived in the lounge in time to see the Foundation's airplane rolling away. If not for the way Andy's heart-pounding urgency compelled me to keep moving, it would have been fun to look back and see him stand there in shock.

Clear of both the hangar and thoughts of Arun, I primed the right engine and repeated the startup procedure. She fired obediently, earning my love once more. Both props spun. I goosed the throttles to smooth out the idle and synchronize the engine RPMs. The airplane accelerated across sun bleached asphalt.

For what might have been only the second or third time in my aviation career, I ignored the pre-takeoff checklist. In its place, I deployed an old mnemonic checklist to cover the basics.

CIGARS.

Controls. I rolled the ailerons and pulled the elevator. Nothing locked. Flaps up for takeoff.

Instruments. Deferred. I planned to tune in the airport's automated weather observation service—AWOS—after takeoff to pick up the altimeter setting. The same deferment applied to programming the navigation system.

Gas. Main tanks. Auxiliary fuel pumps checked.

Attitude. I adjusted the trim wheel for takeoff.

Runup. Skip it. I knew the bird well enough to know that the usual engine runup before takeoff served mainly to warm up the engine oil. I snapped the magneto switches through a rapid cycle just to make sure both ignitions on both engines fired.

Seatbelts, doors, and switches. I flipped on the beacon and strobes, then pulled the belts across my lap and chest, and snapped the latch.

The windsock declared runway 24 active. Runway 24 was also the farthest distance to taxi for takeoff—a poor use of precious minutes. The sock also showed the wind at less than 10 knots. I rolled across the main ramp toward the much closer departure end of Runway 13.

In the calm before Andy's siren disrupted an otherwise idyllic summer day, I had heard an aircraft practicing takeoffs and landings in the traffic pattern. My choice of the non-active runway set up a potentially hazardous conflict.

I snapped on the radio master which activated the Primary Flight Display. The autopilot came alive and cycled through a self-test.

I stomped on the brakes. The aircraft stopped. Bristling against the brief delay, I held the aircraft stationary long enough to spool up the AHRS electronic attitude systems. As soon as the Primary Flight Display instructed me to "Push any button to continue" I tapped the knob and released the brakes. The attitude indicator and its gyro-driven backup showed me a digital blue sky over brown earth. The heading indicator settled on the correct heading.

The engines thundered. I grabbed the Bose headset from the hook in the overhead and tucked the ear cups over my ears. I hit the button for noise cancelling. The roar fell to a mutter.

"Test. One. Two." My voice on the intercom confirmed that the headset boom mic worked.

Someone on the radio announced a turn to base for landing on Runway 24. I recognized the call sign for one of Earl Jackson's Cessna 152 trainers—the one I had heard buzzing around the pattern.

I touched the transmit button on the yoke.

"Is that you, Glenn?"

"Hey! Good morning, stranger."

Lately I'd been out of touch with the other pilots and instructors at Earl Jackson's flight school. Glenn, a senior pilot approaching retirement, had eased away from the grind of air charter and selectively limited his flying to student instruction, at which he mastered a calm and encouraging touch.

"Glenn, I need a go-around. I gotta roll on 13. Can you do that for me?"

A moment's hesitation followed, causing me to worry that he would ask for an explanation.

"You got it. Five Four Hotel going around."

I silently thanked him for not asking questions as I crossed the hold short line at the edge of the runway. Because the taxiway joined the runway several hundred feet from the departure end, safe takeoff procedures called for a right turn to back-taxi. The rule is simple: Never waste runway.

Screw it.

I pushed the left rudder pedal and shoved the throttles forward. The Navajo heaved into takeoff position and shrugged off the unused asphalt behind the tail. Deft footwork lined up the nose with the centerline.

Throttles to the firewall.

Dashed painted lines raced under the aircraft. I looked left and saw Glenn on short final for the intersecting runway 24, a definite collision conflict. The Cessna trainer nosed up. Glenn commanded his student to initiate a go-around procedure that would have him climb in a straight line above his runway as he surrendered the right of way to me. A teachable moment and conflict eliminated.

"Thanks, man. I'll explain later. Twenty-one Tango Whiskey rolling for takeoff on runway 13, Essex County."

The tachometers and manifold pressure gauges confirmed full power.

The vacuum system gauge reported proper suction.

The airspeed needle danced to life.

I shot across the runway intersection at the center of the field. The Navajo, carrying nothing but me and full fuel tanks, leaped free of the asphalt. I settled her in ground effect and let the airspeed needle sweep past the appropriately named Blue Line.

Gear up. Go.

I lifted the big twin's nose and rolled into a tight left turn, opposite the direction of Glenn's go-around. The turn and climb quickly pointed me away from the morning sun. Westbound, I dialed a 130-knot cruise climb and a 270-degree heading into the autopilot and hit the AP button. The autopilot wrestled control from me. I adjusted the props for the climb, adjusted the engine mixture, and set out to pull the rest of my act together.

The crystal blue morning sky lacked the slightest hint of clouds. Green squares of corn, hay, and woodland stretched away under my wings. The vertical speed indicator steadied at 1,900 feet per minute. Plenty of power and not much weight. I shot through 2,500 feet over the western border of the airport.

The automated airport weather information reported the barometric pressure. I applied the setting to both altimeters and switched to 122.95 on the number one comm.

"Essex County, how do you hear One Tango Whiskey?"

"Loud and clear, Will. Here's Andrea." Rosemary II wasted no time.

"Will, are you there?"

"Affirmative." I bit my tongue against a tense *What the hell?*

"Can you call me on your phone?"

My Bose headset offers a Bluetooth connection to my phone. I don't often use it. I do not like the cockpit distraction, but this flight had all kinds of *wrong* going for it.

"Can do." I touched the Bluetooth button on the headset controller, then waited for the light to flash indicating that the phone had paired. "I take it I'm supposed to catch up with Pidge."

"Affirmative."

"Is it bad?"

"Affirmative."

"Is this coming from our friend at the FBI?"

"Affirmative. Call me."

Mentally crossing all ten fingers, I pulled out my phone, opened the screen, and touched the contact line for Andy. The connection took its sweet time before ringing in my headset. While it rang, I needlessly pushed the throttles harder against the stops, then tweaked the mixture controls.

"Can you hold for a second?" Andy didn't wait for an answer.

Jesus, Dee, you asked me to call you. I heard a beep and suspected that any second now I'd wind up talking to myself.

I scanned the engine instruments. Cylinder head temperatures in the green. Oil pressure and oil temperature in the green. The exhaust gas temps looked okay, but I fiddled with the mixture controls again to make them better than okay.

"Will, are you there?"

"Burning holes in the sky. What the hell?"

"Are we going to lose this connection?"

"Probably. I'm jumping cell towers at a hundred and fifty miles an hour." While Andy took a second to organize her thoughts, I asked, "Is Pidge in trouble?"

"Yes. Do you remember what she did in Lincoln?"

Lincoln, Nebraska.

I didn't have to dig deep to remember petite blonde Pidge in the street dancing a strip tease in front of a line of white supremacists. The scene would not fade from memory soon, if ever.

A public demonstration had ominously edged toward violence when several dozen hate mongers lined up waving Nazi and Confederate flags. Things grew dangerous when they began chanting and aggressively challenging a huge counter-protest crowd. The skinheads and tattoo canvases spoiled for a fight. Despite a police line separating the opposing viewpoints, I favored finding someplace, anyplace, else to be. Pidge had other ideas. She handed me a Bic lighter and then ran off to recruit a polka band that had weirdly joined the anti-hate protesters. Next thing I knew, the band struck up the old strip tease classic. Pidge strutted into the street in front of red-faced Nazis, dancing, pulling off her t-shirt and waving it over her head. She shook and wiggled everything she had at rows of gaping young men. Hormones overpowered hate long enough to leave them slack-jawed and staring. The white supremacist demonstration made national news but nearly every video clip highlighted a striking blonde doing a striptease dance while Nazi and Confederate flags mysteriously combusted.

One of my finest moments in the vanished state.

"Is she in danger?"

"Hang on. I'm conferencing in Leslie."

I didn't like the idea. Complicating matters with a conference call did not seem prudent.

Andy allowed no chance to protest. A moment later, the voice of Special Agent Leslie Carson-Pelham of the Federal Bureau of Investigation joined the call.

"Are you really flying right now?" Picturing her was easy. Short charcoal hair, dark eyes, a crooked smile over a runner's physique. Always the same black blouse, black slacks or jeans, and black blazer.

"I do what my wife tells me to do. What's going on, Leslie?"

I didn't expect her to share. Ever since a fringe outfit from the mob in Lincoln, Nebraska—a coffee klatch of cosplay soldiers under the banner of Company W—shot up my house, Leslie did her best to stonewall Andy and me on the topic of domestic extremists.

"We have credible intel that Pidge has been targeted."

"You can't call out the local PD and some suits from a field office? Cedar Rapids? Souix City?"

"Will," Andy said, "they've been called. But the threat may already be in play. You have *an advantage* that local law enforcement doesn't."

Andy did not need to spell it out.

"What happened?"

"There isn't time to—"

There it was—the cell tower disconnect I feared. The call dropped faster than the lead weight hitting my stomach.

Going after Pidge. Jesus.

I hit the altitude hold button on the autopilot and leveled the Navajo at 8,500 feet. The nose found the horizon. The throttles remained against the stops. At full power the engines gulped fuel.

A flashing battery warning caught my attention on the engine management system.

Dumbass. This is why we use checklists.

I snapped on the alternator switches I had missed by skipping the startup checklist. The warnings ceased.

My phone rang. I tapped the iPhone screen to take the call.

"Keep it brief. We're going to lose the connection in a few minutes. What's this credible intel?"

Leslie picked up where she left off. "A Tik Tok Detective—"

"A what?"

"An amateur internet detective. I'm cutting to the chase, Will. A young woman who posts on Tik Tok claims to be a detective and says she can identify the Lincoln Striptease Dancer."

"So can I."

"Yes," Andy interjected, "but Pidge's identity was never made public."

That much was true. After a trio of the Nazis tracked her down in a bar and narrowly missed abducting her, Pidge was persuaded not to brag about what she'd done.

"The Lincoln Stripper is an internet mystery," Leslie said. "Pidge's face wasn't clear on any of the videos. She's a cute blonde. There are lots of them. But this girl on Tik Tok has been promoting herself as an investigator and teasing that she found the famous stripper who broke up a white supremacist protest and lit all their flags on fire."

Wrong. That was me.

"She set a date to reveal Pidge's identity."

"When?"

"Tomorrow."

"That's not good," I said. "But if it's tomorrow, why the hair on fire today?"

"Four days ago, the Tik Tok girl was carjacked and abducted in Boulder, Colorado. Yesterday her bo—"

The call dropped.

Crap.

I touched the Direct button on the Garmin GTN750 navigation system and tapped in KMCW, the identifier for Mason City, Iowa. I hit "Activate" and joined a magenta line on the map screen. At the autopilot's command, the Navajo adjusted her heading.

My phone rang.

"Make it fast. I got military airspace ahead."

Leslie continued. "Around 3 a.m. local time, the girl—her body—was found on a roadside near Des Moines, New Mexico. She'd been tortured. We think Company W pried Pidge's identity out of her, then killed her and dumped her."

"So, call the cops. Call the FBI. Meet Pidge at the airport. Better yet, do that thing you did with me. Go through ATC and divert her."

"We tried. A few minutes ago, she cancelled her flight plan and dropped off the Minneapolis Center frequency. She appears to be holding a course for Mason City, but she's not responding."

"Try her on Guard. She monitors it." *Most of the time.* Pidge, like most professional pilots, monitors the emergency frequency of 121.5 on the aircraft's second radio. *Most of the time.*

"The Minneapolis controllers are trying."

Cold fingers squeezed my heart. I pushed the throttles harder against the stops and begged the airspeed indicator to climb.

"Dee, did you find out who the charter is?"

"Someone named Hansen. Rosemary II is getting me the details."

"Are you watching Flightradar24?"

"Yes. It's like Leslie said. Pidge is still on course for Mason City."

Pidge could have had any number of reasons for cancelling her IFR flight plan and dropping off the center frequency. Most were good reasons. At least one wasn't.

"You think someone booked a bogus charter to get to her?"

Leslie didn't reply. Neither did Andy.

I waited.

"You there?"

No reply. No connection.

3

———————

Two hundred knots never felt so slow. Agricultural squares and dark green woodlands crawled under the wings. I leaned into the shoulder belt, physically nudging more speed from the Navajo.

My wheels up time followed Pidge's by thirty minutes. At ordinary cruise power settings, her Piper Mojave flew a few knots faster than my Navajo. By pushing my airplane at full power, I gained a ten to fifteen knot advantage. It wouldn't matter. Even with a couple tricks up my sleeve to close the gap, I had no hope of catching her before she landed.

The break in conversation with Andy and Leslie allowed time for me to call Minneapolis Center and obtain safe passage through the Volk Military Operations Areas looming on my flight path. Center reported none of the airspaces were hot and offered Flight Following services. I politely declined, keeping my options open and minimizing communications. I stayed on the frequency in case something went awry, or in case Leslie used her FBI badge to connect with me through Air Traffic Control.

Andy's impulse to launch me in pursuit didn't make as much sense as having a small army of law enforcement officers meet Pidge on the ramp at Mason City—until I thought about it. What if Pidge's passenger spotted the reception committee and forced her to take off again? It seemed unlikely that the local sheriff or a remote branch of the FBI would have air assets able to chase her through the sky. A bad actor in the passenger seat who tipped to police presence might have the wherewithal to disable the transponder and force Pidge down to an altitude where government radar could not follow.

Company W and its brother organizations like to play with guns. They routinely use violence to deliver messages and advance their racist agenda. Any number of variables might transform the situation from bad to worse. Andy wasn't wrong. If I could catch up to her once she landed, the best move might be making Pidge disappear—right before her captor's eyes, if necessary.

If I reached her in time.

Go!

Andy's urgent command rang in my head. As always, she had been a dozen steps ahead of me.

My wife and the FBI stayed off the line. I imagined them trying to reach Pidge on her cell phone. Fat chance. Pidge religiously shuns cell phones in the vicinity of airplanes. She makes her students power down their phones before stepping on the ramp, and she teaches by example. I estimated that the earliest Pidge might be tipped off by a text would be after she delivered her passenger and stretched out on a recliner in the Mason City FBO lounge.

If she got that far.

The Navajo plowed through vacant blue sky. Alexander Field and Wisconsin Rapids slid past my left wing. I took up a fresh task—the reason I declined ATC's offer of flight following services.

My destination lay 168 nautical miles and 52 minutes ahead. I needed to shed six thousand feet to reach the traffic pattern altitude for landing at Mason City.

I did the math in my head then selected the vertical speed function on the autopilot and dialed in a 120-foot-per-minute descent. The nose dropped slightly. The airspeed needle crawled into the yellow Caution arc on the dial. My ground speed nudged 220 knots. If Pidge adhered to Earl Jackson's company policy of cruising at sixty-five percent power, I could close the gap. The added speed shaved ten to fifteen minutes off the time that would elapse between her landing and mine. I might get close enough to call her on the Mason City common frequency as she set up for landing.

One more trick slid down my sleeve. I reached back for my flight bag on the rear-facing right-side passenger seat. After fumbling with zippers and pouches, I found and deployed my iPad. Bluetooth connected the iPad to a Garmin device resting on the Navajo's glare shield. I opened the ForeFlight map screen and pinched to expand the view until it included Mason City. Tiny green triangles dotted the screen.

Traffic.

I scrolled the length of our mutual flight path and found the triangle representing the Essex County Air Service Piper Mojave flown by air charter pilot Cassidy Evelyn Page.

"Gotcha."

Less than twenty miles from Mason City Municipal Airport, the green triangle bearing the Mojave's N-number crawled across the screen.

There was no way I would catch her before the Mojave's wheels touched the earth.

4

———————

The phone rang in my headphone cups. Andy didn't wait for a greeting.
"She's deviating."

"I see it."

"You can see her?" Leslie asked. Somehow, we were still on a conference call. My wife knows her phone better than I ever will.

"Not visually. I see her on the screen."

I'd been staring at the iPad. Data showed that Pidge arrested her descent
at 4,500 feet and edged to the right of a line that would have taken her to the
Mason City airport. At first, I wasn't sure what kind of approach she
intended to execute, but it soon became apparent that her path wasn't an
approach. She skirted the Mason City airspace and continued westward.

This was not good.

"How far behind her are you?" Andy asked.

"About sixty miles. Seventeen minutes if she lands—but she's not
landing at Mason City. What do you know about her passenger?"

Leslie supplied the stats. "Male. Sixty-something. His registered address
is Hollister, which is near Antigo. No criminal record. No database hits.
Local authorities are on their way."

"Company W type?"

"Fits the profile."

I fruitlessly leaned against the shoulder belt. My ground speed decreased
by several knots, the result of headwinds stirring. I checked for the fortieth
time. Both engines produced full power.

"Well, she's officially off the flight plan and bypassing Mason City," I said. "Leslie, this Tik Tok girl…did anything actually point at Pidge?"

"We're working on it. The authorities in New Mexico only identified the body a few hours ago. She was twenty-two and lived with her parents in Colorado. We're obtaining a warrant for her home and her computer."

Twenty-two. Just two years younger than Pidge.

When I lit those flags on fire in Nebraska, I saw hate up close. Vein popping, spittle spraying hate. The kind of 24/7 hate hobby that blocks all reason, knowledge, logic, or moral doubt. In this moment, I suspected I would see shadows of the same in a mirror.

"Okay," I said. "As long as Pidge stays on the screen and doesn't pour on the coal, I have a chance. If she drops off, I'll be SOL."

Neither Andy nor Leslie replied. The call had dropped again.

5

I gained on Pidge. Substantially. My gradual descent calculations paid off. I leveled off at 2,500 feet adjacent Mason City's airspace. Leveling off caused my airspeed advantage to shrink. Pidge held her altitude. She continued west, now above me. At full power, the best I could do was shave off incremental time and miles.

Military airspace—the Crypt North MOA—spread across our path in the distance, but the chart gave it a floor of 8,000 feet, making it no factor. The map screen showed several airports ahead. If Pidge planned to land soon, her destination options thinned.

The answer came sooner than I expected. Pidge entered a steady descent toward the only airport on the map for twenty miles in any direction.

I tapped a quick text message to Andy.

Descending toward Algona Muni. 50 mi behind.

I stared at the triangle transmitted to my iPad map screen through the FAA's ADS-B system. Pidge's aircraft crawled across the display. If I stayed lucky, her marker would remain visible all the way to landing.

Chuck Yeager, one of America's greatest pilots, was reputed to have vision capable of spotting enemy planes twenty miles away. Except for airliners spitting out contrails, I've never picked out an airplane more than five miles out. Even so, I fruitlessly searched the horizon ahead.

On the iPad screen, Pidge slowed and descended. The space between us diminished.

I tuned the automated weather broadcast for the Algona Airport, caught the tail end of the broadcast, then listened from the beginning again. Winds 170 degrees at 8 knots. If she was landing, she would land southeast on runway 12. Her track aligned with a 45-degree entry to the rectangular traffic pattern's downwind leg. Her altitude readout showed her leveling off.

I texted again.

P Landing Algona.

Forty-five miles and fourteen minutes behind her.

I pushed the nose down for another descent, trading altitude for speed. Throttle balls still to the wall, my airspeed increased. Even so, I would land ten or twelve minutes behind her.

And then what?

At best, I would roll onto the ramp after she unloaded her passenger. Or after they unloaded her. Was someone waiting? What if I arrived and she was already gone? What if I arrived overhead in time to see her shoved into a vehicle and carried off? What then? Land? Stay airborne and chase some unmarked van? What if I saw nothing?

I tapped in the common traffic frequency for Algona.

Do I call her? Do I let her know I'm here?

Pidge would recognize my voice and call sign. What if her passenger was listening? Pidge might not be in command. A warning would be pointless—or worse. Speaking up might erase the slender advantage I possessed in surprise.

Her voice broke the radio silence. Pidge calmly announced entry to the Algona Municipal traffic pattern. The smooth and professional transmission carried no hint of stress.

The next twelve minutes took forever. In that time, I watched the green traffic triangle enter downwind, turn base, then turn final and descend to the runway where it vanished. Pidge made calm radio calls at all the appropriate points in the pattern.

I texted Andy.

She landed Algona.

I blew through the traffic pattern altitude ten miles out. Still roaring at over 200 knots, I sank to less than 500 feet above Iowa's tabletop landscape. The iPad showed no other triangles in the area, but that didn't guarantee an absence of traffic. Any number of aircraft could fly the traffic pattern or traverse the area without transmitting their position into the ADS-B system. I vigorously scanned the air ahead and to each side, upgrading my vigilance since I was the idiot violating standard pattern protocols.

Algona Municipal Airport slid into view. I searched for and spotted the Mojave parked on an empty ramp. Two vehicles nudged the cluster of buildings and hangars. I scanned the road connecting the airport with a nearby highway. No sign of movement. No windowless vans lurking on the ramp or racing away.

I violated half a dozen standard practices on the landing. I flew the downwind leg low and without reducing speed, then cranked into a hard half circle at over 45 degrees of bank. The rollout lined me up on final approach. Despite potential shock cooling to the engines, I chopped the throttles and begged the speed to bleed off. The landing acquired the earmarks of an overshoot.

At the maximum speed allowed, I dropped the wheels into the wind. Drag from the hanging gear and windmilling props produced deceleration that pushed me against the seat straps.

Airspeed bled away. I lowered the flaps. More deceleration. I shoved the aircraft nose down and rode a steep glide path. The runway threshold climbed in the windshield. The airspeed needle took its bloody time wiggling down to a still-hot approach speed. I took the high speed into account and aimed for a collision with the earth a hundred yards short of the runway.

"Final gear check—green," I called out to myself. Wheels down. Full flaps. At least I wouldn't belly land the airplane in my haste. The runway looked uncomfortably short. Skidding into corn at the far end wasn't out of the question.

I raised the nose and flared out. Excess speed bled off rapidly. I planned for it. The painted runway number 12 swept beneath me. Inches above the asphalt, the Navajo ran out of flying speed. The main wheels greased themselves onto the pavement. The nose settled. I pulled back the yoke and stood on the brakes. Despite aggressive braking, the rollout consumed most of the runway.

When speed permitted, I pulled a tight one-eighty and roared into a fast taxi for the mid-field turnoff. Earl's Mojave sat on the ramp looking abandoned. If this had been Mason City and nothing amiss, I would have found Pidge attending to post-flight duties after delivery of a paying passenger. But Pidge was nowhere to be seen.

I abused the power and the brakes and swung into position beside her airplane, killing both engines with a pang of regret that I had not taken the time to open the cowl flaps and let them cool. The flaps still hung from the wings—another sign of carelessness induced by haste.

I clicked out of my seat straps, grabbed my summer flight jacket, and jumped from the airplane with my phone in hand. The warm humid air hung silent in stark contrast to my thunderous arrival. The airport showed no sign of life.

My phone rang. I swiped.

"I'm on the ground. Plane's here but I don't see her. Call you back." Andy and Leslie would have to wait.

I pocketed the phone.

I jogged across the ramp and hopped up the steps of a small building that shared the property with a row of hangars. A screen door raised my spirits. If the building had been unattended, the heavy inner door would have been closed and locked.

The screen door slapped shut behind me. My eyes adjusted to the dark interior of a typical Fixed Base Operation office with all the trappings. The old worn carpet. The chipped Formica counter fronting a cluttered office. Second-hand furniture. A Coke machine that dispensed classic glass bottles. Nicotine yellowed the walls and ceiling.

A shock of bright red hair paired to a freckled face popped up from behind the counter. I cut off his greeting.

"The pilot of that plane that just landed—where did she go?"

The kid blinked at me. "Which plane?" He looked out the window. The Foundation's Navajo faced us beside Earl's Mojave, a fraternal twin.

"The other one."

"You mean that girl?" He sounded like he'd never seen one fly a plane before, let alone one wearing a shirt, tie, and epaulets.

"Yeah. The girl. Where did she go?"

The kid grinned like he'd just encountered the one quiz question he could answer without guessing. He jerked a thumb at the door on the parking lot side of the building.

"They took the crew car."

They?

The knot in my chest tightened. "Please tell me you have some idea where they went."

"Sure. Up to the church picnic. I can give you a ride. I'm going there myself."

6

———

"Just gimme a minute to lock up."

I pressed. "It's urgent. Sooner is better than later."

"Ah, screw it. I don't need to lock up. I'm coming back." The kid grabbed keys from the cluttered desk and said, "Lessgo. I'm Ronnie, by the way."

"Will."

"Nice to meetcha, sir."

Ronnie led me through a back door to a rust-colored Oldsmobile parked outside the office. The second vehicle I'd seen from the sky was gone.

"What are they driving?" I hopped onto the front seat.

"Crew car. My uncle's '89 Taurus. This chariot belongs to my mother." Ronnie started the car and threw the column shifter in gear. We lurched out of the parking lot. Driveway potholes bottomed out the shocks with hard bangs. I pulled out my phone. The rough ride challenged my aim at the screen buttons.

My call connected with Andy. I filled her in.

"What church picnic?"

"What church picnic?" I asked Ronnie.

"The Baptist Church hunnert n' fiftieth annual summer picnic." He sounded surprised that I didn't know. I passed the answer to Andy.

Andy's brief silence reflected my own bewilderment.

"I tried her phone. Straight to voicemail," I said.

"Same here. Are you sure she went with Hansen?"

24

"That's the word here. If she's not at this picnic or I can't get a line on her, you better call in the cavalry."

"I already called the sheriff's office."

"What happened to Leslie?"

"She's on the phone with her people in Colorado."

"And?"

"It's bad, Will. Look after our girl, okay?"

"She does a decent job all by herself, but yeah. I'll find her."

We traded "I love you" signoffs, which Ronnie pretended not to hear. I pocketed the phone.

Ronnie pushed the old Cutlass up to a blazing forty miles per hour. The town of Algona spread out to meet us. We passed an AmericInn, a Dollar General, and a huge lawn fronting sheet metal sheds belonging to an industrial property. At an intersection marked by a Sinclair station Ronnie turned left. A wide highway exited the town northbound. I glanced back at the gas station. A green dinosaur lurked in a small garden at the corner of the lot. It reminded me of another Sinclair station I'd seen months ago in Louisiana. That one had been abandoned.

The association did not give me comfort.

Ronnie rolled on. Iowa's flat expanse spread to the horizon. Sparse properties lined the broad highway. Random homes mingled with businesses I could not identify. Soon the inevitable corn closed in, well past knee high.

"Are you sure they're going to this picnic?" I asked my driver.

"That's what that minister guy said. The one with your lady pilot."

"Minister? You recognized him?"

"Never saw him before."

"What makes you think he's a minister?"

"I think that's what he said."

"Any idea why she went with him?"

Ronnie shrugged. "Uh…'cuz they got a big barbecue? That's why I was gonna go. For lunch. All the other churches in town bring stuff. Cakes and bakery and stuff. Pretty good eats. I skipped breakfast this morning, on account'a because."

Nothing Ronnie said meshed with the fear gnawing at my diaphragm. The whole thing sounded surreal. I could not imagine why a would-be kidnapper relied on an airport crew car for his getaway. Claiming a church picnic as a destination had to be misdirection. Pidge and her kidnapper were probably headed in the opposite direction. I made a mental note to give Andy a description and license number for the crew car.

The nerves at the back of my neck danced when a pickup truck with a Confederate flag decal dominating the back window roared past us.

I've grown paranoid and prejudiced. Since the brave American patriots of Company W shot my house to pieces, parts of the country I once relished for rural flavor and the wholesome lifestyle I grew up in now feel to me like havens for men whose beliefs had been pretzel twisted until they justified opening fire on the home of a law enforcement officer.

The home of the woman I love—the woman carrying our child.

Andy was not pregnant when the bullets tore through our walls last winter, but the fact that she now carried our child colored the past as well as the present and future. I felt a creeping vulnerability and a growing need to protect my wife, my family. I said nothing to Andy about it because she would have patted me on the head, told me I was cute, and explained that she would handle security in the Stewart family.

Rattling up the highway in the old Cutlass in pursuit of Pidge, I wondered how much my new perspective as a future father accounted for the knot in my chest.

7

———————

S everal acres of chrome and glass threw solar glitter back at the empty blue sky. Beside a white wooden church topped with a box-like steeple, a recently cut hayfield augmented the church parking lot. Cars filled half a dozen double rows. Kids in orange vests guided newcomers to parking through a snow fence channel. Ronnie slowed and turned in, then followed artfully orchestrated baton instructions. The Cutlass's shocks beat a steady cadence over rough ground.

"There." He pointed.

I had no idea what he meant.

"That's Uncle Bob's Taurus." We rolled past the trunk of a faded blue Ford.

"That's the crew car?" I swiveled and snapped a photo with my phone. This time Andy could not chastise me for failing to get the license number.

"Uh-huh. It's a piece of you-know-what. Sucks up a quart of oil a week. But it's got almost a quarter million miles on it and it keeps on going." I twisted in the seat and searched the field for signs of a petite blonde in a pilot's white shirt and tie.

Why here? Combinations and permutations of criminal intent ran through my mind. Did they come to rendezvous with another vehicle? To ditch the easily identified crew car and drive off in something unknown? A parking lot offered a good place to swap cars, but a parking lot full of disembarking families guided by teenaged parking attendants seemed a poor choice. And what about Pidge? Was she compliant? Resistant? The girl

27

could be a fireball when provoked. She would have no inhibitions about making a scene.

Each new scenario arrived at the dark conclusion that Pidge's trail ended in an Iowa hayfield.

A girl in a midriff knotted shirt and tight shorts waved us into a parking space. I held up my phone.

"Ronnie, what's your number?"

"Huh?" He stared at the parking girl. She threw him a smile and moved to the next space.

"Your phone number." I waved my device at him.

"Oh." He shook his gaze loose from long tan legs and rattled off the number.

"Thanks." I fished a twenty from my wallet and shoved it into his palm. "Lunch is on me. Do me a favor. Promise you won't leave without me."

"Sure thing. Are you going to—?"

I didn't wait for him to finish. I piled out of the Cutlass and took off across the clover stubble. Despite a temperature hovering in the mid-eighties, I shrugged on my flight jacket and patted the front pocket to confirm possession of a pair of flashlight-shaped devices.

BLASTERs.

Basic Linear Aerial System for Transport, Electric Rechargeable.

Propulsion. The plastic tubes contained rechargeable batteries and a small electric motor. The same pocket contained two six-inch carbon fiber model aircraft propellers that snapped onto the shaft of the electric motor.

I needed to vanish.

Vanishing and kicking free of gravity promised a bird's-eye view from which to search for Pidge. The power units provided the thrust and directional control I needed for a rapid grid search.

I looked around. Not here. Too open. Too many witnesses.

The steady flow of people disembarking from their vehicles angled back the way we had come. I moved with the stream and watched for any vehicle leaving the parking lot. Cars rolled in, but none bucked the tide and lined up to leave.

At the snow fence entrance, I stopped and took stock.

The church stood alone on this stretch of the road. A small gravel parking lot bordered three sides of the white building. The permanent lot seemed tiny compared to the hayfield full of cars. Sunday service attendance probably never hit summer picnic levels.

A riot of color sprouted at the back of the church and spread into another section of the hayfield. An avenue of tents, some striped, some with flags and streamers, some mere pop-up canopies, covered an assortment of tables loaded with garage sale bargains, crafts, and food. The avenue led to a cluster of carnival rides—the small ones, the ones meant for children.

Beside the largest of the tents, smoke rose from a military grade barbeque tank mounted on a heavy steel trailer frame. The big top sheltered rows of wooden picnic tables. At the far end, a trio of graybeard rockers lived out their dream of playing tunes from their youth. Tunes about cars and girls and summer beaches. The music carried throughout the celebrational sprawl via speakers mounted on poles. Backing up the band, outside of the tent, a row of polished chrome and hand-buffed classic cars invited enthusiasts to *Look But Don't Touch*. Owners sat beside their babies in nylon lawn chairs, taking questions and soaking up sunlight.

The crowd thickened among the tents. People of all ages and sizes strolled or lingered over bakery and quilts and crafts. Sprinkled among the colorful throng of men, women and children in summer shorts and t-shirts were people in period costume. Women wore dresses and bonnets appropriate to a night out on the wagon train. Men wore heavy wool suits over stiff white shirts and collars, topped with an assortment of hats, including a few cowboy Stetsons.

The atmosphere said country fair more than church picnic.

In the shadow of God's house, something sinister moved through my plane of vision. Men, some alone, some in pairs, caught my eye. A few traded glances with me. Some wore camo shirts or pants. Some wore hats embroidered with political statements. A boldly imprinted t-shirt told me what I could do with my commie liberal ass. Another displayed the Gadsden flag and its artfully coiled pit viper. A third stretched stars and bars across a bulbous beer belly and declared Dixie would rise again. Others simply wore dusty hats with farm implement logos whose purpose was no more sinister than preventing the sun from burning the forehead—just as I had done as a kid throwing bales of hay from a wagon onto a rattling elevator. I fought my presumptions and paranoia and told myself that these were just folks, just the faithful enjoying church without a sermon.

Yet I had no way to be certain. The skin on my arms sprouted goose flesh.

Pidge was nowhere to be seen.

8

———————

I needed to get off the ground. I looked for a secluded spot to disappear.

A row of Port-O-Let cabinets lined the edge of the grounds. Not the best idea, but better than winking out of sight with twenty people watching. I diverted from the stream of humanity entering the tent avenue. People waited for one of the plastic flags mounted on the blue door handles to flip from *Occupied* to *Vacant*. Business was booming.

While I looked around for another place to slip out of sight, a brown and white Sheriff's Department patrol car rolled off the highway. The marked sedan bypassed enthusiastic baton wavers at the hayfield entrance and crunched across the Church's gravel parking lot.

My phone rang. Andy.

"Hey."

"Did you find her?"

"No. But the crew car is here and so are the cops. I was just about to start a search." The squad car cruised slowly toward me.

"Leslie is coordinating with local officials. They know you're there, so identify yourself to them."

That wasn't my plan. Connecting with the deputy would slow me down.

The sheriff's car rolled directly toward me then angled into a parking space at the back of the church. The deputy took a moment to tidy up his shop before he extracted his tall frame from the unit. Young and handsome in a nicely fitted tan uniform, he snagged glances from passing teenaged girls who flashed smiles and giggled at each other. He didn't bother with a hat or sunglasses, or with returning the flirtations.

We made eye contact. He walked toward me.

"You want me to stay on the line?" Andy asked.

"Please." I saw an advantage to handing my phone to the deputy and letting Andy handle him. "Stand by." I nodded at the uniformed officer.

"Are you William Stewart?" His guess struck me as impressive until I considered my appearance in Ray Bans and a green Air Force summer-weight flight jacket.

"I am."

"Deputy Pat Shelby. Understand we have a possible critical abduction?"

"We do."

He examined our surroundings again. "The FBI alerted our department. Where do you fit into this?"

I explained, including the slow road chase in Ronnie's Cutlass. He cracked a thin smile.

"Yeah, I know Ronnie." He settled an appraising gaze on me. "Lemme nail down a few details before we go off halfcocked here. We're looking for a white female? Early twenties? Blonde? A little under five feet?"

"Affirmative."

"And she's dressed up like a pilot?"

"She is a pilot."

"Right. She's in uniform? White shirt with the stripes on the shoulders?"

"That's her."

"Does she like barbecue?"

Shelby's expression went blank. This was a waste of time. I needed to get away from this useless interrogation and get airborne. If this deputy refused to take the matter seriously—if he thought Pidge got herself abducted because she wanted a bite of church picnic barbeque—things were headed south between me and the local law.

"You mean because she came *here*?"

He shook his head slowly. A thin smile spread on his lips. I lifted my phone thinking I would put it on speaker and hand him off to an officer of the law with more rank and sense, if not jurisdiction.

Jerk. Let Andy deal with him. I needed to get on with my aerial search.

"Look, you should—"

Someone tapped me on the shoulder. I caught a whiff of smoked pork.

"What the fuck are you doing here?"

I turned around.

Pidge took a bite out of a sandwich the size of her head.

9

———————

"It's a crime they're not selling beer here." Pidge used both hands and repositioned the dripping sandwich. She took another ravenous bite. "Mmmff-ufff-uff-gooo."

"Not that you could drink any."

She shrugged.

It had taken a few minutes to mix apologies with explanations for the deputy, who reported all of it back to his dispatcher after he took down names and examined IDs. I gave Andy the news and said I would call her back. The deputy engaged in a phone conversation with his office—at least part of which consisted of taking a food order—before he strolled to the line forming for barbecue. Pidge tugged me under the big tent. The band had gone on a break, facilitating reasonable conversation.

"What the hell are you doing here?" I threw her own question back at her.

Bad timing. Her mouth was full. She signaled for me to hold my horses and then led me to a table crammed with people. Men and women twice my age engaged in animated conversation with a tall, thin man in a suit—the first I'd seen that wasn't a costume. On approach, the man broke his train of thought and looked up at Pidge who chewed rapidly, swallowed, and spoke.

"Will, this is Mr. Hansen. His father was the minister here for—how long did you say?"

"Thirty-eight years." Hansen rose such as the picnic table would allow and shook hands with me. "Nice to meet you, Will. How do you know my intrepid pilot, Miss Page?"

"Oh," Pidge interrupted, "I taught him everything he knows about flying. He's a slow learner, though. A couple hundred more hours and we might let him solo."

I smiled.

Hansen smiled back but with a note of confusion. Questions I did not want to answer teetered on his tongue.

"If you'll excuse us, I need a word with Pi—Miss Page. Nice to meet you." I pulled Pidge to an empty table. We faced each other across weathered wooden planks.

"Answer my question first," she said between bites. "What the fuck are you doing here?"

I rattled off a summary starting with Andy's panicked interruption of a quiet Saturday morning at the hangar. Pidge munched on her dripping pulled pork sandwich. Her expression grew darker by degrees when I explained the part about Lincoln, Nebraska and the Tik Tok girl. I withheld the grim news out of New Mexico.

"This chick says she knows it was me?"

"Sounds like. Tell me about Hansen. What's his deal?"

"Like I said—his dad was the minister here. He grew up in town. He's kind of a celebrity with this crowd so they invited him to the picnic, except it's something like a seven-hour drive, so he decided to try air charter. Ta-dah!"

"Why didn't he book the charter directly here? What's up with Mason City?"

"First time in a small plane. He never chartered before. He thought he had to fly to the big city airport. We got to talking and he asked me if I knew how to get him a rental car. He was going to rent a car and drive the rest of the way. Hang out here for a while, then drive back. I told him there's an airport right in Algona with a car you can use for a few bucks in gas money. He didn't know that. Saved him some money and a few hours of fooling around and I get this amazing barbeque in the bargain."

I shook my head and sighed.

"Seriously, you should get some." She pointed at a growing line at the other end of the tent where Deputy Shelby shuffled closer to his lunch.

I surveyed the Company W types mingling in the crowd and thought about a young woman who died because she knew or pretended to know the identity of the Lincoln, Nebraska Stripper Girl staring at me from the other side of a picnic table.

Pidge read the seriousness in my expression.

"Stewart, you can't really think this shit is real, can you?"

I didn't answer. I looked at hats and read slogans on t-shirts. I studied the faces of young men mugging for cute girls, and old men chatting while wives fingered quilts and read labels on jars of jam. I probed for the malice that had paraded on the capital square in Lincoln, Nebraska bearing flags representing civil war, slavery, and mass murder. Pidge had a valid point. Nobody screamed hate chants here. Nobody looked for a fight. Neighbors mingled. Children darted toward the kiddie rides. Churchgoers gathered for a swell time at God's house.

A Norman Rockwell day in what the pundits and politicals call Real America. Was it me? Was I seeing things?

On tents and poles above everyone's heads, large and small U.S. flags flapped in light summer wind. My flag. Their flag.

Why was I seeing enemies everywhere I looked?

"I don't know, Pidge. I really don't. But here's what I do know: Until we figure this out, you don't leave my sight. And Hansen rides with me back to Essex."

10

Nothing happened.

Hansen, the son of a Baptist minister and—I would learn on the flight home—a retired actuarial for the Wisconsin Physicians Service Insurance Corporation, had never heard of Company W and did not recall any news stories about a private residence in Essex getting perforated in the middle of a winter night. He confessed that his news consumption ended at gossip printed in his hometown shopper. I learned through gentle probing that he also missed the story of a plane crash near Essex where the pilot miraculously survived falling to earth without a parachute. I sensed he was on a short path to figuring out said pilot was me, so I steered our conversation to his childhood in central Iowa. I probed the perils of committing mischief while his father shepherded the community flock down the narrow path of God's Word. He told a thrilling tale of a stolen tractor and hay wagon, a girl, and first kisses in moonlight—although by kisses I think he meant something more intimate—and how a posse of church elders and angry mothers tracked down the smitten teen couple and brought a wonderous starlit night crashing back to earth with talk of a shotgun wedding.

The look on his face betrayed undiminished warmth embedded in the memory.

By the time the Navajo's wheels squeaked onto the paved surface of runway 24 at Essex County Airport, I felt confident that Hansen came as advertised. I offered to fly him to Antigo, near his hometown, but he reminded me that he had driven his car to Essex. We parted on the ramp over a handshake. Rosemary II met him at the office door while I retrieved the tug to push the Navajo back into the Foundation hangar.

Pidge, who had taken off first, used the speed advantage of the Mojave to land well ahead of me. I contributed to the gap by babying the Navajo's engines on the way home to make up for the hard charge west.

Just as I tucked in the airplane and lowered the Foundation hangar door, Pidge ducked under the descending panels. She had changed from her uniform into a t-shirt and cutoff jeans.

"Are you gonna explain this clusterfuck today?"

"You already know most of what I know."

"Fu—!" She interrupted herself. "Wait a minute. *Most* of what you know? What are you leaving out?"

The big door crept down at its slow loris pace. Reaching the bottom and sealing, the motor stopped. My phone chirped.

"Hang on." I avoided answering the question. I read the text then held up my phone. "You need to follow me home. Andy wants to talk to you. She will probably have the FBI on speakerphone."

Pidge shot a glance at Arun's office door. "Uh-uh. I have plans."

"Pidge, the threat to reveal your identity is real."

An argument dangled on her tongue but didn't muster steam to launch. "Dammit."

"You'll follow me home?"

A perfunctory f-bomb answered in the affirmative.

She marched past me and into the hangar lounge. At Arun's office door, she flipped me the finger, then transformed herself into the image of a Disney princess, crowned with a sparkling smile she carried into his office.

11

____

"Let's make this quick." Pidge swiped her car door shut after parking behind me in the farmhouse yard.

"Plans with your British boy toy?"

"He's taking me to Leander Lake for a moonlight paddleboat tour. I need to go home and change." She plucked at the front of a t-shirt that advertised a metal band I'd never heard of. The t-shirt announced a world tour in 1983, which explained why.

"Looks to me like you're dressed for the occasion. Didn't you get drunk and sink one of those bicycle boats a couple years ago?"

"I've never been on a paddleboat. It sounds quite romantic."

"You did. You and some of your friends staged an aquatic demolition derby."

She stopped in her tracks. "Say one word to Arun about that and I will demolition derby your ba—"

"Hang on." I watched a silver Chevy sedan turn into the driveway. The face behind the wheel resolved in the angled sunset light.

"Isn't that your FBI pal?" Pidge asked.

"Uh-huh." Even before she stopped the car and stepped out, I saw something I'd never seen on Leslie's narrow face. She looked stricken. Pale. Her expression did not carry relief reflecting the fact that the object of our high-speed morning search stood safely beside me.

Leslie departed the rental and hooked a satchel strap over one shoulder. She hurried ahead of us and up the back steps.

37

"Inside." Her command carried no greeting. No explanation. No comment about Pidge's safety. Pidge and I traded wide-eyed glances and followed.

We found Andy in the kitchen mirroring our bewildered expressions. Leslie ignored my wife and scrounged our kitchen cabinets.

"I thought you were in Colorado," I said.

"I thought you were in Chicago," Andy added.

"I was. Everybody sit."

Leslie found a tumbler and a bottle of Scotch that had not been touched since before our trip to Key West. She poured several fingers, then doubled it. After a healthy gulp, she slid onto the last seat at the counter-height kitchen table. She downed another gulp then turned to Pidge.

"I'm glad to see that you're okay, Miss Page."

Pidge flared her eyes and shrugged awkwardly. "I never blew up that shit in Lincoln on social. I never posted anything on account it got a little hairy right afterward when those guys followed me into that bar around the time Stewart showed up. I figured it was best left alone."

"Good thinking."

"This Tik Tok thing…did it point a finger at Pidge?" I asked.

Leslie stared down at the tumbler. She shook her head. "No. The girl in Colorado had it all wrong. She was way off."

"Well, that's a supersized relief. I guess I…can…" The words melted away in Pidge's mouth.

We all saw it. Cold glitter in Leslie's eyes matched the frigid look on her pale face.

"Leslie, what is it?" Andy pressed a hand to Leslie's arm.

The FBI agent downed another hit of Scotch.

She pressed her eyes shut.

She said nothing for a moment.

When she spoke, I wished she hadn't.

"Tik Tok girl had it wrong. She didn't ID Pidge. She manufactured a flimsy case around a college co-ed in Texas. A girl who looks a lot like you, Miss Page. Your height. Your build. Your hair. A girl who liked to dance. A girl who posted a harmless striptease dance like the one you did. She … um… they… they got her ID from the Tik Tok girl."

"Is she okay?" Andy asked. "The girl in Texas?"

Leslie shook her head.

"Kidnapped?" I asked.

"No." Ice in Leslie's eyes melted. A drop ran down her cheek. "They burned her."

12

They burned her.

Three simple words seared with heat all their own.

Leslie made no effort to add detail or paint a picture. Andy held her tongue. Pidge glared but could not speak.

Leslie gulped more scotch. I made plans to confiscate her car keys.

"Your life is going to change," she told Pidge. "Steps must be taken to ensure your safety." To Andy she said, "There's an online briefing in the morning managed by the SACs from Chicago, Denver, and Dallas. It will be joined by Texas authorities and by Director Simmons in D.C."

"Am I included?" Andy asked.

"Passcodes for you and Chief Ceeves will be emailed."

Leslie paused. I thought she might polish off the last full shot of scotch, but instead she stared at the glass and stroked her index finger around the lip.

"There's a video."

No one spoke.

"They emailed it to the Texas AG's office in Austin. The video claims to be from Louis Blaze."

"Who the fuck is Louis Blaze?" Pidge demanded.

I knew but didn't reply. Leslie fielded the question.

"Louis Blaze is the head of the snake, Miss Page. He's the self-appointed commandant of Company W—"

"Those ass clowns that shot up this place last December?"

"Yes."

"I thought they were just a handful of jerkoff gun nuts."

"Company W is a consolidation of at least three and probably more hate groups. Louis Blaze congealed the organization after his would-be son-in-law was assassinated five minutes before he was to wed Blaze's daughter. Since the shooting, Blaze has gone to ground, but he hasn't shut up. He's been messaging that the government sanctioned the hit and that he's next on the list. It's a lie that's stirring up the usual breathless hysteria among extremists and on fringe media."

I didn't need to close my eyes to render a Cinemascope image of Louis Blaze's shellshocked daughter sitting on a lawn chair in a white wedding dress spattered with the blood and brains of her fiancé. I floated less than twenty feet from Darryl Spellman when his head exploded.

"We saw the daughter. A few months ago," I reminded Leslie. "In Louisiana."

Andy asked, "Was she the young woman beaten nearly to death on that boat?"

I nodded. A few hours after a meeting that Leslie and I monitored at an abandoned Sinclair gas station—*Sin lair*, the rusted sign read—six men were murdered on a private boat. Given their affiliation with the shooters at our house, I did not muster any grief until Leslie revealed that one of them was an agent of the FBI, deep undercover. Of those gathered on the boat, only Blaze's daughter survived, badly beaten, left near death.

The affair was never fully explained to me. Leslie went dark on the subject. A matter for the FBI, she insisted.

I did not think that was the case any longer.

They burned her.

Someone's child. Someone's BFF. A girl who probably never heard of Louis Blaze or Company W—or of a Tik Tok detective wannabe who cobbled together a conspiracy theory story and pointed a finger at someone whose only crime was dancing a silly striptease online.

They burned her.

Someone cute and funny and full of life.

Someone who might have been Pidge.

Pidge sat ashen and angry. "Are you saying this Blaze motherfucker is coming after me?"

Leslie pushed away the tumbler, leaving the last shot of scotch untouched.

"Only if he realizes his mistake."

13

The words kept me awake—
They burned her.

—or kept waking me. I could not tell. I rolled over a few times, then reached through darkness to where Andy slept. Her mattress real estate lay vacant.

The upstairs bedroom runs warm in the summer. I slept in boxers under a single sheet. Thus attired, I slipped out of bed and padded downstairs where marginally cooler air kissed the sweat on my skin. The French doors to the front porch hung open. Crickets broadcast a Motown *Wall of Sound* chorus outside the porch screens.

Andy stretched her long legs on my lounge chair. Thin starlight rendered her sleek lines and curves as a jeweled outline. She didn't startle when I stepped out of the dark. The creaks and groans of the old hardwood floor announced my coming. She slid over and patted the cushion. I assumed my usual station beside her. She tucked her shoulder under my arm and eased her head onto my chest.

We didn't speak for several minutes. Our shallow breathing synchronized. I stroked the warm skin of her upper arm and lower back.

I thought about the cold silence that concluded Leslie's kitchen table briefing. None of us found words except for Pidge, who issued an f-bomb and stalked out. A moment later tires bit the pavement at the end of the driveway and punctuated Pidge's one-word response to the grim news. Leslie followed her soon after.

Lying beside Andy, I broke the silence with the same word Pidge used.

Andy answered somberly. "Leslie says the video resembles a jihadist execution."

"Don't let her make you watch it."

Andy sighed, balancing her personal life against professional duties.

"I'm serious, Dee. Don't."

She snuggled closer. "You know Cathy? Cathy Wold? She's one of the teachers Sandy works with. Second grade, I think."

"Sure." I had no idea.

"Cathy was pregnant a few years ago."

"Wasn't me. I'm good at this, but I swear it wasn't me."

"Noted. Sandy told me something Cathy shared. She said during Cathy's pregnancy she watched children's movies with her first little boy. Their favorite was *The Muppet Movie.* You know that beginning part where Kermit sings about rainbows?"

"Uh-huh." I knew the movie, the song, and Kermit.

Andy lay still for a minute or two. Or three. Long enough to make me wonder if she fell asleep in the middle of her story.

She resumed just above a whisper as if someone might overhear her. "When she was pregnant Cathy cried during that song. No reason. She couldn't help it. Hormones, I suppose. It never happened before, but during her pregnancy, the song touched her in a way that overwhelmed her with sadness."

"Okay." Sometimes Andy sets me up for a question. If this was one of those times, I had no idea what to ask.

"So, Cathy had the baby—the second baby—another boy. And as he got a little older, this past spring, she sat down with both kids to watch *The Muppet Movie* again. And the little one—as soon as Kermit's rainbow song started—the little one began to cry. Out of the blue." Andy found my hand and pressed our fingers to her abdomen. "Cathy said she asked what was wrong, and he said he didn't know. He only knew that the song made him really, really sad."

Tales from the crib. I didn't comment.

Andy stroked her tummy. "Do you think it feels my emotions? Inside?"

"Maybe. They have no verbal or visual cognition. No words or images. All the baby has is its connection to you."

Andy said nothing for a long time. Then…

"I won't watch it."

14

Headlights swept the yard. The white light flashed red through my closed eyelids. Andy alerted faster than me. She sat up on the lounge chair, a move that harmonized metallic creaks and groans with the grind of driveway gravel under tires. The car accelerated to the side of the house then braked sharply.

A car door slammed. I found my feet and hurried to the side window for a better look. If I hadn't recognized the car, I would have recognized the short blonde hair bobbing toward the back steps.

Andy hurried through the house to meet Pidge at the mudroom door.

A tiny, helpless voice, strained by pain, met Andy in the dark. *"It was my fault…it was my fault…"*

Andy's silhouette merged with the smaller figure. Two women folded into each other's arms. Sobs broke, a torrent of them. The sound stayed my hand from flicking on the kitchen light.

The wounded sound escaping Pidge was like nothing I'd ever imagined possible from this hard-as-nails young woman. She buried her face against Andy's shoulder and cried. Unrestricted. Unabashed. Andy held her tightly against tremors that wracked her body. Neither woman acknowledged me in the dark.

I went to put on pants.

. . .

HALFWAY DOWN THE STAIRS, tugging a t-shirt over my head, a second set of headlights swept the front lawn. A familiar four-cylinder engine note reached my ears. Not knowing the state of things in the kitchen, and thinking Andy and Pidge should not be interrupted, I jogged across the living room floor and onto the front porch. I flicked on the porch light and pushed through the screen door to intercept the driver of a red Corolla. Heavy dew painted the grass, glittering in the light of a quarter moon.

Arun Dewar hurried across the jeweled lawn into the light.

"Is she here? I'm so sorry to bother you, Will—but that's her car." Despite the urgency in his question, Arun's accented inquiry remained crisp and polite.

"Yeah, she's here."

"Is she alright?"

"Why? What did you do?" He tensed. Panic flashed across his face.

"Nothing—I—"

"Relax. She's with Andy in the kitchen."

Arun's tension deflated. He pressed the palms of his hands to his eyes and released a heavy breath. When his hands fell to his side, he lifted his gaze to the sky, searching.

"I don't know what happened. Everything was lovely. Then she—she suddenly—I don't know—"

"I think I do. You better come in."

He followed me onto the porch.

"My god, is she crying?" Arun started in the direction of the sound coming from the kitchen. I put a hand on his shoulder.

"Yes. Give her a minute."

"I swear, we were enjoying a wonderful evening. I said nothing untoward, Will. I promise you. On my life."

"It wasn't you."

I don't think he heard me.

"If I caused her—if I said anything, I am sincerely sorry. I don't know what happened."

"We usually don't."

"She said nothing. She—"

"FUCK!" The outcry blew through the house and startled us both. I had a feeling the crying part of the evening had ended.

Arun froze.

A stream of curses sailed through the dark house. The barrage shot across the living room and dining room, across the porch and for all I know might have awakened our closest neighbor half a mile away.

Pidge denounced the asshats with the flags, their fathers for poisoning their mother's wombs, their mothers for bearing vermin, their ancestors for coupling with swine. She declared Company W the owners of mutated shriveled body parts and promised amputation of the same. She swore to castrate. To maim. To kill. To exhibit trophies in jars. Sharp, foul curses punctuated each new declaration.

Arun grew more and more wide-eyed with each graphic threat.

"I better go see." He started in the direction of the tirade. I squeezed his shoulder. "Stay here. Seriously. You'll be safe here."

I gestured at one of the wicker chairs, but Arun didn't move.

On bare feet, I trotted through the living room and dining room and into the kitchen where Andy kept her distance while Pidge paced a furious circuit. She waved the largest kitchen knife we owned. Spikes of short blonde hair formed an angry halo around her head. Her cheeks glistened and lines of mascara bled from her eyes.

"Motherf…!" The curses continued. The knife sliced the air, punctuating promises of mutilation and death. In stark contrast to verbiage that would have blanched a longshoreman, Pidge wore a light summer dress over bare legs and white sandals. The flowered hem swished and swayed with each spin she made.

She caught sight of me. The knife blade flashed in my direction.

"We're going after them," she declared. "We're going after those murdering bastards."

"Hey," I said. "You might—"

"I mean it. You gotta be with me on this. I've done some shit for you two and you've gotta be with me on this."

"Listen, Pidge. Ar—"

"Don't mess with me, Stewart. Don't you—"

"Hey! *Arun is here.*"

Pidge stopped in her tracks. She blinked and tears splashed from her eyes. "What did you say?"

"Arun. He's…" I jerked a thumb in the poor guy's direction.

"And you didn't tell me?" To my relief, the knife slipped onto the countertop instead of into my ribs. Pidge threw both hands to her face. Panic peeked through her splayed fingers. *"He's here and you didn't tell me?"*

I looked at Andy who looked at me, then at the figure closing in on us through the dark dining room.

Arun arrived at my shoulder. Pidge's eyes bulged.

"Oh, no. *Oh no oh no oh no please tell me you didn't hear all that.*"

"Cassie, I…" Arun took a step. She cringed.

"*No no no no no no...*" she whimpered.

Andy started toward her; arms outstretched. Arun closed a grip on Andy's arm and stopped her.

"Please. If I may." Arun slipped past her. For each step he took, Pidge took a step back until the geography of the kitchen halted her retreat. "Cassie, please. It's alright."

Panic in Pidge's eyes drowned in fresh tears.

"*What have I done—?*"

"Cassie, it's okay," Arun said softly. He took another step. She threw one hand up to stop him.

"*No! It's not! It's not okay!*"

He took another step.

"It is okay."

"*No no no no no—*"

"It is okay," he repeated. "Pidge."

The nickname slipped from his lips and struck her like a knife. She flinched. I had no idea he knew it. Was it me? Had I let it slip? I thought of the degree to which she'd hidden herself from Arun. How she adopted an entirely different persona in his presence. How I had come to realize her masquerade sprouted out of fear not vanity—fear that now enveloped her, crushed her, collapsed her.

"Pidge," Arun said softly. "Pidge, it's okay."

As small as she was, she tried to shrink deeper into herself. Her hands vainly smeared the air between them, a futile attempt to erase this moment.

"*It's not okay it's not okay it's not okay.*"

Arun reached for her.

"Look at me, darling." Arun gently slid his fingers under her chin and lifted her face to his. "It's—it's *fucking* okay."

The word, uttered by Arun, landed like a thunderbolt.

He drew closer.

"Pidge, it's *motherfucking* okay. Do you hear me?"

She stared at him. Wet streaks painted her face.

"Pidge," Arun leaned closer, speaking softly, firmly. "It's *bloody mother-fucking shit bugger bollocks* okay."

The crisp British diction planted every word between them like a flag. He took her shoulders in his hands. She trembled.

"Pidge, it's bloody arsehole motherfucking okay *because I bloody fucking love you.*"

On this, Pidge fell into his arms.

Andy jerked me from the room.

15

"Oh, what new level of Hell spawned this?"

Headlight beams turned the inside of my eyelids red. Again.

I had just dared to close my eyes, which had begun to burn from denied sleep. I lifted my head from the lounge chair cushion to see a third vehicle line up in the driveway.

Andy slipped from under my arm.

"That's the Chief's SUV." She found her feet and hurried in exactly the wrong direction. She whispered as she disappeared into the dark living room. "I need to put on a robe."

Rather than have Chief Tom Ceeves barge in on Arun and Pidge, who had been suspiciously silent for some time, I once again turned on the porch light and opened the screen door.

Tom stomped across the wet grass. At six feet and seven inches, his 270-pound presence emphasizes the enforcement element of the law, even without a uniform. I'd only seen him in his blues at the funeral of an Essex PD parttime officer named Lyle Traegar and in the official portrait that hung in the lobby of the police department. Winter or summer, he wore an untucked flannel shirt over jeans. He never carried a weapon. Anyone dumb enough to shoot at him deserved the lesson in gun safety that would follow.

Despite his size, Tom rarely looks angry. But when he does, the effect is unmistakable.

"Evening, Will." His voice resembled a bear grunting. I opted for discretion and did not point out that it was technically morning. "Andy up?"

"She went to put on a robe. Come in."

"You entertaining?"

"That's Pidge and Arun. It's been a—I want to say—difficult evening."

Tom bobbed his shoebox-shaped head. "Pidge, huh. She okay?"

"Then you know?"

"Yup." Tom said nothing for a moment, then added, "There's some people walking this earth would up their contribution to society by feeding worms."

I didn't argue or attempt small talk. Andy hurried down the stairs and joined us.

"What's going on?"

Tom huffed. "You hear from your pet FBI agent tonight?"

"Not in the last couple hours. Why?"

Tom huffed again, sharp and with finality.

"They pulled the plug on us. We're out."

"Of what?" I asked, though I could see from her expression that Andy knew.

"The Texas AG announced that an in-state task force is taking charge of the Tiffany Vera Callum investigation and does not require outside assistance at this time."

Tiffany Vera Callum. She had a name.

"That gives me a bad feeling," Andy sat down. Her distressed look distressed me.

"The teleconference is off. They don't want the FBI or foreigners from outta state getting in the way. They've deemed it a 'Sexual Hate Crime' and are rounding up all the usual suspects."

"That was no sexual hate crime," she said. "I don't even know what that means."

"It means they're narrowing their investigation to deviants and perverts."

"Hold up," I said. "What about the message?"

Tom lifted a brow. "Then you *have been* chatting with the FBI."

"She came by earlier. Pidge was here," Andy said.

"Oh." Tom is big but he's not slow. His face told me the picture filled in quickly.

"Again," I asked, "what about the message from Blaze? How is it a 'Sexual Hate Crime' when the head of an anti-government extremist group signs his work?"

Tom shook his head. He started to speak, then stopped himself.

"What?" I pressed.

"Sir?" Andy wanted to know, too.

"The official statement from Austin acknowledged that an unverified video of the incident may exist, but video analysis indicates it is an 'AI-generated deep fake.' Their words, not mine."

"That sonofabitch is covering for Blaze."

I looked at Andy. If she agreed with me, she did not say so.

"Who?" Tom asked.

"The Texas AG. He's covering for Blaze and the whole Company W outfit. Jesus, that's twice he's messed with something or someone I care about."

"You know him?"

"I know his work." I looked at Andy. She flexed her eyebrows in a *go ahead and tell him* gesture.

"I'm afraid to ask, but how did you managed to tangle with the attorney general for the state of Texas?"

"This goes back to the whole Amphitriton scam. And Spiro Lewko."

"Guy's a giant asshat."

"Sometimes," I agreed.

"I didn't like him before and now he's hawking cancer cures with that mystery material he's hoarding—" Tom's expression morphed. "Oh, ferchrissakes! How could I miss it? That was you, wasn't it? Holy crap."

"That stuff he's hoarding amplifies the effect, but it doesn't work on its own."

"Shit. So, the cancer cure thing—is that real?"

"Yeah, it's real. Most of the time. And by having Lewko step in and use those pieces of debris, it keeps the focus away from me."

Tom rubbed his temples as if to massage overheating neural connections. "So, if you do that *thing* you do and make some sick kid disappear, then… what? They get better?"

"Pretty much. Remember that Angel Flight? When it was all foggy?"

"Sure. Jesus, *how does that work?*"

"Hell, I don't know."

Tom folded his arms. "North Carolina. That business with Lewko running an illegal hospital. And the Texas AG's injunction. That's where you ran afoul of Pedmann?"

"Who?"

"Pedmann. Willis Pedmann. The Texas AG."

It was the first I'd heard a name.

Andy said, "Calling it an illegal hospital was North Carolina's spin, sir. They couldn't come down on Lewko themselves, but they couldn't let Texas horn in either. Lewko gathered as many children in one place as possible to set up a way to treat them without Will having to come out of the shadows. Pedmann filed for the injunction on behalf of an unidentified Jane Doe—one of the kids. The child's father is now suing Spiro Lewko for one hundred million dollars. Icing on the cake."

"I didn't know that," I said.

"I didn't mention it because I knew it would make you mad."

"Jesus." Tom took a moment. He paced the short length of the porch. "It takes some kind of sick puppy to block kids from a chance to beat cancer, even if it comes from the weirdest shit I ever heard of. *Who does that?*"

"Someone who wants to score political points and doesn't care who it hurts," I suggested.

"Someone with an agenda," Andy offered.

"An ugly one," I said, "if this same sick puppy is whitewashing what happened to the Callum girl."

"Sure feels that way."

Andy looked up at her boss. "And what? Are we supposed to sit on our hands here?"

Tom chuckled. A deep and resonant sound.

"When have you two ever done that?"

16

"That's it." I rolled off the lounge chair cushion, stood and blocked a fresh blast of headlight glare with one hand. "Get the shotgun."

Tom Ceeves had gone. Pidge and Arun were nowhere to be found despite the presence of their cars in the yard. A new set of lights blew me out of what I think had been the first few minutes of sleep.

"We don't have a shotgun, love," Andy said softly. "I told you we should have gone back to bed." She rose and wrapped her robe across her middle and tied the cloth belt.

"Land mines. I want land mines in our yard. Can you order some from Cops'R'Us?"

Andy slid past me and flicked on the porch light. Leslie, who had been headed for the back door, diverted. She climbed the porch steps and slipped through the open screen door.

"I'm going back to Chicago. I stopped to tell you—"

"We know," Andy said. "The Chief came by earlier."

"It's Grand Central Station here tonight," I added sourly.

Leslie ignored me. She shoved one hand in the front pocket of her black jeans and pulled out a small object. She took Andy's hand and pressed the object into her palm, then curled her fingers over it.

"You're a fine investigator, Andrea. This is everything we have in the Company W files, including the boat murders last spring."

"Hold on," I said. "Leslie, what the hell is this?"

"It's me risking my career and my freedom, Will."

"No. This is you dribbling out crumbs that we're supposed to follow to God knows what because the FBI won't. First you refuse to tell us anything about Company W, then you come here and dump this. You pretend you don't know us, and then you act like we're pals. Dammit, Leslie."

Her crooked smile blossomed without humor.

"You don't want the FBI to know you, Will. And I don't want the FBI to know that I know you. I sneak around because I'm scared to death. For you and Andrea. And for what will happen to me and my pension if the Bureau ever finds out that I've been playing footsie with the greatest threat to our national security since Bin Ladin."

"What—*you mean me?*"

"Leslie, you don't really think—" Andy started.

"Don't I? My God, you have no idea what they will do if they ever figure you out, Will. You have no idea the threat you pose to some seriously bad and seriously powerful people. I'm talking about the people who *really* run things. Who sit around sipping scotch and smoking cigars and deciding the next Supreme Court justices. How long do you think they would let you live if they knew you could be hovering in the room while they sidestep everything this country stands for?"

"I think you know that's always been—"

She wasn't finished. "What about the risks I have taken? That I *am* taking? Ever since Lindsay and Siddley Mansion and that whole shit show with your senator, I have had my neck out so far, I can't see my own tits. So, yeah. I dribble information out to you, *because if I get caught handing it to you the government will give me a timeout in Leavenworth to think about what a bad girl I've been.*"

She stopped, breathless.

Once again, in a night filled with them, a wordless moment played out.

Leslie stared at her shoes. I composed apologies in my head for my fatigue-induced outburst. She beat me to it.

"Look," she said, "I'm sorry. You deserve—"

"Stop," I said. "Just stop." Andy and Leslie waited for me to figure out how to get my feet out of my mouth. "First off, I—we—appreciate you more than I have the good sense to say. But second, don't baby me like some temperamental witness, okay?"

Andy jabbed her elbow into my ribs. "What Will meant to say is thank you for not ratting him out to your bosses or DARPA."

"You're welcome."

"Third," I said, "my wife is not just a *fine* investigator. She is a kick-ass-take-no-prisoners investigator. And you know how we feel about the morons who shot up this house and the murderers who did *the unthinkable* to that Callum girl and the Tik Tok girl. So, if that—" I pointed at Andy's closed hand "—is you finally giving us the green light…then, thank you. And I'm sorry."

"Apology accepted." Leslie turned to Andy. "Use this. Go where I can't."

Motion caught my eye in the doorway to the living room.

Pidge, followed by Arun who held her hand, emerged from the darkness.

"Does that mean we're going after the motherfuckers?"

I looked at Andy, who looked at Leslie, who looked at me. I sent it back to Pidge.

"The buttons on your dress are crooked."

PART II

17

———————

Andy hunched over her laptop at the dining room table. I felt guilty, padding across the floor barefoot, squinting sleep from my eyes. The sun had not cleared the horizon, but dawn lit up the windows. My bones said that what little sleep I'd had fell short.

Andy had less, if any. I suppressed the impulse to offer her coffee. That would have been turning the knife on the aroma about to flood the kitchen.

"When did you get up?"

She brushed back a rebellious lock of hair, the bulk of which was loosely bound up in what I think of as her Gibson Girl look, though she employed the style solely to keep it out of the way.

The woman glowed. I always thought that was a bit of myth intended to mitigate weight and shape gain. Nope. The pregnancy glow is a thing.

"Morning," she purred. She offered her lips. I met them with mine, careful not to share morning breath. Her kiss pressed soft and sweet.

"You're evading my question."

"Do you like how I did that?"

I headed for the kitchen and coffee. "Honest answer? Impressive. Will it matter if I ask again?"

"I don't know why you'd waste your breath."

When I returned with a mug of fresh morning glory, Andy pulled a dining table chair around beside hers. She angled her laptop screen and patted the cushion for me to join her.

"Sit. And keep that devil nectar away from me."

I waved the mug in her direction. She stole a long, savoring sniff.

"You are evil."

"I've been told."

She turned to the laptop. "I went through the files Leslie—I mean *someone anonymously*—dropped off in the night." She lined up her hands on the laptop keyboard.

"Hold on." I took one of those hands and held it. "We need to settle something." I turned and zeroed in my best *this is serious* stare. "You're not going."

She met my gaze with something dangerously innocent.

"I'm not going?"

"Dee, I'm serious. You're not going after these guys. I won't have you and the baby exposed to that kind of danger."

I sounded strong and serious, but the dimple suppressing a smile on her face sent a tremor through the steel in my he-man argument.

"I'm serious," I fought on. "These guys are vicious. I don't want them anywhere near you and little Ethel."

"We're not calling her Ethel. This means you're not taking me with you?"

"No." I sensed victory.

"Okay."

A symmetrical dimple joined the first. A smile germinated.

Something wasn't right.

"That's it? No argument."

She shrugged. "Can I ask just one question?"

I should have felt like I had this in the bag. For some reason I didn't.

"Shoot."

"Where are you going?"

She wasn't mean about it. She smiled. She squeezed my hand. She still loved me, even if she was about to ball me up and stuff me like an Antetokounmpo slam dunk.

"Um…Texas?"

She nodded sagely. "Sounds like a plan. How do you file a flight plan for that? KESX direct to…Texas?"

"It's a big state. Hard to miss."

"Right. And when you get there, what's the plan?"

"Find the bad guys? Make them pay? Hey, it works on TV."

She pulled her hand from mine, planted a kiss on my cheek, and turned back to face her screen.

"That's lovely, darling. And I fully support your TV action hero approach. But while you're beating up bad guys between commercials, I'll be following a more methodical albeit boring approach. Care to see?"

Slam dunk.

"Sure."

She wiggled in her seat energized by a college coed aura I'd seen before when a puzzle absorbed her.

"Okay. In no particular order." She maneuvered the wireless mouse pointer over onscreen columns of files. "Leslie has one thing dead to rights. If it ever gets out that she shared this material with us, she will be in very deep trouble…unless she has a guardian angel the size of King Kong."

"Simmons?" FBI Director Simmons flicks back and forth in my mind as an ally and as an enemy. "How do you know this wasn't authorized by the Director himself?"

Andy pursed her lips, lending the lower prominence. She lifted her hand from her mouse and tipped it back and forth. Semaphore for *undetermined.*

"A question for another day. Just so you know, I unplugged the cable and Wi-Fi before I accessed this drive. I've been using my phone's cellular connection for data searches. But this laptop is air gapped and needs to stay that way."

"A little paranoid?"

"One woman's paranoia is another woman's way to avoid indictment."

"Show me what you've got, Enola Holmes."

"Are you familiar with a book cipher?"

"Yeah. Old school spy craft. Literally from Holmes's day, isn't it? A number code references a book—page number, word number—to send a message, right?"

"It's been out of fashion since before World War II, but it's still a low-tech way to encrypt messages. I think that's what Louis Blaze is doing. You witnessed it firsthand. In Louisiana."

"What? Those candy bars Blaze's daughter handed out? I always figured that was some kind of communication trick. I thought maybe there was a message capsule inside the candy."

"Too easy to find if the courier is picked up. No, those candy bars and wrappers were completely innocent. The FBI lab analyzed three of the six you saw handed out. They were found on the bodies of the men killed on that boat. All three were straight off the shelf of the local Speedway."

"But couldn't the message have been hidden in the candy like I said? Already removed?"

"Potentially, but still way too easy to find if they get caught before accessing and destroying the message."

"Okay." I tapped the tabletop eagerly. "So, lay it on me."

"Lay what on you?"

"The eureka moment. The big reveal. What did you find that cracks the case, darling detective?"

"Will, I'm not breaking any ground here. I'm not going to find something that the FBI missed after dozens of trained analysts examined the same material. There are hundreds of files here. Bits and pieces. Documents. I've barely scratched the surface."

"Oh."

"The candy wrappers are a good example. They've been tested, scanned, and examined down to the microscopic level. None were etched or tampered with in any way. Nothing written on them. No marks. No nothing. There is no eureka moment."

"Oh."

"That just means the wrappers themselves transmitted the code against which Blaze is using a book cipher to dispatch instructions to his lieutenants."

"That's kind of a eureka, isn't it?"

"That's an FBI conclusion, not mine."

"Then the FBI broke the code?"

"No. They know it's a code. They suspect a book cipher. But they don't have the key. With a book cipher the recipient must have the book in his or her possession or have access to it."

"Seems antiquated."

"It is. Book ciphers were state of the art in the nineteenth century and before. Radio changed the way information is transmitted. Developments like the Enigma system in Germany and similar efforts by the allies made it possible to transmit coded information via radio wave. Book ciphers remained useful in situations where the agent can't carry around decrypting equipment but can carry a benign book—like a travel guide or The Bible. If they got picked up, a book was just a book."

"In Louisiana, Leslie joked that Blaze used carrier pigeons. I don't get it. Why go to all this trouble? Why not just use some kind of computer encryption?"

"If he did, the FBI or NSA or CIA would be reading his mail. No matter how smart you think you may be in your electronic messaging, our intelligence agencies are smarter. Blaze isn't wrong to go old school. It's clumsy, but without the key to the book cipher, there's no decoding it. And you can't just use *To Kill a Mockingbird.* Which edition? Paperback? Hardcover? First printing? The word flow on the pages differs with each edition. Everyone must be on the same page of a unique book—literally."

Andy opened a file folder labeled "Murphy." Scores of files filled the screen column.

"Devon Murphy—that was his cover name; the files redact his real name—was the undercover agent who was killed along with five members of the Company W middle management—the men you saw at that service station meeting."

"Along with Blaze's daughter."

"Who was not killed but left for dead."

"Time out." I formed the sports signal with two hands. "Can we pause on that for one second? Who kills five—or six, they thought—mid-level leaders in a white supremacist hate militia? Was that ever resolved?"

Andy shook her head. "Nothing in any of these files offers a theory or so much as a list of suspects. But if you think about it, there are only two possibilities once you rule out stock answers like personal jealousy or a robbery gone bad or a drunken family fight. Possibility One, they were killed by a rival organization—which in this case would be the United States of America, and highly unlikely since Blaze has absorbed most of his other rivals. Possibility Two, fratricide. They were killed by their own people or leadership. Sometimes that can be an internal power grab, but in this case, Blaze is still in power. It's more like a consolidation."

"Killed by their own people?"

"I scanned through a ream of support articles on the subject. Most authorities agree that Company W has emerged at the head of a cluster of these groups with Louis Blaze in charge. Sometimes to tighten your grip you must eliminate potential internal resistance or rivals. Like Hitler did with Ernst Rohm and the Brownshirts. Can we get back to Murphy?

"Sorry."

"Murphy was undercover for almost two years. The last three reports he filed suggested Blaze was brewing something big, but that it was religiously compartmented, and he wasn't high enough in the organization for access."

"Big...as in what?"

"Unknown. A big operation seen through their eyes would be a move against the tyrant federal government. Another Oklahoma City, God forbid. I think that's one reason Leslie has been mute. Top people in the FBI and other agencies who are a lot smarter than you and me are all over this."

"Then why is she opening the door now? What can we do that the FBI and Homeland Security can't?"

Andy rolled her eyes at me.

"Besides that," I protested.

She redirected my attention to the laptop screen. "Let's come back to that question."

"Wait a minute. If this code thing is a book cipher, it means they all need to carry the same book, right? A copy of *Dante's Inferno* or *Harry Potter and the Goblet of Fire*, right? Or for these morons, *The Cat in the Hat*."

"Do not underestimate your enemy."

"Are you quoting Sun Tsu?"

"Katie Taylor scheming to skip school in third grade to stay home and watch *Andy of Mayberry* reruns. Yes, you're right. People receiving instructions through a book cipher would all carry the same book."

"Murphy received one of the candy bars. I saw it handed to him. That means he had to have a copy of the book."

"Nothing in his reports indicates he was ever included in the coded transmissions before that night. No candy bar wrapper was found on Murphy. Nor did they find a phone. He used a burner to contact his handler. It was never found."

"Dee, how the hell were you able to do such a deep dive into all this since…what? Three a.m.?"

"Because I'm a kick-ass-take-no-prisoners investigator—thank you for that. Also, I'm not trying to read every document because I don't have to. The FBI has been through everything with a microscope. I'm scanning the broad strokes."

I took a long sip of the coffee that had cooled enough to be consumed. My mind felt thick. Caffeine might help, but I doubted it would untangle the knot Andy found in Leslie's files.

Andy said, "None of the other dead men had phones in their possession, nor were any phones found in subsequent searches of the deceased's homes."

"No burners? Family phones? Nothing?"

"Secrecy is a religion in these groups."

"Are *all* of these folders full of files?"

"Loaded. Why?"

"My god, Dee, it would take you weeks to go through all this."

"Which is why I'm not trying. For example, there's a whole folder tree devoted to field reports from Murphy. Another one starts with a dossier on each murdered man and expands to cover every detail of their lives. Photos going all the way back to Little League."

"What about Tiffany Vera Callum? Or the Tik Tok girl—shoot, I don't know her name. Did Leslie provide anything on them?"

"Tik Tok girl was Brenda Haverstadt." Andy shook her head. "There's nothing in here on either case. Everything Leslie provided on this drive pertains to the men who were killed months ago. The only thing that connects Company W to those two murders are the Tik Tok detective's teasers about the stripper girl in Lincoln, Nebraska, and the video from Blaze, which is being discredited."

"Which is bullshit."

"Agreed. But also remember, those murders happened in the past few days. These files go back years."

"Jesus, what does Leslie expect you to find?"

"I'll get to that."

"Because if you're supposed to search a zillion files for a connection to murders that had not happened when the files were compiled, we're talking about a needle in a haystack."

"A needle in a haystack is easy to find. You simply pluck one piece of hay from the stack at a time. Eventually you will find the needle. This is way harder."

"Impossible."

"Maybe. It might not matter. Will, *all* this material that Leslie gave me has been reviewed by people and computer analysis programs spanning hundreds if not thousands of hours of investigative effort. Using AI alone, they can process accumulated data at light speed. They can sort the wheat from the chaff. Here." She moved and clicked the mouse. "I found one thing that will amuse you. Or offend you. Did you know Louis Blaze was a pilot?"

"Sorry to hear that. I like to think my fellow aviators are better people."

She clicked on an image. A black and white photo of a clean shaven and much thinner version of the man I'd seen in Idaho filled the screen. He wore white corduroy jeans, a flannel shirt, and a denim jacket. Of more interest to me was the big radial engine behind him. It hung on the wing of a classic Twin Beech.

"Looks like he was a freight dog."

"A what?"

"For a while in the sixties and seventies, before FedEx, air freight companies popped up all over. The typical hauler was the Twin Beech, the Beechcraft Model 18. Remember that guy who gave us a ride from Seward to Lincoln?"

"That big noisy airplane?" A smile told me the tease was intentional.

"Yes. The big noisy airplane. Freight companies used them to fly everything under the sun all over the rust belt in all kinds of weather. A rough way to make a living—especially in winter—but it's how a lot of today's senior airline pilots built their logbook time."

Andy pointed at the photo. "I thought that was his airplane."

"More likely it belonged to whatever freight line he flew for."

"No," Andy closed the photo image and scrolled, hunting. The rapid screen hopping started to make me dizzy. I leaned away and sipped some coffee.

"Here. It says here he is the current registered owner of this airplane."

I looked at the onscreen document that listed the FAA registration number and the owner. Louis T. Blaze. There was no photo, but the make and model listed the same type seen in his freight dog photo.

"May I?" I reached for the laptop. Andy slid it under my hands.

I opened Google and typed in the aircraft N-number. The FAA registry came up in the top three search results. The link hopped directly to a Twin Beech owned by Louis T. Blaze of Coeur d'Alene, Idaho. I clicked the back button and scrolled down to another link, which took me to a photo of the very same airplane sitting on a ramp wearing a dull, unpolished gray metal finish with faded red stripes.

"Sonofabitch. You know…that's one way to get around off the grid."

"I am aware. But if the FBI knows he owns an airplane, you can be sure they know where it is and when it moves." Andy repossessed her laptop.

I looked at her. An inexplicably sunny light sparkled in her eyes. Greater than the glow.

"What am I missing here?"

"Leslie. You were a little mean to her, you know."

"I know. And I'm sorry. But after she stonewalled us for months, she dumped all this on you. To what end? You said the FBI has been all over this."

"No." The sparkle did not diminish. "I haven't showed you the one thing she gave me that required no research at all."

Andy clicked her way back to the file menu for the thumb drive sticking out the side of her laptop. At its root, there were only five main folders and a single PDF document with a jumbled file name comprised of numbers and letters.

She clicked open the PDF file. I read the cover page of a legal filing.

"Is this…?"

"The filing for the federal injunction issued against Lewko in North Carolina. Notice anything about this copy?"

I scanned the formally formatted legal filing.

"Unredacted. This version is unredacted. Holy crap. That's big trouble if Leslie—or you—are caught with this."

I took the mouse from her and scrolled until I found the carrot that Leslie dangled.

"Cynthia Leigh Morgan." I turned to Andy. "That's her?"

She nodded. "Yes. That's the little Jane Doe that Pedmann used to file his injunction against Lewko. This is a copy of the original filing. Cynthia Leigh Morgan was there—in North Carolina. She was on the second bus. Her mother took her to Evermore, apparently against the wishes of the girl's father who brought the complaint to the Texas Attorney General who filed for an injunction preventing her and all the others from receiving treatment —the same attorney general who can also be seen in a photo, I forget which folder, chumming with the girl's father on a golf course."

"This is—I mean, this is great and all—but what does this have to do with the people who burned a girl alive because they thought she was Pidge?"

"Will," Andy said, "Pedmann is the same attorney general currently tripping over his own you-know-what trying to cover for Louis Blaze."

The light came on.

"Damn, Leslie. Well played."

Andy kissed my cheek. "And no, I'm not phoning this in. I'm going with you."

18

——————

After a quick breakfast, Andy switched on the television and scanned several cable news stations. The horrific story of a girl burned to death in a remote Texas field topped each segment. I told her to turn it off. She reached for the remote, but clips from an official news conference in Austin stayed her hand. The clips showed lines of uniformed and business-suit law enforcement officers taking turns at a microphone. A spokeswoman for the attorney general's office must have repeated the term "sexual hate crime" half a dozen times. Another official alluded to satanic rituals and witchcraft, citing undisclosed evidence. A reporter asked if the witchcraft aspect related to the way the girl had been bound to a pole and burned. The official answer was "we're examining all possibilities." Another reporter asked if rumors of a video were true. The spokeswoman for the attorney general denied the rumor.

"Who's that guy?" I pointed at the left side of the widescreen frame.

"Stapleton. Oklahoma senator."

"What's he doing in Texas?"

"He's…"

Andy's answer slipped into the same distant ether as her gaze. Once again, her wheels turned. I said nothing.

The press briefing dwelt on satanic rituals to such an extent that the spokeswoman for the attorney general's office gave the microphone to a member of the clergy. Andy flicked the TV off, leaving me wondering if they planned an on-air exorcism.

She stared at the blank screen for at least a minute.

I waited.

When Andy blinked back into the present from whatever alternate universe she'd been visiting, she turned to me and asked the one question I did not expect.

"Want to save water and take a shower with me?"

The cleansing she needed had to do with more than soap.

19

———————

At a distance, the young woman crossing the ramp looked familiar in every aspect except one. She wore a leather flight jacket over a t-shirt and jeans and dragged a wheeled carry-on case. I waited until she approached the nose of the Navajo before accosting her.

"Hold it right there, young lady. You can't be out here on this airport ramp. Didn't you see that mighty security fence? You're in violation of FAA regu—"

"Bite me," Pidge replied.

"What the hell made you do that?" I pointed at her jet-black hair. Still short. A bit more spiked. "You look like something from an anime graphic novel."

"I'll take that as a compliment. It was Arun's idea. He felt that I should distance my appearance from stripper girl. I don't like it, but he says it's sexy. I honestly think he's having an affair with *other* me."

I thought the dye job looked weird but had the good sense not to say so. I wiped down the oil dipstick in my hand and pushed it back into the right engine for a clean reading.

"Quite the night. Boating. Secret identity reveal. Cursing—although it sounds so polite when Arun does it with that accent."

"I know!"

"And then him saying the magic words."

"Shut up."

68

"By the way, there's a blanket missing from my mudroom. You know anything about that?"

"It's in your barn. In the loft. You might want to throw it in the laundry." She wheeled her case to a stop by the airplane nose, then leaned on the wing root. "You remember me telling you he wants to introduce me to his mother?"

"Jeez, that was a while ago. Is that coming up?"

"Oh hell, no. This apparently takes more planning than the Normandy invasion. I thought he meant sometime this summer. He's talking about Christmas—*in London.*"

"Jesus."

"These things must be handled delicately. He says. It's not something a person can just blurt out over an international line. He says." Pidge adjusted herself and adopted a bad British accent. "One must engage the moment when optimum opportunity presents. He says."

"I wouldn't do that around your boyfriend. Look, Arun Dewar is nothing if not a meticulous planner." The dipstick instructed me to add a quart. Oil is cheap. Engines are not. I laid the dipstick on the wing on a spread of paper towel, then settled a funnel over the hole on the top of the engine.

"You don't think he's afraid to have her meet me, do you? Even more so now—after last night?"

"Hard to say. The poor schmuck is smitten with you, but he might be more terrified of Mummy. Just remember, he bloody loves you."

"Shut up."

"He bloody said so."

"Don't make me hurt you."

I tipped a fresh quart of oil over the open top of the funnel.

"So, what's with the bag?"

"I'm going with you."

"No, you're not."

"Yes, I am."

"No. You are not. Not to put a graphic point on it, but there's one young woman matching your description that has already been—" I couldn't say the words.

"I'm aware. But that girl was a blonde. I'm not. And whoever did the deed thinks the job is done. I'm going with you. Somebody needs to be on hand to pull your balls out of the ringer."

"Horrifying image aside, you can't leave. Earl will never let you run off like that."

"Today is Sunday. I'm off tomorrow. Technically I'm not booked until

Wednesday. Besides, Earl's up in Minnesota hanging out with his ex-wife. He says he's helping Candice rebuild her lodge. I'm pretty sure he's erecting something."

"You cleared all this with Rosemary II?"

"She's not the boss of me. Well, she kinda is. But it's all good."

I stared at her long enough to make her uncomfortable.

"What?"

"Are you okay? I mean about what happened. It hit you kinda hard last night."

Her lips formed a word starting with F but she froze with it unspoken. She met my eyes with ice in her own. Her voice went low and cold.

"You know what they did to that girl."

"I do."

"I want to do it to them. I have never wanted anything more—except to fly. I want the sonsofbitches *to burn.*"

"You know that's not going to happen. Don't get attached to the idea because there's nothing but disappointment at the end of that road."

"We'll see. I'm coming with you."

"As am I," Arun joined the conversation by ducking under the Navajo's tail. He dragged his own small bag.

"No. Absolutely not." I glared at Pidge, hoping to remind her that there was a certain something Arun was not aware of, and that his presence would put a damper on my ability to use that certain something as needed.

She ignored me. She rolled her bag around the left wing and joined Arun at the airstair. He loaded his, then hers into the cabin.

"Afraid I must disagree, Will," Arun said. "I've already informed Miss Stone that we are embarking on a trip to Texas. Austin, Texas, to be precise."

"What makes you think we're going to Austin?"

"Your wife, of course. I spoke to her half an hour ago. She will be here posthaste. Which tells me you already know the destination. I assume you've already filed. Please update the number of souls on board."

Pidge stood beside Arun. She beamed a smug smile at me.

20

I made Pidge fly. If she wanted to ride along, let her earn her way. She invited Arun to the flight deck, an invitation he accepted with enthusiasm rarely shown when I make the same offer. Andy and I took the club seats on the right side of the Navajo cabin. She wore jeans and a loose sweatshirt bearing the Waukesha County Technical College logo, which looked like a white gazebo on a blue field above the WCTC lettering. The sweatshirt from her days as a police cadet hid her bump, which I took to be intentional.

This was the first time she'd flown since the pregnancy. I wondered if her morning sickness, thankfully receding, might be reawakened. The late afternoon flight encountered light turbulence, but the minor jolts produced no ill effect. I suggested that she use the supplemental oxygen we carry. She declined until I slipped a pulse oximeter over her finger and the digits dipped to 90 at our cruising altitude. She reluctantly let me arrange the tubing over her seatback and help her fix the cannula beneath her nose.

Essex direct to Austin Executive Airport flight planned at a little over five hours of flying time. Too much for comfort and too thin on fuel reserves at the end. We split the flight with a stop at Sedalia Regional Airport in Missouri for fuel and bladder relief. Andy studied files on her laptop screen throughout the first leg. I grabbed a nap.

As we reached a cruising altitude of 8,000 feet for the second leg, the sun slipped below the western horizon, painting cirrus clouds above us bright orange and casting a warm glow into the cabin. Andy gestured for me to join her at the laptop. We slipped on headphones and switched the intercom to cabin only. I liked the intimate sound of her voice in the center of my head.

"I have an address for the mother. According to court records, she has custody of our Jane Doe."

"You said it was the father who brought the complaint."

"Dad's a high roller in the part of the insurance industry that specializes in oil and gas facility coverage. Industrial policies. He carries a lot of weight in a state where the energy business and politics are indistinguishable. Mom and dad are separated. Mom has custody. Dad brought the injunction case to the AG's office because of his connection to Willis Pedmann. Looks like he had help from groups affiliated with several churches."

"So, mom believes in Lewko's Cure and dad believes in the Almighty?"

She gazed out the window.

"What?" I asked.

She sighed and shook her head. "Leslie knew you would go after the child. She's using that to get us to look at Pedmann."

"Seems that way. Why?"

Andy didn't answer. She returned to the company of her own thoughts.

I tried to avoid mine.

21

———————

"There's a flaw in Leslie's scheme." I spoke before I realized Andy had eased her headphones down around her neck. I pointed. She slipped them back on. "There's a flaw in Leslie's scheme."

"What scheme?"

"Leslie points us at the girl in the injunction, which points us at the parents, which points us at the father specifically, which connects to Pedmann who *might* be covering for Blaze and therefore could lead us to the Company W people behind these killings."

"Convoluted, but I wouldn't call it a scheme."

"It is a scheme because it's an investigative path she and the FBI cannot or chooses not to pursue."

"That's not entirely true. The FBI has been investigating Pedmann. For quite some time, in fact."

I blinked. "News to me."

"It's been ongoing. Pedmann has been evading a corruption indictment for several years now."

"Years?"

"The wheels turn slowly, dear. Where's the flaw?"

"Oh. That. If mom has custody and she freezes us out, we're done. The path ends there. Nothing connects us to the father who is connected to Pedmann who is connected to the cat that ate the rat that scared the horse that blew up the castle."

Andy smiled.

"Then we don't let it end at the mother. We make her invite us in."

She closed the laptop cover and reached across the aisle to where her carry-on bag lay on the seat. She unzipped the bag, reached in, and pulled out a piece of Styrofoam the size of a shoe.

I grinned at her.

22

———————

The Uber rolled to a stop at the curb. Lamplights on both sides of the tree-lined street provided security without obnoxious glare. The house number Andy gave the driver rose in brushed bronze from a marble plaque beside steps that might also be marble. The steps ascended from the sidewalk to a plateau of lawn that, at first glance, looked like carpeting or sports turf. The house shared the elegance of the approach. Cool white slabs of stucco spoke a design language contemporary to the 1930s. Dark trim outlined the roof and windows. If the gardens hugging the house had been any more manicured, they would have worn nail polish.

The Tarrytown neighborhood oozed wealth. Twice as we zigzagged toward our destination, we passed fenced off lots sprouting lavish new construction. Old homes surrendered to new, more extravagant homes. With properties running to seven figures, the cost of demolition and new construction guaranteed a return, assuming one could afford the price of entry.

I expressed reservations about Andy's full-frontal approach. If it were up to me, I would have vanished, scouted a way into the house, and located the girl in her sleep. Making her vanish while unaware of my presence served a cold calculation. If *the other thing* failed to help her, no one would know. Failure would not become evidence justifying the federal injunction.

At the hotel, after parting from Pidge and Arun (who booked separate rooms at Arun's insistence in what I considered a pointlessly chaste charade), I produced two BLASTER power units and suggested to Andy that we simply launch off the Holiday Inn balcony and fly nonstop across suburban Austin. She refused, insisting instead on traveling via Uber.

I read her stance as intractable and decided there were better hills to die for.

Half an hour later, at the designated address in the heart of the Tarrytown neighborhood, our Uber rolled away after Andy promised the driver a sterling review. Andy stepped onto the sidewalk wearing a white silk blouse over a black skirt. The blouse had a bit of a drape to it, leaving the question of pregnancy in the eye of the beholder. Andy had done her hair in a conservative, businesslike bun. Before leaving the hotel room, she fastened a gaudy bracelet to her wrist. I'd never seen her wear it before, but it supplemented her upscale attire in a way that seemed in synch with the neighborhood.

I checked my watch. Nearly eleven p.m. Rather late to be knocking on doors. When I said so to Andy, she replied that the clock can be your friend. A late-night knock catches people unguarded.

On her approach to the front door, Andy directed me to stay behind her. She swept one hand to her face and rubbed her eye until she was near enough to the doorbell camera to cover the lens with her elbow.

She rang the bell. Despite admiring how she prevented our images from being recorded, I gave Andy's overall effort low odds of success. The owner, at this hour would simply interrogate us through the camera's audio system and refuse entry. It's what I would have done.

I registered surprise when the door opened. I wasn't alone.

"Oh." The woman swinging back a heavy door was equally surprised.

And drunk.

This may be way easier than we thought.

If the half-filled tumbler in her hand wasn't a giveaway, her breath was.

Cynthia Morgan's mother was pretty in a trophy wife way, beautifully coiffed and skillfully made up even at this late hour. She had dark shoulder-length hair, tan skin, ruby but not bright red lipstick, and heavy artificial lashes. Not quite as tall as Andy, she displayed a prominent bosom, possibly enhanced. A tangerine-colored cocktail dress left one shoulder and the top third of both breast mounds bare. A jeweled necklace of considerable value descended into a dark crease of cleavage.

"I thought you were my ride. I left my scarf on the seat."

"No, ma'am. We're from Evermore. May we come in?"

She blinked. "You mean like package delivery?" She looked past us for the distinctive red delivery truck in the driveway.

Andy chuckled. "Not at all. I'm Dr. Ingrid Lazlo. This is my associate, Dr. Rick Blake. It's about your daughter, Cynthia."

I expected the door to swing shut at mention of the girl's name. The woman stiffened.

"What about my daughter?"

"May we come in? There's quite a bit to explain and I can assure you, we are here to help."

"I don't know you."

"Mr. Lewko sent us."

"Spiro Lewko?"

"Yes, ma'am."

"The billionaire?"

"The one and only. He personally directed us to see you." Andy took a step closer. "You took your daughter to Evermore, Mrs. Morgan, but she never got the chance to be treated. The attorney general of this state obtained a federal injunction. I'm sure you are aware."

Morgan stared at Andy. Her expression hardened. Once more, I sensed an imminent door slam.

Andy extracted the Styrofoam piece from her bag and held it up. Morgan's eyes widened as if she found gold nuggets in a flower bed.

"I believe this is what you went to North Carolina for," Andy said. "Because Cindy was denied the opportunity for treatment there, Mr. Lewko insisted we bring it to her."

"Issat...real?"

"It is ma'am. There are no guarantees, but when it works...well, I'm sure you're aware of the potential benefits. May we come in?"

23

We followed the woman into her house, a spotless contemporary home aspiring for a spread in whatever society publication validates money spent on uncomfortable furniture and carefully curated objects of art. Beneath the bourbon breath and a sickly-sweet perfume wafting from the woman, I caught a whiff of cleaning products. The weekly, or perhaps daily, cleaning staff had earned their pay.

"You know Spiro Lewko? Personally?" Elaine Morgan walked an impressively steady line, given her inebriation and the height of her stiletto heels. She led us into an enormous great room that joined the kitchen on one end and worshipped a huge stone fireplace at the other. The room had a bar. Morgan navigated a straight line to it and lifted a cream-colored bottle in our direction.

"Highland Park? It's…" she examined the bottle "…eighteen."

"No, thank you."

A fresh splash joined her drink. She turned and planted an elbow on the bar.

"What's he like?"

"Mr. Lewko?"

"Yes."

"He's like anyone else," Andy said. "His success introduces privacy issues most of us never encounter. Beyond that he's a gentle and generous man. But he does not understand people's interest. For example, he could not imagine you would ask an acquaintance of mine what I'm like."

"Because I wouldn't give a shit." She took a sip. "Because you don't have a hundred billion dollars and a cure for cancer, Doctor—what wazzit?"

"Lazlo."

"Doctor of what?"

"Oncology. Tell me about your daughter, Mrs. Morgan."

Morgan shook her head and shifted her eyes to the ceiling. "What do you want to know? She's supposed to have cancer. She's supposed to be dying."

"Supposed?"

"I misspoke. Has. Has cancer. According to my husband and the doctors he pays."

"You don't sound convinced."

Morgan laughed. "Nobody gives a shit what I think."

"But you took your daughter to North Carolina for treatment…?"

"Well. There is that." Morgan sipped her whisky. "Doctor, do you know what Munchausen by Proxy is?"

"I'm familiar."

"They tell me it's mostly mothers who practice it."

"Are you saying that your husband—"

"Is there such a thing as Munchhausen for Pay?"

"Ma'am, what are you—?"

"I'm not saying a word. Not a word. Yes, I took Cindy to North Carolina. And then my deeply religious husband took my little girl from me and placed her in the loving lap of the Lord Jesus. Surely, Dr. Oncology, you had someone by the name of Jesus Christ in your medical school classes."

"Faith has a value, even if it is not quantifiable, Mrs. Morgan. And I'm not sure you correctly understand Munchausen. Is your daughter at home?"

Morgan took a hard drink. "My daughter is not my daughter anymore. She is the exclusive property of my husband who will not let me near her ever again, so he says. I committed an unforgiveable sin. I attempted to taint her soul with the devil's medicine." She pointed at the Styrofoam. "Does it burn your hand when you hold it, doctor? Satan's tool?"

"People have misinformed assumptions about these objects, Mrs. Morgan. And in deference to your husband's faith, wouldn't he more appropriately consider a tool of this nature one of God's miracles?"

Morgan laughed. She shook with it. "Oh, heavens! I was—" She gasped for air. "I was being sarcastic. The only time my husband ever read a Bible verse it was on teleprompter. No, dearie, if I've been too obtuse for you, let me clarify. The sin I committed was against his holy bank account. Please —" She held up the bottle again. "Have one with me. We'll toast the Father, Son, and Holy Dividend."

Andy said nothing. Rebuffed, Morgan added another splash to her tumbler.

"Okay. Fine. Let's see what you've got. How does it work?"

"I will be honest with you, I do not know what it is or how it works, but I have seen the results. And as I said, Mr. Lewko is determined to make it available to any who would seek it—"

"Suffer the little children to come unto me. Right? I should tell Jake that one. Only I guess it wouldn't apply. I'm—shit—I'm a bit of a mess, Dr. Luh—?"

"Lazlo."

"Lazlo. Right. A bit of a mess, as you can plainly see. No, my daughter is not here. And if my husband gets his way, she will never be here. Ever."

I suddenly wondered if Leslie already knew this. If she did, she could have saved us a trip.

"Show me." Morgan put her glass on the bar, spilling golden liquid across polished mahogany in the process. "Show me how it works."

Andy held up the Styrofoam. "It's not a party trick, Mrs. Morgan."

"Ah." She nodded drunkenly. "I know all about party tricks. My husband has one. He parades our little girl around to his country club friends. Poor little Cindy. She has cancer, you know. It's so sad. He takes her to that gaudy monstrosity of a church so all the Sunday worshipers can pray over her. I wanted to take her to St. Jude. To Mayo. To Evermore. No, he said. No. He takes her to preachers and faith healers and insists that God will bring her back from The Shadow. When I ask him if it wasn't God who put the cancer in her blood and bones, he tells me that Satan puts lies in my mouth. We have such polite conversations." She giggled. "I should warn you. I'm chatty when I'm hammered."

I spoke up for the first time. "I thought you had custody."

She laughed. "I have custody on papers drawn up by his lawyers and his judges and his money and if I open my mouth for anything but to pleasure him, he will see to it that those lawyers and judges and prosecutors drag me through the deepest trough of pig shit they can find before they put me away. All this?" She waved her arms. "Hell's waiting room."

"Ma'am, I don't know what he claims he can do to you, but—"

"*You don't have a clue!*" Morgan hissed. "Show me. Show me how it works. Show me it isn't a scam."

Andy looked down at the object in her hand. The *fake object* in her hand. If it had been real, one of the actual pieces of debris from my midair collision, I would have felt relentless presence throbbing down my center. I would have been able to close my hands on the levers I see in my head and slam them full forward, making myself and anyone touching the object vanish, even across a room.

This chunk of Styrofoam came from packing for a new coffee maker. It wasn't going to do diddly across the room or anywhere else.

Morgan advanced. "Listen to me. I don't care what happens to me anymore. But if that thing is real—*if you promise to use it on Cindy*—I will not only tell you where she is, I will take you to her. Screw Jake. Screw Ray Stroud and Willis Pedmann. I'd like to see the whole thing blow up in their stinking faces."

Bingo.

Andy glanced at me. I nodded. She held out the Styrofoam.

I took it from her and crossed the room to stand near enough to Morgan to pick up a buzz from her breath. She looked up at me and wobbled. I took advantage and caught her right bicep with my left hand.

I held the Styrofoam between us.

"Put your hand on this."

She hesitated. Thin fingers, perfect nails, and rings worth more than the Navajo trembled over the white plastic. She lowered her hand as if she expected electric shock.

"Close a grip."

She complied. I shoved the levers governing *the other thing* to the stops.

Fwooomp!

The Styrofoam vanished. She vanished. I vanished. Gravity released us. To make a point, I pushed the floor away with my toes. We rose.

She gasped over and over. For a weird moment she sounded like a woman consumed by sexual climax.

"Oh God oh God oh God—!"

We ascended. I checked the airspace above us for ceiling fans or other obstacles. The room had a high ceiling with recessed canister lights. Nothing threatened harm.

When the ceiling approached the top of my head, I let go of the Styrofoam and pushed us down. A moment later, my boots touched the floor. I released my grip on the woman.

Fwooomp!

I didn't account for being taller than Morgan. Reappearing caught her a few inches off the floor. She dropped. Her heels betrayed her. She stumbled and collapsed in a heap.

Andy rushed forward and knelt to help, casting a harsh glance my way.

I collected the Styrofoam and moved out of the way.

Morgan made no effort to rise. Andy had the good sense not to strain herself. The woman stared up at me, trembling, gasping. I braced for a flood of tears, but her expression slowly hardened. She squeezed her eyes shut and pressed both hands to her temples.

"Ow!" She winced. "Like ice. I think I had too much to drink, if that's possible."

I held out one hand. She took it and swung to her feet. I prepared to catch her when she flopped drunkenly onto me, but she stood sharp and erect. Her demeanor changed. Her focus intensified. She grabbed my arm.

"Promise me you will use this on Cindy. In front of witnesses. *Promise me!* I want this done in front of a crowd."

The demand surprised me. A dozen complications ran through my head. I looked for a way to suggest something private.

"If we have to." Andy beat me to the punch.

She kicked off the heels and dropped three inches in height.

"I'll go and change." She scooped up her heels and marched from the room.

"Mrs. Morgan," I called after her. "Who is Ray Stroud?"

She answered without looking back.

"Louis Blaze's pit bull."

24

———————

E laine Morgan returned to her great room in white summer slacks and a pink angora sweater. She traded her spiked heels for white sandals with complicated straps. I noticed that the jewelry populating her fingers and neck had changed, gaining both weight and value. Her hair and makeup remained perfect.

Nobody sobers up in a matter of minutes, yet she put on a great act. She walked confidently. She swept past the bar and downed the remaining scotch in her glass, then tossed me the keys to a Range Rover we found in an attached garage. She and Andy boarded the rear seat. I took the wheel.

Her eyes fixed on me via the rearview mirror. Sharp. Intense. I started to wonder if by making her vanish I had sobered her up. The cavalier drunken housewife was gone.

"Where are we going?" I asked after maneuvering for departure from the driveway.

"Jake's club. It's—tap that navigation button on the thing. Up there." She pointed over my shoulder. I activated the vehicle map and navigation system. "Scroll down the list. Look for Lily Club. There. That's it. Third one down. Touch that."

The system painted a blue line on the map for me to follow. A soft female voice told me to turn right and drive three quarters of a mile.

"Bitch," Morgan muttered from the back seat.

"What does your husband have on you, Mrs. Morgan, that gives him control over your life like this?" Andy asked.

"What doesn't he have? I am as unfit a mother as they come. I'm an obvious alcoholic. He has documented every line of coke, crashed car, blown credit card, and of course what he likes to call prostitution."

"Prostitution?"

She laughed bitterly. "Dr. Lazlo, when a man in my husband's position decides to destroy his wife there is nothing he will not do. Nothing he will not make his wife do. With his friends. With his business associates. With people he owes money. Don't look at me like that. I'm not some innocent victim of sex trafficking. I had needs. I had habits. I made my own bad choices. Jake simply took them and ran with them."

"Then how did you get custody of your daughter?"

"I told you. He arranged everything. His lawyers. His judges. His connections."

"Why?"

"Because it plays better. Look," she said, "spare me your concern. I'm not looking for rescue, understand? I am a brass bitch. A whore. I lost any shred of decency years ago. I am the worst nightmare of a mother ever to walk this earth. Honey, don't take it personally, but a woman with your figure and fitness isn't hiding a beer belly under that blouse. If I were in your shoes, I would have that thing cut out of me. Today. Tonight."

"Not in this state," I said.

"Oh, please. My husband and his pals pay for enough off-book abortions to support a Planned Parenthood clinic. It's been a thriving industry since the prohibition started. How many weeks are you?"

I checked the mirror. Andy did not look comfortable. I tried to think of a change of topic, but the female voice reciting directions gave me lane changes and warned of turns ahead.

"Seventeen weeks."

"Easy-peasy. Jake has a guy who will do twice that." Morgan stopped speaking. I hoped she would remain silent.

Andy asked, "Mrs. Morgan. Do you love your daughter?"

Two turns and a lane change came from the navigator before the woman answered.

"She's better off without that love. The trip to Evermore proved that."

25

"What's the Lily Club?" I pulled up to an ornate gate bearing the name.

"Exactly what you think," Morgan replied. "Lily white. Except for the tokens. The ones they tolerate for their money and position. We have a Mexican state senator, a black federal appellate court judge. Couple Asian guys who are richer than shit, and I mean like Koch brothers rich. And we love to show them off. Make no mistake, though. They all joined to be as white as the rest of the membership. You should hear the Mexican state senator on immigration. I think he'd scrape the brown off with a rusty razor blade if he could. Here." Morgan handed me a plastic card. "That'll get us in the gate."

"What's here?" Andy asked.

"Jake. He's a Platinum Member. That means he gets one of the villas by the golf course. Home away from home, what with his unfortunate separation from the troublesome Mrs. Morgan." She whispered loudly, "*There are rumors, you know.*"

"Is Cynthia here?" I asked. Because if she wasn't, I intended to turn this land yacht around and dump this toxic woman at the nearest curb.

"Of course. Childcare is on the menu of services. The printed menu, that is. There are other menus."

I pulled up to the card reader and rolled down the window but did not insert the card.

"What's the plan?" I hoped Andy would take charge.

Morgan beat her to it.

"It's Sunday night. They've been golfing all day. By this time of the night, they're well lubricated and hanging out at the bar by the pool. Another hour or so and the girls will trickle in. They don't have them come all at once. They need time for the wives to clear out. We'll find Jake and his friends at the pool."

"You mentioned a man named Stroud and Willis Pedmann. Are they members?" Andy asked.

"Stroud is. Pedmann is too cheap. He plays here all the time, but he uses his office as a ticket."

"And where's Cynthia?"

"Jake's villa. Number six. Give me that card and I'll go and get her. I want this done in front of Jake, in front of everybody."

I don't. The last thing I wanted was my image or Andy's image caught on a dozen different phones or surveillance cameras, although from the sound of this club's activities permission to carry such cameras would have surprised me.

"No." Andy rejected the idea in her cop voice. "That's not what's going to happen here. Does that card get into villa number six?"

"Yes, but—"

"Then here's how this is going to happen. You want to make a point with your husband, am I right?"

"And his cronies. I'd like to ram it up their—"

"Fine. Dr. Blaine and I will go and get your daughter. You will go and find your husband. Does the pool have a diving board?"

"Uh-huh."

"Find your husband. Tell him something—anything to get him to go with you. Take him to the end of the pool with the diving board. That's where we will take Cynthia. Tell him to watch the diving board. Got it?"

I checked the rearview mirror. Morgan stared at Andy.

"You said Blaine."

"What?"

"You said Blaine. You called him Blaine. You told me at the door his name was Blake."

Did she? I couldn't remember.

"I'm sure you're mistaken."

Now I felt certain Morgan was no longer drunk.

"Who are you?"

Andy took a moment, then pulled open her shoulder bag. She extracted a wallet containing her badge. She showed it to Morgan.

"I'm a cop. Is that a problem?"

I watched Morgan think about it for a moment. I expected anger. A tantrum. Resistance and sudden reversal. I did not expect her to shrug.

"Nah. Actually, that's just fine—as long as you do what you promised."

"We will."

"Okay. Pool. By the diving board. So, what's the deal? You're going to make her appear there?"

"Something like that," I said, still wondering why revealing our deception didn't derail this whole operation.

"Twenty minutes," Andy said. "Be there in twenty minutes."

I could not see Morgan's mouth, but her eyes smiled.

26

———————

Andy and I found villa number six after a longer trek than anticipated. The oversized cottage sat a quarter of the way down the first hole of the club's golf course, backed up against the property's protective twelve-foot brick wall. Heavy tropical vegetation separated number six from number five and number seven on either side. A winding asphalt path wide enough for a golf cart connected to a cobblestone walk leading to the villa.

I handed Andy the key card. She stopped us where we stood.

"We're not actually doing that," I said. "The diving board thing?"

"Or course not. We're here to help this child." Andy stopped at the door. "I want you to disappear. Just until I see what we're dealing with here."

I fixed a grip on her satchel's shoulder strap.

Fwooomp!

I vanished. She towed me to the heavy front door.

Instead of swiping the card, Andy knocked. A moment later the light beside the door flicked on. A few seconds after that, the door cracked open. A girl in her teens peered out at Andy who lit up a radiant smile and held up the card.

"Hi, honey. I'm meeting Mr. Morgan here in a few minutes. He gave me his card, but I didn't want to barge in on you. Is Cindy sleeping?"

The girl, taking it all in stride, nodded.

"Good. Then you can go." Andy pulled a twenty from the satchel and handed it to the girl. "I'll keep an eye on things until Mr. Morgan gets here."

88

The babysitter eyed the twenty like there was something sticky on it. She backed up as Andy gently pushed the door open and let herself in.

"I'll just get my things," the girl said. A moment after gathering a backpack and scooping up an unfinished Diet Coke, she bid Andy goodnight and hurried down the walk. I watched her pick up the pace and disappear beyond the foliage, hustling in the direction of the clubhouse where music thumped, and voices drifted.

Fwooomp!

"Not exactly the kind of security I will be looking for in a babysitter." Andy held the door open for me.

"We're never hiring a babysitter. I've seen too many horror movies."

"Ah." Andy nodded. "So, little Horatio is going to grow up joined at my hip?"

"Our hips. And we're not calling him Horatio."

We entered a plush cottage with dimensions exceeding the first floor of our farmhouse. To our left, a modest kitchen shared space with an immodest bar. To our right, a huge television faced a pit ringed with a proportionally huge semi-circular sofa. Explosive glittering graphics on the screen played out the talent competition that the teen babysitter had been watching. I looked for but could not find a remote. Thankfully, the girl muted the sound when we knocked.

A stairway directly ahead climbed to a loft. I pointed. Andy concurred. We quietly ascended.

The loft above the kitchen overlooked the first floor living space. A king-sized bed dominated an open concept bedroom. Following the line of a low wall, we entered a short hallway with a second bedroom on the left. A bathroom dominated the end of the hall. The whole interior smelled of fresh paint and new woodwork.

Andy eased open the door to the second bedroom.

Cynthia Leigh Morgan, a.k.a. Jane Doe, lay on a fully accessorized hospital bed in the center of four naked walls. If this was a space meant for a child someone missed the memo about stuffed animals and cartoon posters. Nothing but a set of white cabinets adorned the white walls. Detached IV stands loitered in the room's corners. Two wheelchairs—one powered, one hand driven—parallel parked against the wall to our left. A variety of monitors took up space on the far side of the bed.

The girl under the covers wore a cloth skull cap to warm her bald head.

The usual cold fist gripped my chest. *How far gone is this girl? Too far for my help?*

There have been failures. A young woman in Brainerd, Minnesota gained nothing when I made her vanish. I do not know why. Perhaps it was her age. She was one of the few adults I have touched. By contrast, a child that the same dying woman asked me to treat flourished. I do not know why.

I checked on Andy. She shared this experience once before with me, but not like this. Not in this kind of room. And not since the start of her pregnancy. I worried over how the presence of a dying child might affect her.

Reflex brought her hand to her belly as if to protect the life forming there from the disease claiming the child in this bed.

Munchausen by Proxy. This girl's alcoholic mother was clueless.

We passed through the door into the room. At the girl's bedside I assessed the degree to which she slept. It seemed shallow.

I made a quick decision.

"Cindy," I touched her shoulder. "Cindy, are you awake?"

The girl stirred. I tried to measure her body size to come up with an age that factored in her illness. She was not as tiny as some I'd seen.

Her eyelids fluttered, then opened.

She jerked away from my touch and shot upright. The cap warming her head slipped off and flopped on her pillow. She groped after it and tried to pull it back on.

Andy joined me at the bedside. She closed a grip on the girl's forearm, preventing her from tugging the cloth over her skull.

The girl froze.

Andy gently lifted the cap from the girl's fingers.

Cynthia Leigh Morgan stared at my wife.

Andy laid the cap on the pillow then ran her palm over the skin on the girl's skull.

"What?" I asked, baffled by the look on my wife's face.

"Stubble."

27

———————

"Are you hungry?"

"Yes, please. We had pizza before." Cindy Morgan climbed on a stool beside the kitchen island. "There's leftover in the 'fridge."

She seemed remarkably comfortable for someone tugged out of her sleep by strangers. I pointed at the bandages on her left hand. "Do they give you medicine intravenously?"

"I guess so."

Andy shot me a look and the minute shake of her head. No. I made a guess that her assessment followed brief examination of the drawers and cabinets in the child's hospital-like room. The few IV pouches found contained nothing more than saline solution.

Andy pulled the pizza box from the refrigerator and slid it onto the marble surface of the kitchen island. The girl flipped back the lid and pulled a cold slice from a wedge filling one third of the box. She bit into it with both energy and appetite.

Andy and I exchanged glances. I'd never seen either in any of the children I'd encountered; most slept through my visits.

"Cindy," Andy said, "do you live here now?"

She nodded.

"How old are you?" I asked.

In deference to a mouthful of pizza, she held up both hands with all digits extended. She was small for ten, but not sickly small. She did not have the skeletal look of some children I've seen. Andy let her have the

91

skull cap again, but there had been no mistaking the stubble on her skin. A head in need of a shave. Which made me wonder who's been shaving her head.

Munchausen by Pay?

"Do the doctors come here to see you?" Andy asked.

Cindy nodded.

"So, you never go out to a hospital for any treatments or anything?" I asked.

"No. Dad brings them here."

"What kind of treatments do you get?" Andy asked. "Do they make you sick? The treatments?"

She made a face ridiculing the idea of being sick. "Mostly they give me my pills. Sometimes they hook me up to that bag on the pole thing. Do you know my dad?"

"Good question. I'm going to be honest with you. No. We don't know your dad. We just met your mother tonight. Remember when she took you to North Carolina?"

Cindy's eyes widened. "Hooo, boy, do I. Dad was pissed. Totally."

"But you remember why your mother took you, don't you?"

"Sure. She saw that guy on social with the thing he was using to make little kids with cancer disappear. I thought that was so cool. I wanted to try it, but Dad made us come home. He was super mad at Mom for taking me. *Super mad.*"

"Do you still want to try it?" I asked.

I caught her in mid-bite, but there was no mistaking the flash of excitement on her face.

"Honey," Andy asked, gently placing one hand on the girl's arm. "Do you feel sick?"

"Right now?" she asked through a mouthful.

"Now. Yesterday. Last week. Do you feel sick any of the time?"

"Mostly not too sick. They said the medicine makes it so I don't feel sick, I guess. I'm supposed to swallow the pills, but at first it was hard."

"Have they ever told you what you have?" Andy asked.

"Cancer."

"Right…but there are different kinds. Have they—?"

"Primitive neuroectodermal tumors," she replied. "PNET."

Andy nodded. "That's what they told you?"

"Uh-huh. I have stuff growing in my head."

"How did they find out? Did you start feeling dizzy? Did you have any strange episodes?"

She shook her head. "Dad brought Dr. Thurston to see me. They did tests on me. That's when we found out."

"When was this?" I asked.

"In spring."

"What kind of tests?"

"I don't know."

Andy stood.

"Honey, would you give us a minute. Go ahead and get some milk from the refrigerator. Dr. Blaine and I need to talk for a minute."

ANDY DID NOT UNDERESTIMATE the girl's hearing. She led me to the front door. We stepped outside, leaving the door cracked to keep an eye on the child who plowed into her midnight snack.

"I'm no doctor, but…" I whispered.

Andy held up one hand to silence me. She reached in her bag and pulled out a small bottle. She held it up for me to read the label.

Inotuzumab Ozogamicin.

I didn't even try to say it out loud.

Satisfied that I'd seen the medicine name, Andy opened the cap and tapped out a white pill.

"I took this from her room. Here."

"What? You want me to take this?"

She nodded. "She said they make her swallow them, but bite into it."

"You bite into it."

"I already did." She pushed her palm closer.

I picked up the pill and carefully split it with my incisors. Hesitation quickly evaporated. I let the halves fall into my mouth and chewed them.

"Holy crap. Is that Mike and Ike?"

"Close. Good and Plenty. Licorice. That girl is not sick. Which is what the mother suggested."

"Sonofabitch. You mean the Munchausen by Proxy? You think the dad is making her and everyone around think she has cancer just to score sympathy points?"

Andy shook her head. "Something else is going on here. Mom is what she said. A brass bitch. She didn't take the girl to North Carolina to cure her. She took her to prove that she wasn't sick in a way that stuck it to and exposed the dad."

"Whoa. That may be a really messed up family drama, but why would the attorney general for the state of Texas get involved? I mean—they might be golf buddies, but that's one giant leap to take. From golf buddy to coconspirator?"

Andy checked her watch.

"Clock's ticking. Mom's about to alert dad. He's going to be coming down that path very pissed off. I thought we'd be gone by then, but now I think we should play this a different way."

I watched the girl pour herself a glass of milk. From where I stood, her arms and legs looked sturdy. Her movements betrayed no uncertainty. Wrap her up and put her in a wheelchair, and she might pull off the look of a genuinely ill child. Top it off by shaving her head and the image sold.

"Jesus. They have their daughter convinced she's dying."

"Morgan said something. She said, 'Munchausen for Pay.'"

"Yeah. I heard that, too. What are you thinking?"

Andy squinted in the direction of the music floating from the clubhouse.

28

———————

Andy capped the milk carton and put it back in the refrigerator.

"Sweetie, finish that piece of pizza and then we're going to do the disappearing thing."

"Seriously?" Excitement bubbled up.

"Oh," I said, "it gets even better. Wait 'til you see."

Andy hurried around the island to face me.

"You got this?"

"Affirmative."

She pecked a kiss on my cheek and departed at a trot. Cindy watched her slip out the front door.

"She's pretty. Is she your girlfriend?"

"Boy, I sure hope so. Eat up, kiddo." I laid the Styrofoam on the table.

"Is that the stuff from YouTube?" Cindy asked, chewing. She picked it up. "It feels like Styrofoam."

"Yeah. It does. We really need to go. We can leave the pizza out for you. This won't take long."

"I have to wash my hands," Cindy said. She hopped off the stool and went to the kitchen sink. "Germs. They said to watch out for germs. I'm not supposed to get stuff like colds or flu. That's why I can't go to school."

"I'd like to meet your doctor sometime."

In a dark alley.

Cindy lathered the soap and her arms like a surgeon scrubbing for a procedure. I guessed that whoever played the doctor or nurse in this perfor-

95

mance went all out to involve the girl in the theatrics of false illness. Andy and I were prepared to admit to being wrong, but neither of us believed Cynthia Leigh Morgan had anything in her head but the lies she'd been told.

"Come on, munchkin. Let's go." I picked up the Styrofoam.

Cindy finished her scrubbing ritual and dried her hands with a paper towel. I held out one hand and she took it, trusting me.

We left the house. Although the night air remained warm and humid, I wore my light summer flight jacket to accommodate the BLASTERS.

"You warm enough in those pajamas?"

"I wear these all the time."

I checked the golf cart path in both directions. The path remained empty, a winding dark line against grass illuminated by dim light spilling from the distant clubhouse. Dew glittered on the manicured golf course grass.

I handed the girl the Styrofoam prop. She clutched it in both hands expectantly. I leaned over.

"Do you mind putting your arms around my neck? Like I'm going to—"

I was going to say 'carry you' but she didn't let me finish. Still holding the chunk of deception, she threw both arms over my head and hopped up, hooking both legs around my waist.

"Yeah, okay. Like that." I stood up and braced her back with one hand. "Ready?"

"Uh-huh."

Fwooomp!

We vanished. I thought she might shriek. Or giggle. Or something. Instead, she gasped for air.

"Easy, there. Breathe. Just breathe."

"Okay."

"You ready for the best part?" I pulled a BLASTER out of my pocket. Since she had a tight grip on my neck and had locked her ankles behind my back, and she had no weight to drop, both my hands were free. I snapped a prop on the BLASTER and checked the power. The prop spun and threw breeze over my wrist.

"Here we go."

I flexed my ankles against the pavement. We launched.

She gasped.

"Easy. Just breathe like I said."

"Are we flying?"

I held out the BLASTER and applied power. The prop pulled us forward.

"We are now."

She twisted her upper body for a better view ahead. I rotated sideways to make it easier for her to see. We rose along the golf cart path at first, but then I veered out over the course. Why not? I leveled off fifteen or twenty feet above the fairway and accelerated until a steady breeze flapped her loose pajama legs.

"What do you think?" I asked.

"WTF!" she whispered breathlessly. "That's what my mom says, only she says the real words."

"You can say the real words if you want."

"I'm okay."

I aimed for a small tree, then performed a tight hop directly over it. She made no sound. The stranglehold on my neck and around my waist spoke for her.

"Ease up a little. You won't fall. I got you."

She relaxed for a few seconds, then squeezed again.

I curved and zoomed along the course, showing off, giving her a thrill ride. No hurry. She had a lifetime of dealing with grade A shitty parents ahead of her. Why not give her something joyful to remember?

My eyes acclimated to the dark. Stars filled the sky, casting thin light down on the golf course. We skimmed across a motionless water hazard, placing the stars both above and below us. The sparkling limbo tugged a giggle from the girl. I flew a tight circle around the crown of another tree, and she laughed.

"Now, listen," I said when she settled down. "I'm not really a doctor, so I am not the one to make this call, but when we're done with all this, your PNET should be gone, okay? No promises, but it should be. You need to insist on being tested somewhere that's loaded with doctors and nurses and equipment. Not at home, okay? I'm sorry to say this, but—"

"You think my daddy was lying to me."

Her flat, matter-of-fact statement came from someone much older than the child who held up two hands to reveal her age. The child who laughed with abandon seconds ago.

I didn't answer.

"I kinda knew. I did. And Mom knew. That's why she took me to North Carolina. She's mad at Dad all the time so she took me there to stick it to him. She said she was going to show the world. I knew what she meant."

"I'm sorry, Cindy. Truly."

"I'm pretty sure I'm not sick like they said I was."

"Don't let them keep it up. Make them take you someplace legit, okay? You know what I mean? A real hospital. With real doctors. Do you know how to call 911?"

I felt her nodding.

"If they won't take you, call 911 and tell the paramedics everything. Except maybe this zooming around bit. They might have trouble believing that."

"I sure do."

We approached the party lights strung around the pool at the clubhouse. The music grew louder.

She said softly, "He'll have to give the money back," she said. "Or give it to someone who really needs it."

"What money?"

"The GoFundMe. We reached our goal."

"What goal?"

"Five million dollars. We got five million dollars. That's pretty good, isn't it?"

I almost laughed. Instead, I twisted my wrist to the right. We broke away from a line that would have delivered us over a vegetation border separating the pool and patio from the greater golf course. I pulled a tight one-eighty and aimed for the wide-open fairways and greens.

"I'd say that's good enough to get you a longer ride, kiddo."

29

I would later confess to Andy that the scene at the pool was all my fault. By taking the girl on a second swooping and diving tour of the golf course, buzzing water hazards, and hopping over trees, I left too much time for things to deteriorate at poolside.

On our return, skimming the fairway and gliding over the first hole tees, then sailing over the hedges surrounding the clubhouse patio, I saw immediately that things had slipped out of hand.

A small crowd lined the edges of the pool. A group of men clustered around the short ladder attached to a diving board on the deep end of the pool. One man had climbed the ladder and now clutched the rails aligned with the flexible blue Fiberglas board. In his mid-forties, with dark curly hair and matching black chest hair nesting in the vee of a silk shirt open nearly to the waist, he faced off against an astonishingly steady Elaine Morgan who stood halfway to the end of the board. She showed no signs of inebriation.

She presented a problem.

Andy's revised plan had been to land Cindy on the diving board between the silver rails. A safe spot, not out over the water, well in sight of anyone watching. It had been Elaine Morgan's mission to get her husband close enough to the board to witness Cindy's appearance.

Six feet of diving board lay between Elaine and Jake Morgan. Elaine sliced the air between them with what looked like a carving knife stolen from the roast beef cutter at the buffet table—the image of a woman defending herself from the pirates who forced her to walk the plank.

Jake Morgan cursed his wife and called her a stupid bitch as we approached.

I whispered in the girl's ear. *"Call out to your mother, Cindy."*

"Mom!" The girl's voice cut through the thumping music and the unbroken tirade coming from her father. Nearly everyone lining the poolside looked up. "MOM!"

Jake Morgan abruptly stopped shouting.

I reversed thrust to slow down and eventually stop over the clear chlorinated water. The pool glistened with the aid of underwater lights. Illumination from below, bent by ripples on the pool surface, painted Elaine Morgan with wiggling light.

"Cindy?" The girl's mother cried out.

"Mom!"

"Let go of my neck, Cindy," I whispered. *"Give me the foam and hold my hand. As long as you hold my hand, you will not fall."*

I slipped the Styrofoam under my right arm, then helped the girl find my left hand. She slowly released the grip on my neck and unwound her legs from my waist. She grasped my hand and forearm with both of her hands, not fully trusting that she would not splash into the pool below. I eased her out beside me.

"Drop the knife, Elaine!" Jake Morgan took an aggressive step toward his wife. His red-shaded face glistened with sweat. He called over his shoulder without looking. "Cindy! Go back to the villa! Somebody take her back!"

Heads swiveled, looking for a girl who wasn't there. Two of the men at the base of the diving board ladder hurried in opposite directions, searching the small crowd around the pool and the perimeter of the patio. Both men looked starkly out of place in suits and ties. Andy would later tell me she spotted weapon bulges under their coats.

I glanced at my wife at the far end of the pool. Or thought so, if only for an instant. A woman in a white blouse and black skirt with dark hair watched from the shadows cast by a striped umbrella mounted on a table. As soon as I saw her, I realized it wasn't Andy. The face was too angular; the tummy too thin. The hair Andy had captured in a tidy bun hung free around the woman's neck and shoulders, dark and straight.

I found Andy a split second later. She watched the scene play out from a vantage point midway up the length of the pool. Her plan had been to instruct Elaine Morgan to take a position near the diving board and wait. I didn't think for a moment that Elaine challenging her husband with a kitchen knife was Andy's idea.

Jake Morgan took another step toward his wife. The step caused the blue board to bounce, and his estranged wife to wiggle precariously. Less than ten feet from me, I could tell Morgan was as well lubricated as his wife had been. He held the chrome rails of the diving board to steady himself. He shouted over his shoulder.

"Cindy! Go back to the villa!"

"Dad, I'm right here." I suppressed a laugh at the attitude laden pre-teen tone the girl delivered with virtuoso skill.

Morgan jerked his head back and forth.

"Over here, Dad!"

Elaine Morgan relaxed her stance and held out her arm. She dropped the knife, which sliced into the pool with a satisfying plop.

"I'm here, Cin. Show your dad."

I pulsed the blaster. The girl gripped my forearm as if applying a tourniquet. Using low BLASTER power, we glided toward a spot between the feuding parents.

"*Put your feet on the diving board, Cindy,*" I whispered. Morgan reacted to my voice.

"Who's there?"

"It's me, Dad," Cindy answered. "I think I'm all better!"

Morgan searched the air around him like a man being attacked by hornets. His wife adopted a smug, satisfied calm that helped her stabilize on a narrow board six feet above the pool water.

A light bump transmitted through the girl's grip when her feet found the diving board. Fingers crossed. The instant she relaxed her grip on me I retracted my arm.

Fwooomp!

An electric snap coursed through my hand. The girl appeared between her mother and her father, both hands still outstretched in my direction.

"*What the—?*" Jake Morgan gaped at his daughter.

"Fuck," Elaine Morgan filled in the blank for her husband. "That's right, Jake. Our baby is cured. *Just like I said she would be.*"

The woman took two steps and folded her arms around the girl. The mask of rage on her face melted and for the first time during this weird evening, I saw something resembling a mother's love appear on the bitter woman's face. Cindy wrapped her arms around her mother and held on. They bobbed on the diving board.

Jake Morgan clutched the chrome rails with his jaw dangling.

Lights flashed. A dozen cell phone cameras froze the moment. A dozen more remained aloft, recording video of what began as a delicious spat between rich people at a country club pool and ended in a miracle.

That's going viral, I thought.

I looked for Andy. She strode purposefully away from the action, crossing the patio on a line that would eventually take her to the exit. Time to go.

I flicked the power slide control on the BLASTER to ascend, intending to climb high enough to use more power without drawing attention. I planned to keep an aerial eye on Andy and then join her in the parking lot by the Land Rover. The keys lay snug in my pocket. Andy and I would drop the vehicle at Morgan's home, then return to the hotel via Divisible Man Airways. The starlit sky and cityscape would provide a sparkling backdrop to what I hoped would be a romantic cruise back to the hotel. I had news to share.

The plans coalescing in my head evaporated abruptly when a man broke away from the crowd gathered at the pool and walked a determined line to intercept Andy along the pool's concrete edge, not far from where a rope line separated shallow from deep water. He caught up to her and hurried to block her exit.

Noise, be damned. I dove toward the two of them. The man loomed over Andy. Over six feet tall, hard featured and muscular, his arms and shoulders tested the seams of the suit he wore. His square jaw wore fashionable stubble. Lines of slicked black hair hugged his skull.

"Detective Stewart," he said in a sweet-sounding voice that intended nothing of the sort. "I thought I recognized you."

"I can't say the same." Andy made a move to sidestep the man. He matched her move. "Do you mind?"

"I don't mind at all," he replied without moving. "Why don't you join me for a drink? I'd love for you to tell me why you're here."

"I don't drink, and I can't imagine why I would want to chat with you. Please get out of my way."

"Sorry, honey. Not going to happen. Let's keep this civil. I have some friends who would be thrilled to meet you." He reached for her upper arm. Andy reacted sharply. She slapped his hand away and stepped back.

He grinned the way coarse men do when they mistranslate a rejection as a playful challenge.

I fired a shot of BLASTER and descended in position directly adjacent to them, facing the pool. My feet touched the tiled surface of the patio.

Andy, cool as I've ever seen her, met his insolent gaze.

"Let me guess. Friends who visited me and my husband last winter?"

The grin widened. That was enough for me.

Fwooomp!

I flashed into sight beside him. The instant gravity planted my feet, I threw both hands up and shoved a rock-hard bicep. The man had time for a glance at me and nothing else. His high center of gravity threw him off balance. He tried to replant his feet, but the edge of the pool gave him no room.

He split the twinkling surface of the water with a satisfying splash. I watched a deep wave slap over his startled face when he sank.

"Time to go," I said. "Take my hand." I reached for her. She jerked her hand away from mine.

"No. Not like that. People are watching."

Like I cared. Vanishing would have been the safest exit. I didn't give a damn what people saw or thought they saw. I opened my mouth to make the point, but she shot glances back the way she had come.

The two large men who had split off to find Cindy now fixed their attention on the dustup at the side of the pool. They looked neither amused nor likely to remain idle.

"Come on!" Andy broke away from me on foot. She accelerated to the same speed I'd seen her use on the ramp at Essex County Airport.

I took off after her.

We sprinted across the patio, darting back and forth between tables covered by umbrellas, knocking white plastic chairs aside. Shouts broke out behind me. The man in the pool surfaced and sputtered curses.

"Get after her!"

Andy dashed through a gate and raced across an open span of lawn toward the parking lot where Elaine Morgan's Land Rover waited. I glanced back to see the two men race to where I had dunked their friend or boss or whatever he was. They reached out to extract him, but he cursed and threw one arm in our direction.

"Go!"

I didn't look to see if they obeyed.

I ran.

Andy reached the Land Rover first, angling for the passenger side. I jammed the BLASTER back in my pocket and grabbed the driver's door handle as soon as I reached the vehicle. The SUV sensed the key in my pocket, beeped and flashed recognition lights, and released the door locks. Andy and I piled in.

I stomped the brake and poked the Start button. The engine fired. Headlights flashed on, perfectly illuminating the two men pounding through the gate toward us. One of the two held a pistol in his hand. The other jabbed his hand into his coat. I didn't wait to see what he came up with. I threw the Land Rover in gear. Andy snapped her seatbelt.

Tires squeaked and skidded. I threw the wheel over and we cut a tight turn. In the rearview mirror I saw the two men pull up for a moment, then break to one side. Their move told me they had a vehicle close at hand.

Not good.

"Seatbelt," Andy said calmly.

"What?" Adrenaline pumped up my heart rate. My pulse pounded in my ears along with an irritating chime sound.

"Seatbelt, darling. Put on your seatbelt. We're going to wind up in an accident. Please put on your seatbelt."

"Thanks for the vote of confidence."

I threw the wheel back to straighten our path. Several hundred feet ahead, the gate with Lily Club scrawled in wrought iron or steel loomed in our headlights.

I fumbled the belt across my chest and lap. Andy's hand guided the end. She snapped it in place.

"How do we get the gate open?"

Andy looked. "It's either motion sensitive, or we will need the key card."

"I think it's in my pocket somewhere. Shit."

Andy glanced back. In the rearview, I saw headlights swing around after us.

"We don't have time to open the gate," she announced.

"You want me to ram through it?"

"No. God, no. That gate will stop this thing cold." She glanced around. "Go right."

"Where?"

"Right! Go right!"

I cut hard right. The SUV bumped over a curb and across a sidewalk. The vehicle bounded onto the lawn fronting the club. Shadows wiggled and bounced in the headlights. We tore across the grass and through rows of colorful flowers in a vast, curved bed. I swerved around a line of low shrubs. The bumper clipped an empty bench and sent it tumbling across the grass.

"Do you have some idea wh—?"

"There! Go left. There. See it?"

An opening in a tall hedge marked a sidewalk that joined the grounds to the street. Darkness ahead indicated a drop off where stairs descended to the street level.

I stole one last glance at the parking lot. Headlights raced toward the gate. The men following us were taking the traditional route. If Andy was right, the gate would slow them down.

We plowed through the opening in the hedge. Vegetation tore at each side of the Land Rover. The bottom fell out. A sick feeling leaped into my chest. For what felt like forever, the front wheels lost touch with the ground. Unlike the choreographed leaps I'd seen vehicles perform a thousand times on the screen, the SUV obeyed reality's rules. The weight of the engine hurled the front end at the ground. A horrific jolt shot through the vehicle, our seats, and our bodies. My teeth smacked together. My chin hit my chest. My hands broke from the wheel. I feared the impact would bend the frame and disable us. The suspension crashed and rebounded, throwing the front end up and down. The rear wheels thumped and bounced down a set of steps. Sparks flew and chunks of plastic snapped off the body. We bounced into the street. To my utter amazement we not only kept moving, but I managed to get my hands back on the wheel and my feet back on the pedals. The Land Rover responded to both.

I heaved us hard right and stomped on the accelerator. We roared forward. Half a dozen warning lights flashed on the dash. My first concern, the tires, was quickly alleviated. The wheels still rolled.

"You okay? Dee? Are you okay?" I felt a terrible sick turn of my stomach thinking about the impact we had just endured and its effect on her.

"I'm good." She slowly uncoiled the tight upright fetal position she had struck before impact.

"Are you sure?"

"Will, I'm good. Maybe a little bruised, but I'm fine. *We're fine.* Watch the road, please." I realized I'd been looking at her. Looking at her abdomen. "Take a left. Now!"

I almost missed the turn. We nearly sideswiped a parked car. Aligned with a new street, I stomped on the gas. Andy twisted in her seat to look behind us.

"Left again."

This time I made the turn under control.

"Now pull over. Fast." She pointed. The street was residential. Cars parked randomly along a tidy curb. I swerved hard, picking up on her intentions. The wheels bumped the curb. Before the heavy SUV came to a solid stop, I threw the shifter into park and killed the engine.

"Lights!"

I found the switch and flicked it from Auto to Off. Still the lights remained on, a courtesy function that might last up to a minute. I grabbed the door handle. Opened it. Closed it. The lights stayed on.

"Shit!"

I snatched the keys from my pocket, threw open the door, and piled out into the street. I found the Lock button on the fob and stabbed it with my thumb. The lights flickered and the SUV beeped at me. I hit it again.

The lights went out.

I ducked around to Andy's side and crouched. She looked down at me through the glass. Silence joined the thundering of my pulse in my ears.

Andy grabbed the interior rearview mirror and adjusted it. She watched. A moment later a vehicle roared through the intersection behind us without turning. I waited until the racing engine faded into the distance, then walked back to the driver's door and climbed in.

We studied each other, chests rising and falling, words failing. A lock of hair fell across one of Andy's eyes.

"What the hell was that about? Who was that?"

She let the war flag hang. A spark of feral excitement ignited in her unhidden eye.

"I just met Louis Blaze's pit bull."

30

———————

"Five million?"

"That's what she said."

"Do you think she was exaggerating? I mean—that's a lot for a GoFundMe."

Andy, who had taken over driving the Land Rover, decided not to return it to Elaine Morgan's home, citing the chance that the men who chased us would be waiting there. She also decided that we should abandon the vehicle as quickly as possible, since one of the headlights was toast after our airborne departure from the country club. The last thing we needed was to be stopped by the police in a vehicle that may have been reported as stolen.

She found a busy boulevard and pulled into the first available strip mall. She eased around the end of the building and rolled along a succession of back doors, loading docks, and dumpsters. Two rusty trash containers rested a car length apart. She parallel parked between them. After I climbed out, she spent five minutes wiping down anything we might have touched in the front and back seats.

"Shouldn't we be able to look it up?" I asked when she backed away and spent a moment contemplating her work.

"Look up what?"

"A GoFundMe account for Cynthia Morgan. That's public, isn't it?"

She backed away from the driver's door after another round of wiping down the armrest and window controls. Lastly, she rubbed the key fob with a tissue before tossing it into the console cupholder. She kicked the door shut.

"I think so. Unless the account has been closed. Are you sure she said five million?"

"She's a child. She's probably exaggerating." I pulled a BLASTER from my pocket and snapped a prop blade on the shaft. I held out my hand. A look at the stars confirmed my sense of direction. Our hotel lay that-a-way.

Andy hesitated. "Can we go around to the other side? I saw an all-night diner and I'm starving. Plus, I really need to find a bathroom."

I could not argue so I pocketed the equipment. We set off through pools of light cast by security lamps at the back of the buildings.

"It's Rick Blaine, by the way," I said. "Owner of the exotic Café American in Casablanca. And it's not Ingrid Lazlo, her name was Ilsa Lund. Lazlo was her husband."

"You're the movie buff. Next time *you* come up with names." Andy reached up and tugged on her hair. The tidy bun she wore for her role as a doctor slipped free. Her long auburn hair tumbled onto her neck and shoulders. For a flash instant, I remembered the woman I had mistaken for Andy at the pool. Something in the imprint of that moment suggested to me that the woman had not been watching the drama on the diving board. She had been watching Andy, who now stroked her fingers through her hair as much to set it free as to release tension.

It wasn't unusual. Attractive women often study my wife.

"So?"

She glanced at me. She knew what I was asking. I gave her a minute to put it together.

"Little Cindy's sickness was faked. It was exactly what Elaine Morgan said. Munchausen for Pay. They ran a GoFundMe to raise money off the cancer story. Only, I think it's more than that. Much more. If what she said about the amount is true, I don't think this was a garden-variety fund-raising scam."

"If what she said was true, it was anything but garden variety."

"Not what I meant. I think this was more like money laundering. My guess is they set up the GoFundMe around Cindy to move money without having to connect where it's going to where it came from."

"Yeah, but this is obviously a scam based on fake cancer."

"Scams on GoFundMe are rare. They have safeguards. You can report a scam if you think you've seen one. But it's not a scam if the donors know precisely where they're sending the money. And if the fundraiser isn't soliciting from strangers. It's not a scam if no one reports it as one."

"Now you've lost me."

She hooked one hand inside my arm and tugged us together. I felt her excitement over a revelation building.

"Think about it, Will. Leslie has us in the dark poking the elephant in the room. Touching a piece here or there. The injunction. The Morgans. And now a money-raising—no, a money-transferring scam. All of it orbiting the horrible killing of a girl someone mistook for Pidge—vengeance for the flag burning in Lincoln—which in turn connects to Blaze."

"Right, but didn't we know all along the elephant is Company W?"

Andy didn't answer. I could tell she hadn't really heard the question, or she didn't think it relevant. Her thoughts were momentarily elsewhere.

"Using a kid as a cancer victim?" Andy muttered to herself. "I suppose it beats robbing banks."

She lost me. "Who's robbing banks?"

She waved one hand in the air, her erase-the-blackboard gesture. "Blaze built a coalition. He absorbed or destroyed rival groups. Turned it into something more sophisticated than a bunch of gun nuts talking government overthrow. What does that sound like to you?"

"Gun nuts talking government overthrow."

"I'm going to use the T-word. Terrorists. And what do terrorists need more than anything else?"

"Idiots? Gullible true believers?"

She shook her head.

"Weapons? Bombs?"

"Close. They need money. One of the most effective ways the U.S. and our allies have fought terrorism across the globe has been to dry up their sources of funding. Confiscating or cutting off hundreds of millions of dollars being channeled to the groups. Look at the relationship between Iran and the proxy terrorist groups they sponsor. It's not about weapons or explosives. It's about the cash. The sanctions against Iran are all about freezing the flow of cash."

"You think Morgan ran a scam using his daughter so he could raise money for Louis Blaze?"

"I think Louis Blaze ran a scam using Morgan and his daughter. I think that's why Ray Stroud was there tonight."

"Stroud? That goon from an ad for gym membership?"

"Elaine Morgan knew him. She called him Louis Blaze's pit bull. He sure seemed like a pit bull to me. Remember Devon Murphy's undercover reports about something big? Something big takes big money. But that raises a question."

We rounded the end of the building.

"And then what?" I put some pride in knowing and delivering Andy's favorite investigative question.

"No. I was going to ask what if Cynthia Leigh Morgan wasn't the only one? What if there are two—or five—or ten Cynthia Leigh Morgan GoFundMe cases out there? And each one is raising five million dollars?"

I whistled, adding it up. "Ten or fifteen or fifty million?"

"Uh-huh. And that raises the next question."

I didn't bite. I turned and prompted her this time.

"And then what?"

31

———————

W e turned another corner and walked along the storefront side of the strip mall. My watch told me midnight had already snuck past us. The diner Andy had spotted was the sole storefront showing lights. The scent of grease and fried onions joined the pale illumination spilling onto the sidewalk.

A bell announced our arrival at an empty establishment. The rectangular layout stretched toward the back of the strip mall. A counter lined with fixed round stools took up the left side of the building. A row of red vinyl-cush-ioned booths took up the right side. They offered decent cover. Where the counter joined the back wall at the far end, an open doorway accessed the kitchen. Another doorway opened on a hall. A sign above the doorway said Restrooms.

The bell brought a stout middle-aged woman from the kitchen. She issued a friendly smile and told us to sit anywhere we liked. Andy selected a booth near the back. She took the seat facing the entrance.

"Coffee?" The woman running the show arrived with a pot in both hands. One pot featured an orange plastic pour spout. She made the offer to me.

"Hit me. Full strength." I flipped the cup sitting on the table.

"Kin ah getcha anything sweetie?" she asked Andy. "Water? Lemonade?"

Andy smiled, recognizing that she'd been made. "Just the water, thanks."

"Betcha."

Our server disappeared. Andy glanced down. "I guess it shows more than I thought."

"It's the glow. You're like an airport beacon."

"I'm not sure that's a compliment. Although for a while there, I was alternating white and then green. Get it? White and green? Like the airport bea—"

"I got it."

She pulled out her phone and tapped the screen. When she finished, she returned the phone to her satchel.

"Uber in twenty minutes. We might have to order to go."

The woman returned and took my order for a cheeseburger and fries. Andy requested a Reuben sandwich with a side of coleslaw. Ten minutes later both plates arrived. I was about to land a shark bite on a cheeseburger when Andy's face froze, fixed on the glass storefront.

"What?" I turned to look.

"Down! Slide down!" She leaned over and dropped below the lip of the table. I didn't wait to ask. I did the same. We looked at each other across the bottom side of the table. "It's them. They just pulled into the lot."

"Them who? Those guys from the club?"

She nodded. She maneuvered her satchel into position against the bench seat. A moment later her Glock 17 fit snugly in her hand.

"I didn't see. Are they coming in here?"

"No. I saw them pull into the lot, but they were rolling slowly. Checking it out."

"How did they—?"

"Tracker. On the Land Rover. Dammit. I should have thought of that. Morgan keeps tabs on his wife." She issued a sigh that sounded more like kicking herself. "They're looking for the Land Rover. That gives us a couple minutes. Once they figure out that we're on foot, they'll look for us and this will be their first stop."

"Okay. No problem. We can just…"

Andy shook her head and glanced across the aisle. The woman who served us stood behind the counter, casually wiping the surface with a towel. Without looking directly at us she spoke.

"You kids avoiding the law? 'Cause I don't want no trouble here. The till's just about empty."

"I am the law," Andy replied. "Just not from around here. We're avoiding that black SUV cruising through the parking lot. They are most certainly not the law. I don't think they'll come in here right away, but we might have to leave in a hurry if you wouldn't mind giving us the check."

She scanned the front glass. "I don't see no black SUV, but there's a white minivan just pulled up. Appears to be looking this way. You got somebody else after you?"

Andy popped her head up and looked. "That's our ride. We have to go."

"Hold on," the counterwoman said abruptly. She hurried into the kitchen and then returned with a large cardboard to-go box. While Andy dug out two twenties, the woman shoved our food into the box and snapped the lid. Andy held out the cash. The woman carefully plucked one of the two twenties from her fingers. "Let's not get silly here, darling."

Andy hurried to her feet and slipped her hand and weapon into her bag. I grabbed the food box.

"Been a pleasure, ma'am." I swiped a last gulp of the still too hot coffee and regretted it. Andy called to me from halfway to the door.

"Let's go, Will." She scanned both directions. "I think they went around back. We're good."

I waved one last time at the kind woman, then hurried out the door behind Andy. In a flash, we both settled on the rear bench seat. I finger-stabbed the door button. The sliding power door performed its painfully slow closing motion.

"Go. Go-go-go," Andy commanded.

The driver correctly interpreted Andy's tone and dropped the van in gear. I twisted in the seat and kept watch out the back window. I didn't see the vehicle, which must have driven around to the back of the building. We drove well out of sight of the strip mall without seeing another set of headlights.

I settled on the cloth minivan seat.

I had a question for Andy but decided it could wait. I had a feeling it might spark a difficult discussion.

After asking the driver if she minded us eating, and promising to keep it tidy, we went to work on our late dinner.

32

Dinner remained with me in the morning. Heavily. I limited breakfast in the hotel restaurant to coffee and an English muffin. It's rare for Andy to sleep in, but she remained motionless when I slipped out of the room. I thought I'd use a little quiet solitude to contemplate the question I wanted to ask my wife, one that was fraught with potential marital dissonance.

"You're up early," Arun broke my train of thought. He slipped into the booth I occupied in the hotel restaurant. The server, a young woman with purple hair, arrived as if conjured. Arun ordered politely. "Tea, please."

"Bit of a cliché, isn't it? Ordering a cuppa?" I asked after our server hustled toward the kitchen.

"Only here in the colonies."

He looked fresh and sharp as always. Even his white short-sleeved safari shirt had creases. He wasn't wearing a tie, but he might as well have been.

"Where's Pi—er, Cassidy?"

I got a patronizing look. "Pidge," Arun said with emphasis, "is probably sleeping. I have no idea. You may drop the pretense. I thought we'd rather established that."

"Habit."

"Apparently for some time."

I sipped coffee and decided that Arun distracting me from my thoughts wasn't all bad.

"Sleep okay?" I asked.

"Quite. And alone. Let's establish that, since you will be winking at me all day if I don't inform you of my slumber whereabouts."

"Hey, your relationship with Pidge is your own. Leave me out of it."

Arun made a face that mixed a painful expression with pursed lips. "I'm afraid it's not going to be that simple. I've noticed a bit of a father-daughter dynamic between you and Miss Page."

"Instructor-student."

"Yes, well, you may see it that way, but I think she has a different perspective. She does not talk about her family. Her actual family. Not to me, at least. But she talks about you constantly."

"She does?"

"Exceedingly."

"It's…" I was about to say *complicated* but since I consider that to be the worst movie line ever written, I opted for something more precise. "…shitty. The thing with her family, that is."

"I gather."

"Look, Arun, I know you well enough to know that you will be quick to blame yourself if she seals you off from her past. Don't. If Pidge doesn't share her family with you, I can assure you that it's not about you. Just so you never get the wrong impression, no matter what she says or how she covers it up, you need to know that her mother and sister are raging racists."

"A bit harsh."

"No. It's not. They are actual Nazis. With swastikas. And flags. They have a portrait of Adolf Hitler in their living room."

"Bloody hell."

"Exactly. If Pidge doesn't rush to take her new beau home to mama and refuses to explain why, that's the reason. I wouldn't press the issue if you want to build a good relationship with the girl."

"Woman."

"Right. That's what I said." He formed his pained expression again. "What?"

"Well, Will…to be precise, you said, 'girl.' Which is something I've noticed about you and Pidge. Once again, that father-daughter dynamic."

"Is this coming from you? Or from her?"

"I would never presume to speak for her. I don't think you intend it, but sometimes it appears you, quite inadvertently I'm sure, minimize her as a woman. As an adult. It's entirely understandable. You first knew her as a teenaged girl. And she looks up to you. Immensely. That sort of thing forms the DNA of a relationship."

Arun's tea arrived. He engaged in the rituals associated with teabags and tiny kettles of boiled water.

"And here I thought I was having English muffins with my coffee. Turns out I'm having muffins with my English."

He started to speak, then stopped. I waited and let his thoughts steep like his tea.

"It's all over the news again this morning," he finally said. "National and local. Horrible. A young woman burned alive at the stake like that—"

I shot a hand up to cut him off. "If it's all the same to you, I'm trying to keep the more graphic aspects out of my head."

"Sorry."

I looked out the window at wisps of morning cloud rising against a blue sky that, like the brochure said, sprawled bigger in Texas.

"Not your fault. I just—I can't carry around an image like that without knowing there's nothing I can do about it."

"Whatever would you imagine that you can do about it?"

"Stop it. Prevent it. Punish the people who did it."

"Save her?"

I didn't answer. Arun broke into a thin smile. "Cassie says you have a hero complex. You're always trying to save someone."

A ridiculous notion.

Weighted silence fell between us. Andy appeared and saved us both.

"Scoot over, love."

She slid onto the booth bench beside me. She planted a kiss on my cheek and inhaled the scent of my coffee, not in that order.

"They've arrested three suspects." Andy dropped the announcement with the dramatic effect it deserved. She let it hang for a moment. Once more, the young server appeared, making me wonder if I was alone in the ability to simply appear out of thin air. Andy waved her off. "Nothing for me."

"You're not going to eat?" I asked.

"Not right now. We need to go. We can get something when we get there."

I blinked at my wife. Arun's expression reflected my bewilderment.

"Get where?"

"Dalhart. Tiffany Vera Callum's funeral is this afternoon."

33

The Navajo covered most of the vertical dimension of Texas in a two hour thirty-six-minute flight from Austin to Dalhart Municipal Airport. It seemed like a long flight over just one state. I remembered reading that when Texas was annexed by the United States in 1845, they were given leave to remain a single state or divide into up to five smaller states. Crossing a few extra borders would have added nice diversity to the flight. By car the same trip would have clocked in at close to nine hours. Clear skies and smooth air accompanied us, although light turbulence materialized on our descent, and prairie thunderstorms populated the afternoon forecasts.

Andy rode up front with me. I noticed that she kept one eye on our surroundings right up until I raised the gear on takeoff. At the hotel. On the way to the airport. Even on the ramp as we loaded. She didn't relax until we launched. I wanted to ask if she worried about another encounter with Ray Stroud or Jake Morgan, but she kept up a small-talk conversation with Pidge and Arun, and pointedly avoided mentioning the events of the previous evening.

Pidge had been surly about leaving. I blamed her mood on shaking her out of bed and telling her we were wheels up in twenty minutes, which stretched out closer to forty. Arun had been truthful about spending the night in separate rooms, which made me wonder if sleeping solo contributed to Pidge's dark mood.

She dashed my theory when she brightened up in Arun's presence. I told her where we were going and suggested she might contribute to the effort by checking the weather and filing the flight plan. Her single digit response told me what I could do with that idea. She grabbed a coffee to go and rode in the cabin with Arun. They chatted for a while before she curled up and slept.

I'd been to Dalhart, Texas once before, a long time ago when building time for my commercial license. I flew a rented Cherokee 235 from Essex to San Diego for no reason other than I needed to log the hours and I'd never been to San Diego. The flight fulfilled my commercial pilot cross-country requirement. Dalhart had simply been a fuel stop on a leg that I hoped would take me as far as Albuquerque on the first day. After gassing up and launching westbound in the late afternoon, the daily march of mountain thunderstorms blocked my path. Being a flatlander pilot, I executed a prudent return to Dalhart to spend the night.

Two things remained embossed in my memory of the place. As a former bomber training base in World War II, the Dalhart Municipal airport possessed enormous runways and ramp spaces, largely empty and deserted decades after the end of the war, and far greater than the scant general aviation population using the airport required. The second memory was of the sense of vast space. My landing in Dalhart was the first in my career in the part of Texas where wind and drought scraped millions of tons of dirt from over-tilled farm fields to create the American Dust Bowl. The Texas sky stretched farther than I'd ever seen, touching distant horizons in every direction. The land possessed dimensions both beautiful and lonely. The concept of roaring winds and relentless dust came easily to the imagination. Just as easily, I imagined Tiffany Vera Callum caught alone in that landscape. Helpless. Miles from hope of rescue.

Bound. Burned.

The image ambushed me.

"Hey." To shake it off, I switched the intercom to Copilot and broke the headphone silence in the cockpit. I needed to hear Andy's voice. "Fill me in. What's the deal with these arrests? And how did you find out about them? Arun said he watched the morning news, and nothing was said."

"He's right." Andy adjusted the supplemental oxygen cannula at her nose. I knew from experience it can be awkward and uncomfortable at first. I gave her credit for not refusing it. "I'm sorry, but I didn't want to get into the details in front of Arun. I spoke to Tom this morning. He called. Checking up on me."

"Pressure to get back to the office?"

"The opposite. He has me listed as TDY to the FBI. Keeps the city manager off his back about me being MIA."

I bounced my eyebrows at her to show I was impressed by her acronyms.

"He also had intel. You know Tom. He has connections everywhere. He talked to a friend here in Texas law enforcement."

"Texas Ranger?"

"Actually, Texas Highway Patrol. It would have been nice if he knew someone in the Rangers. They're the crime scene investigators in the state. I wouldn't mind a fraternal hookup there. But no, this was someone in the Highway Patrol."

"So, not really inside the investigation."

"But still valuable. Tom said his friend's unit and a bunch of other units were put on standby for prisoner transport connected to arrests in the Callum case. The rumor is they're extraditing three suspects from Dalhart to Austin."

"Isn't that a change of venue issue?"

"Probably. The kind of thing that typically gets hashed out in the county court system. For it to be granted this fast is unusual. I guess that speaks to the control the state attorney general is imposing. On the other hand, this case has generated massive public and media interest. Pretty much every nutball out there is coming out of the woodwork since the AG's office let it slip that they were focused on occult angles."

"Which is bullshit."

"Probably. But it gives Pedmann plenty of plausibility for covering for Blaze. It's bad policing. They're violating the first rule of investigation, which is to let the evidence define the theory, not the other way around. It's also self-fulfilling. Whoever they have in custody will be painted with all kinds of guilt if they're transported hundreds of miles from their home. This will become a circus."

"With intent."

"Maybe…"

"Dee, it's obvious they're covering for Company W."

"You and I look at this from the Company W angle because that's the part that touched our lives. We need to be careful not to let our theory shape the evidence, too."

I made a disapproving sound over the intercom.

"Anyway, Tom said there have been three arrests. All three suspects had links to the girl. All three are from Hartley County. That's all he knows. That and they're being held in Dalhart but may be transported soon."

"Austin?"

"Yup." She absently twisted a lock of hair around one finger.

"Dee, you can't think you're going to get anywhere near these people. Tell me that's not your plan."

"I think there's very little chance anyone will be allowed near the suspects except a court-appointed lawyer. A very carefully selected, court-appointed lawyer who—I'm guessing—may have connections in Austin." She cast a knowing look at me. "And you're right. I won't get anywhere near them." She held that knowing gaze on me.

Crap.

34

"Wait," Andy stopped Pidge and Arun as they gathered themselves to climb out of the airplane. I had rolled to a stop at the Larson Aviation gas pumps. For the moment, no one appeared from inside the FBO which, I was delighted to see, stood beside something called the Red Baron Restaurant. Airport restaurants are priceless gems. Last night's late meal may have been heavy, but the morning's light breakfast left my tanks nearly as empty as the mains on the Navajo. Lunch called out to me.

Andy twisted in her seat.

"Will and I get off here. You don't. I have a job for the two of you."

Pidge dropped back into a seat. Her eyes lit up. I could not get used to the black cap of hair she wore. It was like having a stranger on board. Her icy blue eyes, the flawless skin on her face, the petite and near perfect balance of her narrow nose and lively lips all looked new to me thanks to that one change.

Jesus, I'm seeing her differently.

Not the blonde pixie I counted on to blow up the status quo of any given situation. Not the foul-mouthed ball of fire I've seen drink men twice her size under the table. A woman. An adult woman.

"Tell me we're going to have a chance to seriously fuck these guys up." At least the voice and explosive impulses remained unchanged.

"In the long run, yes," Andy said. "But I'm counting on you to be discrete in this assignment."

"I am a raging volcano of discretion."

Andy ignored the comment.

"Louis Blaze owns an airplane. A…" Andy looked at me.

"Twin Beech."

Pidge grinned. "Round engine taildragger. Nice."

"I did some digging. As much as the internet would allow. There's a good chance Blaze keeps the airplane at a small airport in Green River, Utah. I'd like you to go there and see what you can learn."

"Probably a hangar queen," I said.

"If the airplane is there," Andy continued, "find out who's paying the hangar rent. And anything else related to licensing, maintenance, expenses."

"That should not be difficult," Arun said. If something stood to be learned, the kid's dagger-sharp instincts would ferret it out.

There it was again. *The kid.*

Fresh out of college, yes, but was he really that young? Or was I really that old? I caught my mind wandering while Andy continued talking.

"…paperwork or connections to other partial owners because sometimes fractional ownership comes into play."

"Of course."

"Listen," I said, "Andy will probably make a point of it, but I'm going to say it out loud. Don't do anything stupid. Don't draw attention to yourselves."

Andy interrupted Pidge's protest. "Precisely. Be careful. Keep a low profile."

I said to Arun, "If you get in the hangar, and you have a chance to get on board, Pidge knows what documents are required by law to be carried in the aircraft." I turned to Pidge. "If you find the POH, check the supplements. Avionics upgrade paperwork will show who did the work, which could be valuable. Look for anything. Avionics shops. Maintenance shops. Who did the last annual. Any third party that touched the airplane."

"That's an excellent idea," Andy affirmed. "Take pictures of any names or companies and send them to me."

"On it," Arun nodded.

35

―――――――

"You did that to get them away from here."

The clerk at the FBO desk slid the rental keys in my direction. I scooped them up and claimed the driver seat on the tiny Buick. It took a minute to power the seat far enough to the rear to allow me entry. Andy buckled herself into the front passenger seat. The car was tiny.

"Absolutely. Having them along complicates things."

I steered a rented vehicle out of the Red Baron Restaurant parking lot. Like the car, I was fully fueled after a well-made lunch.

"It's getting worse."

My mind incorrectly leaped to Andy's bout with morning sickness.

She scrolled her phone screen. "This is awful." She flicked her finger across the device.

"Media coverage?"

"Uh-huh."

Andy spent half of our lunch on her phone. First trading text messages with Leslie. Then scanning updates on what was being called by the cable news networks *A Burning in Texas*, complete with lurid graphics.

After two or three screens, Andy abruptly darkened her phone screen and dropped the device in her bag.

"I don't understand. How can people sit in their homes or their basements or their rat holes and post this *unfounded crap*? Some of these lies are so over the top—so outrageous—it's like someone is conducting an experiment to see how stupid and gullible people can be. With every lie swallowed a new low is achieved, but they don't stop. They invent something crazier. It's insane."

"Dee, they've been doing the same thing about you for over a year."

"But I can ignore it. That poor girl can't fight back."

"Reasonable people will see it for what it is. Have a little faith."

I should have shut up when I had the chance.

36

———————

The faith I cited took a hit fifteen minutes later when we rolled up to the drab little church on the outskirts of Dalhart, a simple one-story white rectangle with double doors at the front and a modest wooden cross at the apex of the roof.

"What the hell is this?"

I killed the Buick engine. A roadside sign named the one-story building *Christ Our Savior Christian Church*. A bible verse on the sign, attributed to Matthew, said something about love and tolerance.

Andy and I assessed the situation through the windshield. People milled about on the wooden deck fronting the small church's dual front doors. A few held signs fashioned from cardboard shipping boxes. On more than one, the Evermore logo underscored sentiments scrawled in marker on the sign.

BURN IN HELL

ABOMINATION

MAN + WOMAN AS GOD INTENDED

"Not what you expect to find at a funeral," I commented.

"Dear lord."

There weren't many demonstrators. Half a dozen men. A few women. Two preteens whose enthusiasm for holding up signs seemed wilted by the afternoon heat. Part of the group loitered on the deck in front of the church doors. A few sat on the steps. Several trudged back and forth across the side-walk in a lackluster picket line. It struck me as odd that the scene lacked media presence. After what Andy found on her phone, I fully expected the funeral to be covered by hungry reporters and relentless cameras.

I scanned the street in both directions. Except for a pickup truck slowly crossing at the next intersection, the barren street reminded me of the scene in *To Kill A Mockingbird*, minus one rabid dog.

"The *Dalhart Texan* said—"

"Who?"

"The local paper online. It said the service was at 1 p.m. this afternoon." Andy glanced at her watch. "If that were true, it would have started a few minutes ago. I'm not seeing any cars." The gravel and dirt lot wrapped around the church building lay empty.

"If a service has started, the crowd is a bit thin." Two well-aged pickup trucks and a rusted sedan nudged the curb in front of the church.

"Come on." She popped open her door.

I followed. Heat hit us when we stepped out of the rental's air conditioning. We crossed a span of what could only be called lawn by someone with a generous disposition. Dry grass crunched underfoot. Above us, the thin leaves of an old tree whispered in a warm breeze.

A woman in a pink baseball cap proclaiming Jesus as her Savior assumed a position blocking Andy.

"Are you here for the harlot? The demon shall not violate this house of the Lord."

Andy stopped and looked down at the poor breathless creature.

"Oh, darling," she said softly. "That is so sad."

Andy's sentiment sailed right over the pink baseball cap. The woman wiggled a sign at Andy proclaiming that God would smite all sinners.

"I'm so sorry!" A voice called out from the church doorway.

A tall man dressed in a black shirt topped with the white square of a clergy collar hurried across the deck and down two steps. Although young, his hairline had receded too soon in life. He wore glasses and had hands that looked like they could palm a basketball. If he'd been out of seminary more than a year, I would have been surprised. Tall and thin, he had the look of a growing boy whose body had not caught up with his bones.

"Please," he said to the woman in the hat, "Mrs. Conner, would you just go home? The Callum family has already cancelled the service."

The woman glared at Andy, oblivious to the young pastor's suggestion. The two preteens, however, tucked their signs under their arms and started across the barren lawn.

"Father Jason Wallick." He offered Andy a hand. She took it and shook.

"Detective Andrea Stewart. This is my husband, Will."

"Pleased." I waved. He nodded.

"Are you here for the Callum service?"

"Yes." Andy looked past Father Wallick at the church doors. "You said they cancelled?"

"I'm sorry. The family has elected to hold a private ceremony."

"Can't imagine why." Andy flashed a smile at the woman with the sign, who had not moved.

Father Wallick addressed the cluster milling at the front of the church. "Honestly, Henry. Ted. Mary Jean. Nothing is happening here today. Don't you have something better to do?"

"The Lord's work is never finished," the woman in the pink hat declared.

"Amen to that. But I sincerely doubt this is what He has in mind. There is no service here this afternoon, Mrs. Connor."

She squinted up at him. "'Thus I shall punish the world for its evil, and the wicked for their iniquity.' Isaiah 13:11."

"'…and I will cause the arrogancy of the proud to cease, and I will lay low the haughtiness of the terrible,'" Andy said, smile still shining. "You forgot the second part."

"And you forgot the Levitical Law," the woman snapped at her. "'Thou shalt not lie with mankind as with womankind; it is an abomination.' This house of the Lord will root out abomination from our midst." Her face grew red. Sweat oozed out of her skin, seeking the folds and creases surrounding her eyes and running down into her collar.

Andy nodded. "Silly me. I thought the message was 'judge not, lest you be judged.' I guess I missed the part about rooting out abomination."

The young pastor squeezed his lips to suppress a smile.

Andy tugged my arm. I took the cue to tag along as she wished Mrs. Connor a blessed day. Father Wallick followed us to the car.

"They're not terrible people," he said when we reached the roadside. "These are difficult times for many of my parish members. So many voices lie to them these days. Too many seek solace in the lies."

"Satan?" Andy asked.

He smiled and shrugged. "The internet. So, yeah, I'd say so. May I guess that you're not from around here?"

Andy produced her badge. "City of Essex, Wisconsin."

He raised his eyebrows. "You've come a distance."

Andy didn't answer the unasked question. "Do you think the family would be open to a visit from strangers?"

"The Callums are good and kind people, Detective. They did not deserve this tragedy." He looked askance at Andy. "Please understand that I feel protective of Mr. and Mrs. Callum today. This is their darkest hour. Your journey here suggests that you either want to ask them something or tell them something."

"Tell them."

"Police business?"

"Personal, with a tangent to police business."

"Is it something that may give them peace?"

"Father, I'm not sure anything anyone would say can give them peace at this moment. But if the moment is right, I may be able to reassure them that this…" she gestured at the faltering protest that just lost the two preteens "… utter madness has nothing to do with their daughter."

"Well, then," he said, nodding and folding his hands, "all I can do is beg you to be gentle and respectful."

"Of course."

"I was just getting ready to drive over to the Callums' home." Wallick pointed in an easterly direction. "I'll get my car. You're welcome to follow me."

I took several steps toward the front of the church.

"Hey!"

The sputtering picket line stopped. Faces turned in my direction.

"Let he who is without sin cast the first stone."

Nobody moved for a comedic moment, then the slow sidewalk shuffle resumed.

I caught the young pastor looking at me. Something in his expression suggested that he wanted to offer me a nice little ribbon just for showing up at the game.

"I'm sorry, it's the only Bible verse I can quote."

"Perhaps you should work on that." He headed back in the direction of the church.

Andy opened the Buick door and hopped behind the wheel. I took shotgun. She tossed me a look that inscrutably blended criticism with compliment.

"You are such a twelve-year-old."

THE PASTOR PULLED onto the street driving a vintage Honda Civic with rust lining the wheel arches. It looked like rodents had chewed away the steel. Andy followed.

"A local church is forced to cancel a service for the child of one of its member families," I said. "What do you make of that?"

"Told you it's getting worse."

Wallick made a turn. Andy followed. I twisted in the seat and looked out the rear window until Andy asked what I was doing.

"I dunno. I feel like that pickup just went around the block."

"Darling, every other vehicle in this town is a pickup truck."

Which is why they all look like they're after us. I twisted to face forward.

"Nice battle of the Bible verses back there, Dee. What was that Leviticus Law stuff?"

"Levitical Law. Old Testament commandments. A lot of the social media posts implicate Tiffany Callum in gay sex."

"The girl was gay?"

"No. At least not from anything I've seen. And for the record, The Bible really doesn't take a position on homosexuality except for that one passage. I guess the question of orientation wasn't top of mind in those days, what with, I don't know, starvation, and disease, and conquering armies to worry about."

"Not to mention dental hygiene."

"What?"

I spread a wide smile and pointed at my teeth.

"You think about that a lot? Ancient dental hygiene?"

"Every time I see a period movie, I ask, How do these people even have teeth? Anyway, you were saying...battling Bible verses..."

"I was saying that the Isaiah quote is one of the only references to sexual orientation. It gets used by people who condemn same sex anything, and by the same brush stroke, anything transgender."

"Transgender?"

"Some of the posts claim she wasn't originally a girl."

"Was she?"

"Originally a girl? Of course. She wasn't trans. Or gay. Nor do I think she was a witch. Nor do I think she worshiped Satan or participated in ritual animal sacrifices. I think she was a bright and promising college student who was burned alive because some fool on Tik Tok posted the groundless theory that Tiffany Vera Callum torched a row of racist flags in Nebraska."

"For which said fool on Tik Tok also paid with her life."

Andy sighed.

"But why go to the trouble of destroying the girl's reputation after they went to the trouble of murdering her?"

Andy didn't answer for a block or two, then she said, "You know, you ask a good question now and then. We're here."

The Honda pulled over and parked behind a line of cars at the side of the road. The line stretched away in both directions. Andy parked behind Wallick's Honda and killed the Buick engine. The focal point of all the visiting traffic was a small house on a block dotted with small houses sharing the same Dust Bowl era architectural style. Wooden clapboard construction fronted a tidy porch with gingerbread accents. In addition to the cars parked on the street, a row of cars, pickup trucks, and SUVs lined a narrow driveway leading to a shed at the back of the property. Whatever service or gathering had been planned for Tiffany Vera, it had been moved to or concluded at her family's home. Several small children, oblivious to matters of life and death and probably bored with the somber grownups inside, played on a rusty swing set in the back yard. One little girl wearing a dress over white tights pumped tiny legs as she grasped the chains and soared higher and higher. She closed her eyes and let the empty blue sky reach for her at the peak of each cycle.

Was that Tiffany Vera when she was small? Flying for a split second at the apex of each pendulum arc?

My imagination morphed girlish cries of joy into terrified screams.

"Jesus," I said aloud. I shook it off.

Andy looked at me. She knew. I knew that she knew.

"What's the plan here?" I asked.

"No plan. We pay our respects and hope someone will talk to us. I'd like to speak with the parents. If they throw us out, we go quietly."

We exited the Buick. Father Wallick waited on the dusty sidewalk. I felt grateful for the escort. His presence enhanced our chances of entry.

A waist-high gate hung open. The lawn lay as dry as any we'd seen, but someone had been religiously watering beds of flowers on each side of the front steps. Blooms in a dozen different colors and shapes flashed in the sunlight like gentle fireworks. Against a backdrop of tragedy, the blossoms carried on a sad celebration.

Getting into the house required no introduction or explanation, or even the company of the clergy. The front door hung open. A steady hum of conversation carried from within. Wallick led the way into an atmosphere scented by potato salad and casseroles and fresh bread. To our right, a dining room table appeared ready to collapse under the weight of contributed food. To our left, a packed sitting room hosted friends, family, and neighbors, many wearing black. In one corner, an easel mounted a framed color photograph of a smiling young woman with short blonde hair. The studio image suggested recent graduation. The resemblance to Pidge struck me viscerally.

And now you have a face to populate the nightmare.

Someone in the living room doorway greeted Father Wallick and tugged him into a conversation. Strangers glanced at Andy and me, openly questioning.

A woman in black appeared directly in front of us. She emerged from a kitchen where half a dozen other women chattered. She passed us carrying a casserole dish with both hands protected by heavy red oven mitts.

"Come in, come in," she welcomed us. "Let me just…"

She found a spot on the table, a minor miracle. She nudged the dish in place on a hot pad, then pulled off the mitts. She turned to face her two new guests. Red accents rimmed her eyelids. If she started the day with makeup, most of it was gone. Her nostrils had the ruby hue of someone either enduring the third day of a nasty cold or who had been crying. Her dark hair displayed the first streaks of gray. I wondered if they had been there three days ago. Despite the grief coursing beneath her skin, she offered us a smile and her hand.

"I'm Donna Callum. Are you from school?" she asked Andy.

"No ma'am." Andy folded her left hand over the handshake she held. "Mrs. Callum, nothing I can say can begin to touch what you're going through. I'm so sorry."

The smile wavered. Fresh glitter dampened the woman's eye.

"Did you know Tiffy?"

Andy maintained her grasp. "Ma'am I did not. I know this is an incredibly difficult time for you and your family. I promise you I am here with the deepest respect. My name is Andrea Stewart. This is my husband Will."

Andy didn't release the woman's hand. I dipped a respectful nod.

"Then…how do you know my daughter?"

Andy took a deep breath. She stole a glance around the room. Wallick continued his vigilance over the exchange despite an energetic monologue heaped on him by a white-haired woman. One or two other people watched protectively but from far enough away that Andy was sure her next words would be heard only by the grieving mother.

"Ma'am, I'm a police officer and if you're up to it, I have something you should know about what happened to your daughter. It may not be what you've been told."

Tiffany Vera Callum's mother asked us to wait outside by the swing set where the children eyed us with suspicion until an older girl, perhaps eleven or twelve, came and gathered up the brood. The girl hustled the kids into the house using freshly endowed authority and threats to tell on one resistant little boy. Mrs. Callum emerged from a back door with a man close behind. He shared his wife's strained and worn appearance. Like the children who departed, he regarded us with open suspicion. The screen door slapped shut behind him.

"You're a cop?" He crossed the small back yard and stopped facing Andy.

She produced her badge and let him take it from her.

"Detective Andrea Stewart of the City of Essex Police Department. It's in Wisconsin. But I want to be clear. I am not representing myself as an investigating officer. I do not have jurisdiction here. I'm here on a private matter that connects directly to what happened to your daughter. That's to show you that I take the law seriously."

He handed back the badge.

"My daughter has never been to Wisconsin."

"No, sir, I suppose not."

"Donna says you know who killed her."

"Not precisely. Is there someplace we might sit down?" Andy gestured at the obvious, a picnic table under a shade tree centered in the back yard.

We seated ourselves facing the Callum couple.

"How many weeks?" Mrs. Callum asked before Andy could speak. She gestured at Andy's belly.

"Seventeen."

It brought a weak smile. "How has it been?"

Andy offered a humble shrug. "A little rough. It's my first. Every day is new."

"Do you know if it's a boy or girl?"

We both shook our heads. "We're going to wait."

"If it's a girl," I said, "we're thinking of calling her Ethel."

"We're not calling her Ethel," Andy affirmed.

"Jesus Christ. Don't saddle her with that," Mr. Callum said. An unexpected smile twitched at the corner of his mouth, but the suspicion never left his face.

"I knew Tiffy was a girl right from the start," Mrs. Callum said. "I felt it in my heart. We picked a girl's name, but we never picked a boy's name. She was Tiffany Vera long before we ever said hello."

"It's a beautiful name," Andy said.

"My mother's name was Vera. She did so love that child. She's passed now, my mother. A year ago. It was such a loss, but now…now I'm glad. I'm glad she didn't—"

Tears flooded the woman's eyes. Mr. Callum wrapped his arm around his wife's shoulders. She leaned into him.

I checked the back windows of the house. They didn't make it obvious, but a few faces watched us through the glass. Women in the kitchen.

"This town," Mr. Callum said bitterly. "They knew our girl. She grew up here. She volunteered at the food drive. She was a model student. *The things people are saying.* Horrible things. I don't understand it—this *social media.* They're calling her terrible names. Saying she did things. Did this to herself. Our church—those folks refused to allow—to have our little girl—to have —" He swallowed. "That kid—"

"Father Jason," Mrs. Callum admonished her husband.

"He's just a kid, but I give him credit. He stood up to it. He said to ignore them. He said he would hold the service regardless, but I won't have my baby given into the arms of our Lord with that bullshit parading outside." He bit his lip. *"I will never ever set foot in that church again."*

"I don't blame you," I said, thinking of how it would be for Callum to stand with the Connor woman lifting her face to her savior every Sunday morning.

Mrs. Callum pulled a handkerchief from the pocket of her dress and dabbed her eyes. She slipped from her husband's protective arm. He planted both elbows on the table and folded his hands into a double-layered fist. He narrowed a gaze on Andy.

"You said you can tell us who killed our baby. Tell me. I want to know."

Andy leveled her gilded green eyes on the wife, the mother—a woman who had lost, in the most horrifying way possible, that which Andy now carried and nurtured inside.

Are we wrong in doing this, especially now?

Andy reached across the table and took the woman's hands. Her posture and expression mixed resolve with deep compassion.

"Do you remember a news story from about a year ago? A story out of Lincoln, Nebraska involving a rally of what most people refer to as 'hate groups' that ended with a bunch of their flags catching on fire?"

Mr. Callum glanced at his wife, then back at Andy. He nodded.

38

If nothing else, Andy's description of events ushered the Callums through the door to the second commonly accepted stage of grief. As Tiffany Vera Callum's father listened to Andy the muscles in his jaw tightened. A dark vein emerged above his right eyebrow.

Andy asked if the authorities had discussed this with them. They said no, they had been told nothing contrary to the line delivered to the press and cameras. They had been shocked by suggestions of a sexual hate crime and outraged by allusions of occult practices. Such unfounded claims bore no resemblance to their baby girl. Ever. When they said so, the police refused to discuss the matter. Local police said the investigation was in the hands of state authorities. State authorities advised them to contact the local police.

Mr. Callum asked Andy for the identity of the girl who lit the flags on fire in Lincoln. Andy replied that revealing her would only increase the chances of her meeting Tiffany Vera's fate. Andy's answer did not satisfy. Mrs. Callum told her husband that what happened was not that girl's fault.

Mr. Callum rose and took several steps,. He whirled back to face us.

"They killed my baby because—because of what? *Because of some stupid mistake?*" I don't think I've ever seen a face so stricken, so horrified by the malice rooted in raw ignorance. "Why should we believe you?"

Andy gave it a moment's thought. "My role—our role in this doesn't matter. Someone needs to speak for your daughter. The lies being told about your daughter cannot stand. I never knew Tiffany. But you did. You know the girl you raised. That's why you know I'm right."

Callum seethed.

"Bull. What's in this for you? Because if you're looking for fame or to cash in on this, I will not have it. *I will not.*"

"Mr. Callum, I've already had too much fame in this matter. The worst kind. Fame is the last thing I want." She paused to ensure he was listening. "You're not wrong. There's something in it for us. We *owe* the men who did this to your daughter, and I mean to see them brought to justice. But it's no longer about what they did to us. It's about what they did to Tiffany."

Andy tossed a glance and the narrative to me. I explained how Company W joined an attempt to defame my wife and end her career, and then attacked us in our home.

Andy added, "The attack on us was nothing compared to your loss. I just wish—maybe if we had done something sooner, maybe this horror never would have fallen on you and your family. And for that I am sorry."

If a moment called for unleashing Callum's rage, I thought this was it. I prepared for a wave of blame. A command to get out of his sight. A shift of his anger in our direction.

I prepared to grab my wife and make us vanish, and I didn't care who was watching. Violence throbbed through the vein in the man's forehead.

Rage did not come. Or blame.

Mr. Callum issued a heavy sigh as if the air was let out of him. He staggered to the table and dropped onto the bench beside his wife, spent.

Andy spoke softly. "I was told, in my police training, never to promise justice to the victim, but I swear to you, we will find these men and—"

"Not if I find them first," Callum muttered.

Andy surrendered a moment to him, then continued. "I believe in law enforcement, Mr. Callum. *We* will find them—the law will find them—and they will know justice. You have my word. But as a police officer, Mr. Callum, I am obligated to warn you *not to do anything on your own*. It will not go well. What follows will only multiply your pain. Your wife needs you here with her. Not sitting in prison. You need her by your side if you're going to get through this. Do not take that away from her. Or from yourself."

Callum stared at the woodwork between us. He gave no hint that the words registered. "I think you should go."

"Wait," Mrs. Callum said.

She rose from the picnic table bench and hurried to Andy who also stood. She put her arms around Andy and held on. I heard her whisper.

"You protect that child. Protect that child with your life."

39

I buckled my seatbelt. Andy did the same, but she did not reach for the start button on the dash. I knew better than to speak. Andy pulled a tissue from her satchel and poked it in the corner of each eye before putting on her sunglasses. We sat in a thick silence.

Which I eventually felt compelled to break.

"You did a good thing there, but I'm not sure that helped them or got us anywhere."

"Just wait."

The car interior sweltered. I wanted to ask if she would at least start the engine to run the air conditioning, but I had been asked to wait.

I waited.

Less than three minutes later Mr. Callum rounded the back of the house and stalked toward us. A tall man, fit and muscled, he struck me as having regained a degree of lost determination. Sun brought out color on his face. For the first time, I wondered what he did for a living. The dark suit he wore did not fit well. His arms were a bit too long, a bit too muscled. Perhaps the suit only came out at the best and worst of times.

At the end of one of those potent arms, in his fingers, he carried a business card. He crossed in front of the Buick. Andy rolled down her window.

He held up the card.

"This fella. He's got a sheet metal business in town. Does a lot of shooting up at the range. Talks a lot of smack about the Negroes and the Mexicans and the government and a bunch of that conspiracy crap. I always ignored him and the idiots who hang with him. Most people around here—good people—ignore the nonsense from guys like him and the politicians down in Austin and the dummies on the radio." He handed Andy the card. "Out at the range, he likes to dress up in fatigues. He wears one of those patches. That Company W bullshit."

Andy tucked the card in her bag.

"Thank you."

Callum leaned down. He planted one elbow on the lip of the open car window and lowered his head until he could see us both.

"Donna made me promise. Six months. Six months for your law and justice. If he's still walking around after six months, he won't be in seven."

The grieving father pushed off the side of the tiny Buick and walked away, never taking his eyes from the empty swing set in the back yard.

40

"Leslie said the FBI is tracking three more GoFundMe accounts with profiles nearly identical to the one for Cynthia Morgan. Four, five, and seven million. All three accounts met their goals in just a couple weeks and have now closed." Andy delivered the update without looking at her phone, which meant she got the report back at lunch, two hours ago. I didn't question the delay. She likes to let the bits and pieces simmer. I appreciated that she kept her eyes on the highway.

"Twenty-one million bucks. Not a bad haul."

"But no complaints. No donors reporting fraud or asking questions."

"Money laundering?" I asked. I adjusted my air conditioning vent. We were southbound. The sun beat down on my side of the car.

Andy drove her usual fifteen over the 55-mph speed limit. Despite that, another tall pickup truck roared past us when a straight stretch and traffic allowed. I wondered if the locals knew something about speed enforcement that we didn't. The Ford F-250 was the third of its kind to pass. I wished I'd taken a closer look at the one I'd seen lurking in Callum's neighborhood.

Logic suggested that someone following us would not pass us. I pushed my paranoia aside.

"I wouldn't call it that," Andy replied. "I think GoFundMe is blameless in this. In fact, it's the fact that there have been no complaints that feels out of place."

"Isn't that just because no one has exposed these people as faking their kids' illnesses. No revelations. No reason to cry foul. Can the FBI track the money?"

"Probably. If they weren't on it before, they're on it now. At the very least, they can interview the subject of the fundraising. Maybe the money went for medical bills." She took one hand from the wheel and pushed her hair back; except her hair didn't need pushing. Before pulling away from the Callum home, she produced a hair tie and pulled everything into a ponytail. The ponytail comes out when she's setting herself to a task. The push-back gesture happens when she's thinking. It told me that despite her statement, the last place she thought the money went was toward medical bills.

I decided to show her I was keeping up.

"What do terrorists buy with 21 million dollars?"

She threw me a look.

"Hey, you're the one who told me that the number one item on the terrorist wish list is money. This is a lot of money. So, what are they doing with it?"

"Nothing good, love. Nothing good."

THE DECISION TO drive south was not unanimous. I wanted to find a hotel and a cold beer, and not in that order. Andy had other ideas. She drove through the heart of the small town, past the courthouse, and past the county jail. At the jail building a string of media vans camped along the curb. It explained the absence of interest in the canceled funeral service. News that the three suspects had been arrested in the vicious burning of an (alleged) occult follower eclipsed services for the victim.

Uniformed officers loitered outside the jail. A cluster of people, some with camera equipment, mingled on the sidewalk. The double door entry seemed well protected.

"If we're going to get in there, it needs to be in the middle of the night," I said as we drove past.

Andy barely looked sideways at the single-story structure.

I waited to ask until she passed up two potential hotel options, drove past the police department without stopping, and then finally turned onto Texas State Highway 385 at what seemed like Dalhart's busiest intersection. The Toot'n Totum gas station, home of the *Which Wich Superior Sandwich,* slipped by on my right. A sign said we were on our way to Amarillo. Andy accelerated on the green light. A flat landscape of parking lots and one-story buildings streamed past us. Random grain silos constituted a city skyline.

"Where are we going?" A Best Western floated by on Andy's side of the car.

"I need to look at something."

"Okay. Anything in particular?"

She hesitated.

Her reluctance to show her hand told me something was off. I contemplated letting it hang. I had nowhere else to be, although the day had grown long, and a cold beer would have been welcome. The sun had been relentless all day but building clouds on the western horizon promised relief soon, perhaps even a cooler evening. Cumulus towers reaching jet flight levels would bring an early sunset. Everything looked white and puffy for now, but I remembered the forecast for afternoon and evening thunderstorms. Then again, for as dry as the landscape looked, the prospect of rain falling and actually hitting the ground seemed slim.

I tilted the seat back and gave her silence to fill.

"Tiffany Vera Callum left the university in her own car after her last class on the day she died. She promised her parents she would be home before they turned in for bed. She never arrived. Leslie sent me a map pin."

"The scene of the crime?"

"Uh-huh."

We gradually departed the broad streets, storefronts, parking lots and fringe strip malls of Dalhart. State Highway 385 hit its stride at the city limits where it grew two more lanes and joined a railroad track on its journey toward Amarillo. Wide fields bearing circular irrigation discs spread out on either side of the road.

"You don't have to come," Andy offered.

"Are you telling me to jump?"

She pursed her lips and flicked a glance at me over the rim of her sunglasses.

"No. I just mean you don't have to come with me when we get there." She struggled. "It's just…you seem…more affected."

"By what?"

"The news. The images. Descriptions. And I understand about things you can't unsee. I'm completely with you about the video. I never want to see it."

I looked at the endless road ahead, which did not so much as twitch one way or the other as far as my eye could see.

"You can stay in the car."

She said it gently and without judgment. She wasn't wrong. I felt like I was physically holding a door shut in my mind. Something behind that door wanted to burst into the room at any moment. Something I didn't want to see or imagine.

"Did you see the photo?" I asked.

"I did. She looked a lot like Pidge."

And there it was. In a split second I saw it. A girl alone. Men taunting her. A post driven into hard earth. She had a face now. Desperate. Drained of hope. Did she beg to know why? Did they tell her? Did she deny it?

"Will."

Did they ask her if she'd ever been to Lincoln, Nebraska?

"Will."

"Yeah." I tugged my vision back to that which my eyes could see through the windshield. "I'm here."

"Love, it's a given that you would care about anyone who suffered this. But this is so close to home."

"Why do you need to see where it happened?"

She concentrated on driving and on composing an answer. Another pickup truck roared past us. I checked. Andy cruised at 73 mph. The guy had to be doing 90.

She said, "I don't have a good answer. It's one piece of a picture. I need all the pieces if I'm going to see the whole. Does that make sense?"

Not for the first time the contrast struck me. A woman of such beauty drawn to the intricate details of something so ugly.

"For you? Yes."

We let silence hang between us for a few miles before I went for the last word.

"If you think I'm going to let my pregnant wife go hiking offroad by herself, you are mistaken. I'm all in. Always."

41

Andy used her phone to chase the pin that Leslie dropped. Our route followed Texas 385 southeast from Dalhart. Many miles later, a turnoff took us across the railroad tracks that mimicked our route. A dirt road pointed west toward … nothing. Flat nothing. Farmland without farms.

Vast fields stretched to infinity. Some green. Some brown. All of them laden with emptiness.

More disconcerting was something I noted when Andy slowed to make the turn. Half a mile down the highway a vehicle at the side of the southeast-bound lanes parked with one set of wheels far enough off the road to give the vehicle a slight tilt. Pickup truck, I guessed, although it was far enough in the distance that I left a margin for error. Either a pickup with a cap on the bed, or a big SUV. Possibly a Chevy Suburban, the "national car of Texas."

It looked a lot like the guy who raced past us. But then again, they all did.

Maybe it was nothing.

I felt a twinge of the paranoia that infected me in Iowa where men with ball caps were either hunting for Pidge or hunting for a bite of barbecue at a church picnic—and I could not tell the difference.

We rolled up and over the railroad tracks, then accelerated on the rough dirt road, headed west toward that endless horizon and the wall of towering cumulus rising from it. What had been white and puffy acquired a dirty leaden look.

I twisted in the seat to watch the parked vehicle. It grew smaller and remained motionless and therefore less discomfiting. Probably just someone wise enough to pull over before taking that important phone call.

We drove several miles on a dirt road listed as County Road K on Andy's phone. I considered the tag generous. Except for being the width of a vehicle and roughly flat, I would not have qualified this as a road.

What looked like a dead end approached. Instead of ending, the road hooked 90 degrees to the left. The change in direction meant something to someone once upon a time. An abandoned shed marked the turn. Rusting equipment—some kind of conveyor—lay in the weeds around the shed. Two cement cistern cylinders poked out of the ground, choked with weeds.

Andy made the turn.

Fields with circular irrigation patterns streamed past us on either side. The sun on my shoulder along with the digital compass in the rearview mirror said we headed south. The road dipped and ascended, but not much more than a foot or two either way. This was seriously flat country.

It should have been easier to see the trouble ahead, but we traversed one of those stretches that dipped for the better part of a mile before a slight rise took us back to level ground.

"Okay, this is not good."

Two parked pickup trucks broke the flat horizon ahead.

The road appeared to intersect another dirt track marked by a stretch of leaning and tangled wire fence. Directly ahead, on the other side of the intersection, one parked truck angled across the full width of the road under our wheels. There was no misinterpreting his position. His companion did the same to the left of us on the dirt track we approached. The drivers sat behind the wheels of their vehicles.

"That's one of the guys that passed us." I pointed.

"I know."

Andy slowed but did not stop. She took the 90-degree turn to the right and accelerated. She tightened her belt, adjusted her seatback more upright, and checked her mirrors.

"They're not moving."

"Did you get the feeling we're being herded?"

"A little."

"Great."

She said nothing.

The Buick claimed to be a compact SUV but there was next to nothing sporty or utilitarian about it. It struck us as a kiddie car the moment we approached it in the airport parking lot. The front-wheel drive and cushy suspension were not made for the rough ground we covered. The entire vehicle rattled and shook from the abuse the road dished out. Andy ignored the vehicle's protests and kept her speed up.

I twisted in my seat and watched through the rear window.

Andy checked her mirrors. "Still not moving. Maybe they're farmers. This is all agricultural land. They might be looking at us like we're lost tourists."

"Or trespassers. Is this the only way into the crime scene?"

She glanced at the phone in her left hand. "Not sure. Probably not."

I reached in the back seat and pulled my flight jacket onto my lap.

"What are you doing?"

I pulled a BLASTER from the jacket pocket and retrieved one of the six-inch carbon fiber props. I snapped the prop onto the shaft at the end of the power unit. Andy glanced at my handiwork.

"Getting ready. Just in case. If these guys are Company W morons, I want a quick way out."

"They're probably just the farmers who own this land. They could also be state cops. For all we know, we're not the only ones here today. State investigators might be guarding the scene. There could be any number of officers holding a perimeter, especially for a national news story like this."

"Well, that would be good," I turned around and leaned down to check the mirror on my side, "because the farmers just fell in behind us."

Andy confirmed the sighting by pushing for more speed. The oversized grille of at least one of the trucks raced after us ahead of its own cloud of dust. The Buick's digital dash readout said 57 mph. It felt like twice that thanks to the thundering and rattling of the wheels over the rough track.

"This would be a great road for a chase," I said, "if we were in an Abrams tank."

Andy swerved to follow a bend in the track, swerved back again, then resumed our original line westward. I saw no good reason for the s-turn in the middle of nothing.

An intersection presented itself. We were too far away to see the crossing track, but not too far away to see two more pickup trucks parked on either side, waiting.

"Dee, this is getting serious. I have an idea. Those guys behind us are a quarter mile back. Pull up now. Stop. We get out and beat it out of here." I held up the BLASTER and flicked the prop. "Leave 'em wondering."

"No." She pushed hair behind her right ear and then fixed a determined two-handed grip on the wheel. We accelerated. The digital speed readout displayed 66.

The vehicle vibrated and shook. Fifteen miles per hour would have been jarring on this road. Anything over that wanted to remove the fillings from my teeth. I gripped the handle above the door, then dialed the climate control knob for my side of the car down to 60 degrees. I was sweating.

I made a note of the sunroof control in case we needed a vertical exit. Leaving the vehicle would confuse our pursuers, but it also meant abandoning my flight bag and both of our overnight bags. I wasn't keen on either.

"How far?"

"Another mile or so."

We shot through the intersection. This time the two waiting trucks did not hang back. Even before we passed, dirt flew from all four wheels of the gunmetal gray truck on my side. He wasted no time pulling in directly behind us. I watched him fishtail violently and hoped he might lose it and block the road for everyone that followed. No such luck.

A sick feeling washed over me. What if they start shooting at us? Buick's little compact SUV was anything but bulletproof. It would only take one round drilling through the thin skin and through the upholstery into—

"How many? In the trucks. How many did you see?" Andy demanded.

"My side, I only saw a driver."

"Same here. That's good." She pushed the Buick to go faster.

"How is that good?"

"They can't drive and shoot at us."

"Jesus, Dee!"

She glanced at me. "What?"

"Fine. If you're going to read my mind, what am I thinking now?"

"You're thinking we should pull over and make out. That I should surrender my desperate aching loins to your tender touch." She glanced at me and laughed. "You said to read your mind."

"Not that part, for God's sake. Go back and read the part about them having guns. You really think they can't shoot at us?"

"Not if there's only one per vehicle and he's driving."

I held on. Ruts in the road threw the wheels. The steering wheel jerked in Andy's hands. She pushed for more speed. 78 mph.

The very real possibility of losing control and rolling this little tin can across an irrigated field now replaced gunfire as the violent death I envisioned.

The road dipped and lifted. We entered a landscape with actual terrain. Like modest ocean swells. We descended, then climbed a hill not much higher than the Buick, then dove into another shallow dip.

Flying up the other side, we crested a shallow incline onto a fresh span of infinite flat.

Andy slammed on the brakes. The anti-lock system chattered violently. The Buick shuddered over the rough dirt track. Ruts bit and grabbed the steering. Dust flew up around us. The stupid little rental refused to stop. I braced to T-bone the white pickup truck blocking the track ahead of us. Andy swerved to miss it, but that only put us on a line toward another a two-tone Suburban. She cranked the wheel. We departed the dirt track. Fortunately, there was no ditch. We missed the second vehicle and bounced into an open field, and careened across the untilled ground outside the irrigated circumference before we entered the circle defined by the center-pivot irrigation system. Freshly tilled earth acted like glue. The wheels sank. We heaved to a stop. Dust billowed around us.

I hit the sunroof switch, a useless effort. The glass panel above us crawled just far enough for an escape hatch I doubted Pidge would fit through.

"We gotta go." I unsnapped my seatbelt and threw open my door. "Take my hand."

Vanishing before the dust cloud revealed we were gone would cause beneficial confusion. I figured I could pull Andy across the front console. After that—

"No."

I reached for her hand. "Let's go."

"No." She jerked her hand away.

Stunned, I tried again. She ignored me and grabbed her satchel from the front floorboards under her legs. She popped open her door. I reached for her.

"*Don't!*" She pulled away and stepped out of the car.

Dammit! I threw open my door and stepped out after her. My boots sank in soft ground. Choking dust drifted away from the sunken Buick. In the dim near distance, two men climbed out of the parked trucks. Both lifted bright white cowboy hats to their heads. The trucks that had chased us pulled up and stopped. Four more men emerged. The first two walked toward us. One of the two placed his hand on a gun holstered at his hip.

This can't be happening.

Andy faced them in a naked line of fire on the other side of the car. I tried to run to her. Soft dirt absorbed my steps like beach sand.

Rounding the tail of the Buick, I saw the decals on the sides of the pickup truck and the Suburban. They differed, as did the paint jobs, but the meaning was unmistakable. My guts froze.

Of all the stupid clichés to die from. The Company W killers were cops.

Gold star decals marked the side doors of the two vehicles that had road-blocked us.

That's how easily Tiffany Vera Callum had been taken. Pulled over by the sheriff. Flashing lights and a friendly face bearing a badge. *What seems to be the problem, officer?* She didn't have a chance.

I pounded across the back of the car. No matter what Andy had been thinking, no matter who was watching, there was only one way out of this now. Up.

In just seconds one of these two trained officers would spot the BLASTER in my hand and shout a weapons warning that would start the shooting. I shielded my hand from view as best I could.

Andy moved away from me and the stuck Buick holding both hands high.

"I'm a police officer," she called out.

"We know," one of the two men shouted back.

Crap!

I stomped through the dirt to catch up to her. Clutching the BLASTER in my right hand, I prepared to grab Andy's right arm with my left. The men formed a menacing firing line at the edge of the field.

I fixed a grip on the imaginary levers in my head and readied myself to throw them full forward with all the extra effort I had.

Just as soon as I pulled Andy into my grasp.

"We know who you are, Detective Stewart." The shorter of the first two men took off his hat the way a man does when meeting a woman. "I oughta give you a speeding ticket, but Tom Ceeves says that's just the way you drive."

Tom Ceeves…?

42

———————————

Don't.

Andy mouthed the harsh word at me as soon as I reached her. She took a step to her left, away from me. Her avoidance posture hit me like a Canadian cold front.

The man who spoke Tom's name doffed his cowboy hat and held it in his hands as he looked over the Buick. "Well, you buried that little clown car up to the axles. You know that Al Dorian out at the airport was just messing with you, giving you that thing. He keeps it around as a joke to play on folks from up north."

"It does stand out in a town where every other vehicle is a pickup truck," Andy said. "I'm sorry. You are?"

He approached. Shorter than Andy, he had weathered skin and a cowboy mustache topped with friendly blue eyes. He wore boots like mine, well-traveled and creased. I guessed him to be about my age if you looked past early wrinkles at the corners of his eyes.

"Sheriff Dalton. Hartley County, on which you stand. You can call me JB." He extended his hand. Andy walked to the edge of the dirt circle and took it. He gestured at the taller man beside him, considerably older with a gaunt face and restless eyes. If he had hair, I could not see it under his hat. "This here is Sheriff Jefferson Willard, our good neighbor from Dallard County, from whence you have come."

Another round of handshakes.

"You know my name," Andy said. "This is my husband—"

"Will Stewart," Dalton said. He gave me his hand. Dry and calloused. The man did some real work when he wasn't driving a sheriff's unit. "Pleased to meet you." His eyes suggested he wasn't lying.

"I guess I'm just as pleased," I said. "Sorry about the chase. We thought you were someone else."

Dalton dropped his hat back on his head. "Yeah, about that. Maybe we can discuss who's who and what's what over supper. That sky tells me we don't want to be the tallest objects out here when that squall line arrives."

"You know Tom Ceeves?" Andy asked.

"Indirectly. I know Sue Kresky, sheriff of Bear County, up by the North Pole there in Wisconsin. She and your boss have been an item lately. I guess they got to talking about you coming here, and one thing led to another. She told him about me, and he asked her for an introduction. I talked to him just this morning."

"Then you knew we were coming," Andy said.

"Was that you keeping tabs on us back in town?" I asked.

"Tag team with Jeff's boys." Dalton gestured at the strong silent type standing beside him. "That part of Dalhart is Dallard County."

Willard touched the brim of his hat.

"Then you know why we're out here," Andy said. "We've come this far. I'd still like to see it."

Dalton traded a glance with Willard, who had yet to speak. I found myself eyeing the drivers of the other trucks. They watched us from the edge of the field. None of them wore badges on the mix of chambray and t-shirts they wore. I did not fully trust the situation. The BLASTER remained jammed in my back pocket.

"You mean where it happened?" Dalton asked. "There's just one problem. It's not out here." Dalton shrugged at the landscape.

"I was given this location by someone with the FBI."

"Who got it from someone in Austin." Dalton flashed Andy what sure appeared to me to be a *say nothing about it* look. It was gone as fast as the lightning now flickering in the darkening sky. A few seconds passed, then thunder stomped across the fields. I suddenly felt very tall. "That's something else we can chat about on the way to supper. Whyn't y'all hop in with me. We can leave this little joke where she sits. Let Al Dorian come and get it hisself."

"Our bags are in the back," Andy said. She fished the key from her satchel and remote-opened the rear hatch.

"Boys, lend a hand here!" Dalton called out.

Two of the young men at the edge of the field trotted forward. Neither, I noted, was armed. The only weapons present belonged to Dalton and Willard, and Andy. If it had come to a firefight, knowing her skill, and the distances involved, I put the odds in her favor. I thanked God it didn't come to that.

God answered with thunder that rumbled ahead of the approaching squall line. Thunder sounds louder in Texas. A gust of chilly air swept the irrigated circle, picking up dust.

"Guess we best move it." Dalton made an ushering gesture toward his truck. Willard tipped his hat and marched off, closing out the conversation with his record of silence intact. After closing the hatch and depositing the key in the cupholder, we left the little Buick to its fate.

Andy took the front seat. I climbed into the back seat behind her.

43

———————

"You leapfrogged us back on 385," Andy said.

"Once we knew the general direction you were headed, we figured out your intentions. It was easy to scoot on out in front of you." Dalton drove at a far more reasonable twenty-five miles per hour over the rough dirt road. We were last in line behind the other three trucks. Their dust raced away in the gusty wind. I was surprised by how dark it had become. The automatic headlight feature of the pickup trucks kicked on.

"But you knew we were going to the wrong location."

"We knew you were headed to the location that the AG's office used in their reports. We didn't know they gave it to the FBI, except maybe for spite. You made a bee line to a whole lotta nuthin' out there."

"Why?"

Dalton chuckled. "Folks down in Austin came right out and said it. They don't want the federals poking around. They believe that nuthin' leaks like the good ship Federal Lollipop. The sleight of hand has an upside, though. Nobody wants the press and the public stomping around out where it really happened."

"Are you taking us there now?" Andy asked.

Dalton made a show of looking up at the sky through the windshield.

"All the same to you, with this weather coming in, I'd just as soon we go home and get that supper. I need to stay close at hand in case the network spots tornados. Y'all understand. There ain't much to see there anyway.

There's a pole in the ground. There's some burnt grass. That's about it. The Rangers have been over it with a fine-toothed comb."

I sat back and watched the gunmetal colored clouds boiling toward us. Scale clouds told a tale of violent turbulence, the kind that tears airplanes apart. The big sky of Texas generates big weather, and it moved rapidly.

Not as rapidly as the cold front coming from the front seat. Andy radiated a chill that brewed up faster than the squall line tearing across panhandle Texas.

Don't.

For a word not said aloud, it reverberated. And since boarding this land yacht, she had not met my eye. This was not the dreaded game of *Guess What's Wrong Now*. I knew what was wrong. I just didn't know why.

Dalton diverted the minimal conversation to small talk about the town, the weather, the history of northern Texas during the Dust Bowl. Andy exchanged monosyllables with him. I sat in silence in the back seat staring at her hair.

44

Sheriff Dalton drove us to his home, a low-slung ranch-style house set at the end of a two-mile dirt driveway. I had to squint to see the nearest neighbor. The ranch house shared the property with two ancient trees and half a dozen outbuildings. He pulled up in front of one of the outbuildings, a wooden structure that might have passed for a good-sized shed on a Wisconsin farm. Close up, I could see it had tidy siding and high-quality windows.

"Mel and I will put you up here in the bunkhouse," he announced. He hopped out of the cab and lifted our bags from the pickup truck bed. "Don't let the rustic look fool you. We fixed it up real nice. There's a brand-new shower, a kitchenette, and the big screen TV gets satellite. Mel comes from a huge family and there's always some cousin or aunt dropping in. A couple times we put it out on Airbnb, but I think folks were a little disappointed that we're not a dude ranch and it's five miles to the nearest Starbucks."

"Really, this isn't necessary. We were planning on finding a hotel in town," Andy protested.

"Yup. And if you can find a hotel in town, so can some of the fellas I think you were running from today." Dalton set our bags on the bunkhouse front porch and leveled a serious look at Detective Stewart. "We need to talk."

"Yes, we do."

"You get yourself settled and then come on over to the house and meet Mel. I don't talk business in front of her and the kids, so we'll have a nice supper, then us grownups can have a drink on the veranda—God willing we don't get blown away, although we could use a good soaking. We'll talk then." He took a second to regard us, then added, "Take all the time you need. Looks like you two got things of your own to talk about."

Ha! I wasn't the only one who felt The Big Chill on the ride over.

Dalton hopped back in the cab and rolled the truck fifty yards to park in front of his house. He waved one more time on the way to his front door.

I picked up the bags, all of them, and bumped my way through the unlocked bunkhouse door.

The interior lived up to its billing. Varnished wood met the eye in every direction. A stone fireplace anchored a broad first floor room. A wooden staircase climbed to a loft bedroom. I dropped the bags inside the front door and hiked a straight line to the refrigerator.

"The man is a god," I said. I pulled a cold Corona from a squadron of them. An opener stuck magnetically to the side of the refrigerator, as it should. The first slug went down like liquid heaven.

Andy stepped into the room and looked over the furnishings. I sat down on a stool fronting a counter that separated the sitting room from the kitchenette. I took another drink and then fixed a steady gaze on my wife.

She felt it.

"What?"

"You tell me."

She dropped her eyes for a moment, then said, "I need to use the rest room."

I pointed at what I figured to be the correct door, but she had already assessed the floorplan. She disappeared inside. Her move made me realize that I also needed to go, but not so much that it couldn't wait.

Andy took her time. I carried the overnight bags up the steps to the loft where I found a king bed, two small dressers, and skylights that gave a splendid view of the boiling clouds that had chased us all the way back to Dalhart, then east to Dalton's homestead. The tormented sky had yet to produce rain. Gusts of wind rattled something against the roof.

I made it back down to the stool and my half-empty beer before Andy emerged from the restroom. She freed her hair from the ponytail. Rich auburn waves twisted and flowed to her shoulders, framing her face. The light sweater she wore over jeans wasn't low cut, yet it still drew my attention. Andy has a figure that snags the eye of nearly every male with a pulse. Pregnancy supercharged her contours. Not staring challenged me.

She strolled across the room and pulled out a stool beside me. I gave her credit for getting face to face, although initially her eyes did not meet mine.

"You noticed." She stroked my leg but did not reach for my hand.

"Yes."

She swallowed. Ordinarily I'm the one who screws something up between us. Seeing her struggle put me in uncharted territory.

"Dee, what the hell? If those guys hadn't been who they are, what was your plan? Were you going to shoot it out with six men?"

She shrugged. "True, the odds were not in their favor…"

"I'm serious. *What the hell?*"

She silently worked on an answer for a moment, then heaved a heavy sigh. At last, her eyes met mine.

"I'm scared, Will. I'm afraid of your touch. I'm afraid of *the other thing.*"

There it was. Precisely as I suspected.

"I had a feeling. You've been…reluctant. More than usual. I think this is something I think we need to clear up before we go sticking our necks where they don't belong."

"I know."

"If using *the other thing* is not an option, then I don't want to get into situations like that. Is it because of…?"

She nodded. "Seventeen weeks. I can't believe I'm that far along, but I also can't believe it's not over until next winter. The past feels like a blink; the future feels like forever." She touched her abdomen. "What does it say about me that I am having moments when *I am terrified.* Not just of…you know."

She abruptly threw her arms around me. Her head pressed my shoulder.

"*I don't want to be afraid of you.*"

I returned the tight squeeze that accompanied her whispered words.

The question that had been nagging me for several days had its answer. "Jesus, Dee, I should have realized. I'm sorry."

"We just don't *know.* I mean…what if…? This *thing* is inside you. We've seen the scans. What if it's inside our baby?"

I chuckled. I didn't mean to. It escaped uninvited. She did not take it well.

"Dammit, this isn't funny."

"I know. That's not what I was—never mind. What's funny is that I had this conversation with Stephenson. Right after we found out."

She leaned back to look at me. "You never told me."

"Well, of course not. I mean, just bringing it up was scary. I asked the doc if he thought I would pass this on. Genetically. I asked if DNA programming could cause our baby to be born with *the other thing*. You know what he said?"

Of course she didn't. She let me continue.

"He asked me if I had any fillings in my teeth. Or crowns. He asked if I had any pins in my bones, you know, from a break."

"What does that have to do with anything?"

"Everything. His assessment agrees with mine—that when I collided with that object, it deployed a life support system. Automatically. Or out of compassion. Or because of some Prime Directive. We may never know. All we can be certain of is that it's something technologically outside the bounds of what we know."

"You're not reassuring me."

"Dee, think of it like putting on an inflatable life vest before the ship sinks. A life vest is no more a part of my DNA than a silver filling or a gold crown or a pin in a broken tibia. Babies aren't born with any of those, no matter what modifications their parents carry around."

"I'm not sure it's the same."

"Granted. We don't know. Here's what else we don't know: There might be a way to remove this life support system just like unbuckling a seatbelt. I just don't know what that is. *I'm not sure I want to know.* So, for now, I walk around with the life vest attached. The point is, Stephenson said there's practically zero chance of it being transferred to a fertilized egg via sperm."

"He's sure of this?"

"I suppose there's a margin for error, but you know Doug. He seemed certain and he didn't get where he is by making wild guesses."

Andy didn't show the relief I hoped she would.

"Look, sweetheart, I honestly don't think we have anything to worry about genetically."

"Okay…" Her hand stroked her belly again. "This is a fetus in development, Will. What happens to it if you deploy this *life support system* on it while it's growing? What did Boyd call it? Matter in an altered state? For God's sake, I won't even take a sip of that beer, I'm so afraid that alcohol might knock a genome off kilter. Or coffee, which is killing me. I don't take acetaminophen or ibuprofen and I've had headaches that were blinding. What happens if you use *the other thing* on me and alter the matter of our developing child?"

"Yeah," I said solemnly. "Can you imagine? The kid pops out and vanishes. The nurses chase him around the room like a balloon at the end of an umbilical cord."

She slapped my leg. "Stop it. I'm serious."

"The baby's been crying all night. We just can't find it."

"Don't do that." She jabbed her fingers into my armpits, her ultimate weapon. I nearly spilled the remainder of my beer by dodging her pit attack.

"Okay, okay, okay. But seriously, you put on a seatbelt when you get in the car, right?"

She didn't answer.

"So, are you expecting the baby to be born with a seatbelt?"

"That's not the same. And—" She stopped.

"And what?" She would not look at me. I touched her chin and raised it until her eyes met mine. "And what?"

"What if…the baby…what if *the other thing* sees the baby the same way it sees the cancer in those children? What if it *removes it?*"

Game over. Like hitting a steel wall. The impact dug into my bones. The table turned so fast it gave me vertigo.

How could you miss that? I cursed myself. I felt like I left a loaded gun in a toddler's crib.

"Jesus, Dee…" I didn't know what to say. I should have thought of this. "I'm so sorry."

"This is new territory for us," she said. She lifted one hand and stroked the side of my face. "We just need to be careful. Right?"

I nodded.

She kissed me. Forgave me.

45

Mel Dalton moved like a woman powered by a nuclear reactor. She greeted us in a whirlwind of herding four small children, preparing a meal with an unspecified ETA, sidestepping her husband in a small kitchen, and gushing over Andy, whose sweater, to my eye, did not confirm or deny her condition, but which the sheriff's wife instantly assessed the same way Mrs. Callum had. I began to wonder if women had baby radar.

A sturdy woman with reddish-gold hair and charming freckles, she beamed at Andy. "Oh, my Lord, you are just the most beautiful thing. It's your first?"

"Yes."

"Oh," she exclaimed, "the first is unforgettable. Just like the first time doing it except the experience lasts for months and months. Moments of pure pleasure mingled with moments of ridiculous discomfort."

"Speak for yourself, honey," Dalton muttered.

"If only I could, sweetcakes." She pecked her husband on the cheek. "Now you go on and remind the children who their daddy is. Lord knows, I have trouble keeping track."

He pecked her back and added a quick grope of her backside that Andy and I weren't supposed to notice. He then handed me a fresh Corona, but not until he had wedged a slice of lime in the neck.

"You're a civilized man, Sheriff." I tapped his bottle.

"And you're both uncivilized," Mel scolded us, "drinking in front of this poor woman who can't have one. Let me get you a glass of water, dear." She darted to another corner of the kitchen. "The kids have all been fed and they get an hour of screen time, so we can have a nice supper without World War Three breaking out. I set a table on the veranda. It's covered and shielded, so it don't matter if the rain comes and the wind won't bother us unless there's a tornado. Have there been any warnings, hon?"

"Nope."

"You two go on out and I'll bring everything. Go on!"

Andy hesitated. "Is there something I can help with?"

"Shush. Absolutely not. If your husband isn't waiting on you hand and foot, then he'd best pay attention. Now, go on!"

Andy hooked my arm. "Pay attention, love. There will be a quiz."

The Big Chill had melted.

46

———————

After an insanely delicious meal of empanadas and fresh fruit, Sheriff Dalton poured himself a bourbon and offered the same to me. I waved it off. He disappeared for a minute, then dropped a fresh Corona beside the one I'd been nursing. Protest did not strike me as polite.

Mel excused herself to attend to the dishes and the children. Once again, Andy offered to assist. Once again, our hostess ordered her to stay put.

We hovered on the verge of a comatose state at a heavy wooden table beneath a covered veranda. Wind shook the leaves of a huge tree in the back yard and wiggled the adjustable slats of walls on either side of us. The air over Dalton's round table remained calm. White Christmas lights strung overhead grew brighter against the storm's darkness. Lightning flashed at regular intervals. A charge hung in the air. Gusts kicked up dust in the fields around us. That it had not rained made the storm more menacing for lack of purpose.

Dalton tipped his glass to the sky.

"Sometimes they're like this. My granddaddy lived through the Dust Bowl. Months and months without a spit of rain. He said storms like this would brew up and give folks hope, but then all they got was another wall of dirt thrown a mile high. I've seen photos. You just can't believe something like that is real."

"Sheriff," Andy leaned forward, lowering her voice, "please forgive me if I am being rude, but can we talk about Tiffany Vera Callum?"

He brushed off her apology. "Not rude at all, Detective. I figured we'd be talkin' business."

"Did you know the girl?"

"Not personally. I know her daddy, Frank Callum. Mel was on a school committee with her mama, Donna. Good people." A frown tugged at the corners of Dalton's mustache. "I know you see it all the time in this line of work, but things like this shouldn't happen to good people."

"We both know who did this."

Dalton examined the swish and swirl of golden liquid in his glass. "It ain't cut and dried. Staties have a pile of evidence and three suspects in custody."

Andy waited. Her silence dismissed Dalton's weak implication that the case was solved.

"My office wasn't involved in the arrests," Dalton muttered as disclaimer.

"How was she found?"

"Highway boys got a tip, they said. About a fire. They're the ones found the site and the body. They're the ones sent it straight to the state and that's when the AG's office got involved. There was some Feds involved early on, but they've been sidelined."

"A tip?"

Dalton sipped, then looked at Andy over the rim of his glass.

"Not sure I like your tone, young lady." The twinkle in his eye said otherwise.

"A tip? Really? Have you investigated the source of this 'tip' they're talking about?"

"Do you know what will happen if I stick my nose in the state investigation? If I start investigating the investigators? Especially if they find out I'm in cahoots with some smalltown police detective from Wisconsin?"

"Essex is twice the size of Dalhart."

Dalton chuckled. "I thought you might say that. Yes. A tip, they called it. Do you know what I'm talking about?"

"I do. A video."

"Rumor has it."

"A video made by the people who murdered that girl, and another girl up in Colorado.'

"That's the whisper."

"You know who I'm talking about, Sheriff. The question I'm asking myself is are they potential suspects or are they your friends and neighbors?"

A cool settled between my wife and the county law officer and it did not come from the marching storm. Andy is rarely impulsive. She just appears that way when she sinks her teeth into something, or she wants to elicit a response. Even so, I wasn't certain this was the time to bite the hand that just fed us.

"Got something on your mind, Detective?"

"Extremist groups attract ex-military, and sometimes—too often—law enforcement. Men and women who want simpler solutions to the hard problems we see and deal with every day behind the badge. People who have lost faith in institutions. I don't know you, Sheriff. You seem grounded in your community. I'm guessing you grew up with half the people you interact with daily. And here we are, strangers visiting your town, on our way to look at a crime scene, and there you are to intercept us."

"What is it you're trying to say?"

"I'm asking you to give me credit for looking at things from every angle, including who we can and cannot trust to follow the evidence."

Oh crap. Now she's done it.

Dalton stared at the weather. Shafts of rain fell widely spaced on the landscape like pillars that held up the granite gray clouds.

"You know," he said distantly, "it ain't always the redneck."

He let the comment hang. I wondered if he suffered prejudices the way I had in Iowa. The way I tensed and worried about malice at a church picnic when the men I saw were just as likely mere citizens with a taste for barbecue. Did he see us the same way from the other side of that fence?

Dalton locked his gaze on the horizon.

"Folks here love this country. We send our boys to fill the ranks of the armed forces—more than any other state. Yeah, we like football. We listen to country music and drive pickup trucks. But let a handful of assholes dive down conspiracy rabbit holes headfirst and the whole country figures we're all crazy. One or two nutballs rant about Texas seceding from the union, or some clowns lead a convoy down to the border to make noise about immigrants, or some loonies hang around Dealey Plaza waiting for both John Kennedys to wander back from the dead—and it makes the national news. Nobody says boo when our kids raise reading levels statewide, or our universities produce authentic rocket scientists. Yeah, this Company W outfit has been on the fringes around here for years under a dozen different names. Setting up their training camps. Playing with guns on weekends. They stink up the internet with talk of racial purity and complaints about poisoned blood—yeah, I seen the stupid civil war shit they put out there—and when they make news, right away people think everybody in a John Deere cap is a Nazi. A redneck. A racist. On the late-night TV they laugh at us for having pride in our flag, our laws, and maybe thinking life shouldn't be so goddamned complicated."

Andy and I held our silence. Dalton took another sip of his after-dinner drink.

"And now I got a choice. I can let the state run with their sexual hate crime witchcraft occult bullshit theory or I can team up with a pair of Yankees and prove the rednecks really are the bad guys—*again*—which just feeds what the whole world already thinks. Helluva choice."

He stopped. Said nothing for a full minute.

When he did, his voice was thin. "You know what? It ain't no choice at all. You want to see the crime scene, Detective? I can take you there. But I got two little girls in the other room being told stories about princesses and unicorns and shit slidin' down rainbows, and I gotta tell you, what's out there I ain't ever going to unsee or ever stop thinking about. Not on the days surely coming when I gotta watch those girls grow up and go out on their own. I don't need to prove anything to you, Detective. But I sure as hell gotta prove something to those girls. And to Tiffany Vera Callum. Does that answer your question?"

We watched the storm. I sensed that the one brewing over the veranda table had passed.

"Boy howdy," Andy said, forcing Dalton to grin. "Tell me about the suspects in custody."

47

D alton reeled his focus back to the table. "Sorry. That was my redneck speech."

"It's a good one." I lifted my Corona and tapped his bourbon glass.

"Well, coming from a commie liberal snowflake Yankee, I take that as a compliment."

"Who are they?" Andy asked again.

"Kids," Dalton said. "Well, I think of anybody under thirty as kids. They're kids who knew Tiffany Callum from school. Around the same age. Three of them got the notion to squat at an abandoned farm a few years ago and nobody seemed inclined to tell them they oughtn't. Two brothers and a girl the brothers seem to share. Those boys have always been goofy. I'm not sure where they picked up the girl. The town gossip started a couple years ago. Occult stuff. Witchcraft. Holistic medicines and stuff. Me? I figured they were just out there getting high."

"How do they connect to the murder?"

"Detective, you gotta remember, I'm not invited to all the state seances. The AG's investigators and the Rangers, they don't tell me shit. I hear rumors, is all. They make an arrest and tell me to hold open the cell door and when I ask questions, they say they cannot *divulge*. They like that word. Divulge. Makes me think of someone squatting on the thunder mug. They keep their evidence secret so as not to taint it, they say. For court. Thing is, I'm not the local yokel they think I am."

"You are if you use the term 'thunder mug,' Sheriff." I grinned before drawing from the cold bottle of Corona.

"What do you know about their investigation?" Andy asked.

"I know they collected a rash of social media that implies that Tiffany Callum partied out at that farm, but if you get right down to it, half of that girl's graduating class probably partied out there. I'll take her daddy's word that she never set foot on the property. Yeah, I asked. The state boys didn't think to ask, but I did. I know there are some gas cans locked up in an office we gave over to the Rangers. I know they took tire track castings. And I know they have her car."

"Her car?"

"Yeah. They found her car in the barn where those kids were living. All kinda paraphernalia in the car. Shit for casting spells and whatnot. Devil worship stuff. Least that's what they were willing to *divulge.*" Dalton glanced at the screen door that separated us from the kitchen. His wife transferred dishes from the sink to the dishwasher. He lowered his voice. "Rumor has it they found more occult shit spread out on the ground at the scene near where they—" He glanced at Andy. "Well…you know."

"Terribly careless of them," I said.

"Not from somebody stoned out of their minds. That's the theory." Dalton sipped his bourbon. "Now it's my turn. What's a detective from the big city doing here in rural Texas poking around this case—and don't tell me it's because this thing gets more airtime on the *Today Show* than fashion week. You don't strike me as one of those bloodthirsty scandal chasers."

"Big city? Sheriff, our worst traffic hazard is deer. And I'm talking about in town."

"Didn't you tell me Essex was twice the size of Dalhart?"

"Which tells you how small Dalhart is. The truth is, Sheriff—"

"JB."

Andy nodded. "JB. The truth is, we have skin in the game."

Perhaps because she felt the conversation bypassing me, for the second time today Andy let me tell the story of the attempted recall in Essex, the intent to see her fired from the police department, the picket line in front of our home on a winter night, and the shooting that followed. I left out my connection to Louis Blaze and any mention of my pal in the FBI.

"Tried to get you fired, did they?" Dalton leaned on his elbows and leveled a direct stare at Andy. "On account of that thing in Detroit?"

Andy raised her eyebrows.

"Yeah, I do my homework. Did you really take a potshot at the President?"

"If I had, he wouldn't be upright today."

"A recall seems like a lot of trouble to go to. Round here they'd just vote me out. They best not think about coming out here to shoot up the place, though. I can't hit shit with a gun, but Mel's a dead shot."

"My husband and I have a debt to collect from Company W. People say we should let it go. They call what was done to us *high level vandalism* but that's only because we weren't murdered in our bed. I might have accepted that we would never see justice because dealing with extremist groups is whack-a-mole. But then Tiffany Callum happened."

"I'm gonna go out on a limb here and say you know about Lincoln." He maintained his steady gaze at Andy, which was good because my cheeks would have burned if he turned his investigative eyes in my direction.

"I do. Do you?"

"Yup. And I know that Tiffy Callum wasn't the girl on that street in Lincoln. I seen the video when those flags got burned. That girl wasn't Tiffany."

"No, she wasn't."

Dalton squinted. "But you know who was."

Andy didn't answer. I made a guess that was the answer he was looking for.

"So, maybe you got a little more skin in the game than a bunch of bullet holes in your siding?"

"Maybe," Andy admitted. "Sheriff, I told you before, we both know who did this. I think we also *both know* that the truth is being influenced—"

"Whitewashed," I interrupted.

"—by some high-level political interests."

"Pedmann." Dalton said the name as if it tasted bad.

"What do you know about him?"

"I know I ain't discussing him with someone I just met."

"Fair enough. And I'm a big girl. I know how political influence plays in criminal investigations. If it were just a matter of steering the investigation, that's one thing. But thanks to his office and influence, those kids his people arrested are being railroaded."

"Yeah, well, that office and its influence keep me awake at night and you both would do well to treat Pedmann like the coiled snake he is."

"Can you get me inside to talk to them? The kids?" Andy asked.

"Not a snowball's chance in hell."

"What about just getting us into the building? Maybe into your office? Then let us take it from there."

"You'll get caught which means I get caught."

Mel Dalton pushed through the screen door and dropped into the chair beside her husband. To his surprise, she poured another splash of bourbon into his glass.

"Plying me with alcohol, woman?"

"If that's what it takes for you to do something crazy and help Detective Stewart help those kids."

"Been listening in?"

Mel patted her husband on the arm. "Honey, you should only know."

"There's something else." Andy pulled a business card from her bag and handed it to Dalton. "Frank Callum gave us this card. He said he's seen this man wearing one of those Company W patches. Do you know him?"

Dalton made a face. He showed the card to Mel.

"Oh, Lord." Mel rolled her eyes.

Dalton handed the card back to Andy. "That's Cole Winters. Mel's cousin Aldo works for him. Aldo walks and talks whatever dribbles outta Winters' mouth."

"Is Winters a wannabe or a true believer?"

"Who can say? Last I heard, Winters was all over that anti-government shit. He talks big. Can't say I think he'd plant pipe bombs, but you never know."

"Do you think your cousin would know if Winters was involved?"

Dalton traded a look with his wife.

"If Winters is involved, sure as shit he's dragging Aldo along. The kid… he ain't got the brains God gave—"

"He's an asshole," Mel interrupted. "Would anyone like pie?"

48

Dalton turned off the lights and rolled his truck to a stop at the side of the narrow road without touching the brakes. We sat in the dark pickup cab with the windows open. Cricket song infected the warm night air with tinnitus.

"You're sure about this?" he asked Andy again.

I knew she wasn't, but I gave her credit for pretending. "I think it works out best for all concerned. Whatever we learn, we share. This way, you don't have to get your hands dirty."

"I have no trouble getting my hands dirty."

"I stand corrected. This way you don't have to lie to the state investigators. And if it turns out Aldo is not involved, having us talk to him instead of you avoids awkward encounters at the next family reunion."

Dalton tapped out a contemplative beat on the steering wheel.

Four small houses clustered at the intersection of a pair of county roads. Three of the four structures burned interior lights, the kind people keep on at night to feel secure or facilitate trips to the bathroom. The fourth hunched on its corner in darkness, black from the tip of the roof to the foundation. No interior lights. No exterior yard lights. A late eighties Cadillac slumbered in the driveway on a sagging suspension.

Lightning flickered high in the sky. The storm line had passed, but trailing unstable air sustained the light show. It did not rain. Not on the Dalton ranch, at least. Or here on the fringe of Dalhart. Broken pavement and barren yards remained dry.

Dalton heaved a weighted sigh. "I ain't worried about the state investigators. But Aldo's mother is hell on wheels and if she catches me harassing her idiot baby, she will auger me and Mel a new one at every family gathering from here to eternity. Fine. If y'all want to take a crack at him and keep me off the radar, that works for me. If he coughs up anything solid about Winters, though, then you folks are done. Got it?"

"Got it," Andy said. She opened the front passenger door. The interior light did not switch on. Cop vehicle. I jumped out of the back seat and reflexively tapped the side pocket of my summer flight jacket. Two fully charged BLASTER units answered my touch.

Andy slid out of the cab, then leaned in.

"We'll walk up to that next intersection when we finish in case any of the neighbors wake up. The last thing we want is for someone to see a big truck with a star on the side. You're not exactly inconspicuous." She looked at her watch. "Pick us up at one?"

"That enough time?"

"More than enough. One more thing. You may hear a single pistol shot. If you hear one, everything is fine. More than that, come running."

"This is Texas. Not sure I'd notice gunfire." He said it deadpan. I thought he was serious until the mustache twitched.

"See you at one." She closed the cab door quietly and stepped away. Dalton pulled a tight U-turn and headed back the way we had come. He drove a quarter mile before switching on his headlights.

"I don't like this," Andy whispered.

We walked an angled line across the empty road toward the lightless house. Andy's dissent was not news. She had been unhappy with the plan from the moment I suggested it after our return to the bunkhouse.

"No."

"Why not?" I pleaded. "It doesn't involve making you disappear. It's not something the guy can complain about. Who's he going to tell? And who would believe him? Besides, the experience might give him a fresh shot of that old time religion."

"Don't mock someone's faith."

"Dee," I stopped her just inside the bunkhouse door. "You know I respect your rules. Dalton can do everything by the book in due course. I'm just suggesting we loosen the guy's lips. We both know that if Dalton hauls the guy in, he will just clam up and then nobody learns anything."

"We could get his mother to beat it out of him. Sounds like she would."

"Right?" I liked that Andy saw a glimmer of humor, but the light faded quickly.

"There's nothing to say that he wouldn't reveal vital information under formal questioning."

"Maybe. But what if he doesn't? What if he runs back to his boss who takes it to his boss, and someone up the chain in Company W decides he's a liability? Especially if they really are on the verge of something big. We wind up knowing nothing, and he winds up in a shallow grave."

She frowned. "You watch too many movies."

"This is what we came here for," I countered.

She pulled a hard breath. Her lower lip gained prominence; familiar signs that appear when she reluctantly surrenders to one of my harebrained ideas. I shut up because I nearly had her.

Her phone chirped.

Dammit.

She stepped away from me and checked the device screen.

"It's from Pidge. Does 'No Joy' mean what I think it does?"

"Pilot talk. She's not seeing the airplane we sent her to look for."

Andy tucked her phone back in her bag. "She said they're calling it a day and will be back here in the morning."

"Then we're getting nowhere faster than usual."

"I wouldn't say that. We're keeping her out of harm's way."

I fought the change of subject. "Come on, Dee. Let's turn over a rock."

She took my hands and wrapped them around her lower back. She pulled me close, pressing. The gilded flecks in her green eyes twinkled in the partial darkness of the bunkhouse.

"You know you're crazy," she said.

"I wasn't until I met you."

The kiss sealed it.

"Have I mentioned that I don't like this?" We edged past the Cadillac. The vinyl Landau roof peeled like it had a bad sunburn.

"I vaguely recall."

We reached a sun-bleached front door. Andy issued one last audible huff of discontent, then reached into her satchel. She tapped her phone screen. I adjusted my Bluetooth earpiece. She secured her phone and extracted her weapon, checked to confirm that the chamber was empty, then handed her Glock semiautomatic over as if I had asked for her citizenship.

"Finger outside the trigger guard. Period." She would not let go until I confirmed.

"Finger outside the trigger guard."

"And if he comes to the door armed, this deal is off. Do NOT let him see this weapon if he's carrying. Understand? If he's carrying, let me handle it."

"Affirmative." I gripped the pistol and showed her how my trigger finger pointed straight along the barrel. If my gun safety practices satisfied her, she did not show it.

She asked one last time, "Do you seriously think he will fall for this crazy judgment thing?"

"He'll have his own eyes to believe. Trust me."

"Right. Those are the two words that make everything better."

She positioned herself squarely in front of the door. I noted the location of the door hinges and moved to the opposite side. I pressed my back to the wall. She issued one more head shake in the dark, then opened the screen door.

She hammered on the house door with her fist. She pounded relentlessly. Chips of peeling paint came off and fluttered to the concrete stoop. Unless Cousin Aldo was dead drunk, he stood little chance of sleeping through the nonstop concussions.

A yellow light beside my head snapped on.

Andy adjusted herself. She wore a navy-blue blouse and dark jeans for this night operation. In the amber glow, she flicked her hair back over her shoulders and fixed a come-hither smile on her face. She tugged at the low vee of her blouse, exposing generous cleavage.

Hell, I'd open the front door at midnight for this woman.

Heavy footsteps approached. The door had no deadbolt. Cousin Aldo twisted the knob. The door opened.

"Hi!" Andy launched her sticky sweet monologue before he could speak. "Could y'all help me with my car? I'm just over there. I think the engine blew up or the transmission or some such. I don't know the first thing about cars." She reached and put her hand on Aldo's forearm and tugged.

The young man she drew onto the front stoop looked like every high school's resident stoner. Straight blond hair hung to the bottom of his jaw on both sides of his head. A thin goatee, also blonde, suggested at an attempt to imprint maturity on a face that would look boyish well into his thirties. Drooping eyelids signaled interrupted sleep or recent drug use. I bet on the latter. His thin frame filled a ratty t-shirt over baggy shorts. He wore no shoes.

Andy pulled him toward her. Ensnared by her open collar and the deep vee of her shirt front, he never saw me.

I pressed the tip of the pistol to the side of his head as Andy converted her alluring forearm touch to a snakebite grip. She twisted his arm and stepped behind him, bending the skinny forearm halfway up his back. He cried out.

"*Ow!*"

"Move." She pushed. I grabbed his other arm to keep pace and maintain contact between the pistol muzzle and his temple.

She shoved him off the sidewalk and onto the dirt.

"On your knees." She bent both her knees which rapped the back of his legs and broke his stance. He dropped. Andy released his arm.

"Wha—wha—?"

I switched to a grip on the long, greasy hair at the back of his skull and added pressure to the pistol at his temple. Andy stepped aside and let me take a position directly behind Aldo. He tried to look up at her. I shoved his head forward so that he stared at the ground.

"*Hey! You can't—*" He had a high, squeaky voice.

"Shut up," Andy hissed. She gestured at me with her hands. I moved the pistol to the back of the man's head.

"*Wha—I—who the f—*"

"Shut. Up." Andy bent down. "We're here to kill you for what you did."

"*I didn't do nothing I swear I don't know what you're—*"

"Kill him."

"*What?! No!*"

Andy took the pistol from my hand. I slipped a grip around his thin sweating neck. His body went rigid. I bent my knees and let her know I was ready.

She snapped back the Glock slide to chamber a round. She turned and aimed the weapon at the dirt several feet away.

She fired. The gunshot punched my ears.

BANG!

Fwooomp!

I vanished. Under my grip, Aldo vanished. I pushed hard with my legs. Holding his neck with his weightless body extended away from mine, we shot into the black sky.

HE WIGGLED AND SCREAMED. I don't think he detected the grip on his neck.

The colliding awareness of being killed and sensations of rocketing into the sky may have overloaded his senses.

When we cleared treetop height, his body went rigid. Dalhart sprawled on our left. Dark empty land expanded in every other direction. The sky above us flashed occasionally, but the lightning remained high and distant. At least I hoped so. The steady flashes lent a sinister atmospheric touch to the unfolding dark drama. All the same I didn't fancy being struck.

The occasional flash had a benefit. If he collected his wits to look at himself, Aldo would see that his body was missing. On takeoff, I pushed extra hard for a rapid ascent so that he wouldn't have time to notice that his dead body wasn't decorating his front yard. Best I could tell, he didn't look down.

A steady whimper reached my ears. I felt his arms move, touching himself. I imagined him holding his hand out and seeing nothing.

"What the—?"

"You're dead," I said gravely. He jolted at the sound of a new voice. He tried to look around, but I held his neck tightly. "Settle down. That woman and her partner shot you."

"Oh, my Christ—what's happening?"

The earth fell away. Dalhart's streetlights laid a jeweled pattern at our feet. Highways stretched to the horizon displaying a thin trail of departing taillights and a counterbalanced parade of approaching headlights. Thunder rumbled.

"Aldo Bryant, I am The Collector, and we are on our way to The Gates of Judgment. Have you lived a righteous life?"

"What are you talking about? What's happening?"

"If you keep interrupting, you're going to use up your allotted time. Let me recap. That woman's partner killed you with a single shot to the back of your head. Straight to the amygdala. Lights out. Your dead body is watering your lawn right now. Your immortal soul is being escorted to The Gates of Judgment. And by the way, don't break my grip or you will spiral directly into the jaws of Hell."

"What are you talking about?!?"

"Aldo, I will give you a minute to challenge all this because that's what you dumbasses always do. You get one minute to say I'm full of shit and this can't be happening, and this must be a dream and all the usual crap that I've heard ten thousand times. Take a minute and explain to me your version of why your body is gone and we are headed for the heavens. Have at it."

He snapped his head back and forth. He touched and patted himself. I heard heavy breathing. One hand found my hand on his neck.

"Uh-uh," I warned. "It's a straight shot to Hell if I let go." That much was true.

He pulled his hand away as if burned. He made a sound like a kicked dog but made no attempt at a counter explanation.

"Okay," I said. "I didn't think so. We have about five minutes before you reach the Gate where you will be judged. Got that?"

He hesitated, then nodded.

"I need your answers to be verbal or they're not part of the contract."

He cleared his throat. "*Got it.*" He sounded like a frightened little girl.

"This is how this works. In those five minutes your Creator allows you to spill your guts and beg forgiveness for any sin. Big or small. Doesn't matter. Anything you miss or skip or hide is held against you and will determine if you ascend to Heaven or spend eternity burning in Hell. Clear so far?"

"*This can't be happening!*"

"Like I never heard that before. Clock's ticking, Aldo. Got anything on your mind that might cause you to wind up eating Satan's toe jam day after day for the next million years?"

"*I didn't do it! I didn't do any—*"

"Aldo."

"*I swear I swear I didn't—*"

"ALDO! Listen to me. There's one more thing about your five minutes. We already know everything. So, this isn't so much a confession as a test of your integrity. Got that?" I estimated we were a thousand feet up. Our ascent had slowed thanks to wind resistance. The cloud base remained well above us, occasionally laced with lightning. Except for the rumble of distant thunder, the sky wrapped us in silence. "What I'm saying is that lying will land you in a lake of fire with eels chewing on your balls. We will know if you're lying, and it will count against you."

"*Puh-puh-please, I didn't—I didn't know what they were going to do, I swear to you!*" He sobbed.

I waited a moment for the emotional collapse to pass.

"Aldo? You with me?"

He sniffled loudly.

"Take a breath and tell me. This is about that girl, right?"

"*I swear I didn't know. They said she was the one and we were just gonna scare her. But she was naked when I got there, and all tied up and everything. I didn't touch her! Honest to God, I wasn't one of the ones who— you know—she was tied to the post by the time I got there. I never touched*" *her! This is the worst thing I ever did in my life and I'M SORRY! I SWEAR I'M SORRY!"*

I clenched my teeth. The image of Tiffany Callum's final minutes assaulted my mind's eye.

Dropping him would be easy. Listening to his screams all the way down might block out the screams in my imagination—like humming a favorite tune to kill an earworm.

It. Would. Be. So. Easy.

He wept. *"I—I—I left—when they poured gas on her. I left. I never thought they would do it! Oh, God—oh, God—I'm so sorry!"*

"Who else was there, Aldo? Clock's ticking. Settle down and tell me. You need to save your soul."

He coughed, choked, swallowed. His voice, already strained, soared a few notes higher.

"It was Cole. He was there. And a couple guys—Lanford, and Joe Lake and his brother, along with that guy they always hang out with, I dunno his name—I swear. Guys from Cole's unit. And some others."

He gasped. His body spasmed.

"Aldo. Aldo! Take a breath. Just talk to me. Who else? Nice and easy."

He paused. He fought with and subdued his breathing. His voice remained high and girlish. *"That scary guy. He was there. And a couple guys with him. When I saw what was happening, I told Cole I wanted to leave. I was afraid they wouldn't let me, but Cole—he stood up for me. He told them I would keep my mouth shut. He told me to take off and never say nothing. And that scary guy—he said if I opened my mouth I'd be next."*

Andy spoke softly in my Bluetooth earpiece. "Ask him who told him to be there in the first place."

"Fact check, Aldo. Who told you to be there?"

"Cole."

"And who told Cole?"

"He said the orders came straight from the man hisself."

"What man?"

"Blaze. Louis Blaze hisself."

"And who was the scary guy?"

"I dunno. Cole called him Rory—er, no—Ray, that's it. I left. I left—*oh, God, I didn't know they would do it. I saw the light. When I drove away. I saw the light in the rearview."*

"What light?"

"The fire. Jesus, the fire. I heard her screaming. I'm SO SORRY!"

. . .

A MINUTE OR TWO PASSED. Aldo lost control and wept. I ceased to hear him. The empty sky stuffed cotton in my ears. I heard my own breathing, harsh and short.

I heard Tiffany Vera Callum's desperate pleading. Her screams.

Her screams blended into the screams I imagined coming from Aldo.

When I let him go.

Andy's voice brought me back, repeating my name in my ear until she broke through.

"Will?"

"Will?"

"Are you there?"

"Yeah, I'm here." I reflexively touched my phone in my pocket. "Did you get all that?"

"Yes. I got it. Will?"

"Yeah?"

"Don't drop him."

49

———————

I dropped him.

Ten feet above the dirt yard where Aldo Bryant thought he'd been murdered by a stunning female assassin and her partner I issued one final command from The Collector to Aldo Bryant before I shook his sweaty neck out of my grip.

Wind drift must have been stronger than I thought. A thousand feet up, I struggled to find the same street, the same cluster of houses, the same yard we had launched from. The sparse housing at the edge of Dalhart had little to distinguish it. I tracked the road we'd driven to the outskirts of town, then found the intersection with four homes. Locking down my bearings, I pulled out a BLASTER and spiraled down. I flew an approach across Aldo's roof. We almost hit a tilting aluminum TV antenna that likely received its last signal when The Beatles played the Ed Sullivan Show.

On the way down, I laid out Aldo's instructions.

"New plan, Aldo. What you and your friends did to that girl—that's unforgiveable. If you live to be a hundred, you probably won't be able to redeem yourself and I'll be hauling your ass from the nursing home to Lucifer's Sea of Snakes."

"*I know—I know—I'm so sorry!*"

"But you get to try. I have orders to return you to your mortal body, and you're gonna try every day for the rest of your miserable life to make it right. And you're gonna start by spilling your guts to the first cop you can find. Got it?"

He nodded.

"Say it out loud because this is a contract."

"*I'm gonna spill my guts. I'll tell them everything!*"

"Damn right you will. Because if you don't, they're gonna make me come back and if I come back, you get a one-way trip up Satan's ass where you will swim in hot diarrhea for eternity. I hate that delivery. Got it?"

More nodding.

"Out loud, dumbass."

"*I got it. I swear.*"

I issued a final command.

"You will dedicate your life to that girl, Aldo."

"*I will. I swear.*"

Ten feet over the dirt, I let him go.

He shrieked when he hit. Something snapped. He clutched one leg and writhed in agony.

Andy walked out of shadows cast by the attached garage wall. She held her weapon in one hand and her badge in the other. He paid no attention to the dark figure standing over him until she used one foot to roll him on his back. He gripped his right knee.

At the sight of her, Aldo shrieked.

"DON'T KILL ME AGAIN! PLEASE!"

She held up her badge. "I'm not going to kill you unless you try to get up. I'm a cop. Just lay there."

I pulsed the BLASTER and maneuvered to a nice touchdown at the end of the driveway where the car blocked me from Aldo's sight.

Fwooomp!

I reappeared. Andy put away her badge and extracted her phone from her bag. She tapped the screen to close her connection to me. A moment later she lifted the phone to her ear.

"Sheriff? Change of plans. Come and pick up a cooperating witness."

50

"Did you folks get any sleep?" Sheriff JB Dalton caught soft morning sunlight outside the door to the bunkhouse. He had rapped so quietly I nearly didn't hear him. He tucked his thumbs in his belt and shuffled his feet. "I wasn't tryin' to wake you, but Mel sent me to fetch you for breakfast. I don't think no is an option."

"You didn't wake us. We're both up." I gestured for him to enter. "And yes, we got a couple hours. Coffee?"

"Oh, Lord, I've had six cups if I've had one. It's been a long night." He doffed his hat and stepped into the apartment politely, as if this wasn't his property. "Which is why one more won't hurt."

"Good morning, Sheriff," Andy descended the stairs. How she managed to look the way she did mystified Dalton. His slack jaw showed it. She wore black leggings, calf-height lace-up boots, and a white sleeveless blouse, untucked. Despite less than twenty minutes of prep, her hair swept back to converge in a complex knot behind her head. Her face was photo-ready in that way she has of looking perfectly made up without wearing makeup.

She glowed.

"Morning, Detective," Dalton reached to tip his hat, but then remembered he held it in his hand.

"Did my husband offer you a cup?"

"Right here." I carried a mug to the counter. "Have a seat. I'm going to guess by the shirt you're wearing you've been up all night."

"Doesn't take a detective to figure that one out." He wrapped his hands around the hot mug and inhaled. "I gotta ask. What did you say to that poor dumb sonofabitch? I never had anyone so anxious to unload."

"Just an appeal to his better angels," I replied.

"Any luck?" Andy asked. She had bristled at not being allowed to accompany Dalton and his prisoner to the sheriff's office. She quietly fumed the entire Uber ride back to the Dalton ranch.

"Precious little. Cole Winters is gone. Packed up his gear and took off, his old lady said. And by gear, I mean his go-to-war gear. She said he loaded every handgun and rifle he has in his truck along with a couple thousand rounds."

"What were you saying to me about rednecks?" I lifted a crooked grin over the rim of my own mug.

Dalton rolled his eyes and ignored me.

"We put out an alert. Everybody knows to tread lightly. But that also means the state boys now know something is up."

"That can't be helped," Andy said. "You don't want some young officer pulling him over unaware."

"Winters ain't alone. Aldo spit up the names of three other local fellas he saw at the murder scene. I guess they answered the call of the apocalypse, too. They're all gone. Same deal. Loaded up for bear and took off. There's a chance they crossed the line up into Oklahoma. They had a camp up that way a few years ago. Just a busted up old Airstream, but they called it Fort Defiance or some stupid shit. I got some folks up there checking it out."

"Did Aldo spill his guts about Company W?" I asked.

"As much as he could." Dalton shrugged. "Sounds like they were happy to use him, but he wasn't a fully vested member. I think Winters took him along for what they did to Tiffany Callum out of some kinda twisted logic that if he was gonna do terrible shit, he was going to make certain he wasn't alone."

"What about the one called Ray?" Andy wanted to know.

"Aldo says he never saw the guy before, but that he was scary and in charge. He said he treated the girl like she was nothing. Like she was already dead, even though she was screaming and crying the whole time. Aldo was pretty sure they…well…you know…" Dalton blushed.

"Raped her," Andy said coldly.

"Yeah. Before…you know."

Andy showed no sign of emotion. Dalton fidgeted for a moment before he continued. "I checked with Cole's wife, and some of the folks in the Lake brothers' circle. Nobody knew anybody named Ray that's been running with these boys. Folks are a little edgy talking about Company W. A few anti-government types around here think of them as local heroes 'cuz they don't know any better, but talking out loud about it scares the bejeezus outta them."

"Anybody named Ray on the roster?" I asked.

"I could tell you if we had a roster."

"You wouldn't get very far," Andy said. "These guys are cagey. Nobody knows too much. That way if any one group or cell goes down, they can't take down the whole organization."

"Aldo sure as hell don't know squat."

"Seems a little odd, doesn't it? Going on the run?" Andy asked.

"Not after what they done. I'd be halfway down Mexico by now."

"Why? A lot of effort has been put into painting Tiffany Callum's murder as a sexual hate crime and in cooking up the occult angle. The AG's office did the handoff, and the media ran with it like a high school halfback finding a hole in the line. It's still the lead story on most of the morning news shows."

Dalton produced a grin. "Halfback? Detective, you never cease to impress."

Andy smiled. Mostly, I think, to ease the tension. "I thought you'd like that one. The point is that the whitewash should have given those men comfort. That and the arrests, although it's obvious someone set up those kids by planting evidence in Tiffany Callum's car and parking it on that farm property."

"Looks that way. But—"

"They should—I'm sorry to interrupt—they should have been feeling fat, dumb, and happy. Not like they needed to go on the run armed for World War Three."

"You get no argument from me." Dalton sipped hot coffee and burned himself for it. I waited on mine. "I agree. Double agree. Because the state's not letting go."

"What do you mean?" I asked.

"The state extradited those three kids last night just a couple hours before we paid our visit to Aldo. Midnight Express with no notification. They're well on their way to Austin."

"Bring them back," Andy said urgently. "You've got an eyewitness to the murder who clears them and blows up the entire witchcraft theory."

"Aldo ain't the most reliable witness." Dalton threw up his hands protectively. "Don't get me wrong. I believe him—although his attorney will probably make hay out of that blown out knee."

"He tripped." I tried to look innocent.

"I'm sure he did. I ain't complaining. Like I said, I never seen anyone so enthusiastic about confessing. But until we can grab up one or two of the other perpetrators and get them to corroborate, Aldo is just telling a story, whereas the state can claim hard evidence."

"So, what's next?" I asked.

"Well, I 'spect you folks can head back to Wisconsin for some cheese and let us rednecks take it from here."

"Touché."

Dalton laughed. "Yeah, I can see that's not gonna happen. I can't exactly bring you into the investigation, but since you're not likely to just wander off and see the sights of Dalhart, and since I'm pissing in the wind with the state, and since you make a decent cup of coffee, I got no objection to keeping avenues of communication open between us. You're welcome to stay here as long as you like."

A blank, distant expression washed over Andy's face. She sat motionless. The sheriff looked at me like I was supposed to know where she'd gone. I shrugged.

She abruptly blinked and returned to Earth, mildly startled.

"I'm sorry. Yes. We want to help."

"Mind tellin' me where you drifted off to?" Dalton asked.

Andy rose and crossed the small kitchen to the sink. She leaned on the edge and gazed through a window above the porcelain double bowl.

"JB, have you wondered why Louis Blaze and Company W would shoot a video of the execution of Tiffany Vera Callum and release it with a manifesto-style statement but then go to the trouble of planting evidence to completely reframe the nature of the crime and essentially deny involvement?"

"What're you getting at?"

"Well, think about it. Blaze committed a heinous murder either for political gain or to terrify the public. The state stole his thunder. All anyone in the media talks about is witchcraft and sexual hate crime. Nobody's talking about domestic terrorists."

"The question did come to mind. Up until last night, I credited that to the AG's unofficial position that the video—which they deny exists—was an AI fake."

Andy bit her lip. She pushed the delicate fingers of one hand deep into the waves of her hair.

"What're you thinking?" Dalton asked.

"It's not what I'm thinking. It's what I *don't* think. I don't think the video is a fake. I don't think the people who released the video are the people whitewashing the murder. I don't think the Ray you're looking for is from around here. And I don't think my husband and I will be staying in Dalhart."

51

———————

"Wait…what? We're leaving?" Andy's declaration caught me by surprise.

Before she could answer, her phone rang. She read the screen, then laid the phone on the counter.

"It's Pidge."

"Who's Pidge?" Dalton asked.

"Our pilot," Andy replied. Dalton tossed me a confused glance but not before Andy touched the speaker button. "Hi, Pidge. You're on speaker with me and Will and Sheriff Dalton of Hartley County."

The line stayed silent.

"Pidge, honey, it's okay. We're not under arrest."

"Christ," she said. "You scared me for a minute."

"Are you back?" I asked.

"Andrea, it's Arun." Like we wouldn't have guessed. "No, we are not yet back in Texas. We had planned on returning this morning, but after a bit of let down yesterday, we had a turn of luck."

"Are we—I mean—" Pidge hesitated "—is it okay to talk?"

"Yes," Andy assured her. "You can talk with the sheriff present. He's a friend."

A frantic exchange unwound on the other end. *Do you want to tell? Do you? Would you rather I—? No, go ahead. Right.* Arun resumed speaking.

"When we arrived yesterday, we were unable to confirm that the aircraft in question—"

"The Twin Beech," Pidge prompted.

"Right. The Twin Beech."

"What Twin Beech?" Dalton asked.

Andy quickly explained that Pidge and Arun were tracking down an airplane owned by Louis Blaze. "Go on," she told Arun when she finished.

"We were unable to confirm that it was stored here or had ever been stored here. There was no one on the field, and the hangars are locked."

"I said screw it, we should just—" Pidge stopped herself. "Well, never mind."

"This morning, however, we were taking fuel aboard and we spoke to a maintenance person—"

"A ramp rat."

"Yes. That. I struck up a conversation with the young man who has been working here for several years, and he confirmed that a Twin Beech airplane has been stored here. He affirmed that it was, as you mentioned, Will, a hangar queen—that it's never been moved or flown for as long as he's been here."

"But?"

"Yes, but two weeks ago he noticed activity in the hangar. People with whom he was unfamiliar came to the airport and appeared to engage in maintenance on the aircraft. They did not initiate contact with anyone here on the field. The work was performed inside the closed hangar. From my limited airport experience aviation people are usually friendly and open, which of course could be specific to Essex County Airport, but anecdotal evidence would suggest—"

"Arun," I interrupted.

"Yes, quite right. To the point. These people were not friendly. Not according to the young, er—ramp rat."

"Did they fly it?" I asked.

"Our young observer said he did not see the aircraft fly, but this airport is not far from town, and he thinks he heard the airplane fly over several times one evening after dark. He said the flyover got his attention because the engine noise was unique. He said he didn't think anything of it the first time, but then the aircraft made several flights over the same part of town."

"They were in the pattern," Pidge said. "Crash and dash."

"They crashed?" Dalton asked.

"Just an expression," I said. "For practicing takeoffs and landings."

Pidge spoke to Arun. "Tell 'em the part about the display."

"Yes. Right, then. The ramp person then saw the airplane outside of the hangar just a few days ago. He thinks it was Saturday. He said he came to work, and the airplane occupied a corner of the ramp, away from the airport buildings. Someone was there with it. He said he saw a vehicle pull up and he thought they might be loading cargo or passengers, but the vehicle drove away shortly afterward. Then several more vehicles visited, but he saw no one board and no loading of cargo. In some cases, the driver never exited the vehicle."

"Is it still there?" Andy asked.

"No. The young fellow went to lunch. When he returned, the airplane was gone."

"Gone, as in *gone*," Pidge asserted. "The ramp rat showed us the hangar. Empty. And by empty, I mean cleaned out."

"Do you have any idea where they went?"

"Hell, yes! You tell this part."

Arun resumed. "While Cassidy was supervising the fueling this morning, I happened to see a gentleman pulling his airplane out of a hangar next to the empty hangar. I took a chance and walked over to speak to him. He was quite friendly, and quite helpful. He also saw the Twin Beech airplane on the ramp, which was exciting for him. He is an aficionado. He said he spoke to the pilot who told him he was not the owner and that he was taking the airplane to Oshkosh to display as a vintage aircraft at the big airshow. He said he parked on the ramp for several hours to display the airplane for airport visitors, something he planned to do at multiple stops on his trip to Wisconsin."

"What? This is some kind of tour thing?" Dalton asked.

"It's not uncommon," I said. "People fly to the airshow at Oshkosh from all over the country, all over the world. Sometimes people with vintage aircraft stop along the way and draw a crowd."

"Okay, but here's the weird part," Pidge said. "The fella with the Citabria —the guy with the hangar next door to the one with the Twin Beech—he's not just some guy. He's president of the local EAA chapter and get this. Nobody said anything to him about showing off a vintage Twin Beech."

"What's EAA?" Dalton asked.

"Experimental Aircraft Association," I explained, "and it's a big deal. It's also a big deal that someone would show off a vintage plane at its home airport without at least extending an invitation to the local EAA chapter."

"Yeah. The guy said nobody said a word to him or anyone else about setting up a display. Nobody from the local chapter knew anything about it and they were a little miffed that they were ignored. Yet there was a steady stream of outside visitors."

"So," Andy said, "we know where they're going. Oshkosh."

"Yeah, but don't you think that's weird?" Pidge asked. "If you're not bringing out the locals, then who were these visitors?"

"Good question," I said. "You said that was Saturday?"

"Uh-huh."

"They're probably in Oshkosh by now."

"Nope. Tell 'em," Pidge directed Arun.

"I expressed regret that I was unable to visit Oshkosh this year and that I missed the chance to see a piece of aviation history. The EAA gentleman said if we wanted, we could catch the Twin Beech pilot at his next stop."

"Naturita, Colorado," Pidge blurted out, "wherever in the hell that is. We're going after him."

Andy vigorously nodded her head. "That's excellent."

"Yeah, go for it," I added, sensing that was what Andy wanted.

"Okay. Just wanted to let you know," Pidge said.

"Wait," Dalton said. "What am I missing here? I mean—okay, if the airplane belongs to Louis Blaze, then some mild interest is warranted. But it sounds like you're chasing a vintage airplane that's going to a vintage airplane show. Do I have that right?"

"Yes, that's correct. Good work, you two." Andy seemed in a hurry to wrap up the conversation. Dalton knit his brow.

"A-firmative. We're outta here."

Pidge ended the call.

I looked at Andy. She looked at me. Neither of us said anything for a moment, which was probably our mistake.

"You know," Dalton said a bit too casually, "what with everything that's happening in our little corner of Heaven here, I like to keep an eye out. Talk to folks around the community. Stay in touch, so to speak. You understand, Detective. Keep up that community policing initiative. Some folks around here might be called busybodies. I like to think of them as alert citizens. Got a couple of those out at the Red Baron Restaurant at the airport."

Andy sighed. "I get the feeling you have something to share, Sheriff."

"Hmmmm." He exaggerated looking thoughtful. "A fancy airplane comes in when we've got visitors from all kinda media in town, only this airplane's registered to an education foundation in Wisconsin, which doesn't exactly fit with current events. Two people get off and rent Al's little clown car. Two more people get back in and fly away. One of the latter is a well-dressed brown fella; I'm gonna say Indian and not Mexican. The other one is a cute little thing that's checking the oil and kicking the tires and next thing you know she's in the pilot's seat. Good looking gal with short dark hair."

He tapped the phone in his shirt pocket. "My busybody at the airport sent me a picture."

Andy did not ask to see the photo. She leaned back and made a show of drumming her fingers on the counter. Dalton hiked up the corner of a grin. He sipped coffee to string this out.

"Spit it out, JB. What's on your mind?"

"If I read the room correctly, you two seem happy to send that gal off on a wild goose chase."

Andy drummed the countertop. "Every lead, Sheriff. Leave no stone. Follow the evidence. Etcetera. Etcetera."

"Uh-huh. Guess I'd be barking up the wrong tree then if I said that little girl flying that big airplane sure looked to be the same size and shape as the girl on that Lincoln, Nebraska street video. The same size and shape as Tiffany Callum, except for the hair, of course, what with Tiffany being a blonde."

Andy dismissed his assertion. "Lots of girls fit that description."

"I suppose they do. But it got me to thinking what a genuine tragedy it would be if someone were to misidentify a girl fitting that description—say, Tiffany Callum—as the little wildcat that lit all those flags on fire in Lincoln, wouldn't it?" His grin evaporated. He leveled a cold stare at Andy who did not flinch. "What was it you said about having skin in the game?"

"If your hypothesis is correct," Andy said evenly, "that would mean there are two tasks at hand. Make sure the right girl stays alive. And make sure someone pays for murdering the wrong girl."

Dalton allowed a pause to become the second pregnant thing in the room. He nodded slowly.

"Boy howdy."

52

"Gimme five minutes and then come on over for some breakfast. I'll clear the savages outta the kitchen." Dalton started for the door.

"Sheriff," Andy stopped him, "I meant what I said. I think Will and I need to go back to Austin. Yesterday, you didn't want to talk to us about Pedmann. What are you not telling us?"

He fidgeted with his hat before placing it on his head. "Let's get some food first. I'd rather not take up that subject on an empty stomach."

"Fair enough. Five minutes," Andy said.

He ducked out. My wife watched him go in a way that a less confident man might view jealously. I knew better. She wasn't looking at him; she was studying him.

"Did you catch that?" she asked.

"Catch what?"

She reeled in her gaze and returned to the room, taking the stool beside mine.

"What he said. About Pidge. That's the second time he connected the murder of Tiffany Callum to the flag burning in Lincoln."

"That's why we're here."

"It is. And our information came from a source in the FBI. Where did he get his information? Because the official story here has been bogarted by the AG's office from day one. Witchcraft. Occult. Murderous mischief in the hinterlands with no focus or mention on domestic terrorism. He never asked us why we were interested in Company W, yet he's in lock step with us. How?"

"What are you thinking? Because he's been nothing but friendly. And he comes with a connection to Tom."

"He knows someone who knows Tom," Andy corrected me. She shook her head as if to shake off a bad thought. "Maybe I'm being paranoid. Or maybe he's keeping his friends close and his enemies closer."

She stroked my thigh.

"Are you suggesting…?"

"I don't know what I'm suggesting. But let's pack."

"Breakfast?" I hoped for another taste of Mel Dalton's cooking.

"Yes. And let's see if the Sheriff will share his thoughts on the Attorney General of the Great State of Texas before we go. Because I have a bad feeling that everything wrong with what's being said and done about this murder is coming from the same source."

53

___

Breakfast called to me. Over the sound of my stomach awakening to Dalton's invitation I heard an engine start. Tires kicked up dirt in the yard between the bunkhouse and Dalton's home. Andy heard it, too. We paused the process of packing our bags to listen. The engine revved. Wheels skidded on dirt outside the bunkhouse door.

A police siren chirped.

I hurried down the steps with Andy close behind. We opened the bunkhouse door to find Dalton's truck outside. He leaned toward the open passenger window. Despite the Texas tan embedded in his skin, Dalton's complexion carried an ashen overlay.

"What happened?" Andy hurried past me.

"Aldo killed himself in his cell."

"What? No way," I declared. "He wouldn't."

"How? Who found him?" Andy asked.

"State investigators got wind he was in lockup. They showed up this morning and found him. I don't know any more than that. I gotta go."

"Let me come with you," Andy said.

"No." Dalton squared himself in his seat and hit the power window button. The glass rose between him and Andy.

"Call me," Andy insisted. "Sheriff. *Call me.*"

He dropped the truck in gear and kicked up dust with all four tires. Andy and I watched him go. A breeze swept his dust plume into the cloudless blue morning sky.

"This doesn't make sense," I said. "Aldo *believed* that Hell waited for him. He wouldn't. Dee, he just wouldn't."

She did not answer.

Aldo dead.

I found no room for forgiveness in my heart. Not while Tiffany Callum's pleading and screams lurked on the fringe of my imagination.

But I irrationally hoped I had been wrong about the eels.

54

W atching Dalton's dust cloud dissipate, Andy said distantly, "I have a bad feeling, love."

"I know. I just got the same feeling."

Did Aldo's guilt propel him to punish himself?

Did the dark solitude of a holding cell close in and convince him that burning in Hell was the only justice worthy of burning a young woman alive? If so, I was as much to blame for his decision as he was.

"You think he killed Aldo?" Andy asked.

"What?"

We looked at each other, confused by the disconnect.

"What are you talking about?" I asked.

"What are you talking about?"

I explained my theory that guilt drove Aldo to punish himself.

"Don't be ridiculous," Andy said. "You were right. He wouldn't. He was handed a divine second chance and he grabbed it with both hands. You heard Dalton. He never met anyone so anxious to spill their guts. Aldo swallowed whole that line about redemption that you gave him. No way he killed himself."

"You think it was Dalton?" I asked, utterly incredulous. "That's crazy."

Andy waved me back inside. She looked over her shoulder at the house before we closed the door behind us.

"Okay. Hear me out. Dalton knows about Lincoln. He intercepts us on the way to the crime scene. He takes us under his wing. What better way to

194

keep an eye on us? We led him to Aldo, which he already knows about—and he lets us confront him because he can't risk Aldo recognizing him. He probably expected nothing to come of it, but because we got a confession he was forced to act. That made Aldo a leak that must be plugged. Dalton says he spent all night chasing down suspects who mysteriously bolted—but was he? Or was he warning those suspects to go to ground? Who was the last one to see Aldo in jail? Who had unsupervised access to him?"

Andy paced the floor between the front door and the fireplace. Glass-eyed severed antelope and deer heads watched her from the walls.

"It's not out of the question for Dalton to be with Company W," she continued. "Elements of the military and law enforcement can always be found in extremist groups. If Dalton is with Company W, then he has known from the start who we are. He knew our story before we told him."

"And we walked right into his hands. Dammit." I flashed on the feeling I had for just an instant when I saw the star on the side of his white pickup truck. Cops.

Andy hates the bad cop trope in the action movies I tend to devour. Not surprisingly, she hesitated. "It's a theory. A plausible theory, but still a theory, Will. I think the thing for us to do right now is clear out before he gets back."

What hit me next came as a gut punch. Andy saw the stark horror on my face.

"What?"

"Pidge. We just handed him Pidge on a silver platter. Jesus, we need to warn her." I patted my pocket for my phone, then saw it on the counter between the abandoned coffee mugs. I scooped it up and tapped her line.

Straight to voicemail.

I hit the red button to kill the call and switched to text. I promised Pidge I would never transmit the emergency transponder code to her unless the situation warranted it. I tapped out the four-digit number followed by *Do NOT pursue the Twin Beech. Turn off ADS-B and fly someplace off the grid. You are in danger. Call me!*

I hit Send.

"Will?"

How could I have been so stupid?

"Will?"

The room went dark so suddenly that for a split second I thought my vision had grayed out. Andy stood at the windows facing the ranch yard. She tugged on the cords for the blinds. The slats snapped shut. She waved at me to hurry to her.

"Come and look at this."

I closed in beside her. She pinched open the blinds.

"Did you call for a ride?" she asked.

We watched a black sedan roll up the long dirt driveway toward the ranch house. A plume of dust lifted in its wake, lending it solemn significance.

"No. I thought we were having breakfast first."

"Keep an eye on this," she said. She pulled away and hurried back up the stairs.

I watched the sedan cruise the length of the lane connecting Dalton's ranch house to the road two miles distant. If the driver had arrived a minute sooner, he would have met Dalton speeding away.

The car pulled into the yard and rolled to a stop in front of the house. Two men emerged from the front seats. Both wore dark suits, which struck my eye as an anomaly in Dalhart. Outside of the Callum wake I had not seen a single suit and tie. The men examined the yard and the outbuildings with a trained eye I've seen Andy use.

Cops. Or FBI, if the suits were taken at cliché value.

I let the blinds snap back in place just as the driver's surveillance gaze swept across the front of the bunkhouse.

Andy silently descended the stairs. Her bag hung against her hip with the strap diagonal across her chest. She held her service weapon at the ready, muzzle down, both hands wrapped around the grip.

She slid close beside me and leaned slightly to steal a look through the thin gap between slats.

"If these guys are Company W they'll come straight here. Dalton will have told them where to find us." She whispered even though a wall and fifty yards separated us from the two men.

Mel Dalton opened the door to her home. One of the two men approached her. The other moved to the rear of the sedan and used the key fob to release the trunk lid, which bobbed up. He clasped his hands like a preacher waiting for the Sunday flock.

Mel traded words with the other man. He spoke. She answered. She shook her head. She listened. She asked a question of her own and the man extracted a leather wallet from the breast pocket of his suit jacket. He flipped up the flap and held it up. She stepped into the sunlight to examine the wallet. Her movement seemed guarded.

"Cops," I said.

"Doesn't mean they're not looking for us."

The man talking to Mel returned his ID to his pocket and struck up a companionable pose, one hand in his trouser pocket, the other gesturing. Mel looked wary. I held my breath, waiting for her to casually point in our direction.

I wondered if Dalton's plan had been to catch us unaware at breakfast. Had we, by lingering in the bunkhouse, foiled the timing?

The bunkhouse had a back door. Getting out would be easy. Getting away, less so. Nothing but flat fields surrounded the cluster of ranch structures. For me, hiding was no issue. However, Andy's refusal to vanish with me threw up barriers to escape.

The man chatting with Mel raised his hand to pause the conversation. He pulled his phone from his pocket and lifted it to study the screen. Then he held the phone up for Mel to see. She leaned closer.

It happened fast.

Deploying moves I'd seen Andy use, the man distracted Mel with his phone one minute, and then stood behind her with both of her arms restrained the next minute. He produced a zip tie and closed the plastic loops around her wrists. She bucked and struggled without success.

The second man pulled a paper shopping bag from the trunk. He strolled into the yard and reached into the bag, then tossed small objects onto the dirt as if sowing garden seed. After spreading the objects in both directions, he returned to the car and dropped the bag on the back seat.

Andy moved for the door. I caught her arm.

"Dee, no."

She resisted for an instant, then reluctantly returned to the window.

The situation deteriorated.

One of the Dalton children, the oldest, a girl of about seven or eight years, appeared at the front door. Seeing her mommy pulled and dragged away from the house, she issued an ear-piercing scream. Neither of the men paid attention. Mel shouted at her daughter. When Mel's captor reached the sedan, the second man swept up her feet. In one swift move, she was lifted and dropped in the trunk of the sedan. She kicked but could not maneuver herself to be effective before the lid slammed shut.

The girl on the porch continued screaming.

The second man casually returned to the driver's side of the car. The first man, the one that took Mel, walked to the porch. He hooked a grip on the small girl and dragged her into the house.

"Okay," I said. "This is some bullshit." I grabbed my flight jacket and pulled a BLASTER from the front pocket. Andy started for the door again. "Stop!"

I hurried to her, snapping a prop on the power unit. She looked at me with impatience hanging just short of anger.

"You can't go out in the open like this," I said. Before she protested, I added, "But I can. Stay here. Call for help. Dalhart PD, not the Sheriff's office."

"What are you going to do?"

"The usual. Make it up as I go."

I closed a grip on her shoulders to combine a hug with moving her aside. Despite steel tension coiling beneath her skin, she relented.

I peered through the small glass window in the bunkhouse door. The driver slid behind the wheel and waited. He turned his head toward the house.

I opened the bunkhouse door and slipped through.

Fwooomp!

"Close it behind me. Stay here."

I rotated and prepared to launch when the ranch house door slammed open. The second man hopped off the porch and jogged to the car. In one swift motion, he jumped in the car and slammed the door. The driver punched it. The rear wheels kicked up dust and dirt. The car—

a BMW that looked familiar

—performed a tight half-doughnut, throwing up a dust cloud. It shot out of the yard and onto the long ranch lane.

I had not launched before the door behind me flew open and Andy rushed out. She slammed directly into me.

Fwooomp!

I reappeared and staggered into the dust cloud in the yard.

"Sorry!" Andy collected herself and hurried past me. "Will, follow them! Whatever that was—it wasn't law enforcement. Go!"

I picked up the BLASTER that had been knocked out of my hand, repositioned, and bent my knees. Then stopped.

"I gotta get my goggles," I raced back into the bunkhouse.

Inside, I threw on my flight jacket. Two more BLASTER units, fully charged, lay in the pocket. My flight bag sat on the floor near the front door. From a zippered outside pocket, I tugged out a pair of ski goggles. I pulled the goggles over my head and fixed them in place. I hurried back into the yard and pulled a second BLASTER from the pocket. I fixed a prop in place and posed with a power unit in each hand. I bent my knees to launch when—

"Will!" Andy cried. She pointed.

A thin wisp of smoke snaked out the open front door of the house, hooked the eaves and wiggled away in the breeze.

Andy ran. She reached the house first. I shoved the BLASTERs into my jacket pocket and pounded across the yard and onto the porch after her. I followed her through the front door.

The low roar of flames greeted us. Smoke boiled out of the kitchen and spread across the ceiling. Fire engulfed the stovetop. A bottle of cooking oil lay on the floor. All four gas burners contributed flame to the fire.

Andy ducked to avoid the heat and smoke and reached for the knobs on the stove. One by one she shut off the gas. The oil fire continued to roar and lick the cabinets above the stove.

"Where are the kids?" she called to me over her shoulder.

I glanced into the rooms I could see. No sign of children. Andy raced to the sink and pulled a towel from a hoop beside the sink. She threw open the faucet and doused the towel, then spread it and threw it over the burning oil on the stovetop. Some of the flame disappeared.

"I got this," I told her. "Go get the kids."

Andy darted into a hall that connected to bedrooms. I heard doors slam open. She called out.

I took a shot. Andy and I keep a kitchen fire extinguisher in the cabinet under the kitchen sink. I threw open the doors and spotted the blessed red bottle hiding behind a cluster of cleansers. I grabbed the extinguisher and jerked the safety pin free. I aimed the extinguisher nozzle at the base of the flame and squeezed the trigger. A chemical cloud swallowed the flames. The fire went out. Knowing the hot burners might reignite the oil that had been spread on the stovetop, I continued blasting at the stove. Eventually the cloud of retardant replaced the smoke and pushed me away.

Andy reappeared. With her arms spread she herded four small children through the kitchen and out the front door. The girl who had witnessed her mother's abduction helped guide her siblings, the smallest of which barely touched the ground as two others hauled him by the arms.

I made certain the fire did not reignite. After a minute or two passed, I followed Andy and the children. I left the extinguisher at the door, then trotted clear of the porch. The sunlight felt clean; the fresh air smelled sweet.

Dalton's children clustered around Andy, hugging her, and crying. She pulled them against her and spoke soft words of comfort that contrasted sharply with the look of pure murder on her face.

She had one word for me. It was superfluous. Both BLASTERS had returned to my hands.

"Go."

55

F*wooomp!*
I kicked the ground and shot skyward. I held both arms out and pushed the slide controls on the power units fully forward. Both units screamed. The props threw wind up my arms.

Twin-BLASTER flight is new for me. My first attempt to use external power to move in the vanished state employed two electric motors. The overpowered effort nearly killed me. A gash on my head and brush with death convinced me to limit myself to single-unit power. Eventually I swallowed my fear of tumbling out of control and conducted tests with pairs of BLASTERs. The trick was to hold my hands as close together as possible so that any asymmetrical power differential would not pull me off course. The other trick was to tweak the power to synchronize prop RPM as closely as possible, much the same way I adjust the prop controls on the Navajo's twin engines.

The speed produced by the dual power units surprised me. In tests, I estimated that I reached eighty miles per hour.

I needed that speed now.

The dust plume from the departing BMW had dissipated. The car had reached the paved road and was gone. The ranch lay a dozen miles from the outskirts of Dalhart. The road connecting the ranch to town carried little traffic. Despite time lost dealing with the fire, I held out hope that I could find the car. For one thing, it wasn't a pickup truck. A BMW sedan on the highways around Dalhart wasn't unheard of, but they weren't exactly common.

Wind tore at my clothing. I thanked God for the foresight to grab the ski goggles. I accelerated and climbed. The world sank away, simultaneously expanding. Miles and miles of flatland Texas stretched to infinity.

The sedan had only two directions to travel. I scanned both. To the west, the bleached asphalt road wore dust like gray camouflage against the dry countryside. Nothing blemished the highway on its line back toward Dalhart.

To the east, the road wore a sheen caused by reflection of the rising morning sun. The pavement stretched away like a wet channel.

Several miles down the road a black speck interrupted the flawless line.

Gotcha.

I flexed my wrists. An instant course change followed. A moment later I angled to intercept the highway. I continued a climb into the morning sun, the better to watch the sedan. Five hundred. Seven hundred. A thousand feet.

The wind racing past me took on a solid quality. I extended my body behind my outstretched arms to reduce resistance. The land below flowed at a pace that produced a roar in my ears.

Who are these guys?

They carried badges, but shoving a woman into the trunk of a car and then starting a fire to kill four small children has a disqualifying effect. I wasn't sure where Andy found the kids, but it was clear to me that the man who set the fire meant for them to perish.

What does that mean for Mel?

Andy speculated that Dalton rolled with Company W. If so, the terrorists had turned on their own. Badges or no badges, these guys were not cops.

The power units buzzed loudly. The harsh ripple of my clothes in the relative wind said I was moving at full speed. So was the BMW, still at least two miles ahead of me. The gap showed no sign of shrinking. A new worry crept into the picture.

At full power, I estimate roughly twenty minutes of battery life in a BLASTER. After that, this tail chase would end. If the driver of the BMW maintained his current speed longer than my battery life, they would simply pull away. I had only two options. Catch up and latch on to the vehicle. Or pray that they either ease off the accelerator or reach their destination.

I could not count on the latter of the two. I had no choice but to hope maximum speed would bring me close enough to the car to grab something and hang on. Being a sedan, it did not have a luggage rack. The ubiquitous feature atop America's fleet of SUVs offers a perfect grip. Some other hand hold would have to do.

Twenty minutes. Max.

The car remained in sight. The gap between us did not shrink. Battery power doesn't simply run out; it gradually diminishes. Before my twenty minutes expired, I would lose ground.

My arms began to ache. My back grew sore from holding a straight-legged horizontal posture. Most of my battery-powered BLASTER flying has been unconcerned with speed and therefore conducted in a comfortable upright posture. This business of posing like some kind of flying superhero was a pain.

THE GAP REFUSED TO CLOSE. I felt a change in the vibration of the two units in my hands.

Battery drain.

If I had been in an airplane, a last-ditch dive to produce speed might have pulled me within reach. But standard physics do not apply to *the other thing.* The absence of inertia and immunity to gravity meant that nothing additional could be gained by a dive. The opposite was true. A dive would increase my angle on the car, allowing the vehicle to pull ahead.

Just as frustration mounted, I caught a break. The BMW's relentless speed dropped. A dirt road perpendicular to the two-lane highway approached.

They're turning.

Brake lights confirmed it. The undefeated gap closed rapidly. The car slowed and swung left onto the dirt road. I angled hard left, cutting the corner and aligning on a path to intercept.

I dove for the intersecting road. The sedan accelerated ahead of a plume of dust. Pavement is one thing; smooth highway surface meant for The Ultimate Driving Machine let it sustain what must have been more than 80 miles per hour. A dirt road is another animal. Unless they wanted to risk snapping a suspension component on an unexpected rut or rock, they would be wise to hold the speed at or under 30 miles per hour.

The intercept course worked its magic. We angled together until the car roof passed directly below me. I descended below 200 feet. The dirt road lacked telephone or electrical poles. Wide empty fields and undulating prairie spread in every direction. Structures dotted the distant horizon, miles away. A farm, perhaps. Or grain elevators. Nothing suggested a reason for this dirt road's existence. It didn't matter.

I had them.

Sun arrows flew from the car's clearcoat black paint and chrome trim. Visceral familiarity with the car struck me again, but I wasted no effort examining the feeling. I relaxed my legs. My body appreciated the change in posture. The arm and back pain eased. Had I been visible, it would have looked like someone riding a motorcycle.

I dropped lower. The BMW suspension thumped over the rough road. The occupants rode in air-conditioned comfort with all four windows sealed. No grip there.

I considered dropping behind the trunk and grabbing the bumper, but the dust and dirt flying up behind the vehicle would have been choking. Instead, I maneuvered to the passenger side and eased into formation abreast of the front seats. Looking sideways, I had a clear view of the two men inside.

I've seen them before.

The pool. At the diving board.

These were the two men patrolling the pool at Morgan's club. The two men who answered to Ray Stroud just before I dunked him. The two men who chased me and Andy when we made our escape in the Land Rover.

The pieces slammed together with all but an audible *Clunk!*

Andy's suspicions about JB Dalton weakened.

The driver abruptly slowed. I reacted poorly and shot ahead. By the time I backed off the power, the car had almost stopped. The driver turned onto a pair of wheel imprints scribed in a stretch of dry grass prairie.

I veered left to follow. The new route felt like a destination had been reached or would be soon. Battery power ceased to be an issue. A bigger question loomed.

What now?

56

The car climbed a shallow rise, then dropped toward what looked like an abandoned excavation—a hole the size of a baseball infield, not much more than seven or ten feet deep with a flat dirt floor. Perhaps an attempt at an irrigation pond. A ramp of dirt and gravel descended from the grassland into the shallow pit. The BMW rolled down the ramp and pulled off to the side.

The sinister purpose for the stop revealed itself.

At the center of the pit, a post had been driven into the ground; a steel pipe roughly three inches in diameter. I had no idea how far down it had been driven, but five feet protruded above ground. Except for the pipe and the newly arrived BMW, the pit contained only one other object.

A red gas can.

I reversed the BLASTERs and stopped.

Fifteen feet above the dirt surface, I hung in the air while the two men exited the BMW. They moved to the back of the sedan. The driver held out the key fob and released the trunk lid, which slowly opened.

Gaining a closer look at the two men in daylight, I could scarcely tell them apart. They weren't twins, but they wore the same short hair, had the same thick necks, and sported the same stubble-littered faces that shared the same blank indifference to their task. Thing One and Thing Two. I now understood Aldo's comment about how coldly Tiffany Callum had been treated.

Like she was already dead.

Thing One leaned into the trunk and closed a grip on Mel Dalton's upper arms. She screamed and shouted and wriggled loose.

Thing One paused, closed a fist, and slammed it into her face. The blow stunned her to silence. He reestablished his grip and jerked her over the trunk lip. She flopped on the ground whimpering. Blood poured from her nose.

"Cut her clothes off," Thing Two said. "I'll set up the camera."

He went to the rear door on the driver's side and pulled out the paper shopping bag I'd seen at the ranch. He strolled toward the steel post spreading the same seeds he had planted at the Dalton ranch. Small twigs bound with yarn in human shapes. Tufts of hair. Beads. Objects designed to feed the witchcraft lie. I momentarily counted him out of the equation.

At the back of the car, Thing One reached into his pocket and extracted a knife that he snapped open with a rapid flicking motion of his hand. He straddled Mel who gasped and choked on the blood streaming from her nose. He bent to tug off her shoes, but she kicked. Changing tactics, he sat down on her legs, pinning them. He sliced open the laces of her shoes and tugged them off.

I jammed one of the two BLASTERs into my jacket pocket and used the other to accelerate. Below the rim of the pit, discarded field stones lay in random clusters. They ranged in size from softballs to beer coolers. I picked out an egg-shaped rock the size of a Jack-o-lantern. I pulsed the BLASTER to stop and then lowered myself, bending my legs so that my knees straddled the boulder. I wrapped my arms around the rock which probably weighed 70 pounds. I pushed hard.

FWOOOMP!

The rock vanished. I lifted the weightless object against my chest with one hand. I pushed off and engaged a low power level that pulled me back toward the BMW.

Thing One remained on Mel's legs, taking his sweet time peeling her socks off. His position posed a problem. Dropping the rock on him carried the risk of hurting Mel. I switched targets.

Thing Two shook the last stick toys and voodoo dolls at the foot of the post. He returned to the car and tossed the empty bag in the back seat. He extracted a tripod. He walked to within fifteen feet of the post and spread the tripod's legs. He pulled out a smartphone and inserted it in a clamp on top of the tripod.

I lined up on him and reduced the BLASTER power. Roughly twenty feet up, I silenced and pocketed the BLASTER. I held out the rock with both hands and eyeballed the target.

"Hey, asshole," I said quietly.

He looked up as I passed overhead.

I released the rock. Electric snaps bit my palms.

The boulder appeared.

Gravity jerked the gray granite pumpkin home to Mother Earth. The rock dropped on a line running straight through Thing Two's upturned face. He saw it coming but only long enough to turn his head. The rock smashed into the right side of his face and then into his shoulder. I heard snaps. He issued a clipped grunt and dropped to the dirt. The boulder thumped beside him and rolled a few feet. His legs kicked over the tripod. The smartphone tumbled from the clamp. Blood splashed from Thing Two's head, staining his shirt collar and the dry dirt. He lay on his back staring skyward through huge, shocked eyes. His right shoulder no longer aligned with his left. His right arm lay on the dirt, immobile. With a shaking left hand, he reached up to touch a flap of skin torn from his right cheek. His fingers stroked exposed teeth. I expected screams, but instead a clicking, gurgling sound came from his open mouth. His breath came in short, desperate gasps. I saw why. His snapped collar bone pushed against his skin and into the side of his throat and windpipe.

Thing One leaped to his feet and pulled a gun from his coat. He swung it sharply from side to side. He stepped away from the BMW and tried to make sense of the scene near the pole.

"What the...?"

Scanning the dimensions of the pit, he moved carefully toward his partner. On the ground, Thing Two gasped and gurgled. His good hand trembled in front of his torn face.

Thing One looked over his partner but offered no aid. He read the disaster as an attack and the threat as imminent. He aggressively swept the rim of the pit with his handgun. Twice, he focused sharp assessment on the boulder, trying to make sense of it, trying to determine its origin.

My bombing run carried me away in silence. A slow glide took me to the pit wall. I rotated to form a fresh plan of attack.

A bombing approach was unlikely to work a second time. Thing One moved on high alert, dancing and shifting his stance to cover 360 degrees of potential threat. A moving target. On the bright side, Thing One abandoned Mel. She lay near the rear bumper of the BMW with her jeans most of the way down her legs. I considered grabbing her, making her vanish, and flying us both out of harm's way; an easy escape but one fraught with problems afterward. For starters, we were miles from any aid.

Better to eliminate the threat.

I applied reverse BLASTER power and dropped down near another collection of discarded field stones. Touching my knees to the dirt, I lifted softball-sized rocks and tucked them in my jacket. One by one they vanished, igniting a sharp tickle against my skin. I loaded five good-sized stones.

Careful not to draw attention, I pulsed the BLASTER just enough to set up a path toward Thing One. My toes skimmed the dirt.

Thing One held his weapon in firing position and continued a fruitless search for the enemy. I closed the distance to within twenty feet and stopped. I tucked the BLASTER in my back pocket and pulled the first stone from my jacket.

It felt weird, but I locked my position facing Thing One using the core muscle generated by *the other thing* whenever I vanish. With the rock in hand, I wound up a pitch. My leg came up major league style. My arm came forward like lightning thanks to the weightless stone. The speed I produced on an inertia-free stone translated to a pitch I never could have thrown on a baseball diamond. I would love to know how it clocked because when that stone slipped my grip and appeared, it whistled through the air. High and outside, the ump would have said. The rock clipped Thing One's cheekbone. I heard a crack. The rock changed course and sailed on.

Thing One went down hard but not out.

I didn't wait. I kicked the ground and shot skyward.

As expected, a second after Thing One hit the ground, he rolled into a crouch and fired wildly in the direction he held suspect for the assault.

BANG-BANG-BANG-BANG!

Bullets bit into the sides of the pit wall. Thing One screamed obscenities at his attacker over the sharp gunfire. Blood flowed from his face.

"WHO'S THERE? SHOW YOURSELF!"

I wondered how he thought his request made sense, but then again, the guy just took a fastball to the face. A new opportunity presented itself. Halting my ascent with the BLASTER, I repositioned directly above his head. I pulled out another stone and gave it my best guess. I let go. The granite softball snapped into view and dropped.

I fired up the BLASTER and accelerated away.

The rock hit him square in the lower back. He shrieked, rolled to his side, and fired into the blue sky.

BANG-BANG-BANG-BANG!

The echo of the shots raced away on the breeze.

That's eight.

I repositioned near the rim of the pit and launched another stone, which missed entirely but drew his fire in the opposite direction. His aim was not bad. Three shots blasted and chipped the stone as it rolled away.

Thing One screamed at the ghost attacking him.

"SHOW YOURSELF, YOU SONOFABITCH!"

Yeah. Right. Eleven.

I wound up a fresh pitch and fired another fastball. The core muscle held my alignment on target. My arm came forward like Roger Clemens working magic from the mound. The pitch repeated its incredible speed. The stone slipped my grasp with an electric snap, appeared, and nailed Thing One in the ribs under his left arm. Bones snapped.

Thing One uttered a feral howl and spun to his left firing.

Directly at me.

BANG-BANG-BANG-BANG!

The air on either side of me rippled. I felt a tug on my jacket. My heart stopped.

Thing One continued firing. *Snick-snick-snick.* Empty.

Jesus Christ!

I frantically patted myself to feel for holes. For pain. For damage. My heart and breathing started again. Pounding and ragged. My hands shook.

Well, that was stupid.

Thing One attempted to rise, but collapsed in pain, gasping. Blood dripped from his face and painted his white shirt. He wheezed and clawed at his ribs.

I regained control over my shaking hands. After extracting the last stone I set a course straight for him. Even with the gun empty, I nursed the power to stay as silent as possible.

Below me, Thing One grunted and wheezed. He doubled over clutching the empty gun in his hand.

I cruised directly overhead and held out the last stone; this one approached the size of his head.

Released from my grip, the stone appeared and raced for Earth. His skull tried to stop it. The sound reminded me of someone rapping on a coconut shell.

Thing One flopped to the dirt, motionless.

I maneuvered to where Thing Two remained flat on the pit floor facing the sky. I lowered myself to the ground, checked to ensure that Mel could not see me, and—

Fwooomp!

—popped into sight standing almost directly over Thing Two. His glassy eyes remained open. They stared blindly at the high cirrus clouds overhead.

He gurgled and gasped. His good hand tremored near his torn face. I doubted that he saw me staring down at him.

I dropped to one knee and poked into his jacket. With two fingers, I removed his gun from a shoulder holster and tossed it against the pit rim. Then I fished out the badge wallet he had shown Mel. I shoved it into my flight jacket pocket. I left him where he lay.

Thing One lay face down. The rock put a visible dent in the top of his skull. Blood gushed freely. I didn't think he was dead. Yet.

I rolled him over. His eyes were closed but he breathed. I pulled out his badge wallet and pocketed it. Then I patted his pockets until I found the BMW key fob.

I kicked his gun away and left him at the foot of the post.

Near the gas can.

THE SAFETY KNIFE I carry in the shoulder pocket of my flight jacket easily cut the zip ties binding Mel's wrists. I helped her roll over and gave her a moment to tug her jeans back up. Despite the wound to her face and a nose that would need surgery, modesty overpowered other concerns. While she recovered her dignity, I fetched her shoes and helped her into them.

She spit blood, then looked up at me. "Where did you cub frub?"

"Back seat. They threw me in after they threw you in the trunk. I managed to break the zip tie and got the drop on them." I held up the BMW key fob. "We can go."

She blinked at me, uncomprehending. I helped her to her feet. She balled up her shirt and pressed it to her face. She blinked wide-eyed at the two men lying on the dirt.

Then at the post.

Then at the gas can.

Without a word, she turned and threw her arms around me.

She smeared blood on my jacket.

57

———————

"How is she?" Andy asked.

JB Dalton did that thing people do when attempting to leave a hospital room quietly. He tried not to open the door too far and then slipped through the narrow gap. His effort made no difference because the door did not creak and in the middle of the afternoon, light was no factor. He paused halfway through and fixed a long look back at his wife.

"Asleep." The word came hard to him. Fury. Fear. Desperate gratitude. A multitude of emotions erupted from the moment he arrived at Coon Memorial Hospital where I'd driven Mel. Andy joined us shortly after he arrived, delivered by Dalton's sister who had been enlisted to race to the ranch to gather Andy and the children. After a long stint in the Emergency Department, transfer to a room, visits from a physician, paperwork, and administered care, Mel Dalton slipped into medicated slumber while her husband clutched her hand.

Dalton stepped into the hall where Andy and I waited on gaudy orange vinyl chairs. "She's gonna need surgery. Her nose is mostly smashed." He absently stroked his moustache. "She always talked about getting a nose job …"

If the words had been ground glass, they would have passed with less effort through his lips. Bright tears bubbled from his eyes.

"Jesus Christ," he said angrily, wiping them away with his sleeve. He drew a deep breath and huffed it out. "Sonofabitch. I'm not usually such a wimp, but that gal in there, she's—she's the sun that rises and sets—she's—"

"Let's go get a cup of coffee," Andy suggested.

"God," he muttered, "if I never see another cup of coffee."

Andy smiled and closed a hand on his shoulder, the professional facsimile of a hug. He sniffed loudly and wiped his eyes again. "Aw shit. I ain't never gonna hear the end of getting all blubbery in front of a darn Yankee."

"Hell no, you won't," I said. "Let's skip the coffee. There's gotta be a bar near here. If what the nurses gave her does what I think it will, she'll sleep until sunup."

"I can't. I can't leave her."

"Yes, you can. Come with us." Andy hooked Dalton's arm. She gestured at the two Dalhart PD officers waiting nearby. "Nobody gets in there to see her. Nobody except those ladies at the desk. Understood?"

They answered a woman they never met like cowed recruits. "Yes, ma'am." The uniformed duo took up station on either side of the door.

"You shoot any sonofabitch tries to get in there," Dalton added. He stopped at the nurse's station to give them his phone number and a promise he would be back soon and for the night. The nurse told him his wife would be sleeping for hours, then told him to skedaddle.

We walked down the sterile hallway toward the hospital exit. Short of our destination Dalton suddenly stopped and peered into an empty patient room.

"Hang on a sec," he said. He turned and stepped inside. I threw Andy a questioning look and then heard a muffled outcry from within. I started into the room where he had dropped to one knee, but Andy stopped me.

"He's not going to want you to see him like this," she whispered. "Give us a minute."

"I'll wait out front."

"Good plan." She patted me on the chest, then slipped into the room where Dalton wept.

58

———————

Fifteen minutes later the Sheriff of Hartley County escorted Andy out of the hospital emergency entrance. He wore sunglasses and pointed at his big pickup truck, parked askew in the nearly empty lot. We followed him to the truck bed where he used a key to access a locker. From it, he produced a tackle box. From the box he extracted an expensive-looking bottle of golden liquid and three of four whiskey glasses tucked in a foam template.

"County's got some rules about selling and serving alcohol. Best we tap my emergency supply."

"No rules about public drinking?" I asked.

"Plenty. Remind me to arrest myself."

Andy waved one of the glasses back into the box.

"Sorry," Dalton apologized after an embarrassed glance at her midsection. She produced a small water bottle from her bag. I borrowed her Aquafina and poured a few drops into my glass to cut whatever was being served. I offered the same to Dalton. He resisted. I splashed water into his glass anyway, then dumped it.

Dalton poured us both a shot.

Andy lifted her water. "To Mel."

We tapped glass to glass to bottle. Dalton threw back his drink and downed it. He poured himself a refill.

"That's good stuff," I admitted after a taste. "Doesn't burn or peel paint." I checked the bottle. Scotch, not bourbon. "Twelve-year-old McCallan? You haul this around in your truck? Jeez, JB. I really ought to have you arrested."

"You and Santa Anna's army." He downed the whole shot again; drew a breath; blew it out and bowed his head. He spoke just above a whisper. "*Jesus H. Christ.*"

He shook his head angrily, then refilled his glass.

"Go easy there, cowboy," Andy warned him. "Your wife needs you clearheaded tonight."

I offered a diversion. "Clue me in, Sheriff. You called me a 'darn Yankee.' Why not a 'damn' Yankee? I don't qualify?"

Dalton chuckled. "A northerner who visits Texas is a darn Yankee. If you stay and steal my job, you're a damn Yankee. If you stay and steal my woman, you're a God Damned Yankee. Course...I wouldn't have a woman to steal if it weren't for you, so..." He lifted his glass. "I'm making you a provisional redneck."

"Boy howdy." I toasted my new status.

He cruised his own thoughts for a moment and then spoke flatly.

"Sheriff Willard and his boys found 'em. They're both alive but not by much. One's got a pretty good dent in his skull. The other one mighta' had the oxygen to his brain cut off for a while. He's breathing but that's about it. They're being transported to Amarillo." He cast a dubious eye in my direction. "You gonna tell me how you managed all that against two armed sons-abitches?"

I shrugged. "Like I told Mel. I saw them throw her in the trunk and I tried to stop them. They put a gun to my head and pushed me onto the floor in the back seat. We got where we were going, and they didn't take me too seriously, so I picked up a rock and pelted one of them. When he went down, the other one started blasting away, but I got down behind the car and found another rock and got off a lucky throw. It put him out of action long enough for me to score a few more hits. That's all there was to it."

"Rocks against guns?" Dalton oozed skepticism.

"It's funny. Shoot at somebody and they don't know what just happened. Throw a rock at somebody and they freak out."

"Lucky throws, I'd say."

"Will pitched for his high school team. They won state," Andy said. She tossed me a smile that would have eclipsed the shine on a state trophy if her ad lib story had been true.

"Still got the arm," I gilded the lily.

"Sheriff Willard said you dropped a damned boulder on one of the two."

"He was trying to get up. I figured he'd pull his gun if I let him."

"Uh-huh. You do know this is a load of unfiltered bullshit."

"Goes down easy with fine scotch, though."

"Amen."

Andy reached for her satchel and pulled out the two badge wallets I recovered. She tossed them on the truck bed. Dalton picked them up one by one and examined them.

"Holy mother of God," he muttered.

"Uh-huh. We thought you should know."

Dalton read the names and examined the official seals, then looked around the empty parking lot. The afternoon sun lengthened shadows, but none were attached to people.

Dalton tossed the wallets back on the steel bed like they were hot. Andy picked them up and returned them to her bag.

"You took these off those asshats?"

I nodded. He whistled.

"Damn, Will. These are Special Investigators for the Office of the Attorney General."

"That's what the fine print says," Andy tapped her bag. "Aldo said there was a scary guy with two other guys at Tiffany Callum's killing. I think these are the two extras. I also think the scary guy was a man named Ray Stroud. Name mean anything to you?"

Dalton shook his head. "Is this the Ray you was asking about?"

Andy looked down at her hands before she spoke. "JB, this morning, I leaned into a theory that you're a member of Company W." She glanced up to read Dalton's expression, which hardened. "After what happened to Aldo, I couldn't ignore the possibility. If you were a member of Company W, then you would know that Ray Stroud is Louis Blaze's trusted lieutenant."

"You still think along those lines?"

"No," she said. "But at the time, I reasoned that because of us, you were backed into a corner and had to arrest Aldo, and then killed him to take him off the board."

"Still think so?"

"No. I do not think that anymore."

"I appreciate that. I put Aldo in holding at the courthouse, not the city lockup, to isolate him. My mistake."

"What happened?" I asked.

"If I were to guess—and as of thirty seconds ago it ain't no guess—I'd say *those guys* happened to him. The courthouse officer told me he was found by two special investigators from the state."

"You think *they* did it?"

"I'd bet the farm on it. Aldo pushed his knees into his pants with his legs folded up against his ass. He cinched up the pants, then threw himself off the top bunk with his shirt tied around his neck. The weight of his body snapped his neck. At least that's how it was supposed to look."

"Why the pants thing?"

"That way his feet couldn't hit the floor. The cell ain't tall enough to hang yourself. With his legs bound up like that, he wouldn't wind up standing. His neck broke from the weight of his body in the fall. That's how it was meant to look, anyway. Only Aldo wasn't that smart."

"No way," I protested. "Aldo feared death. He would have put up a fight. When was he found?"

"Around 6 a.m."

"How long between when those guys arrived and when Aldo was found? Because it would have taken time to get him rigged up like that. I can't imagine he didn't resist."

"Not if they broke his neck first, then arranged the rest," Andy explained. "Think about it. His knee was swollen. There's no way he could have bent his leg back. He was already dead when he supposedly *threw* himself off his bunk. They only needed a couple minutes."

That made sense but prompted me to ask another question. "I don't understand the attack on you and your family. What was the point?"

"Jeff said they found a smartphone and tripod at the scene. They were either fixin' to send me a warning of what might happen, or a video of what they—what they was gonna—"

"It wasn't a warning." Andy spared him the words. "It was prevention. It was meant to take you out. Arresting Aldo caused them a problem. It messed up something. Something big. It caused Winters and all the others to bolt, and it caused you to start asking questions about more than witchcraft. They needed to erase Aldo and end your involvement. Easy to do if Aldo is dead and you're devastated by the loss of your family. And for icing on the cake, the scene plays as another occult killing that throws the community, the media—heck, the whole country—into a frenzy and off the track."

"Those were Pedmann's boys. His investigators,"

Andy shook her head. "I strongly doubt you will get confirmation of that. I expect his office never heard of them. I'll keep those IDs safe. If you delivered them to Austin, you would likely be told they're fakes—and worse, they'll disappear. Like the Tiffany Callum video."

"Don't matter. That sonofabitch is to blame, and I aim to make him pay for everything. *Every damned thing.*"

"Sheriff," Andy said, "you've got children and an injured wife to protect. Whoever did this nearly pulled it off. If you go after them, they *will* try again."

"I can't let this go."

"Nobody's asking you to. But your priority is to make sure no one gets near your family. You're no good to anyone if you're busy planning funerals."

"Jeff's out by my sister's place. City PD is here at the hospital. I'll be in her room all night with my sidearm. Ain't nobody getting past me."

"That's fine, as far as it goes. But if they were my family, I'd take them far away—out of state."

"I ain't running from these sonsofbitches. Goddammit."

"That's not running. That's protecting the ones you love and living to fight another day."

"Will's right. We told you we have skin in the game. Now more than ever. I've only known you and Mel for a day, but you're our friends now. Company W came after us and they came after our friends. Will and I are not letting this go. We're heading down to Austin tonight."

Dalton huffed disbelief. "What? You think you can take on Pedmann?"

"I do," Andy replied. "We have allies you don't know about. Tools we can't discuss. As soon as Mel can be moved, you pack up her and the children and get out of here. Protect your family. Let us do what must be done. No argument."

Dalton swished the last of his scotch in the glass. He tipped it to his lips and downed the liquid, then planted his glass firmly back in the box.

"You need to know what you're up against. Lemme tell you about Pedmann."

59

Andy and I sat on the pickup truck tailgate like two kids at a backfield bonfire. Dalton leaned on the side of the bed resting his arms on the rim. The prairie sun bleached the western sky and beat down on our skin. I felt myself becoming a redneck in the original sense.

"Texas has a border problem. You might'a heard about it."

"Which version?" I asked.

Dalton chuckled without mirth. "Right. It's an invasion or it's an economic boom. It's desperate people escaping horrible violence in pursuit of the American dream or it's terrorists and rapists. It's fleeing families or it's animals and snakes. From what I've seen, politicians on both sides generate a lot of noise but don't give a shit about solving real problems. But embedded in all this is the other kind of traffic crossing the border—in both directions. The drugs and the guns. I'm a Second Amendment guy all the way, but I fail to see what producing and shipping thousands of civilian versions of military grade weapons to the cartels has to do with hunting elk in Montana or defending your home. Point is, there's a real problem with hardware going south and a combination of drugs and cash coming north. Ever hear of Alejandro Ruiz?"

I shook my head. Andy nodded. Dalton explained.

"Millionaire. Prominent player in southwest politics. He gets trotted out by TV pundits because he's second generation Mexican and rabidly anti-immigration. Hates the wetbacks—that's what he calls his own people. The liberals hate him back for that. The conservatives show him off whenever they can. For a long time, he's been under scrutiny from the federales who suspect him of exporting weapons to the cartels across the border and supplying the militia camps on this side. Estimates run to half a billion in guns gone south. He denies it, and he gets thrown a lot of cover from fancy offices in Austin. Of course, that has nothing to do with the big checks he writes to both political parties."

"I thought Ruiz was under indictment," Andy said.

"You're not up on current events, Detective. Pedmann's office filed a dozen different injunctions against the federal investigation. He landed all that paper before judges who are friendly to the state. All but one got rubber stamped. Pedmann also sued the federal government citing jurisdictional dominance or state sovereignty or some bullshit. He claimed the federal investigation into Ruiz conflicted with ongoing state investigations. Some of that nonsense made it to the Supreme Court and got twisted around into a ruling protecting states' rights—which coincidentally hamstrung the DOJ. Funny, isn't it? Protecting us from investigating criminals."

"Is Pedmann investigating Ruiz or shielding him?" Andy asked.

"Lemme tell you a story. About a year ago, we had an eighteen-wheeler roll through. Southbound. It was after midnight. The driver was a bean popper and had been running twenty-six hours straight when he drove the rig off the road and tipped it over. Jeff took the call and got there first. He found busted open crates of weapons spilled all over. Next thing we know special investigators from Pedmann's office show up. Jeff's assigned to crowd control. The people he was told to keep away included the FBI and ATF. I gotta say, he was not happy to be given those instructions, but thankfully the feds never showed up. The truck got tipped back on its wheels, and the evidence drove away right quick. A few weeks later, Jeff went to wrap up his report on the incident. He called the AG's office and asked questions no one knew the answer to. Couple days after that, another special investigator showed up and demanded all the county records related to the incident, including any photos or handwritten notes. He also collected Jeff's draft report. He told Jeff the investigation was closed and said all the paperwork had to be filed in Austin, you know, in case they wanted to cross reference it with other cases. You met Jeff. He don't talk much but he is a wiz with a computer. He found out that the rig belongs to a trucking outfit that belongs to a holding company that belongs to an offshore company that belongs to a syndicate that had Alejandro Ruiz's name buried in the filings. The same Alejandro Ruiz making campaign contributions to our esteemed attorney general's reelection campaign."

Dalton leaned on his pickup's sheet metal. Andy held him in a penetrating squint. She drummed her fingers on the tailgate.

"Pedmann." She spoke as if the name left a bad taste on her tongue.

"Yeah," Dalton agreed. He examined the callouses on his hands. When no one spoke, he packed up his emergency scotch and returned it to the bed locker. He cast a long look at the hospital. "I best be getting back inside. I feel a need to sit in the dark and hold that gal's hand. But here." He fished in his pocket and held out a key fob. "If you're going down to Austin, you sure as hell can't drive that BMW. Take my truck."

"We couldn't possibly," Andy protested.

"No argument."

I reached for the key fob, but Andy snatched it from Dalton's fingers.

"Designated driver."

"We gotta make a stop first," I said.

"The ranch?" she asked. "No need. I brought our bags. They're inside."

"Not for that. If I'm a provisional redneck I need a cowboy hat."

PART III

60

"I parked over on the other side of the Ashmore next door. That truck sticks out like a clown at a funeral director convention." The Marriott room door latched behind me with an overly loud snap. I dropped the GMC key on the desk that Andy claimed for her laptop and our phone chargers. The room contained two queen beds. Both looked inviting. I felt an urge to flop on the nearest and play dead.

We departed Dalhart after Andy promised to keep Dalton informed and emphatically assured him that I would not buy a cowboy hat. She repeated her insistence that he protect himself and his family. Her effort may have made a dent. He reluctantly conceded that a visit to California might double as consultation with a good plastic surgeon for Mel.

Dalton and I would have comfortably bid each other *adios* without any fuss, but Andy threw him a hug. When they parted, his handshake with me carried a lingering grip and wordless thanks transmitted by damp eyes. I had been counting on his gratitude because I had one final request. The time seemed right to ask it.

"JB, there's something you can do for me."

"Oh, boy. Here it comes. I guess you know I owe you."

"Keep my name out of it. Give Mel the credit for throwing those rocks." His expression grew incredulous as he imagined his wife beaning her own kidnappers. This was a big ask, but he carried a bigger debt. I gave it the full court press. "I already had this conversation with Mel. She'll do it if you'll do it."

Dalton elaborately lifted his hat and scratched his scalp. "I don't know, Will. You're putting me in a tough spot."

"JB, the only folks you need to lie to about it might be the same people who tried to kill her."

"Oh, that ain't it. It's just..." He shuffled his feet for a moment. "Hell, the woman's gonna be impossible to live with when a story like that gets around town."

HOW WE MANAGED the three-hour drive as far as Lubbock, I do not know. Andy and I were bone tired. We fought fatigue down the endless and feature-less miles of Interstate 27. Andy did better at fighting drowsiness because she was driving, and because I kept stirring her up with baby name suggestions based on Texas landmarks, sports teams, and town names. She would not admit it, but on this trip, she had resisted the sleep demands of her pregnancy. In the weeks before this trip, her body often induced dozing early in the evening. Since departing Essex, she had pushed herself. Payment was due.

Incredibly, despite our exhaustion, Andy floated the idea of going farther. I drew the line at Lubbock. Fifty miles out I pulled my phone. After checking in vain for word from Pidge, I searched for a hotel. I needed sleep. The day's adrenaline high and inevitable crash drained the last of my stamina. JB's whiskey didn't help.

As highway exits for Lubbock approached, I rattled off the names of hotels. Andy favored one- and two-star dives. I picked the Courtyard by Marriott, which cost triple the room rate of Andy's choices. I told her the higher rate meant the hotel was three times cleaner, and that the Marriott offered the added advantage of being off the path of Interstate 27 on some-thing called the Texas 289 Loop, in case anyone conducted a serious search for us. Andy brushed off my paranoia but caved to my refusal to sleep anywhere for less than $100 a night.

A shower washed away whatever held me up. A room service meal ordered before we cleared the front desk finished me off. I sprawled on the sheets letting the mattress absorb my fatigue like a sponge.

Andy found her second wind after the meal. She changed into her night-gown and studied her laptop screen at the room desk. Occasional comments sprang forth without explanation. I knew better than to ask.

"Huh."

"Seriously?"

"Unbelievable."

"Utterly shameful."

I closed my eyes and welcomed the glide into sleep, but her one- and two-word commentary kept coming like distant radio calls. At last, I heard the laptop snap shut. She disappeared into the bathroom. Then the lights went out and she slipped into the bed beside me. She laid her head on my chest. I stroked my fingernails up and down the baby-smooth skin on her back.

"Want to hear what I found?" Her voice vibrated against my ribs.

"Nope."

"Pedmann has been elected the top law enforcement officer of the state of Texas, not once, but three times. Did you know he's been under indictment in a real estate fraud case for almost five years? He got reelected *while under indictment*. Can you believe that?"

"Nope."

"The guy has dozens of lawsuits against him, both as an individual and as attorney general. He picks fights with every group and faction that finds their way into the crosshairs of his religious beliefs. I have no quarrel with faith, but for this guy church subsumes state. His manipulation of the law for persecution of his enemies would make Pontius Pilate blush. Want to know what else?"

"Nope."

"He's got roots going back to David Duke's Knights of the Ku Klux Klan. His father was an attorney for the people who harassed and threatened the Vietnamese refugees in Galveston and the Gulf Coast. Straight out of law school, Junior advised some of the civilian militia outfits that popped up after the Gulf War, but he was smart enough to never put his name on any filings. I would not be surprised if Pedmann had a prior acquaintance with Louis Blaze. There's a direct through line between Company W and early groups like Civilian Military Action. Did you know that they were the mercenaries on the helicopter that crashed in El Salvador and triggered the Iran-Contra scandal?"

"Nope."

"He skirts direct connections to the white power movement but as a prosecutor, he slow-walked prosecutions against racists involved in attacks on immigrants. He did a term as a state senator and authored bills to prohibit transgender medical services. Are you still awake?"

"Nope."

"Since becoming attorney general, he's sued the federal government eighty-six times. Nothing ever sticks or gets to trial. He files, holds a presser and a couple of exclusive interviews with fringe media, then lets the whole thing slide into obscurity until some judge drops it off the docket or he with-draws the suit without explaining anything to anyone. He spent millions on these filings. Do you think anyone ever held him to account for the cost of all that?"

"Nope."

"He's rah-rah on human trafficking. He established a special office to combat human trafficking eight years ago. Made big headlines. Hired a squad of special investigators and set up SWAT teams. Do you think that in eight years they've secured a single conviction?"

"Nope."

"He's anti-labor, anti-environment, anti-voting rights, anti-literacy, anti-vaccine, anti-immigration. You name it. He's used the AG's office to carry on what he calls his 'crusade for decency.' But at the same time, he rubs elbows with political donors like Clancy Barton, who was convicted of a massive securities fraud that cost hundreds of Texas voters their savings. Or Niles Yarwell. Remember him?"

"Nope."

"Sure you do. Yarwell published newsletters declaring that Hitler merely 'disarmed' the Jews in Europe, and that there were no murders. But his crowning achievement was sexually assaulting a young male intern at a state party fund-raiser. He nearly strangled the boy. Do you think the state prosecuted?"

"Nope."

"Plus, just like JB suggested, Pedmann claims to have an open investigation into Alejandro Ruiz, but the case never moves forward. He just keeps saying his office continues to develop leads and evidence. Somehow the evidence he presents to the press always alludes to malfeasance by the federal government rather than criminal behavior by Ruiz. He's filed for two dozen injunctions against federal action in the Ruiz case. People call him Ruiz's public defender. Can you believe that?"

"Nope."

"You don't? Or you do?"

"Nope."

She slapped my leg.

"Pedmann has publicly demanded that Texas secede from the union, which is against Texas law. Six months ago, he declared that federal law has no authority in Texas. He demands that the President suspend the Constitution. And he has praised 'patriots' who defend the rights and freedoms of the citizens of Texas, which sounds great except it was in the context of an incident in which Company W goons beat up a group of Muslim worshipers at a storefront mosque in Fort Worth. He ordered officials not to prosecute a Company W shooter who killed three unarmed Pakastani tourists because they strayed onto the shooter's land by accident. The story made national headlines. Remember?"

"Nope."

"Want to know what else I found?"

"Nope."

She lifted her head and rolled to face me. Her hair fell on both sides of her face, framing elegant features in the near dark common to most hotel rooms.

"Photos of Pedmann on social media. With politicians. With donors. With supporters. Including one *very interesting* image of Pedmann cozying up to Jake and Elaine Morgan and their daughter Cynthia Leigh. Remember them?"

"Nope."

She shoved her fingers up into my armpit. Her attack jolted me out of a comfortable near sleep state. I rose up and grabbed her wrists, then rolled her onto her own pillow and held her.

"You know what I think?" I asked. I slowly released her and with my right hand found the top button of her nightgown.

"Nope."

I popped the button. "I think…"

I popped the next button. "…that you've done enough talking…"

And the next. "…for one night. And you know what else I think?"

"Nope."

"I think…" I shifted so that my body pressed against hers, with obvious intent.

"Oh my."

"I think I know how to make you stop."

And I was right.

Sometime later, during an intensely wordless conversation in the dark, Andy's phone dinged. Against my sincere wishes, she stretched for the nightstand and read the screen notification.

"Pidge," she whispered breathlessly. "She and Arun just landed."

"Here?"

"Yes. Go back to what you were doing."

61

"**W**ake up!"

I dropped hard out of a dream in which I skimmed the treetops behind the farm fields surrounding our house. In the dream, I couldn't get the BLASTER to work. I drifted helplessly through the air without propulsion control. I've had the dream before. The situation resolves in a variety of ways, none of them good or logical. This time it evaporated under Andy's urgent grip on my shoulder.

"Put some pants on. We've got company."

I heard it. Low rapping on the room door. Steady. Urgent.

Andy moved in the dark. She didn't need light to find her bag and the weapon inside. She edged silently away from the bed.

I spun my legs off the mattress and into my jeans. As I tightened the belt I heard the loud snap of the room's door bolt.

Jesus, she's letting them in.

Light shouldered its way past two dark figures that slipped through the door. Andy hurried the door shut behind them.

"Dee, wh—?"

"*Shhhhhh.*"

No one moved. Andy hovered at the peep hole in the door. The two new figures held statue poses. Seconds ticked by in my head. I unconsciously forced my breathing to go shallow, as if it might be heard through the walls. Thinking someone could burst through the door at any moment, I prepared to vanish.

I wasn't sure if I heard or imagined the footsteps passing our door.

A moment later Andy said, "Okay. For now."

A light switch snapped. The recessed lighting around the top of the room flickered on. Andy hurried to the windows to tighten the room-darkening curtains.

Pidge and Arun stood on the patterned institutional carpet looking tense.

"Fuckers followed us."

62

"Does this joint have a minibar?" Pidge stalked past the bed and searched the cabinet under the flatscreen TV. She found a small fridge containing nothing. "Shit."

"Please sit down," Andy commanded.

Pidge hopped on the undisturbed queen bed. Arun pulled the chair away from the desk and dropped into it. A light sheen of sweat glittered on his forehead, pasting down a lock of black hair. He looked worried.

Andy snapped off the lights. She pulled apart the joined curtains and studied the parking lot from end to end.

"Anything?" I asked.

"Look for a black SUV," Pidge prompted her. "Big thing. Tahoe or Suburban."

"Only five or six of those out here," Andy said. She closed the curtain.

"Oh, they're out there."

"Who?" I asked.

Pidge and Arun volleyed back and forth.

"You wanna tell?"

"No, you—"

"Because you saw—"

"Yes, but who was—?"

"Hey!" I interrupted. "Abbott and Costello. I don't care who's on first. What the hell is going on? Arun. Go."

He cleared his throat.

"We know where they're going."

"Who?" Andy asked.

"The twin Beechcraft airplane. They're not going to Oshkosh. They're going to—"

"They're hopscotching their way to Danville, Virginia," Pidge interrupted, the words bubbling up. "I got a picture of their flight plan. The whole thing. Oh! I almost forgot."

She rustled around on the spare bed. I heard cellophane crinkle. Something flew out of the dark and hit me on the leg. I reached down and found it, long and glossy. Andy produced her phone, activated the screen as a light, and shined the light over the object in my hand.

Pidge bobbed excitedly on the bed.

"Candy bars. They're flying all over the country giving out candy bars. Who does that?"

63

Andy picked up the Clark bar and turned it over. After studying every inch of the king-sized confection, she positioned her phone over the barcode and snapped a picture. She tossed the candy bar back on the bed and thumbed her screen to—I assumed—send the photo to Leslie.

The Pidge and Arun chorus broke out again.

"They had hundreds of those—"

"We think they were—"

"Giving them out. Like—"

"At the airport—it wasn't what that—"

"Jesus!" I tugged my shirt over my head and tucked it in. "First things first. What do you mean Virginia?"

Pidge started, "I got a pi—"

"That can wait," Andy interrupted harshly. She scooped up clothing from the occasional chair in the room and used the dim phone light to guide herself to the bathroom. "We have to go. I'll get dressed and get us packed. Will, go out and see what we're dealing with. Earpiece."

"I wouldn't recommend going out there," Arun warned. "Two very large men were waiting for us when we landed. They followed us here."

"Waiting for you?" I asked.

Pidge answered. "Couple guys sitting in the FBO pretending not to notice us. We caught a cab, and I could feel those baboons staring at my ass —and not in a good way. Sure as shit, when we got in the cab those guys got in a big SUV and pulled out after us. I mean…one minute they're sitting in an FBO lounge like a couple lost hillbillies pretending they can read *AOPA Pilot*, and the next they got someplace urgent to be? Bite me."

"Immediately after we arrived here, they drove past the lobby and—"

Pidge bounced to the edge of the bed and cut off Arun. "Big ass black SUV with the same two gorillas inside rolled past like they were tourists. We thought we better let you know. In case you want to kick some ass."

"Nobody's kicking anybody's ass." Andy slipped into the bathroom taking her thin phone light with her. As she closed the door, she caught my eye and head gestured at the room door. I pulled my boots on, edged past Arun, and pulled open the closet.

"Wait!" Arun sounded panicked. "You can't go out there."

"He can," Pidge said. "They won't spot him. They're looking for us."

"I'll be right back." I pulled my flight jacket from the closet and slipped it on, confirming the presence of two BLASTERS in the pocket. From another pocket, I extracted my Bluetooth earpiece. The device fit snugly in my ear. Lastly, I stroked a small shoulder pocket and felt the flat escape knife I keep handy to slice through seatbelts—and lately, zip ties—in an emergency. "Keep the door locked. Do whatever Andy says. Arun, would you grab Andy's bag and put it on the desk for her? It's kinda heavy. It's over there, on the floor."

He crossed the room in the dark. The move momentarily took away his line of sight with me and the room door. I snapped back the security bolt and grabbed the door handle.

Fwooomp!

I vanished and pulled the door open, then grabbed the outside handle and heaved myself into the hallway. The door snapped shut behind me.

The room we had been assigned on the second floor had only two doors between it and the stairs at the north end of the building, a factor I considered when parking Dalton's truck. In a pinch, a short descent to the first floor and escape out the fire door put us less than 100 yards from the sheriff's pickup.

Rather than deploy a BLASTER, I shoved myself off the door handle and coasted to the end of the empty hall. At the stairway door, I grabbed the handle and wedged my feet against the carpet for leverage. I pushed open the stairwell door and pulled myself through. The door snapped shut behind me. I grabbed the steel railing and heaved my legs over. A short descent took me to the first floor. The door to the first-floor hallway was a pull, not a push. Opening was easier. I shoved off the frame to glide down the first-floor hallway. In short order, I reached the centrally located lobby. Chlorine odor betrayed the hotel's swimming pool nearby.

No one lurked in the common areas. No one lounged on the scattered contemporary furniture facing the check-in desk. Nor did anyone attend the front desk. The low banter and intermittent laughter of late-night television floated from the back office. I pushed off a wall and crossed the hardwood floor toward the front door. On the way, I passed a flatscreen TV mounted on the wall. Hotel notices and promotions cycled silently across the screen. In the lower left corner, I found what I was looking for.

12:38 AM

Not as late as I thought. Andy and I had only been asleep a little over an hour. I thought I'd feel greater fatigue, but the adrenaline rush of being jolted awake and the simmering anger of being freshly hunted by Company W energized me.

At the hotel entrance, I ran into trouble. Automatic double doors failed to detect me approaching. I looked for but did not find a handicap pushbutton that would activate the doors. I floated up against the glass panels and stopped.

The unblinking eye of a security camera watched over the entrance. Popping into sight to activate the door was not an option.

Crap.

I turned around. A small self-serve snack shop beside the front desk offered a cubby hole, but it too enjoyed the protection of 24/7 surveillance. A high-mounted camera watched for would-be shoplifters.

A visit to the first-floor bathroom adjacent to the lobby solved the problem. Ducking inside, I reappeared, then reversed and walked through the automatically activated lobby doors like I owned the place.

Warm, humid night air contrasted with the cool sensation that wraps my skin when I vanish. I strolled away from the hotel entrance like someone with someplace to be. I gambled that Pidge and Arun's tail didn't know my face and would dismiss my unhurried departure.

A row of guest parking faced the hotel and offered the most likely place to park and watch the entrance. I casually noted each black SUV. Windshields coated with reflections of the lighted building obscured the vehicle interiors. Someone could have easily lurked unseen behind the fragmented and glossy glare.

I aimed for the corner of the parking lot. To sell the charade, I pulled Dalton's truck keys from my pocket and used the key ring to twirl the fob around my finger. Just a guy headed out to the rental in search of a late-night snack.

My path took me right past them. Two men hunched down in the front seats of a gloss black Chevy Tahoe. Ballcapped heads swiveled as I strolled within inches of the massive vehicle grille. Caps. Denim collars. Beard stubble and a hint of ink on at least one neck. Company W types. The very redneck stereotypes that Dalton bristled at. I wished he were here to have a chat with these good old boys and then tell me the redneck isn't always the bad guy.

My bootheels suddenly sounded too loud on the asphalt. I held my breath. At any moment, I expected a truck door to open followed by a command to stop. There are times when I don't give a rat's ass whether someone sees me vanish or not. This was one of those times.

I closed my mind's hand on the comforting knobs atop the levers in my head.

Ready.

No snap of a door latch.

No boots dropping to pavement.

No call of, "Hey, buddy. Hold up."

Nothing.

I walked on, trying hard not to appear so casual that I looked ridiculous. I cut between a minivan and a pickup truck. The minivan briefly blocked me from their view and would have been a good place to vanish, except failing to emerge at the back of the minivan might have raised suspicions.

I crossed to another row of vehicles and zigzagged between parked SUVs, building distance that I hoped built proportional disinterest for the men in the truck. When I reached the last row of the lot, I strolled to the end and turned in behind a jacked-up pickup that blocked their surveillance.

This time I vanished.

Fwooomp!

I pulled out a BLASTER and fixed the prop on the shaft. I tested the power. A light stream of air rode up my wrist. The test pulled me forward and upward. I let myself rise past the roofline of the pickup truck.

The men in the black Tahoe remained static.

My phone jangled in my earpiece. I touched the button to accept the call.

"You there?"

"Yeah. I see them. Two Company W goons in a black Tahoe. They're watching the front of the hotel. They saw me. Fully visible. Didn't do anything, which tells me they're following Pidge, not us."

"Any movement?"

"No."

Andy thought for a moment, then said, "They're waiting for reinforcements."

I didn't like the sound of that. "Where are you?"

"In the room. Leaving now."

"Is that the best idea?"

"It is if they're waiting for backup. Where did you park?"

I described the location of Dalton's pickup. "Crap!" I kicked myself.

"What?"

"I have the key."

"No, you don't. It's here on the desk."

"Okay. You three head out. I'll meet you there. I need to do one thing first."

"Darling…" Andy's tone carried a warning.

"Nothing crazy. See you in a minute."

I touched the button to end the call. Andy probably would have preferred to keep the line open, but I didn't want to have to explain anything to my wife.

I had ascended to thirty or forty feet above the lot, almost even with the roof of the hotel. I aimed the BLASTER for the rear of the parked Tahoe. A moment later my boots touched the asphalt. I gently gripped the rear window wiper.

Two heads broke the silhouette line of the front seat headrests. The SUV's occupants did not move. Low conversation within could hardly compete with the low hum of passing traffic.

I pocketed the BLASTER, then crouched and transferred my grip to a trailer hitch. Changing to a horizontal position, I pulled myself to the rear corner on the passenger side where I reached for the wheel well. After tugging myself around the corner, I drew up at the right rear tire.

The side mirror showed a pair of eyes looking straight at me, causing a momentary jolt. The eyes lingered, then shifted back to the front windshield. I unsnapped the shoulder pocket flap and drew my knife. After opening the knife, I used my left hand to grope around the rim of the wheel. Careful of the blade, one of the sharpest I've ever owned, I found the tire stem at the bottom of the wheel. I brought the blade up against the inflation stem. The knife went through the rubber like butter, faster and easier than I expected.

Air hissed from the severed stem. The vehicle settled.

That ought to wake them up.

I heard a curse. The driver's door opened. Boots landed on the pavement. I prepared to push off the asphalt before both vehicle occupants rushed to the scene of the crime.

The passenger did not get out. The driver marched toward the back of the vehicle. I waited for the passenger to make his move, but he remained seated. Confronted with a second chance to strike, I grabbed the wheel and heaved myself forward along a narrow running board, just inches above the pavement. Knife in one hand, I floated beneath the arc of the passenger door —praying it would not swing open.

If he stepped out now, stabbing him in the leg offered a creditable Plan B.

He didn't climb out. At the right front wheel, I groped for the inflation stem. Upper right. The blade cut through the soft rubber without resistance. Another satisfying hiss ended when the wheel sank on the flat tire.

The passenger door latch snapped.

Here he comes.

I pulled hard on the wheel and heaved myself forward just as the door opened above my prone body. Boots landed where my legs had been seconds earlier.

I shot past the front of the SUV and skimmed across the pavement. My phone rang again. This time I could not answer it. I still had the open knife in my right hand, but the sharp blade was the least of my concerns.

Headlights swung over me, momentarily blinding me. A car approached the hotel portico. For an irrational instant I wondered what the driver must think of me zooming across the road at bumper height.

Behind me, two angry men examined my vandalism and searched the parking lot in vain for the perpetrator.

"Inside!" one of them snapped. Hard footfalls charged my way. The approaching car bore down on a collision course with me.

I punched both palms against the asphalt. Grit scraped and stung my skin. The strike sent me upward. I kicked both feet against the pavement, accelerating the hard launch.

The car swept beneath me. I jerked my legs up to avoid being struck by the windshield. Just as quickly as the danger approached, it departed. The car completed a casual loop under the hotel portico and stopped.

The men in ball caps trotted across the road below. One wore a denim vest. The other wore a denim jacket. Lumpy weapons in belt holsters broke the lines of both garments.

Ringing fought the hammering of my pulse in my ears.

The phone. I tapped open the call.

"*Sorry!*" I whispered, "*Are you out?*"

"In the stairwell. Why did you—?"

"Hurry. You've got two men coming through the lobby. No reinforcements that I can see."

"Go, go, go." Andy's command wasn't meant for me.

"I'll meet you at the truck."

"Remember, Arun is with us," she reminded me.

Right.

I put the knife between my teeth and fetched the BLASTER from my jacket pocket. Nothing is ever easy.

64

Andy wheeled the big pickup truck out of the parking lot and onto the frontage road. Pidge and Arun kept watch out the rear from the crew seats in back.

"Where to?" I asked as I snapped the seatbelt.

"It's six hours to Austin," she replied.

"Screw that," Pidge said. "Let's grab our bird and get in the air."

"We can't. If they met you at the FBO, they're watching to be sure we don't do exactly that," Andy explained. "Flying is out of the question. At least, for now. And I can't drive six hours in the middle of the night to Austin. I'm beat."

"I can." Pidge again. "Lemme drive this bad boy."

"It's not just that. I want to hole up somewhere and sort things out. I want to call Leslie."

"We should stay away from the interstate," I offered. "Pidge, grab my iPad from my bag, would you?"

She passed the tablet forward. I spent a few minutes searching while Andy drove and everyone but me threw glances at the road behind us.

"Okay. It's probably a bedbug colony, but I got something. Take a right at the next light."

65

The Alamo Motor Court and RV Park five miles northwest of Post, Texas might have slipped right past us if not for a quivering neon Vacancy sign mounted beneath the eaves of a freestanding one-room office centered between two flat-roofed wings of motel rooms. Forty droning minutes from Lubbock on Highway 84 had been enough to tap into our fatigue and nearly hypnotize us. Andy had to stand on the brakes to catch the turnoff into the dirt driveway and parking lot. She pulled up in front of the office, then opted to drive around to the back of the building. Behind the motel structure, a network of dirt paths fanned out into an open field. The extravagantly named RV Park showed no signs of occupancy when our headlights swept across dry grass and dirt lanes. Andy stopped at the back of the office.

The rear door was locked.

Stretching kinks out of my legs, I rounded the building and tried the front door. Locked. Weak illumination cast yellow puddles of light at intervals up and down the motel façade.

"Might not be as open as the sign says." I tugged on the doorknob.

"Here," Andy said. She tugged on my arm and pulled me to face a cubby box mounted on the office wall. A plastic label tape offered instructions. Andy read it. "*After hours take key. Pay in the morning.* My, my. Trusting people."

"Jeez. Where was this place when I was in high school?" Pidge asked.

Andy plucked two keys with large flat fobs from the cubby box.

"You take six. We'll take seven." Andy handed Pidge a key. "That puts us on either side of this office. I didn't see back doors for the rooms, but we'll leave the truck behind the office just to be on the safe side."

A narrow wooden boardwalk separated the office from the rooms Andy had selected. Quick getaway if we needed it.

"Dump your stuff and then come to our room," I told Pidge and Arun. "We need to talk."

66

Pidge hopped on a corner of the bed and sat on her crossed legs like a girl sharing the first ghost story of the sleepover. Arun carefully examined an armchair in the corner of the room before sitting on it. Andy leaned on the doorway to the room's tiny shower and toilet.

Andy opened the meeting with a recap of our two days in Dalhart. The Callum wake. The failed attempt to find the crime scene. The encounter with both sheriffs. She skirted the specifics of how we persuaded Aldo to confess. Pidge grew agitated when Andy told her that the men Aldo identified had gone on the run, but she brightened when I described disabling the two who were about to murder the sheriff's wife. Arun sat looking stunned, a hint that we might be pushing his limits. Andy wrapped it up with the story Dalton shared with us introducing the connection to an arms dealer.

"Arms dealer," Pidge muttered. "This is some shit."

"What about you?" I asked.

"Okay, so you remember we found out they were going to Natchamacallit in Colorado, right?"

"Naturita," I filled in from my spot at the head of the bed. The room wasn't the Marriott, but it was surprisingly tidy. The carpet was frayed, and the sink was rust stained, but the sheets and towels were clean, and Andy found no signs of bedbugs.

"Right. We followed 'em. But we got there and guess what—no Twin Beech on the ramp and nobody at the airport. Only—"

"The entire time enroute to Naturita," Arun joined in, "Cassidy asked me

242

to monitor the moving map feature of her ForeFlight program on her iPad. Remarkable technology. I watched the traffic flow at the Naturita airport and surrounding area."

"Like, who's flying in and out of Nowhere, Colorado, right?" Pidge threw her hands up in a shrug.

"An assumption that served us well," Arun confirmed. "I was able to see a single aircraft depart while we were yet some distance away. We—"

"We landed anyway," Pidge said. "But I had him keep an eye on that departure. We checked out Naturita. Absolutely dead. But that departure—I said we should take a shot and go after it. Go ahead, you tell 'em."

Arun squared himself in the armchair.

"As she indicated, I monitored the aircraft's progress on the moving map. We departed and engaged in pursuit. Quite exciting. Rather like an old movie. Pushing it a bit, our aircraft had a slight speed advantage over the older Beechcraft, but they had a substantial lead on us across a significant distance. I've always been rather taken by the Battle of Britain, so it was thrilling when we caught up—"

"I turned off the transponder. Like you suggested," Pidge said. "That way they wouldn't tip to the fact that we were flying up their ass."

"To be clear, I suggested you turn off the transponder and get the hell off the grid. Not go chasing after the very people who were more than likely trying to kill you," I replied.

"Tomato, to*mah*toh."

"If I may," Arun continued, "we took all necessary precautions, Will. I should say, up to a point. However, using the technology at hand, we spotted the bogey at twelve o'clock—God, I've always wanted to say that—and confirmed it was a twin-engine Beechcraft."

"The dumbshits were running with their ADS-B. Why do that? Because I'm pretty sure they're up to no good."

"Maybe to avoid violating any FARs," I offered, "kinda like not speeding on the way to the bank robbery."

"Meh."

"The point," Arun said, "is that we were able to maintain visual pursuit all the way to—what was the next airport?"

"Mineral County Memorial—and holy crap, Will! This is smack in the middle of some serious mountains. Like, 12,000-foot peaks all around this one-strip hole in the wall. Something like an 8,000-foot field elevation. Serious shit."

An understatement. A knot of worry formed in my mind, but Pidge, on a whim last summer, spent two weeks bouncing around airports in the Rocky

Mountain states looking for people to teach her the lifesaving basics of mountain flying. As usual, between the two of us, I would have trusted her more than me to handle the situation.

Arun continued. "Cassidy suggested that we should let them land. I concurred. No reason to engender suspicion. We circled the area, keeping watch. Incredible scenery. Spectacular vistas with—"

"And it's getting dark now, and I got clouds moving in and there's granite in some of them. So, finally I said, screw it. We're landing. One hot shit approach, let me tell you. And there it is, the Twin Beech, just sitting on the ramp. I mean, I'd give a sloppy bl—I mean, give just about anything to fly one of those beauties."

"Quite the classic," Arun mused. In the dim single nightstand light, I thought I saw a hint of blush flood his cheeks. He caught me staring and lowered his voice. "Right. As we landed, we saw a vehicle driving away from the airport. When we parked on the ramp, we found ourselves utterly alone. We waited inside the aircraft, thinking that if someone was curious or intended to welcome us, they would approach. None of the buildings seemed to have occupants. The fuel system is self-service. After twenty or so minutes we felt confident that enough time had passed that we were the sole occupants of the airfield."

"So, I broke into the airplane."

"What?"

"Yeah. Piece of cake. You know how bad old airplane door locks are. All I needed was my pocketknife and a piece of wire I keep in my bag for exactly that kind of emergency."

"You broke into the airplane?" Andy repeated. From her lips the words carried admonishment.

"Had to. How else were we supposed to get this?" Pidge tugged her phone from the pocket of her flight jacket. She thumbed the screen, then tossed it across the bed covers to me.

"What am I looking at?"

"Edit screen for the ForeFlight map screen. That's the whole thing, right there." She pointed as I used my fingers to expand the screen.

She had photographed the screen feature into which a pilot enters airports and waypoints to lay out a flight plan. In the GPS age a flight plan often consists of two points with a direct flight between them. Not this time.

"Jesus Christ," I muttered. Andy leaned in for a look.

U34 KAIB C24 KANK 4V1 KLAA KLBL 104 9K8
KOWP KJLN KDYR M20 7A8 KDAN

"What is all this?" Andy looked over my shoulder.

Pidge hopped off the bed and unzipped the flight bag she had carried into our room. She pulled an iPad shielded by a lurid pink leather case from the bag and flipped it open. She tapped the screen, then held it up to show me a map of the United States. A blue line zigzagged from the Rocky Mountains to the east coast, separated by dots with airport identifier captions. She had duplicated the plan.

"That's where they're going, handing out candy bars like Saint Nick. We found two big cartons of those Clark bars in the back of the airplane. They sure as shit aren't going to Oshkosh."

I let out a low whistle. "You see where this is pointing?"

"A-firmative."

"What?" Andy asked, alerted by Pidge's intense expression.

"Danville is the last point on the NavLog." I replied. "Extend the line. That's Washington, D.C."

67

———————

Despite a flurry of questions from Arun and Pidge, Andy declared our meeting closed. We need sleep, she announced, and we would take up their questions in the morning. She practically pushed our guests out the door.

"Power your phones down," she called after them. "Just a precaution. Get some sleep."

"Should we pull the batteries out?" Arun held up his phone.

"Not necessary. Just power down. Without power it's just plastic and metal. Untraceable."

His skeptical expression, tinged with worry, told me he would be pulling the battery and putting it under his pillow for the night. Andy closed the room door and hooked the flimsy chain latch. A moment later, urgent knocking came through the thin door.

"Gimme the truck keys," Pidge held out her hand when Andy opened the door. "You old toads will probably sleep all day. I'm gonna want breakfast."

Andy handed over the key. "Be careful. And don't play with the lights and siren."

Pidge's grin was not reassuring.

"Bring some for all of us!" I called over Andy's shoulder. "Coffee!"

Pidge flashed a jaunty wave over a devilish look that confirmed she was more interested in getting behind the wheel of a powerful law enforcement vehicle than in delivering carryout.

Andy closed and relocked the door. She reached up and released her hair from a hastily tied ponytail. She shook it out on her shoulders.

I like to think I can read the signs. Her body language and the appeal in her gold-flecked green eyes told me to take her in my arms. She affirmed the move with a deep sigh. Her head came to rest on my shoulder, tucked in against my neck. Her hands pulled me tightly against her body. We traded wordless signals full of need and love and comfort.

She spoke first, but without releasing her hold on me.

"How did they know?"

I'd been wondering the same thing. Two men appearing at the hotel like that might have pointed at something she and I had missed, but it wasn't us they had followed. They had intercepted Pidge and Arun at the airport.

"Not sure. Lubbock is in controlled airspace. Pidge would have no choice but to operate the transponder. Maybe they tracked her ADS-B signal. Our registration is listed as Private with the FAA, but someone knowing what to look for can still track it. Potentially all the way back to when she left Dalhart. Jesus. I can't believe Pidge broke into Blaze's Twin Beech like that."

"No? Seems on par for her."

"What if it's not Pidge that led them to us?"

Andy pulled back and looked at me, brow lined with questions.

"You mean us?" she asked.

"Yeah. What if it's that truck? Or worse, what if it's Dalton?"

"No." Andy shook her head. "They were waiting for Pidge at the airport. They followed her to the hotel. It's not Dalton. We both know it's not Dalton."

I said nothing, which caused Andy to emphasize her point.

"Will, they almost burned his wife alive. I know it feels like we have chased shadows ever since we got here, but we can't lose sight of what got us here. They burned a girl at the stake. Alive. A girl that was meant to be Pidge. And they meant to do the same to Mel. That's real to Dalton. And it wasn't just his wife. It was his children, too."

"Boy, do I want you to be right about him. Are you sure it's not Dalton's truck?"

"Tracking a vehicle isn't as easy as they make it look in the movies. Remember, those guys were waiting at the FBO. They followed Pidge to us at the hotel."

"I guess…but I still wonder about the truck. Maybe it has LoJack."

"LoJack has to receive a signal from law enforcement to activate."

"My point exactly. Dalton is law enforcement. Maybe that's why he wanted us to have his truck."

She wasn't buying it. Frankly, neither was I.

"It's Pidge by way of the airplane. That's the only thing that makes sense. So, then… how?"

I shrugged. "It's like Dalton said. Busybodies at the airport. Somebody watching Dalhart airport saw her, saw the airplane, saw us, tied the whole package together and came up with the idea to track where she flew. We thought we were taking her off the board by sending her off to find that Twin Beech. I think we put her in more danger by pointing her at a key component of whatever they're planning."

"The candy bars?"

"Carrier pigeons. That's how Blaze does it. That candy bar is a message."

"A message to whom?" Andy released her embrace and slipped out of my arms. She paced the small confines of the room for a moment.

"Guys like Cole Winters. Company W foot soldiers."

"Guys who have loaded up their arsenals and hit the road," she added. "I think you're right. I think a call has gone out, and the message in those candy bars is for anyone answering the call."

She stopped and stared at me. We both knew what she meant. Something big brewed in the ranks of Company W. A stroke conceived and carried out by True Believers, the kind that leaves innocents dead.

I glanced around the room, then grabbed the armchair Arun had used. I pushed it up against the door and wedged it against the knob. Andy broke into a bemused smile.

"Think that's going to help?" She stepped up to me and touched my cheek. "You're cute. We should sleep. You take the bathroom first. I want to try Leslie again. And I want to try the Wi-Fi."

SHE WAITED until I stepped out in my boxers and t-shirt. I tossed my clothes in a heap on the top of my overnight bag. As an afterthought, I moved the pile to the foot of the bed. Handy for rapid departure.

"What?" The serious expression on her face prompted me. She swiveled her laptop to show me the screen.

"Two things. First, there's a press release on the website for the Texas Attorney General that announces that he's receiving a civic leadership award from a coalition of Texas communities. The awards banquet is tomorrow— er, tonight at his home."

"Okay."

"It goes on to say that from there he's headed to Washington, D.C. for a think tank summit on human trafficking. It keynotes with a banquet at the White House."

"When?"

"Day after tomorrow—er, God, what time is it? Tomorrow night. I might be able to find it on a White House press site." She moved the mouse and clicked a new tab on her laptop screen. "Second, there's this."

A fresh window filled the screen. A blue box in the upper left corner of the screen displayed KVUE and the ABC network logo. A headline spread below the menu bar under a notation for "Local News."

FOUR DEAD IN AMBULANCE CRASH

Beneath the headline, video played inside a frame. Distant smoke billowed at the side of a four-lane highway. Emergency vehicles in the foreground flashed warning lights to drivers diverted into a single lane around firetrucks at the side of the road. The video cut back to a pair of on-air personalities at a news desk. Andy left the sound on mute.

"Is that…?"

She nodded. "Rolled over and caught fire. An EMT up front was thrown clear. Two more perished in the fire along with the two men being transported."

I did not say it aloud because Andy subscribes to a higher concept of justice than me, but two of the men who burned Tiffany Vera Callum to death and tried the same with Mel Dalton got exactly what they deserved. The video switched back to the accident footage and wiggled as the camera tried to zoom in on roiling flame and black smoke consuming the crushed ambulance body box. Given the arrow-straight line of the highway and the flat, expansive terrain, I seriously doubted the crash was accidental.

Andy closed the screen window, then her laptop.

"Did you connect with Leslie?" I asked.

"No."

68

"We have a job for you two," Andy announced.

Pidge finished distributing tall coffees in paper cups bearing the name Coffee Wizards. Arun laid out a selection of pastries and bagels. Manna from heaven, both. I grabbed a bagel and lowered myself to the floor near the door. Morning sunlight angling through the room windows did no favors for the old carpeting.

"We need you to retrieve the Navajo and meet us in Austin," I finished Andy's preamble pointedly at Pidge.

"How are we supposed to do that? Won't those guys be watching?"

"They might," Andy conceded. "Or not. Keep in mind that Company W may be true believers, but they also recruit weekend cosplay wannabes. Twenty-four-hour surveillance requires dedication and resources. Most of these guys squeeze government overthrow in between their day jobs and bar nights. They might be watching the airport..."

"Then how the f—"

"Easy," I said. "Sterile ramp." I looked at Pidge, who instantly flashed on the obvious solution.

"I'm not following," Arun said when he saw her grinning.

Pidge ignored Arun for the moment and asked me directly, "How?"

"We have you two booked on a scenic flight out of Lamesa Municipal with a guy that flies a Piper Comanche," I replied.

"It's about an hour drive from here. We'll take the back roads," Andy tag-teamed in.

"The guy takes you up in his Comanche for a wander around the panhandle that just happens to land at Lubbock where you give him a fat tip and thank him for the ride."

"That way it's not a charter…and not on any manifest," Andy said.

"And we hop out right next to Tango Whiskey. Nice." For Arun's bewildered benefit, Pidge said, "Nobody gets on the ramp without authorization."

Arun picked up the cue. "Of course. And if they're waiting in the FBO for us, or outside in the parking lot, they'll never see us pass through. Clever."

"I called the FBO in Lubbock and had them top the tanks," I said. "Get in the air as quick as you can. Clear the Lubbock airspace and point the airplane anywhere but Austin. As soon as you can, drop down into uncontrolled airspace and kill the transponder. Do a little low-level meandering, then fly down to Austin. Text us when you get there."

"Low-level meandering…" Mischief danced in Pidge's eye.

"Yeah, don't let anyone on the ground read the N-number or see the color of your eyes," I warned her. Not that it did any good.

69

Time became an issue.

Fifteen minutes to pack and check out of the Alamo Motor Court and RV Park despite the owner's best effort to draw us into a lengthy conversation about our point of origin, destination, planned activities and favorite foods. The small office was open and she worked hard to sell us on visiting the local rodeo and getting lunch at Holly's Drive-In. We promised to do our best.

Just short of an hour to drive to Lamesa Municipal Airport and another fifteen minutes to locate the owner of a faded blue and white Piper Comanche who had not checked his voicemail and wasn't aware that he had a scenic flight scheduled. The retired Delta pilot made up for it with unabashed delight at having paying passengers—and more when he learned that Pidge was a pilot.

Five-and-a-half hours to reach Royal Tuxedo in Austin, Texas.

"You need a tux," Andy asserted as we passed an *Austin 110 Miles* sign.

"A what?"

"It's black tie."

I realized she meant the event at the Attorney General's home. After dropping off Pidge and Arun, we discussed the pros and cons of crashing the party. The pros won, but I had assumed the crashing would be done via *the other thing*.

"Pretty sure nobody will see what I'm wearing," I said.

"No. You need a tux and I need a dress." Andy looked at her phone, which she had been thumbing for the last hundred miles while I drove. "We'll do the tux place first because they close at seven. There are two options for a dress that are open until nine. 'Fraid I'll be hitting the company credit card. It will be tight, but we should have time to check in to the hotel to get dressed, then hit the party by ten."

"That's cutting it close, don't you think?"

I caught a distinctively devious glint in her eye. She leaned across the console and flipped two toggle switches mounted at the bottom of the dash. The siren startled me. The light bar over the cab cast flickering blue and red reflections on the big truck's sheet metal. Andy sat back and smiled.

"Step on it."

I'M NOT sure we cut all that much time off the run into Austin or that I ever want to drive a pickup truck at close to 100 miles per hour again. Eventually, Andy felt we were more likely to lose time by being pulled over by a county or state patrol car and she switched off the noisemaker and lights. Almost as amazing as the speed run was the fastest tuxedo fitting in history. Andy barked measurements and made snap selections at a bewildered sales associate, and in short order we scurried from the store with a garment bag over my shoulder. Her crowning achievement, however, came with selecting an evening dress. She told me to stop at the curb in front of a store called Couture de Austin and all but said to keep the engine running, as if she planned to rob the place. Twelve minutes and fourteen seconds later—I timed her—she jumped back into the cab of Dalton's pickup with a wrapped bundle of dress and a shoe box in her arms.

"I am in absolute awe of you," I said.

"You should be." She handed back the Education Foundation credit card and issued the next order. "Hotel."

IT TOOK THREE TRIES. Dressing without gravity was hard enough, but the damned tuxedo kept disappearing when I slipped it on after I vanished. Finally, concentrating intently, I succeeded. I looked over my masterpiece in the mirror. Just like the old movie.

She's going to love this.

I gripped the hotel bathroom door and pulled it open. With the tux weighing me down, I was able to walk gingerly. I swung myself out into the room.

Andy worked the finishing touches on her eye makeup in the mirror above the desk. As ever, she had magically sculpted her hair into a master-piece of flowing swirls and tantalizing curled accents.

"Sweetheart, I'm ready." I held a tense grip on the levers in my head. It seemed to help.

Andy looked over at a headless tuxedo that carried a goofy grin she could not see. I lifted an empty sleeve to wave at her. She slowly drew herself erect. She frowned. Her mild exasperation at the juvenile trick tickled me, until she spoke.

"Who taught you to tie a bowtie?"

70

W e parked Dalton's truck as far as possible from the mansion entrance. The residential neighborhood tolerated curbside parking in two-hour increments, but the law enforcement star on the cab door suggested we needn't worry about being ticketed. The evening air remained warm, too warm for a tuxedo but comfortable for Andy's bare shoulders and bare back. The dark red dress she wore shimmered in the subtle streetlamp glow. The deep vee on the front of the dress tugged at my attention. Once more I wondered if the baby bump showed, or if I just saw it because of my investment in the project.

"Come on," I said. "It was hilarious."

"Yes, love. It was hilarious." She patted my arm. Suppressed dimples peeked from her cheeks and told me whatever humor she saw had nothing to do with haunting a hotel room as an empty tuxedo.

"I've been wanting to do that ever since this started."

"Of course, you have."

"You didn't think it was funny at all, did you."

"Don't be silly. I think you're quite funny." She smiled up at me in a way that delivered zero satisfaction.

"Fine. I still don't see why we had to go to all this trouble. Crashing this party is no problem."

"For you."

She had a point.

"Trust me, Dee. Someone looking like you will have no trouble gate crashing a political hoedown like this. Bat your eyes and claim you're the *niece* of senator so-and-so."

"There's an ugly image. I have a better idea." She opened the small clutch that she had miraculously accessorized with her dress in under thirteen minutes of shopping. She lifted out two familiar wallets. "We're special investigators for the Office of the Attorney General."

"How do you know there won't be people guarding the front door who know these guys?"

"The people at the front door will be office staff. Maybe an aide or intern. People running around with these credentials don't mingle with the errand staff."

I glanced at the clutch after she handed me one of the wallets and slipped the other back inside.

"Not carrying tonight?"

"It's not practical. Besides, this is a well-lit public place full of powerful people with social images and political interests to guard. I suspect being armed is very little defense against the weapons these people wield."

71

We passed through an open wrought iron gate that granted access to a circular driveway. The obligatory fountain at the center of the circle sprayed water and white noise around a Greek or Roman goddess. Something in the garden bloomed and thickened the night air with fragrance. Hedges and carefully manicured gardens fronted the imposing two-story mansion. I wished I knew more about architectural styles, but also guessed that this ostentatious pile would probably offend anyone with actual knowledge. Elements of classical, modern, Spanish, English Tudor and God only knows what else made it into the finished design. The mix conveyed the only impression that mattered. Money.

Warm incandescence from within and garden spotlights from without lent the property a Disney theme park aura. Light classical music drifted across the front lawn, cementing the cliché. A string quartet, perhaps. Or a good facsimile of one. Here again my limited education failed me. Music by a composer whose name starts with a B, no doubt.

Two people guarded the open front doors. My faith in Andy's assessment grew. Both were young. Staffers, probably. Interns if we were lucky. A young man and a young woman. They looked intent on avoiding conversation or eye contact with each other. Andy strolled up the broad steps with me at her side. Given the late hour, I suspected that the bulk of the arrivals had been hours ago, and door duty had long ago grown boring. The young woman beat her associate to the punch when she stepped forward to greet us.

"Good evening." She slapped on a smile that contrasted with the way she positioned herself to block the entrance.

Andy pulled the wallet from her clutch and flipped it open. I followed suit. We purposely obscured part of the ID with our fingers, in case they knew the men whose names appeared in laminated form.

"Boss had us working late," Andy sighed. "Told us to come by for a drink before the party ended."

The gatekeeper glanced at our IDs but without much enthusiasm. I snapped mine shut and pocketed it.

"Good luck with that," the young man said flatly. "Most of the good booze is long gone." He showed no interest in our identification. His companion stepped aside.

"There's still plenty," the young woman countered. "The buffet has been taken down, but the dessert table is still up." She pointed at a large dining room to the left of the foyer. "Everyone is in back on the patio. The inside bar is closed, but they're still serving on the patio. Enjoy."

Andy paid her a polite nod and moved on with authority. She did not offer me her arm. Work colleagues, our stolen wallets said. This wasn't a date.

High ceilings on the first floor explained the impression of height seen from the outside. The interior layout and style reflected the exterior's confused architecture. A wide foyer divided the center of the house with classical curved marble stairs climbing to the second floor. The dining room on the left had an English manor feel. The path to the right opened to a huge room that may have been meant as a ballroom. Native art and cowboy arti-facts decorated the walls. Adhering to open concept design, the ballroom touched on a sprawling kitchen at the back, but also shared a row of French doors that opened onto the promised patio. Multi-colored paper lanterns hung in rows around a broad tiled patio and in the avenues of an extravagant garden. The source of the music became clear. A group of string musicians occupied a small stage set up on the side lawn. Men in tuxes like mine. Women in black dresses. The rich warm wood of their instruments glittered in the lantern light.

Guests clustered around a bar opposite the musician's stage, far enough from the music to permit comfortable conversation. Men in tuxedos loitered around high-top tables. Women hung on their arms, if not their every word. A few couples wandered the garden paths. A few crisp cowboy hats bobbed in the crowd looking incongruent over formal wear, at least to my eye.

Andy led me through the ballroom, which had a stage of its own, a podium with the Seal of the State of Texas affixed to the front, and double rows of chairs filling two thirds of the room. This had been the scene of Pedmann's high honor, an award for community service, Andy told me, that seemed to have no history predating this event. I imagined a gaudy gold star hanging on a striped ribbon lifted over Pedmann's head to thunderous applause.

When we reached the French doors, Andy abruptly stopped and spun around to face me.

"That's Morgan," she said quietly.

"Who?"

"Morgan. Cindy's father. End of the bar facing the garden."

I spotted the man. He held a glistening tumbler with ice and golden liquid. The woman deeply charmed by his smile and conversation was not his wife. I wondered if Elaine Morgan had been invited. Andy stole a cautious look at the crowd.

"And that's Senator Drew Stapleton. From Oklahoma. Same group. Tall guy with the hair."

"I see him. This feels like the same bunch from the country club. I don't want to run into that Stroud character without warning. See him anywhere?"

Andy ventured a casual search, then shook her head.

I leaned close to Andy and asked, "Who's the woman with Stapleton?"

"No idea. Why?"

"I think she was at the club." I tried to congeal strands of vague memory. The night we splashed Ray Stroud into the club swimming pool I had seen the same woman. For an instant I mistook her for Andy, but largely for the similar outfit she wore. She had long hair, but hers was jet black and straight. She had a slim build with generous breasts, a narrow waist, and strong hips that looked slightly out of proportion to the rest of her. Andy's figure is striking for naturally alluring geometry I find cohesive and hard to describe. Something about this woman struck me as irregular. She wore a sparkling gray dress with a plunging neckline and a slice up the side of the skirt closed at her waist. Men clustered around her, clearly the Senator from Oklahoma—one of the younger in the Senate and a media favorite for his bachelor status—held her attention.

My subconscious wanted to see her as plain, yet her features looked perfectly proportioned. Symmetrical. Beautiful. From a distance.

"Will, you're staring."

"Sorry." I shook it off. "It's just...I feel like I've seen her before."

"Where?"

"No idea."

"Well," Andy said, "just try to avoid kissing her."

Andy's reference to Olivia Brogan and a completely not-my-fault moment at a Washington, D.C. party sounded playful. Mostly. "You're not going to let that go, are you?"

"Good heavens, why would I?" She flashed what I would call a ninety-percent smile.

"I threw her in the ocean, I'd like to remind you. That should count for something."

"Yes, you did. And I appreciate the thought, love." Andy looked around. "We need to find Pedmann. I'd like time alone with him."

"He's the guest of honor. You'd think he'd be here somewhere."

"Not seeing him."

"I have an idea. It's a crazy guy thing, but it just might work."

"What?"

"Let's ask for directions."

72

"Do you know where we can find the boss?" I asked the young woman at the door. She'd taken to leaning on the jamb and since we were just staff, same as her, she did not adjust her posture.

"I do," she said, "but he was pretty clear about not being disturbed."

"Very clear," her associated emphasized.

"And he was just as clear to us that we were to report to him as soon as we arrived," Andy said. "But I can always let him know that you countermanded his orders to us. What did you say your name was?"

"It's Beverly. Go ahead. I'm happy to tell him Rennie and I followed his instructions as they were given to us."

"Whoa, whoa." Rennie, her companion, held up his hands. "Back up the truck. Don't drag me into this."

Andy swung her attention to Rennie. "Oh, I think you're already deep into this, Rennie."

Color drained from the young man's face.

"Upstairs. He's in his study."

"Rennie!" Beverly snapped. "If this bites us in the ass, it's entirely on you."

"Buzz off, Beverly." Rennie head-gestured at the stairs. "I wish this damned party was over. My feet are killing me."

Andy flashed a cold thank you smile at both door watchers and made for the curved staircase. I followed. Halfway up, Beverly called after us.

"Why don't I call and tell him you're on your way up?" She held up her phone. "What are your names again?"

Andy ignored her. I glanced back, then raised a single-digit gesture in her direction, which caused her to huff loudly in my direction.

"What did you do that for?" Andy asked after we reached the top and entered a hallway that spanned the width of the building.

"Staying in character with the office culture here. Now what?"

Andy looked both ways. I half expected to see the standard hulking bodyguard standing outside a door, but the long upstairs hallway was empty.

"You take that side. I'll take this side. Listen at each door to see if there's a meeting or phone call or anything inside."

We split up. Plush royal blue carpeting silenced my footsteps. I strolled casually in case someone popped out unexpectedly. At each white painted door, I leaned in to listen. There were four on my side of the house, two on each side of the hall. When I reached the end, I turned to signal Andy that the search revealed nothing.

She was gone.

73

I spent a moment of disbelief double-checking the length of the hallway. I jogged across the center stair landing and down the long blue carpet past four white doors, all closed. I did not test the doorknobs.

At the end of the hall, a new passage went left toward the back of the house. Andy must have explored deeper. I followed.

The short hallway ended with a ninety-degree turn to the right into another hallway. Double doors on the left stood open. Sounds but not voices flagged the room as occupied. I walked through the doors trying hard to look like I belonged.

A woman in business attire looked up from behind a land yacht of a desk. Drapes of dark blonde hair hung in swept curves on both sides of her perfectly proportioned face. Forties, I guessed, but carefully fit and holding on to her twenties with all ten bright red fingernails. The desk featured dark polished woodwork, delicate dovetail joints, and enough carving on the front panels to qualify for a museum display. The piece added to the weight and authority of the office, a windowless study and library. Between tall bookshelves, framed sports jerseys and at least three Texas flags splashed color against dark wood paneling. The woman startled to my sudden appearance. A scatter of file folders littered the leather-cornered blotter. She held several in her hands.

"They leave already?" I asked, hoping to BS my way past a barrage of queries.

"Ten minutes ago," she replied. She hesitated. "And you are?"

I pulled out the wallet and flashed it at her but didn't wait for her curiosity to rise. "I'll see if I can catch them."

"Hold on," she called after me when I hurried away. I kept moving.

The short hallway ended at a set of stairs that descended to an exterior door. At the bottom of the stairs, I looked through a window at a rear parking lot bordering a six- or seven-car garage. Figures hustled across the pavement, crossing through pools of light cast by ornate carriage lamps attached to the garage. The woman in the gray sparkling dress. The tall senator from Oklahoma. Several men in tuxedos. The group boarded a black Cadillac Escalade that waited with its V8 engine running. The instant the passenger door closed, the driver rolled.

When the Escalade pulled forward I saw Andy.

On her knees.

Handcuffed.

Three men in dark suits stood over Andy. One spoke on a phone. One aimed a gun at my wife's temple. The third stood back and watched.

White hot fury flooded my gut.

Fwooomp!

I vanished on instinct or out of anger or out of thundering urgency. I grabbed the doorknob, twisted, pulled, and angled through the opening, leaving the door ajar. Until now, the power unit in my coat pocket had been an awkward bulge in a tuxedo not designed for storage. I simultaneously pulled it from my pocket and shoved myself away from the building. The launch established a glide across the asphalt. I found a prop for the power unit. Tension, fear, or fury—I could not distinguish—ignited tremors in my hands.

Cool it, I commanded myself. *You won't do her any good by dropping this.*

The blade snapped in place. The unit responded to my touch. Air blew up my arm. I surged forward and upward.

It would take only seconds to reach her, grab her, make her vanish and make our escape.

Don't. Her word. Her voice. Her worry. The echo of her warning rang in my head. *Don't do it,* I warned myself. *Not unless you absolutely have to.*

Now what?

The weapon pointed at her did not waver. The man on the phone looked at Andy as he spoke. He held her stolen special investigator wallet in his free hand.

Plan B. Grab the guy with the gun. Make him vanish. When he goes weightless haul him fifteen feet up and drop him.

And what if the gun goes off when you grab him? Or when you lift him, blowing us both out of the sky? Previous experience with gunshots while in the vanished state said I would wind up on the pavement half paralyzed.

My options slipped from bad to worse as I bore down on the trio in suits.

To avoid a collision, I angled the power unit up and soared overhead. I let the BLASTER whine like an intruding drone. All three men looked for the source of the sound despite the string quartet still earning their pay on the lawn behind a wall that separated the parking lot and garage from the party.

Short bursts of power altered my trajectory and carried me over the roof of the garage. The man holding the gun backed away from Andy. He split his attention between Andy and the mosquito noise overhead.

Andy glanced up as well. *Good. She knows I'm here.*

Glints of silver light sparkled between Andy's wrists. Handcuffs. Metal handcuffs.

I pulled around and swept down past the eaves of the garage. I killed the BLASTER. The ground came up quickly behind Andy. The instant my feet touched asphalt I bent my knees, careful not to bounce off the hard surface. A ricochet would have meant colliding with Andy. I spread my knees to straddle her feet. My knees hit the hard asphalt.

I grabbed the silver chain connecting the two bracelets of her handcuffs. She involuntarily jolted.

"*Dee.*" I whispered the word against strands of her hair at her ears. She stiffened. Her light perfume used my senses to remind me of what I might lose if this could not be resolved.

"Don't." She said it loudly, clearly. That word again. That warning. All three men glanced in her direction. She looked up at them. Any hope of convincing her to let me make her vanish went up in smoke.

Plan C.

I spoke scarcely above the sound of a breath.

"*I won't. Pull.*"

She nodded.

Clutching the chain in my hand, I pushed the levers hard against the stops. *The other thing* flowed over the handcuff chain like water sucking the links under. The central links vanished. Where they joined visible links, the steel looked blurred, frayed.

Andy tugged. A link snapped. Although freed, she held her hands together behind her back. Two of the three men stared at her. Phone Man turned his back and walked a short distance, lowering his voice.

Now what?

I considered a billiards approach. Line up on two of them, collide, make the first disappear, then collide with the second. If I got lucky, I could make the second disappear and scoop them both up high enough to drop them. It would require maneuvering to gain a line on—

"HANDS WHERE I CAN SEE THEM!" Before I could move, a shout came out of the darkness behind me. All three men swept their attention over Andy's head.

I knew the voice.

He came slowly into a pool of light behind the biggest revolver I've ever seen. The business end of his hand cannon pointed at the man with the gun aimed at Andy. On JB Dalton, the cowboy hat made sense.

"Drop it." Dalton left no ambiguity in his tone.

Andy glanced over her shoulder at Dalton, then quickly took to her feet. She jerked her hands apart with a gentle *Ooomp!* sound—theatrics that paid off. Two of the men looked wide-eyed at her hands, still bearing the bracelets, but with broken chain dangling. Snapped links tinkled on the pavement.

Let them wonder, I thought. *If she can do that…*

Andy didn't hesitate. She closed one hand over the slide of the gun that had been pointing at her, twisted it away, then freed it from its owner. She pulled the slide, checked the chamber, then handily swept the gun up in the face of Phone Man.

"End the call. Now." She backed away, nearly stepping on me. I put a hand on her hip to alert her and to push clear.

Dalton, in jeans and his white chambray shirt, walked into a pool of light. His rolled sleeves revealed corded muscles in his forearms. His face glistened with exertion sweat. He worked to control his breathing. He'd been running.

"You don't want to do this," Phone Man warned. "We're police."

"Well, ain't that a coinkydink," Dalton replied. He lifted his sheriff's badge from a shirt pocket. "Then you might explain why you're treating a fellow officer, a lady at that, like a criminal."

"This woman threatened the attorney general. She's also impersonating an officer of the Texas Department of Justice. I suggest you put that weapon away, Sheriff, or you will find yourself in the same straits as her." Phone Man tried to lower his hands.

"Up!" Dalton waved his gun. "We'll figure out who's who when I say so."

"I'm Detective Andrea Stewart," Andy told Phone Man. "City of Essex

Police Department. I simply asked to speak to the Attorney General. You're the ones who pulled a gun."

Phone Man wanted to argue. "You falsely identified yourself as a—"

Bright lights and racing engines cut him off. Headlights swept across the group. A trio of dark SUVs raced to a stop on the garage asphalt. Doors popped open. More men with guns spilled out, weapons raised.

"FBI. PLACE YOUR WEAPONS ON THE GROUND. NOW." The voice roared from a loudspeaker mounted on one of the vehicles. The harsh command cut the night air. Chamber music on the other side of the fence abruptly stopped.

Party's over, folks.

Andy let the semiautomatic handgun dangle from one finger until the muzzle pointed skyward, then carefully lowered it to the pavement. Dalton eased his gun to the ground. Figures from the vehicles hurried forward to collect the arms. I gave the earth a gentle push and rose clear of potential collision with the many bodies moving about. I ached to take Andy with me.

Men in ballistic vests and black military web gear spread out around the group, weapons raised. The three men who had surrounded Andy frantically called out that they were police.

Andy turned and looked at the lead vehicle, then broke open a wry smile. The driver stepped out. Short, dark hair. Black blazer. Black jeans. An FBI badge dangling on a lanyard. She was joined by two men wearing ball caps. One in a denim jacket. One in a denim vest.

Special Agent Leslie Carson-Pelham strolled up to Andy and shook her head at the scene.

"What have we got here? Cops arresting cops arresting cops?"

74

Leslie insisted we wait for her in the dining room. She joined a loud argument outside the front door. A state police captain tore into Leslie and the FBI. The captain cursed and ordered the federal officers to leave the state property immediately. The men on the AG's protective detail were *his* men, *his* responsibility, and Hell was about to be paid. He backed his bluster and threats with a promise that the governor would call in units of the Texas National Guard if the FBI did not immediately comply. Leslie held her own, claiming the federal officers were merely responding to reports of the captain's own law enforcement officers in trouble.

"What the hell are you talking about?" the captain demanded.

"We heard a woman had three of your men surrounded," Leslie replied.

From inside the building, I could have sworn I heard veins popping. The captain stormed off.

A steady stream of party guests flowed through the foyer and into waiting cars that could not depart fast enough. Beverly and Rennie, the door guardian staffers, were long gone; the presence of the police and FBI provided excuses aplenty to end their evening.

Leslie threaded her way back inside sporting a smug smile.

"Looks like you won that round," I said.

"A draw. State Police command refuses to let us interview their guys without a senior officer present and those three cops refuse to be interviewed without their union representative. I didn't know they allowed unions in

Texas. Are you gonna eat that whole thing?" Leslie pointed at a bundt cake the size of a softball sitting on a plate in my hands.

"Try reaching for this and you could lose an arm." I plunged a fork I lifted off the dessert table into the cake. Andy and I hadn't eaten since the hasty bagel breakfast. I tried to get my wife to take something from the decadent table, but she turned a cold shoulder to the sea of sweets.

Leslie turned her attention to Dalton, who lounged on a small sofa near the dessert table.

"Who are you again?"

"Redneck Rescue," he offered with a little extra Texas drawl. "I been keepin' an eye on those two. That was a wild run down Highway 71, by the way. Ever consider NASCAR?"

"You were following us?" I asked between bites.

"No, he wasn't," Andy said. "What was it, JB? LoJack?"

Dalton smiled. "Redneck LoJack." He plucked a phone from his shirt pocket. "I put Mel's phone in my emergency supply box when you weren't looking. We like to keep an eye on each other so we know who can pick up groceries over't the DG or get Caroline from her dance lessons."

"Leslie," Andy said, "this is Sheriff JB Dalton of Hartley County, which is way up by the North Pole of Texas in a place called Dalhart. JB, this is Special Agent Leslie Carson-Pelham of the FBI."

Dalton politely found his feet and traded handshakes with Leslie.

"That's a mouthful of name. Pleased, ma'am."

"It's Leslie. Call me ma'am again and you'll find out that FBI stands for Feisty, Bitchy, and Indignant. Pleased likewise."

"Why did you follow us?" Andy asked Dalton.

"You headed out to take a poke at Pedmann. I wanted in on that."

"And Mel?"

Dalton returned to the sofa. "Mel got released this morning. Her sister has a fifth wheel. She took Mel and the kids and hit the road. No phones. No credit cards. No plan. I figure they're safe out there lost in America. Darlene knows all the outta the way places. We're set to meet up in L.A. in a few days to get her nose fixed. Got her an appointment with one of those Hollywood doctors."

"Sheriff, what exactly is your interest in Attorney General Pedmann?" Leslie asked.

Dalton lifted a single eyebrow in Leslie's direction. "Are we talking formally here? 'Cuz I might also ask what interest the FBI has in our top law enforcement officer. I thought the feds were froze outta investigating our daisy fresh AG."

Leslie engaged in a five-second stare down with Dalton. She broke it off by grabbing a plate from the dessert table and shoving it at me.

"Gimme a piece of that bundt cake. That looks amazing."

I sliced off a generous portion and scraped it onto her plate. She sat down beside Dalton and downed a few bites. The deeply satisfied look on her face met my expectations. The cake was phenomenal.

Leslie's two denim wearing agents walked in from the front foyer and flagged her attention.

"Ma'am, we don't have a line on the attorney general yet. I've got his senior executive assistant waiting upstairs. She's not saying much." Leslie waved her fork in the air and the denim twins ducked back out.

"Those guys are yours?" I asked.

"Yes," Leslie said through a mouthful of cake. "And you owe us for a couple tires."

I shrugged. "Don't know what you're talking about."

Leslie made a face at me that said exactly what she was thinking. I pulled a chair away from the long and dessert-laden table and gestured for Andy to sit, but she continued to pace with two silver bracelets jingling on her wrists. The state cops had been collected by their supervisor before either of us thought to ask for the key. I thought the darn things were univer-sal, but no one on Leslie's crew had a match. I offered to finish the job of removal, but Andy waved me off. She had other things on her mind. I knew the look.

Andy's encounter with the state police guards happened as I had guessed, just as Pedmann was leaving his study. Andy saw him hurrying from the room under escort. She followed the entourage to the parking lot where she called out for him to stop. Pedmann shouted to his protection detail that this woman has been stalking him. The detail shoved him into his waiting SUV then pounced on Andy while Pedmann's vehicle took off. I arrived a moment later, just as the dark-haired woman I'd seen at the party made her exit with Senator Stapleton.

The skirt of Andy's expensive gown bore dirty marks where her knees pressed the pavement. The damaged fabric made me wish the three cops were still on hand. I wanted to teach them to fly.

"Leslie, how did your guys know about Pidge and Arun?" I asked.

"We have friends with the FAA. We've had an eye on your girl all the way. There's still a team watching the airport in Lubbock."

"You might want to check in with them."

Leslie stared at me for a moment, then walked to the foyer and shouted up the stairs for someone named Clarence. One of the two denim agents trotted into sight.

"Call your guys in Lubbock and get me a sitrep." Leslie left it at that and walked back into the dining room. She looked at me. "Are you going to make me wait for them to trip over their own dicks?"

"Pidge picked up the Navajo hours ago. It's parked out at Austin International. For the moment, she and Arun are staying with the airplane."

"Sheesh." She shook her head, then paused to look me over. "Gotta say, Will. You clean up nice. The tux gives you a real British spy vibe."

"You didn't answer my question," Dalton said.

"Which one?" Leslie asked.

"Are we among friends here? Or am I talking on the record to an open federal investigation?"

"Can't it be both?" Leslie asked. Dalton stiffened. "Oh, relax, Sheriff. I'm not the bad guy. Will and Andy can vouch for me."

"Never seen her before in my life," I muttered.

Dalton chuckled. "Well, they did say they had allies I didn't know about."

"Glad you see it that way. Your turn. Explain yourself."

Dalton gathered himself. "A couple of operators carrying special investigator IDs from Pedmann's office tried to burn my wife and kids alive. Kinda left me with a grudge if you know what I mean. These two seemed to have a fix on the sonofabitch, so I thought I'd tag along. Discretely. See if they might shake him up a bit."

Leslie looked aghast at Andy. "Is he serious?"

Andy nodded.

"And it's connected?" Leslie asked Andy.

"We think the same two operators JB mentioned were present when Tiffany Callum was murdered," Andy replied.

"They're also dead," I added. "The two operators."

"How?"

"Poetically."

"Is that why you're here?" Leslie asked Andy.

"I was hoping to have a word with the AG in that gray area off the record."

Dalton raised one hand like a schoolboy. "Special Agent, how 'bout answering my second question? Why are you here? And don't give me any of that *divulge* crap."

"Divulge?"

I leaned toward Leslie. "It's a thing with him."

Dalton waited for her response.

Leslie finished off the cake and slid the plate and fork under the sofa. "I was in California a couple years ago, right before one of those big quakes. Ridgecrest, I think. Anyway, right before it happened—I don't know how to put this—things just felt strange. And they say it's not scientifically documented, but I swear the birds went silent. Birds and insects. You could *feel* something coming." She looked around the room at three skeptical faces. "Okay. That's a lot of crap but the analogy works. Things are happening. Disconnected things. Company W goes old school radio silent. A girl is tortured and murdered after she identifies another girl who gets burned alive. All over the country, persons of interest connected with Company W— including people we had under surveillance—up and disappear. People who—"

"What do you mean, disappear?" Dalton interrupted.

"Gone. Poof! Gone. Some of them walked off their jobs. A couple wives we interviewed said their husbands drove off without a word—as in, didn't even say they were going out for cigarettes."

"Winters." Andy looked at Dalton when she said it. To Leslie she said, "One of the men we suspect in the Tiffany Vera Callum murder."

"Loaded up his guns and ammo and took off." Dalton said. "Him and a couple other losers. And I don't think it was because we were closing in on him."

"Tsunami," I said.

"Come again?" Leslie asked.

"Your analogy. It's not an earthquake, it's a tsunami. When the water goes out—disappears—it's time to run because it's coming back as a tsunami. Company W guys disappearing all over means they're coming back big time."

Leslie squinted at me, nodding.

"Is that why you're here? All these disconnected pieces?" Andy asked.

Leslie laughed. "Darling, the top floors at FBI headquarters don't traffic in Leslie's Disconnected Pieces. I only got permission to follow the money."

"What money?" I asked, already knowing the answer.

"The GoFundMe money you found. It added up to over thirty million dollars. It's been moved around so much it's getting frequent flyer miles. The bean counters at the Bureau who work financial magic tracked it through half a dozen shell companies. Last night, it was cashed out of a Cayman Islands account and wire transferred to a bank in Virginia. I go comatose when our guys explain it all to me, but at least one of the pipelines the money went through is connected to a trust belonging to...guess who?"

"Pedmann," I said. Leslie shook her head.

"Stapleton."

"The senator?" I asked. "No shit. He was here tonight."

"Indeed, he was. And I don't think they meant for it to happen but buried on the authorization that set up the transfer whatzit—I don't know what it's called—is an attorney listed as the entity's original registered agent. And that attorney is…wait for it…"

"Pedmann."

"No."

I threw up my hands. "Jesus, Leslie." She grinned.

"Well…no, and yes. Pedmann's old man. His father."

"That's not possible," Andy said. "Pedmann's father died years ago. It was in the—er, in certain files I read."

"And you would be correct. His father was a nasty piece of work in life, but he's one hell of an attorney after death, because the registry was filled out six months ago under his signature."

"How is that possible?" I asked.

"Someone allowed it to be back dated. Someone who has a lot of juice with the Texas Department of Banking. I wonder who that could be…"

"Pedmann," I tried one more time.

"That's our guess. That's why we're here. There's a ton of plausible deniability to wade through, but we're not looking to make a RICO case. We have bigger problems. We have reason to believe that the Attorney General of the Great State of Texas and the junior senator from Oklahoma are working their fevered little fingers to the bone to move over thirty million dollars into the ether. But here's the other disconnected piece. Our sources are whispering that a known arms dealer is closing a big sale. For thirty million."

"Alejandro Ruiz," Dalton said.

"Give the man a kewpie doll," Leslie said with honest admiration. "You folks at the Texas North Pole certainly keep up on current events."

"Thirty million buys a whole lotta trouble," Dalton said.

"And who would you guess is getting thirty-million-dollars-worth of early Christmas?"

"Company W," Andy said. Her gold-flecked green eyes were alight for a moment. But only for a moment. Seconds later they rolled and revealed the whites beneath her irises.

She dropped.

I grabbed her and caught her before she hit the floor, limp and unconscious.

75

"Hey."

Andy blinked at me.

"What happened?"

"I'm not sure. I think you fainted." I knelt beside the sofa onto which I swept her when she went down. Dalton and Leslie hovered over my shoulders. Andy looked up at the two of them, taking a second to let her comprehension catch up.

"Don't be silly," she said. She tried to rise but I politely pressed her back against the cushions.

"Just stay put," I said. I touched her forehead. No fever. "How are you feeling?"

"Fine."

"Dizzy? Queasy?"

"I said I'm fine."

"Check her fingernails," Dalton said. I glanced up at him. "I dunno. Saw it in a movie. If there's…you know…poison."

"I'm not poisoned, for heaven's sake."

"Will's right," Leslie said. "I think you did. Faint, I mean."

"That's ridiculous."

"It's not that farfetched," I said. "You haven't had enough sleep. You barely ate today. You're probably dehydrated, too. Oh, and by the way, I don't know how to break it to you, but you're pregnant."

Leslie pressed a bottle of water into my hand. I held it up for Andy who knew better than to protest. She drank.

"How do you feel?" Leslie asked.

"Actually…amazing." Andy tried to rise again. I repeated a gentle embrace that made the point. "Seriously. My God, I feel—it's weird—fully refreshed. How long was I out?"

"Seconds," I said. "Long enough to catch you before you hit the floor and put you here."

"I've seen this before," Leslie said. "It's like a kind of reset button. My partner fainted like that once. Out for a few seconds. Ready to run a marathon when she woke up. Weird."

I glanced up at Dalton and Leslie. "Maybe you guys could give us a minute?"

They muttered apologies and shuffled out of the dining room.

I leaned closer to the woman who nearly stopped my heart. Nothing prepared me for what had just happened. It had not yet fully caught up to me. I took her hands in mine, partly to keep mine from shaking. I breathed her scent. I gazed at her soft skin and brilliant eyes, at the strands of hair coiled in glyphs on her forehead. I tried desperately to draw her in and ached to quash the latent terror that still had me screaming inside.

"Will, I'm fine," she said. Always the detective, reading the clues on my face.

"You scared the crap out of me," I whispered.

"Please don't go overboard, love. I'm not a porcelain doll. I don't need a doctor. I don't need a trip to urgent care." She pulled one hand free and laid it on her belly. "Everything feels fine. I mean it."

"Dee," I sighed, "what are we doing here?"

"Sweetheart, I admit. I overdid it today. The last couple days. I don't need the lecture."

"That's not what I meant. I want to know, where are we going with all this?"

"What do you mean?"

"This. Pedmann. We came roaring down here because someone did something unspeakable to an innocent girl who was meant to be Pidge, and I get it. I get that we all felt like we had to do *something*. We let our pal Leslie yank our chain with that Cindy Morgan business. But that's over. The injunction against Lewko is as good as dead. We turned over a rock on the people who killed Tiffany Vera Callum. We did what we came for. What are we doing *here*? *Tonight?* This business with Pedmann? The guy's a turd. Let the people of Texas deal with him."

"What are you getting at?"

I looked down at the woman carrying my child—a notion still light years from my grasp. Half an hour ago a man put her in handcuffs and pointed a gun at her. And while there is no one I would rather face danger with, I could not suppress the image that played and replayed in my mind's eye.

And now this.

Andy will never accept the role of damsel in distress. Nor would she ever tolerate me seeing her that way. But her limp body in my arms imprinted something on me that would not be shaken off.

I could not live with losing her.

"You need to go home," I said firmly. "I'm calling it. We did what we came to do. Hell, we can't compete with the FBI. You always tell me how much you hate those movies where the rogue hero outfoxes the world's largest and best equipped law enforcement agencies."

"They're stupid."

"So, let's not pretend that we can do anything more than we have. Let Dalton go after Winters and his pals. He's got Aldo's statement. Pidge's identity is safe. Leslie and the entire FBI are hot on the trail of financial clues you and I can barely understand, let alone access."

She smiled. "Cut to quirky sidekick playing a computer keyboard like Chopin. *I'm in. We have the proof.*" She laughed.

I laughed. We both laughed. We stopped. We kissed.

When our lips parted, she sighed. I dared to hope for her surrender.

Instead, she said, "Thank you."

"For what?"

She looked down at herself. "Thank you for not playing the medical card. The whole *what if something happened to the baby* card."

A fresh wave of fear rippled through my guts. I may not have played the card, but it was right there in my hand staring at me. She knew what I knew. Texas was the last place either of us wanted to be if this pregnancy developed complications.

I kissed her again and said, "Let's get to a hotel and get some rest. Tomorrow you and Arun will catch a flight home."

The question formed on her face.

"Yes, Arun," I said, "because I don't want you to travel alone."

"What about you and Pidge?" She read what I didn't want to say. "You know you can't lie to me."

"That's a serious disability in this marriage."

"Not from where I sit."

I attempted to avert my eyes, but she touched my chin and pulled me back. Heat flooded my cheeks. My cursed blush response. She saw it. Like always it amused her. Dimples appeared at the corners of her lips. She fought to hold in the smile that came with knowing she could lay bare my heart and soul with a few blinks of those damned beautiful eyes.

"Fine," I said. "You got me. I want to take the Navajo and catch up to that Twin Beech. There's something going on there and I think I'm the best option to find out what it is."

"Aren't you putting Pidge in the sights of the people who started all this?"

"Or you could say I'm keeping her close so I can watch out for her."

Andy's gaze can be ruthlessly penetrating. She can also be charitable. That she didn't argue granted me the latter.

76

"Come with me." Leslie infused the request with urgency. I did not jump to her beck and call. Instead, I lingered on the front steps to watch the cab pull away with Andy's face framed in the rear side window. Pidge and Arun would meet her at the hotel and Leslie had assigned one of the denim twins to stay with them. My pulse still throbbed. My breathing remained choppy. From halfway up the curved staircase, Leslie called out again. "C'mon."

I took the steps by twos and caught up to her on the landing. She hiked a straight line on the same path Andy had followed to Pedmann's study. We heard the blonde woman inside before we made the last turn onto the short hallway. Her voice carried severity that I easily pictured on her face.

"You have no right to detain me. You're standing on property of the sovereign State of Texas, and you have no jurisdiction here. I can think of a dozen Texas state statues you have violated. Unlawful detention, unlawful search, denial of my rights, impeding an officer in the conduct of her duty, and—"

"Ripping the tag off a mattress?"

I smiled. The other denim twin had a sense of humor.

Short of the dual doorway, Leslie stopped and spun around. She put a hand on my chest to bring me up short.

"Do it."

I knew what she wanted. I didn't know why.

"The *thing*," she whispered.

The executive assistant's outraged monologue continued. Leslie answered before I could ask. "I'm going to go in there and wind her up. Then I'll leave. I want you to see what she does. Who she calls. Or if she starts shoving docs in a shredder. Okay?"

Easy enough.

I shoved the levers to the stops and—

Fwooomp!

—vanished. The move caught me off guard. My boot soles lost their grip on the carpet. The hallway was too wide for me to touch both sides. Leslie, after an instant of looking startled, turned and launched herself into the office. I floated above the blue carpet feeling stupid for needing something to grab.

"Ms. Brandt, thank you for your patience." Leslie's breezy greeting interrupted the woman's rant. "Thanks, Clarence."

"I'm leaving," the woman announced. "You cannot detain me. You have no authority here."

"Are you saying that the Federal Bureau of Investigation has no authority to ask you a few simple questions?"

"This is tyranny! This is the weaponization of the Department of Justice that is being corruptly used against every citizen of America. You people—"

"Ma'am, calm down. Put the revolution on pause for a moment. First off, your impression of the authority of federal law enforcement needs a tune-up, but I'll leave that to someone else who wants to poke sharp sticks in their own eyes. Second, no one is detaining you. My colleague here was simply asking if you would stay for a few minutes to help us clear up a few things. No one is arresting you."

"I have nothing to say to the Gestapo."

I gave up trying to get a grip and pulled out the BLASTER. As I fixed the prop on the shaft, I smiled to myself. *Here it comes.*

"Excuse me?"

"You heard me," the woman doubled down.

"Ma'am, let me see if I understood you. You work in law enforcement, correct?"

"I work for the Attorney General of the Great State of Texas."

"Okay. You do understand, that's law enforcement, correct?"

"Texas law enforcement."

"Uh-huh. Sworn to uphold civil and statutory law. Can I ask you a question? Have you been detained? Thrown in a cold cell? Denied food and water? Tortured for days on end and threatened with execution?"

"You're being—"

Leslie's voice rose. "Have you been beaten? Raped? Have members of your family been arrested? Have the people of the town where you grew up been rounded up and shot? Has anyone you work with or associate with been sent away to a government facility to be systematically starved and tortured and ultimately hanged or shot or gassed?"

"I refuse to—"

"Because before you dare to compare my profession as a dedicated federal law enforcement officer with a sworn duty to the Constitution of the United States of America—*which guarantees you protection from precisely that kind of treatment—TO THE MOST HEINOUS NAME IN HISTORY* you better make room for my fist in your mouth along with the word you just called me. *Do I make myself clear?*"

I pulsed the blaster and floated into the open doorway. Pedmann's executive assistant stood behind the desk, her skin drained of color. Leslie faced her across the plateau of polished mahogany. Whatever words the woman planned to throw back at Leslie remained locked up in her slack jaw.

Leslie abruptly shifted her tone and posture as if she had just joined the woman for afternoon tea among friends.

"This was such a beautiful party. Was that you? Did you plan it? I am a disaster with that sort of thing. I wonder…is there any chance you can find a guest list? Also, I hoped you might tell me if Attorney General Pedmann has been in contact with a man named Alejandro Ruiz. Does that name sound familiar, Ms. Brandt?"

Brandt stood frozen. Leslie waved a hand in front of her eyes.

"Alejandro Ruiz? Ring a bell? Because we're investigating the transfer of a significant amount of money through certain financial instruments with your boss's fingerprints on them. It would be just peaches if you would shed light on what we're finding."

"I—uh—I don't know the name."

"Ma'am, just a small point of order. It is a federal crime to lie to an officer of the FBI in the performance of said officer's official duties. You may not be a fan of the Department of Justice, but I can assure you they are Johnny on the spot when it comes to prosecuting people who F-I-B to the F-B-I. Care to revise your answer?"

Brandt cleared her throat. "The name may be part of an on-going investigation by this department in which circumstance I really cannot comment, as it is the policy of this department not to comment on an active investigation. I would be happy to relay your inquiry to the proper authorities, Agent…?"

"Oh. Sorry. Leslie Carson-Pelham." Leslie put out her hand. "Pleased to meet you."

Brandt returned a hesitant handshake.

"And what role did you play in the transfer of these funds, Ms. Brandt?" Leslie asked.

"I—uh—I don't—you really need to discuss this with General Pedmann, ma'am. I'm sorry, I don't—"

"Were you the registered agent of any of the entities the funds passed through?" Leslie pressed.

"I—"

"Were you a signatory to the transfer?"

"No, I—"

"How much do you know about an illegal arms purchase? We estimate it involves around thirty million dollars in weapons. Ring a bell?"

I drifted toward the bookshelf on the right side of the room, opposite where Clarence the Denim Twin watched his boss in virtuoso form. Leslie planted her hands on the desk and leaned forward.

"What are you *not* telling me, Ms. Brandt?"

"*I want a lawyer!*" Brandt took an involuntary step backward. The bluster and fury we heard in the hallway deflated. Panic set in.

Leslie leaned closer.

In for the kill, I thought.

Instead of eviscerating the woman, Leslie abruptly pushed herself upright, sharpened the fit of her blazer, and looked at her watch.

"My lord, look at the time. I had no idea it was so late. I apologize, but you *must* excuse me. I have a hair appointment first thing in the morning. I will never get enough sleep at this rate. That means I'll be sitting in that chair staring at the bags under my eyes for a solid hour. Don't you just hate that?"

Brandt said nothing.

"Ma'am, it's been a pleasure chatting with you. I'm sure we will be speaking again in the future—so much to talk about—but for now…well, you just have yourself a wonderful evening." Leslie flashed a brilliant smile, gestured at Clarence, and led him from the room with the energy of two kids released for recess.

Brandt collapsed in her boss's office chair. The springs squeaked in unison with a sob that broke from the woman's broken composure. She huffed heavy breaths. For a moment I feared she might hyperventilate. She stared at the doorway as if the demons that had just departed might perversely reappear shouting *psyche!*

Nothing happened.

After a moment she jumped to her feet and hurried to the office doors.

She checked the hall, found it empty, and then pulled the twin doors shut. She snapped a deadbolt lock between the doors and engaged two latches at the floor. She backed away until the desk blocked her retreat, causing her to jolt.

I fixed a grip on a bookshelf loaded with tomes on the history of Texas. There seemed little chance of Brandt crossing my path, but I had to account for the possibility. A quick tug on the shelf would hoist me to the ceiling if she came my way.

She did not. She used the desk the way a person uses furniture in the dark, gripping it as she moved to where she stood earlier. She drove one hand into her purse and pulled out a set of keys. Fumbling through them, she found what she needed and unlocked the middle drawer on the left side of the desk. She pulled the drawer all the way out and bypassed the clutter of pens, stamps, and office debris at the front of the drawer. At the back, she used her fingernails to lift out a tightly fitted panel. Beneath the panel a row of small mobile phones lay in two lines. She lifted one and placed it on top of the desk. Once more into her purse, she lifted out an ornate silver makeup compact. She laid the compact beside the phone, flipped open the lid, and turned over the applicator pad to reveal a small white label imprinted with a phone number.

A moment later, after dialing the number, she held the phone to her ear.

"*Pick up pick up pick up...*"

I shoved off the bookshelf and rode a slow glide to the desk, close enough to smell her perfume. Thick silence in the stuffy office made it possible to hear the call ringing on the other end until a voice broke in.

"Why are you calling me on this line?"

"Willis, the FBI was here. *They know about the transfer.*"

"Get off this line. Get out of my office. Get out of town."

Three beeps signaled that the connection was severed.

Pale and panicked, Brandt looked down at the phone. What happened next nearly put her over the edge.

I reached out and carefully jerked the phone from her grasp. The burner was small, not even a flip phone. As fast as possible, I closed my fingers around the device. A snap bit the skin of my palm. The phone vanished.

Brandt uttered a sharp shriek. She blinked at the empty air, then launched a frantic search of the desktop, the open drawer, the floor. I pushed away from the desk and returned to the bookshelf in case she might start moving around the office. Growing panic induced frantic muttering.

"*No no no no no no!*" She searched the floor, the chair, the thick plastic carpet protector. She dumped the wastebasket and spread the meager paper contents, flipping pages over as if the phone might have skittered under them. She laid her head against the carpet to scan spaces beneath the desk.

"*DAMMIT!*"

Her hair fell into her face. Her skirt became skewed. Her skin turned a papery pale shade. I counted on her rational mind discounting the impossible —that the burner had vanished in front of her eyes. The only possible explanation was that it had fallen. On hands and knees, she scoured under the desk, muttering and eventually sobbing.

When she rose, she took stock of the situation and allowed *flight* to win over *fight*. She slammed the wooden drawer panel back in place, shoved the desk drawer closed, locked it, secured the keys in her purse, and fled the office. She took the route I had used to reach the back lot where I found Andy. A few minutes later, I heard a car start and the chirp of tires biting pavement.

"HERE," I handed the burner to Leslie. "She used it to call Pedmann to warn him that you were here. She said, 'They know about the transfer.' Are you going to pick him up?"

Leslie took the phone—without gloves on, I noted, which meant that my fingerprints did not matter either—and dropped it in her shoulder bag. "Ah, if only you were admissible in court, my friend."

"Seriously? You're going to let him get away?"

"Not at all. In fact, I know exactly where he is headed."

"Where?"

"For dinner with the President of the United States."

PART IV

77

———————

Arun booked himself and Andy on a Southwest Airlines flight that departed Austin at 11:15 and arrived in Milwaukee at 4:10 after a plane change in Kansas City. The schedule allowed time for them to see me and Pidge off from the luxurious Million Air lounge at Austin-Bergstrom International before trekking to the less glamourous commercial passenger terminal.

"Good thing we fueled up in Lubbock," Pidge said sipping on the complementary Starbucks provided by the FBO. "Gas is almost ten bucks a gallon here. They must mix in Chanel No. 5."

I didn't comment. Most of the clientele passing through the richly appointed facility boarded corporate jets. Sitting on the ramp, our Piper Navajo looked like a farm girl at a cotillion dance. The Million Air services and amenities were first class as advertised, but so was the bill at the front desk when I paid our ramp and tiedown fees. I saw Arun wince.

Andy greeted the day both fresh and energetic. She had been asleep when I finally arrived at the hotel. Try as I did, I could not avoid waking her. After crawling into bed, we talked in the dark, mostly about fainting. It was a new experience for both of us. Just as Leslie described it, Andy said she went from feeling worn and fatigued to a state of feeling completely cleansed and refreshed.

"It was the strangest thing," she said, "to recharge like that in a matter of seconds. I've never felt anything like it."

"Sounds nice, but let's not do that again. I might not be there to catch you."

"You caught me?"

"Sweetheart, you dropped like a sack of flour. I caught you before you hit the floor."

"A sack of flour, huh. Nice way to describe your wife."

"Did I mention I swept you off your feet?"

The save earned me a kiss. The kiss might have spun into something more, but we reigned it in and both fell asleep without further exertion.

Over a full and hearty breakfast, I asked Pidge to program the Twin Beech flight plan on her iPad. When she finished, we scoured the route lines hoping to find a traffic marker representing Louis Blaze's airplane. Nothing showed up, but the day was young.

"Let's aim for Leitchfield." I pointed at the third-from-last route point. "That way if they get past us, we can cut out Avery County and hop straight across to Danville."

Pidge poked at her screen. "Austin to Leitchfield…714 nautical. We'll need gas."

"It'll be expensive here. Pick someplace that doesn't require us to take Andy along and sign over my first-born child."

"You would trade our baby for fuel?" Andy produced a pout and pretended to look hurt.

"Not for fuel, love. For an airplane, maybe."

"Aim higher. An airplane with full fuel," Pidge suggested. She lifted her iPad to show me the screen detail page for Harrell Field in Camden, Arkansas, a stone's throw from Little Rock. She touched the FBO button. "Gas is $4.50. God bless self-service."

"Looks good. Go ahead and file it." Roughly four hours of flying with a fuel stop break would put us in Leitchfield, Kentucky around mid-afternoon.

At the Million Air FBO, before hoisting our flight bags and setting off through the security door to the ramp, Andy pulled me aside.

She said, "I hope you don't find anything. I don't want you and Pidge mixed up with those guys."

"We don't even know if Blaze's airplane has anything to do with Company W. Did Leslie say anything about that candy bar photo you sent her?"

"No. Just…please be careful."

I gave it some thought. "I don't think so. I checked the calendar. This is not a Be Careful week."

She made a fist and lightly punched me in the chest.

"Okay, fine. I'll swap weeks on the calendar. We'll be careful. Pidge will stay in the Navajo and be ready for a hot start. I will do all my recon discretely."

"And you take no action on your own."

"And I will take no action on my own."

"If there's anything there, you will call Leslie."

"If there's anything there, I will call Leslie. Why Leslie?"

"Because she'll be in the neighborhood. She left for D.C. this morning."

"Really? Is she going to bust Pedmann between courses at a formal White House dinner?"

"I would not be shocked. I swear that woman is her own bureau within the Bureau." Andy slipped her hands around my waist. She pulled me close. "JB said he will work to make a case for Tiffany Callum. He's motivated. And he's a good man."

"For a redneck. We need to send him a photo of me in a cowboy hat."

Andy smiled up at me. "I would take one of those. Shirtless. Tight jeans." Her smile crossed a line that belongs only to the two of us. I pulled her tighter.

"Maybe I'll oil up and pose for you up in the barn loft. Finally get that on a calendar."

"Maybe."

FIFTEEN MINUTES LATER, after receiving a straight-line clearance to Arkansas, as the Navajo's wheels parted with the surface of the earth, I could still feel Andy's kiss on my lips and the press of her body against mine.

78

"You think they can really get them?" Pidge asked through the intercom after we stabilized the Navajo at her cruise altitude of nine thousand feet.

Her question carried the tone of casual conversation, so I didn't really listen. Cockpit duties supersede casual conversation. I finished setting up the power, closing the cowl flaps, switching fuel tanks, and adjusting the fuel mixture. I manually synchronized the props. When everything looked and sounded good, I made a note on my knee pad of the time for the fuel tank change, along with the fuel consumption quantities.

"Who?" I asked.

"The men who killed that girl." She hesitated, then said, "The men who *burned* that girl." The distinction mattered.

"Two of them are dead." She cast me a surprised look. "Didn't have time to tell you. It was on the news. Two of the men who killed the Callum girl tried to do the same thing to the sheriff's wife. They're dead." I explained how it happened and how Andy found the news report online.

"Jeez, Will." Pidge's admiration carried through the intercom. "Throwing rocks. That's old school. They got what they deserved."

I thought she might offer more, expressed in her colorful vernacular, but she fell silent. When I looked over at her in the copilot's seat, she aimed a long gaze over the nose; blue eyes fixed on the hazy horizon line suspended under endless pale azure. I left her to her thoughts.

Pidge said little more for the rest of the ride to Harrell Field in Camden,

Arkansas. The air stayed smooth. The sky remained clear. Sixty-five hundred feet of smooth asphalt welcomed our wheels back to earth. The City of Camden managed the field and the fuel and kept a small office with clean restrooms. I fueled the airplane, topping three of the four tanks. Pidge did her business, then finished gassing the last tank while I hit the head. We were back in the air in less than twenty minutes.

"I want them all dead," Pidge broke her intercom silence after we cleared Memphis airspace halfway through the trip leg.

"Understandable."

"Not to Arun. He got upset with me for saying so."

"Your first argument? Aw, that's cute."

"Shut up. No, he said that I was hurting myself. He quoted something that Ray Nitschke said."

"The Packer linebacker?"

"Yeah. Some shit like…don't fight with monsters or you will become one and fall into the abyss or some BS like that. Like he was telling me I'm a monster for wanting those dickheads dead."

I laughed. She fired a deeply earnest look at me. "It's not funny. He was really worried about it."

"Not *Ray* Nitschke. *Fredrich* Nietzsche. German philosopher. 'Beware that when fighting monsters, you yourself do not become a monster…for when you gaze long into the abyss, the abyss gazes also into you.'"

"He didn't play for the Packers?"

"Not hardly."

"Okay, well that was what he said—what Arun said. The thing about monsters. Like he's calling me a monster for wanting them to burn. But—I can't—I can't see what they did in my mind without wanting to light a match on them for it. I can't."

"I know. I've been feeling it, too. You're not alone."

She said nothing for a few minutes. Then, "Do you ask yourself if we were wrong? If we shouldn't have done it?"

"The flags?"

She nodded.

"We were not wrong."

There was no point in sharing the doubts I carried. They would not bring her any peace.

SEVENTY MILES past Memphis we hit clouds; a vast wet veil dragged itself behind a slow-moving warm front. The radar image transmitted to my iPad painted seas of green rain ahead, sprinkled with islands of yellow intensity and one or two red thunderstorm cells. Nothing serious blocked our path, but our arrival in Leitchfield would be a wet one.

For a while we cruised between gray layers, a sensation that leaves a pilot feeling isolated and alone. Beads of moisture raced up the windshield. The wingtip strobe lights flashed on raindrops sailing in the opposite direction at 200 mph, freezing them in white light for an instant.

Pidge turned the center-mounted iPad to face her and studied the lines marking the Twin Beech's flight path. She zoomed in and scrolled slowly, examining each small triangle that represented air traffic sharing the skies with us. Her meticulous effort yielded nothing. I began to wonder if something had changed—if the airplane had a mechanical issue somewhere back along the segmented flight plan line. Maybe Louis Blaze's Twin Beech sat on a ramp somewhere with a blown exhaust valve or fouled spark plugs. Or had our phantom already flown this path, leaving us to play catch-up?

Memphis Center issued our initial descent clearance a few miles past Campbell Air Force base.

"Twenty-one Tango Whiskey out of niner thousand for four thousand," I acknowledged.

"Got 'em!" Pidge suddenly called out. "Got the bastards!"

She flipped the iPad to face me and pointed. The screen had been zoomed in on Leitchfield, our destination. A small triangle bearing the identification number for Louis Blaze's Twin Beech arrowed away from the airport. The altitude number beside the aircraft showed them climbing.

"You sure that's them?"

She tapped the screen. The info box for the aircraft appeared and displayed the registration number, altitude, heading, and speed. The flight plan origin of M20 was listed above BE-18, the model number for the Twin Beech.

"Oh, yeah, it's them. Do we go after them? Ask for amended?"

I contemplated the complications of asking for an amended clearance to bypass Leitchfield and fly direct to the next marker on the flight plan, a small airport called Spruce Pines near the western end of North Carolina. ATC might give us a *present position direct* clearance which stood a chance of putting us there ahead of the Twin Beech. If so, there were advantages to sitting on the ramp before they arrived, but how much before? If it was only minutes, they might become aware of us. I was not 100 percent convinced that the people operating Blaze's airplane were oblivious to being followed by Pidge and Arun in a recognizable Piper Navajo. If they knew our call sign, if they recognized the airplane, we were screwed.

Fuel complicated the calculations. If we deviated to Spruce Pine, we would be landing with the tanks largely empty. Did we want to be gassing up when Blaze's plane arrived? Tied up with an operation that would put us out in the open? What if sight of us prompted them to go 'missed approach' and climb back into the soupy conditions while we sat on the ground with a fuel hose sticking out of our tanks? The instrument weather conditions meant we would need a clearance to follow, and the delay along with ATC separation would prevent us from catching up.

All this rushed through my head while Pidge hung on my decision.

"No," I decided, "we land and load fuel, then bypass Spruce Pine and go straight to Danville."

"What if they don't go there?"

"Then it would be their first deviation from this flight plan. Fingers crossed that they stay on course. We can land well ahead of them, top off again, and scout things out. Maybe even park this bird out of the way. Sound good?"

Pidge gave me a thumbs up.

"Good. Set us up for the approach."

We landed. Fueled. Called for a clearance to Danville, and then took off. Seven hundred feet above the airport we penetrated dense white mist. We remained enveloped until we dropped out on final approach to Runway 04 at Danville Regional.

79

Andy told me later that negotiating the terminal, security, and the hike to the gate at Austin-Bergstrom International felt like a wrestling match with Arun. He took her bag, pushed open doors, and fell all over himself helping usher the helpless pregnant lady along every step. He hovered anxiously and offered to fetch water while she presented her credentials and completed her PCFA forms for the airline, affirming her qualifications to fly in possession of her service weapon.

"You don't have to do this," she gently suggested when he rushed to gather up her carry-on bag, her coat, and her shoulder bag from the steel rollers where such things are spit from the x-ray machine.

"It is entirely my pleasure," he insisted, loading himself down like a pack mule. Fortunately, the trek to the gate was short. With over an hour to wait for initial boarding Arun established base camp near the windows. When Andy looked with longing at a café they passed, Arun leaped to his feet and took her order for cranberry juice and an oversized pastry. She insisted that he ignore her deeply unrequited desires and treat himself to the coffee she suspected he was craving.

Settled once again, Andy found herself quietly amused at the degree to which Arun felt awkward in her company. Reasoning that it couldn't get any worse, she asked, "Arun, how are you feeling about Pidge?"

"I beg your pardon?" His tan complexion blanched.

"About Pidge. I don't mean your relationship. That's private, of course. But how are you feeling about things since Saturday night at our house?"

"Ah. Yes. That." He found something of compelling interest in the top of his coffee cup. "I mean—yes, of course—it's quite alright—it's—"

"May I offer an observation?"

"Of course."

"I think she adores you," Andy said. Visible relief melted the young man's tense demeanor. "I do. I admit I had a concern. It's not my business, of course, but she's a dear friend and so are you."

"Thank you, Mrs. St—"

"Andy. Please. Honestly, Arun, if I had a nickel for every time I have told you to please call me Andy."

"The wealth of Croesus, I'm sure. Thank you, uh, well…thank you."

"I was concerned," Andy continued, "that you would be disappointed in the girl you met in our kitchen. That she was not the girl you knew up to that point. I was concerned that you might feel she tried to deceive you."

"Oh, no," he insisted. "No, nothing like that."

"The thing is…I've known Pidge since I met Will. I know her background. You know how she got her nickname, right?"

"She told me."

"I think that's who she thought she had to be in a profession dominated by men. Of course, matters were made worse by her natural talent. If Will hasn't told you—and he should—he thinks Pidge is the best pilot he's ever seen. Bar none."

"I was not aware."

"Ask him sometime. He'll tell you stories. But what I don't think Will has ever recognized is that her skill and natural aptitude come at a price."

Arun let his gaze drift out the windows at a point thousands of miles from the rush hour-busy airport. "Yes. My mother is fond of saying that competent women must conceal. Did you, Missus—er, Andrea? Did you do the same to succeed in your field?"

"I didn't have to. When Chief Ceeves brought me to Essex directly out of the academy he made it clear to me and to everyone else—and there were a few skeptics—that our department has only one level to the playing field. I never had to conceal or overcompensate. Doing the job was enough. And I am good at the job."

"Do you think Cassi—er, Pidge—er—"

Andy laughed. "Call her Pidge. Half the people around the airport will have no idea who you're talking about if you call her Cassidy."

"Do you think Pidge overcompensates?"

Andy gave it a moment's thought, then said, "I think there is no question that she does. Not just for the flying, but because of her circumstances. Her past. Her relationship with her family…it's, well…"

"Yes, I understand it is fraught."

"In a word. She'll tell you when she's ready. But here's the other half of the observation I'd like to offer. I think the girl she presented to you initially —the polite, pretty, attentive creature, all soft edges and flower pedals—I think there's a chance that somewhere in that fluff you'll find the real Pidge. The real Cassidy. I think that girl may be closer to who she really is, and the girl you met a few nights ago is the façade."

Arun stared blankly at Andy for a long, long time. Andy took a sip of her beverage. Arun nodded thoughtfully, then shook his head.

80

"Is that Pidge's iPad?" Andy asked. The hot pink cover was hard to miss when Arun pulled it from his carry-on bag.

"Yes. On loan. She's teaching me the ForeFlight application that she and Will use for navigation and flight planning. I've been asking Will, but he never seems to have the time—not that—I mean, he's quite—"

"It's okay, Arun." Andy laughed. "Will is a master procrastinator. I believe his motto is 'never begin a job until you've exhausted—'"

"'—the last possible extension.' Yes, I've heard him say that." Arun flipped open the iPad cover and propped the device against his crossed leg. He tapped the screen. Andy saw the familiar VFR Sectional map appear. "I want to learn more about the aviation component of what we do, the flight planning, the weather influence. The amount of data available to pilots is astonishing. I believe I can assist Will in some of the travel planning attendant to our work."

"That's a polite way of saying it's easier to manage your scheduling without having Will defer the flight planning until the last minute."

Arun smiled. "I would never—I mean—well, when you put it that way…"

Andy let him return to his screen. She sipped the last of her juice, regulating intake and timing her consumption to allow for a trip to the restroom across the hall from the gate just before boarding. A new feature of life with a bun in the oven was the way her wristwatch and her bladder conspired against her.

Just before she gathered up the empty bottle and pastry trash to make the restroom run, Arun looked up from his studies and asked an unexpected question.

"Excuse me, Andrea, but did you take a photograph of that candy bar?"

"I did," Andy affirmed. "I sent it to Leslie to share with her codebreakers at the FBI."

"Codebreakers?"

Andy explained the running theory about Louis Blaze's means of communication. She started to describe the book cipher method when Arun interrupted.

"I'm familiar with book cipher coding. A bit of side study in school. I've always been fascinated with the history of Bletchley Park and Ultra and all that. Do you really think they're using a book cipher?"

"I don't know what I think. It's one of the theories the FBI is working on."

"Did you hear back from them? The FBI?"

"No. Why do you ask?"

Arun dismissively brushed the air between them with one hand. "Oh, it's nothing really."

Andy knew it was more than that. "Do you have an idea, Arun?"

"No. Certainly not. Well, nothing worthy of consideration."

"Arun…?"

Arun blushed deeply. "It's—well it's just a bit of amateur sleuthing. Nothing at the level of the FBI. Childish by comparison, if I'm honest. Never mind." He refocused on the iPad screen but the tint in his cheeks and the wrinkles on his brow remained.

"Tell me." Andy pulled out her phone. She tapped the screen and scrolled to find the photo in question. "Here. Is this what you're looking for?"

Arun leaned closer and squinted at the image of the barcode on the Clark bar wrapper. "Yes, but I honestly can't imagine this hasn't already been considered."

"What?"

"Nothing. Nonsense. Rubbish on my part."

"Arun, don't make me drag it out of you. Tell me." She held out the phone.

Arun hesitated, then took the phone from her and pinched the screen to zoom in on the image of the barcode. He silently mouthed the numerals, then laid the phone down. He returned his attention to the iPad screen, keeping it angled so that Andy could not see it without overtly leaning across the empty seat between them. He tapped the screen. Regarded his effort. Then tapped more.

Eventually, Arun finished his work. He stared at the screen and ran his fingers through the black waves of his hair.

"I'm quite sure this is coincidental. It's far too simple."

"Spill it."

Arun wiggled in his seat, squared up the iPad on his thighs, and picked up Andy's phone, his dark eyes alight. He took an extra moment to rehearse his thoughts.

"Right," he said. "Once more, this is utter rubbish. I am quite certain that Agent Carson-Pelham's colleagues have considered this and dismissed it out of hand. However, look at the barcode number."

He held up the phone.

0 72938 89770 6

"Okay," Andy said.

"If you think of the way the digits are grouped as irrelevant, then look at the first four digits. Zero. Seven. Two. Nine. What does that represent? Or I should say, what is one possible meaning one might attach to those four numbers?"

Andy touched one finger to her lips, thinking.

"One too many for an area code. One short of a zip code. Maybe the last four of a social? I don't know."

"Look again. Read the first two together, then the third and fourth."

"Zero Seven. Two Nine…twenty-nine." Andy lifted the phone from his fingers and scooted sideways onto the seat beside him, her expression bright. "A date. July 29. Arun, that's today."

He shrugged modestly. "I thought of it because you may recall when we first learned of Louis Blaze taking his airplane out of the hangar, we were told he would be traveling to Oshkosh for the big airshow. But the airshow takes place this week. It began three days ago. Doesn't it seem strange that they would travel to such an event to arrive in midweek? Of course, it's irrelevant because Oshkosh did not turn out to be their destination. Still…the date stuck in my head, and that's what made me think of the first four as a date."

"Today's date," Andy reiterated. "That could be significant. Especially with all the talk of Company W planning something…something consequential."

"God, I certainly hope not. I'm quite certain that it means nothing of the sort. That I'm being completely mental about this."

Andy ignored him. "Last night Will said something. Tsunami. When a tsunami is about to hit, the first sign of serious trouble is the way the water recedes. In the past few days, known members of Company W have been receding—disappearing from view." She gestured at the map screen. "What else? What about the rest of the numbers?"

"Oh," Arun shrugged, "I think—well, I mean—it's absolutely mental."

"Arun, don't make me hurt you. Tell me."

"Alright. I do have an idea but it's so obvious it would be impossible for the authorities to overlook it."

"Which is?"

He held up the screen. "I've been learning how to plot points on the map in ForeFlight. It's rather amazing. You can simply touch the screen, and it asks if you wish to plot that point as part of a flight route. When you do, it shows you the latitude and longitude of that point. Here. Like this." He showed Andy, then continued. "The same feature allows you to plot a point by entering the latitude and longitude numeral sets in degrees, minutes, and seconds. May I?" He took the phone from her fingers and held up the Clark bar photo for them both to see. "Look at the remaining numbers. Again, ignore the grouping on the barcode. Group them in two sets of four."

3889 7706

"Okay."

"What if that's 38 degrees and 89 minutes north, and 77 degrees and 6 minutes west? A point on a map? I tested the theory. I programmed those coordinates into ForeFlight, and the program marked that point on the map." He held up the iPad.

Andy examined the result. Any shred of patronizing amusement with Arun's decoder-ring sleuthing evaporated. She stared intently at the map box on the screen.

The map was scaled to show a huge swath of the east coast with Wisconsin visible at the top of the screen and the Carolinas sliced off the bottom of the screen. A yellow dot with the latitude and longitude tag landed in a triangle formed by Philadelphia in the northeast, Pittsburgh in the northwest, and Norfolk to the south.

Andy lifted the iPad from Arun's grasp. She pinched and spread her fingers to zoom closer, closer, until a set of concentric airspace circles filled the available screen box.

"Is that…?"

"Yes."

Both she and Arun recognized the significance of the most intensely guarded airspace in North America. Andy zoomed in tighter, tighter until the graphics on the VFR Sectional map became giant blurs.

"Where is that?" Arun asked.

Andy tapped the top menu and turned off the U.S. VFR Sectional map selection. From the same pulldown menu, she touched Street Map. She pinched and zoomed tighter and tighter until a blue band of river filled the screen, divided laterally by the white line of a bridge. The map point landed in the center of the bridge where it crossed the river.

"Good lord," she said softly.

She handed the iPad back to Arun and stood abruptly. "Gather up our stuff. We have to go."

"Go where?"

She didn't wait. She marched off between the rows of gate seats. Arun scooped up their carry-on luggage, stacked it, and wheeled the pile after her. She weaved through passengers assembling for the flight to Kansas City.

"Go where?" Arun asked when he caught up. Andy marched resolutely down the center of the tiled terminal aisle. She ignored his question as she thumbed a message on the screen of her phone. Satisfied with whatever she typed, she hit Send and looked up. She searched for the nearest flight message board.

"Go where?" Arun repeated.

"Washington D.C.," she replied. "If you're right—and I think you are— the action Company W has planned is today and it's in Washington, D.C."

"But," he protested, hustling to keep pace with her, "it can't be that simple. The code, I mean. It can't be that obvious. It's absurd."

"Is it? Blaze eschews technology, and with good reason. He can't hope to compete with the resources of U.S. counterterrorism. He communicates by word of mouth. By carrier pigeon, Leslie likes to say. Why can't it be simple? He's not sending complicated messages like the Germans did with Enigma." Andy shot him a knowing glance. "Yes, I'm familiar with the history. If all Blaze needs from his troops is for them to show up at a certain place on a certain day, why not go with simple? Date and location. A rendezvous point. It's juvenile but it's elegant."

"Juvenile enough to be dismissed," Arun muttered. "But, I don't under-stand. How did he get the candy bar to have the right numerals."

"He didn't. There are tens of thousands of barcodes. Millions. Every possible combination. All he had to do was look for the product that had the number he needed."

"That's…that's mental!"

"Willis Pedmann is going to Washington today for a formal dinner at the White House. I pray I'm wrong, Arun, but I think it's connected to the action planned by Company W." She stopped at the message board, found what she was looking for, and pointed. "That way."

For a moment, Andy did not move. Arun saw the distant, worried expression she wore. After a moment, she fixed it uncomfortably on him.

"I just pray that Will and Pidge don't stumble into this."

81

"Hey asshole. You've got five seconds to show yourself or we blow a hole through this little bitch's brain."

"Who're you calling little, you bloviating eunuch?"

The man shouting was Ray Stroud. The retort came from Pidge.

I recognized Stroud the instant I saw him. Tall and muscular. His stubbled square jaw rested on the top of Pidge's head. Slicked black hair and a thick brow gave him the look Hollywood likes to cast in the brute role. Second thug from the left. When I last saw him, he was sinking into blue chlorinated water at a country club pool.

He posed in the center of the hangar, just ahead of the pointed nose of Louis Blaze's Twin Beech. The crook of his left arm squeezed the small and delicate neck of Cassidy Evelyn Page like a python. His right hand pressed the muzzle of a heavy semiautomatic handgun to Pidge's temple. Forty-caliber, I guessed. His finger massaged the trigger. Electric jolts of fear coursed through my entire body.

Charge him. No. He'd shoot.

Sneak up and grab the gun. Same outcome.

Crap!

Pidge gasped for air that the python arm around her neck denied her. Blood ran from her upper lip. A dark purple and yellow contusion spread around her left eye. She clawed the arm around her neck. She swiped at Stroud's face. He brushed her arm away as he might have dismissed a cloying toddler.

303

In a moment or two, she would pass out. What then? Would he simply put a bullet in her brain to spare himself the dead weight?

"Five! Four! Three!..."

We had royally screwed up.

82

Pidge and I landed at Danville comfortably ahead of the Twin Beech. An RNAV approach dropped us below low-hanging mist for a smooth landing and rollout on Runway 02. I took time to refuel at the self-service pumps but declined an offer of parking at the FBO. Instead, I taxied back along Runway 02 to a narrow strip of asphalt in front of a row of hangars. A single hangar occupied ground between the row of hangars and the runway. Betting on no one minding, I rolled the Navajo onto the ramp in front of the free-standing building and u-turned to a stop facing the exit. The spot was quiet, off the beaten paths, and served to keep Pidge safely distanced from the matters at hand. If the Blaze airplane followed form, it would park on the distant main ramp, draw visitors, hand out Clark bars, and be on its way.

I planned to vanish, cruise across the airport to where the Twin Beech parked and try to find out what the crew of the airplane was up to. It was not lost on me that the next potential point on the flight route was Washington, D.C. I hoped to gather meaningful intelligence, then leave them to their business with no knowledge that I'd ever been there. Or, if opportunity permitted, see if I could throw a wrench into the works of whatever they were planning. A flat tire on an airplane is a much bigger deal than a flat tire on a parked SUV.

The plan went awry immediately after the big twin-engine airplane landed. Rumbling with a hypnotic sound only round-engine airplanes can make, the Twin Beech taxied back from a landing on Runway 02, bypassed the main ramp, and rolled directly at us. I irrationally hoped they intended to return to the departure end of the runway, but they followed the same route we had taken, trundling into the taxiway devoted to hangars.

Directly toward where we sat watching.

"Where the hell are they going?" Pidge asked. We sank in our seats and used the high instrument panel to hide from view.

After the airplane passed less than fifty feet from our left wingtip, I stole a glance through the window on my side of the cockpit.

The Twin Beech rolled to the end of the taxiway. There, a huge hangar showed signs of new construction. Recently filled-in dirt and new gravel fringed a jet-black asphalt ramp. From the outside, I would have guessed that the new hangar's interior contained a pristine business jet. I would have been wrong.

As the airplane approached the head of the taxiway, the huge door lifted high enough for the Twin Beech to roll in. Risky business. The pilot cut both engines but used the airplane's momentum to swing to the right of center. Inside the hangar, he locked the left wheel brakes and spun the airplane to face outward. Nice trick. I heard the tire shriek on the concrete hangar floor.

The huge hangar door immediately descended. I expected them to seal it. They seemed in a hurry to keep the airplane out of sight, but they stopped the door just above the height of a man. I wondered why until three gunmetal gray pickup trucks hurried onto the taxiway from the airport access road. They cruised past us and into the hangar, scarcely clearing the semi-closed door.

Pidge poked her head up. "You think they saw us?"

"Of course they saw us. At least the airplane. The question is whether it means anything to them or not. Are you sure no one saw you break into that thing in Colorado?"

"Positive. Mostly. Maybe…"

I shook my head. "Jesus, Pidge. These days I think you need to live your life as if you're on a camera at all times." I powered up the iPad and opened the screen to the Danville Regional airport diagram. "Here. See this?" I pointed at the departure end of Runway 02. "There are two hold short lines. Wait ten minutes, then fire this bird up and taxi down to one of those lines and hold with the engines running."

"What are you doing?"

"I'm going over there. I'll join up with you, but if anything gets funky, and I mean *anything,* take off. Just go."

"What—and just leave you?"

"I'll catch an Uber."

I climbed out of the pilot's seat. Pidge shifted over. She looked back at me when I popped the cabin door.

"Do you think these are the ones? The guys who did it?"

They burned her. The words had been Leslie's but they were imprinted on all of us now. I heard them in Pidge's voice.

"Maybe. A good reason not to let anybody in here, okay?"

"Affirmative."

It would be some time before I found out how she went from sitting in the Navajo's pilot seat to squirming in Ray Stroud's grasp.

83

"…Three!…Two!…"

"Alright!" I shouted. "Alright, I'm coming out. Just keep your shit together."

I hovered just inside the open hangar door. Dropping and reappearing out of thin air while Stroud and five other men watched would give away the only card I held.

I flicked my wrist and gave the BLASTER a shot of power. Too much power. The men in the hangar alerted to the sound. They looked up at the high ceiling and steel trusses that crossed overhead.

"Drone," I heard one of them say. The other pointed at a side door and two more jogged past the parked pickup trucks to investigate.

I scooted clear of the open hangar door and—

Fwooomp!

—I reappeared where they could not see me, my feet dropping to the asphalt ramp outside. I staggered several steps along the side of the building, then whirled around. I snapped the prop off the BLASTER and shoved both into my right boot top and tugged the leg of my jeans back in place. The parts wouldn't survive a competent search, but it was the best I could do. The sharp prop dug into my ankle when I walked into the hangar with my hands spread at my sides.

"Right here," I called out.

Stroud did not flinch. He pressed his gun to Pidge's temple. His thick arm remained tight under her chin. She fought for breath. Her face darkened.

"Ease up," I said. "She can't breathe for God's sake."

Stroud beamed a sadistic smile at me. I did the math. The ceiling of the hangar looked like twenty-five feet. More than enough for a fall to break him if it didn't kill him. I just needed to get close enough to vanish and grab him.

My boot heels clicked across the polished concrete floor.

"Stewart, right?" Stroud said. "Your wife that cop?"

Pidge's eyes rolled upward, losing consciousness. She began to go limp.

"Let her go, dammit!"

Stroud expanded his grin, then unflexed the corded muscles of his forearm. Pidge gasped. She gripped Stroud's arm and pulled. He resisted, giving her just enough slack to draw air.

"I asked you a question," Stroud said.

"Yeah. I'm Stewart. How was your swim the other night?"

The grin did not waver. "I'd ask what you're doing here, but it's just too much of a coincidence, wouldn't you say? You'd lie to me, and I'd shoot your little friend here. Helluva way to start a conversation. That's far enough."

I stopped fifteen long feet from where he stood. He wanted me no closer. I credited the encounter at the pool with giving him cause for caution. I wondered if he had reconciled the way I appeared out of nowhere. He probably couldn't stretch his imagination all the way to the truth, but it didn't mean he stretched his trust.

"Bobby," Stroud called out to one of the two men returning from a fruitless drone search. "Bring a couple ties. And chairs. Three chairs. There's some in the office."

Bobby, an athletic young man in full camo who could easily kick my ass in a fair fight, hurried to carry out Stroud's command. A few minutes later tight white plastic zip ties painfully bound my wrists. A heavy hand on my shoulder pressed me onto a metal folding chair. I noted several things.

They tied my hands in front, not in back.

Every one of these guys is armed.

Stroud is not relaxing his grasp on Pidge.

The cargo door on the Twin Beech is open.

"Are you one of those guys who has a particular set of skills?" Stroud asked, quoting the popular movie line. Bobby placed a second folding chair six feet away facing me. He placed a third chair equidistant from the first two.

"Not me. I run away from fights. So, what's the deal here, Ray? What's with the D-18? You some kind of old freight dog? You don't look old enough. Blaze would be the right age. Is he here?"

Stroud ignored me. To his man Bobby, he said, "Get behind him and get a good grip on him and put your piece up against the back of his skull." Stroud turned to the other man who had gone drone hunting. "TJ, c'mere."

A man with a huge flop of belly hanging over his cinched belt walked stiffly to Stroud. Back troubles, I surmised, maybe from carrying around that belly. Thin strands of gray combover covered the top of his head. He had a fleshy face and dull, obedient eyes.

Stroud pushed Pidge forward and down into the chair that faced me. She rubbed her neck and gasped for more air.

"TJ, do the same for her. Tight grip. Gun to her head."

TJ cinched Pidge's wrists with a zip tie, then reached into his back pocket and produced a snub-nosed revolver that looked too small for his hand. He stepped behind Pidge, gathered up a wad of her t-shirt with his left hand and pressed the muzzle of his revolver to the back of her black hair with his right hand. He pressed hard enough to make her bow her head. Her chest heaved to pull in air.

The sight of Pidge, bruised and bound, awoke a cold, black impulse in me.

"Okay, now boys," Stroud said like he was talking to a troop of cub scouts, "hold 'em both tight. Bobby, if this little girl flinches or so much as sniffles, shoot *him*. TJ, the same goes for you. If *he* so much as looks cross-eyed, shoot *her*. Got it? Watch her, shoot him. Watch him, shoot her."

"Got it."

"Got it."

"I ain't dickin' around," Stroud said sternly. "We don't need either of them alive. And we can swab up the mess. Brains all over—I don't give a shit. Just don't get it on your clothes. I don't want any action movie bullshit from either one. They ain't faster than bullets, boys."

Both men answered with tighter grips on our clothing and more forceful press of their weapons against our heads.

Pidge lifted her eyes to meet mine. She signaled anger, apology, fear. I blinked once slowly. Something Andy's sister Lydia once told me about cats. Lower your eyes to show them compassion. I thought it made sense. All I got back from Pidge was an expression that translated best as *Huh?*

I took Stroud seriously. I dared not move my head, my hands. I sat and stared. I left the levers in my head alone. Vanishing might buy a moment of confusion, but would more than likely cause one or both of the men to pull their triggers.

The hangar contained the airplane and all three pickup trucks. Men who were not party to guarding us loitered beside their vehicles. Stroud walked over to a man I assumed to be the pilot who waited by the left engine of the Twin Beech. He did not seem concerned that his associates just kidnapped two strangers at gunpoint and threatened to commit murder.

The two men spoke at a level I could not hear. The pilot listened, nodded, made a questioning face, then nodded at whatever answer he got from Stroud, who glanced back at us in a way that did not give me comfort.

The conference continued for a few more minutes. The pilot did a lot of nodding, then he broke away. He jogged over to one of the drivers of one of the trucks. Another conversation ensued. The driver reminded me of JB Dalton when he opened a utility box on the back of the truck and handed over a toolkit. The way it rattled and the way the pilot carried the box, I dropped any hope that the kit contained a bottle of fine scotch and four glasses. Stroud followed the pilot to the plane and ducked inside after him.

I fixed my mind on just one thing: How to vanish and take Pidge with me. If I could get a grip on her, disappear, and kick off the floor they'd never know what hit them. I didn't care if they saw what happened. How would they explain it? And to whom? Grabbing Pidge and blasting off for the steel truss roof of the hangar was all I needed. I didn't care about the airplane, its cargo, the men in the hangar, or whatever they thought they were doing. Screw their plans.

I glanced down at my watch. 1:40. But that was Texas time. Eastern Daylight Time made it 2:40. Andy would be enroute to Milwaukee with Arun.

Thank God. I felt relief that my wife and unborn child were outside the Texas state line and the touch of Texas state law. My relief tripled when I thought about how she wasn't with me here and now—although she probably wouldn't have let me get into this mess.

Stroud walked past TJ and Pidge to a position behind my chair. I felt the pistol at the back of my head change hands.

"Go get your party kit, Bobby. And bring that cooler from the back of my truck."

Bobby shuffled off.

Stroud held the gun to my head and said nothing to me. No trash talk. No comment on the inevitable success of his evil scheme. No interrogation. Nothing. His silence worried me.

"What's the deal, Ray?" I asked.

"Speak again and it will be your last words."

I believed him.

Bobby returned with a small cooler in one hand and a zippered pouch in the other. He carried both behind me so that I could not see. I heard the cooler open. I heard ice shift and bottles clink. I heard the snap/hiss of bottle caps removed.

A moment later the pistol changed hands again. TJ resumed guard duty. Stroud walked around the chair and faced me holding three bottles of cold beer.

"Here." He handed me a condensation coated brown bottle. "Have a beer."

I lifted my bound hands and took the bottle. He turned around and walked over to Pidge. He looked down at her. She looked up at him. I said a silent prayer for her to keep her mouth shut. He lifted a bottle and touched it to her bruised face. She winced.

"A little makeup will cover that right up," he said, rolling the cold beer against her skin. I wondered how often he said those words to a woman. "Here. Drink up."

"Fuck you."

"Ah, don't be like that. Take it." He pressed the bottle into her bound hands. He added. "Drop that and I'll shoot him."

If not for the threat, I think she would have. I was glad she didn't.

Stroud tipped his bottle back and downed roughly half the contents. He smacked his lips.

"No? Not joining me?"

"I'm okay," I said. Pidge said nothing.

"Okay," Stroud said with a light shrug. He turned to Pidge. "Little lady, I don't know your name and I don't care. But it's rude of you not to drink with me, so here's the deal. You chug it. The whole thing. If that bottle doesn't hit the floor empty, he gets a bullet in the head. Go."

Pidge glanced at the gun pointed at my head. Her eyes met mine again. We had another moment. Apology. Fear. Anger. Same recipe. I lowered my eyes again to absolve her of whatever happened.

"Fuck you," she said to Stroud. She used both hands to tip the beer bottle to her lips, raising it nearly upright. Her throat pulsed. The amber contents of the bottle drained. When she finished, she threw the bottle at Stroud's feet. It hit the concrete but did not shatter. Instead, it clattered and spun away across the floor.

"Nice." Stroud turned to me. "Your turn. Chug or she dies." Stroud lifted his own bottle in a toast.

TJ moved his little revolver around to the side of Pidge's head and pressed until she tipped her head to one side.

"Is it that hard for you to find a drinking buddy?" I asked. "Fine. Bottoms up."

I've never been one to chug beer. The cold and carbonation tore at my throat. I downed the entire bottle. The icy contents burned their way down to my stomach which reacted to the chill with a shiver. When finished, I heaved the brown bottle after Pidge's.

I knew why Stroud was entertaining us. The brew tasted funny.

GHB? I wondered. *Or Rohypnol?*

Pidge realized it, too. I saw it in her eyes.

Doesn't matter, I thought. *I can fight it. I can resist it.*

Stroud chugged the last of his beer.

One of the men standing by the trucks called out to Stroud while holding a phone to his ear.

"It's here!"

Stroud put his empty on the floor. He walked to the open hangar door. When several of the other men started in the same direction he waved them to stop.

"I got this."

Neither TJ nor Bobby moved. The grip on my shirt did not slacken. The press of a gun barrel against my head, if anything, intensified. I probed my senses for any hint of the drug's effect. Maybe I was mistaken. Maybe there was nothing in the beer.

I started feeling like things would be just fine.

I faced the wrong direction, but with the pressure from the gun at my temple, I had an excuse to turn my head just enough to see what was happening.

With the high-revolution engine sound a truck makes in a low gear, an 18-wheel semi rolled most of its length past the hangar door. The driver stopped with the tailgate of the truck even with where Stroud stood. Air brakes hissed and snapped.

Stroud pulled a key ring from his pants pocket and opened a padlock on the trailer's rear doors. He unsnapped the latch, then swung one half of the door open. He reached into the trailer and pulled a long wooden box into his grasp. It had weight. Stroud's muscles corded and flexed. He carried the box just inside the hangar and laid it on the floor. Twice more, he repeated the move. No one advanced to assist. He returned to the trailer and closed the door. After dropping the latch, he reinserted the padlock.

He walked to the driver's side of the truck and waved. With a diesel roar and the lurch of low-gear startup, the truck pulled away.

"Alright," Stroud called to the waiting men. "Load 'em up. Carefully."

By twos, the men carried three green wooden boxes to the cargo door of the airplane. The pilot hopped up in the plane and guided the loading. In short order they were finished.

Stroud strolled back to the three-chair meeting. He looked at me the way a scientist looks at a rat in a maze, then kicked his empty bottle. The clatter and ping of the empty glass on concrete hurt my ears.

A wave of confidence washed over me. I felt less worried by the minute. *I can fight it.* Whatever they put in the beer was having no effect on me. None.

In fact, I was feeling pretty good.

84

S troud swung one leg over the third chair and sat.

"The fellas and I have about a four-and-a-half-hour drive to the rally point, but we got a few minutes," Stroud said. He sat on the empty folding chair. "Your wife is the one that tried to kill the president."

"You watch the wrong cable news."

He chuckled. "Well, I don't watch that fake news, if that's what you mean. Besides, that's all gonna change. They won't be on the air with their lies much longer. You two walked right into history. When they find your bodies, it's gonna be all over the Real News. And that bitch you're married to will be in Leavenworth, if not executed."

"What's the plan, Ray?" I asked. I sounded friendly, like we were old pals. It felt weirdly comfortable chatting with him.

"The plan is for the true patriots of this great nation to take back our country, that's the plan. People like you and your wife who are running America into the ground are gonna pay. We're a goddamned third-world nation, thanks to you."

"Me personally? Wow." It struck me as funny. So did the floor of the hangar, the way it rose and fell in uneven swells. "I can see where that might really piss you off. Warm beer. Crappy internet. No air conditioning."

"I don't get pissed. I get even. There's a whole lotta gettin' even coming down the pike." Stroud's face made me want to laugh. He reminded me of a cartoon character—I couldn't think which one. A pompous rooster. Any second now he would call me 'son' with a southern accent. Stroud looked

315

over at the man with the jelly belly. "Jesus, TJ, how much did you put in them beers?"

"Double dose," TJ said from somewhere far away. His voice carried like someone on a stage. Testing a mic. Testing. Testing. One. Two.

"Check it out," Bobby said. He walked over to Pidge whose chin dropped against her chest. He put one hand on the top of her head and gathered a handful of her hair. He lifted her head up. The lids of her eyes hung at half-mast. With his other hand, Bobby reached down and closed a grip on Pidge's left breast. He grinned in a way that made me want to peel off his face and throw it on a stove burner. "Nice and firm."

Stroud abruptly stood and walked over to where Bobby groped. For a moment, I thought he planned to scold his subordinate for his crude sexual assault. Bobby made the same assumption. He quickly released his grip on Pidge and stepped back.

Stroud plucked at Pidge's hair. He looked closely.

"Well now, honey. Looks like your roots are showing."

"Huh?" Bobby asked.

"She's a blonde, Bobby boy. A cute little certifiable blonde. Sonofabitch. I've seen her before." He had no doubt. I wondered if I'd seen Stroud before as well, perhaps holding a flagpole on the street in Lincoln, Nebraska.

"You think she's the one?" TJ asked. He played catch-up, but he had it all over his pal Bobby who broadcast a stupid look from his face.

"Well, that would kinda make stupid sense. Her being here poking into our business and all."

"Well," TJ struggled with the concept, "what about that other one?"

"Well, TJ," Stroud said, "I guess she *wasn't* the one, just like she said. Too bad for her."

"You think we oughta light her up?" Bobby asked, coming abreast of the conversation.

"I wish," Stroud said, "but we can't leave that much mess in here. We stick with what we got worked out." Stroud looked at his watch. "Time for us to go. Load these two in the airplane and then we'll help Lou push it out. He'll have to kill some time. TJ, give Lou your kit and tell him to give 'em each another dose before he takes off. Another double dose, if he can get it in 'em."

Pidge slumped, but Bobby threw an arm around her before she hit the floor. He went out of his way to grab what he wanted.

Stroud walked up to me and tugged my chin up to aim it at his face.

"Have a nice ride, asshole. I'll be sure and give my very best to your wife."

Andy. He meant Andy. He meant more.

I told him to burn in Hell. I told him his mother copulated with swine. I told him he and his Company W companions were gullible useful idiots for corrupt politicians whose lies wouldn't pass muster in a third-grade class.

Or at least I would have told him all that if I could have made my mouth work.

No effect.

None.

Except for the comforting darkness that folded over me.

85

"Can't figure out why I ended up liking you. You always struck me as a little full of yourself. I chalked it up to the pilot thing because every pilot I've ever known thinks he's king shit." Lee Donaldson leaned back against the dark red vinyl booth upholstery and sipped his beer. He drank the same beer as Ray Stroud, but I could not quite make out the brand. "Then again, that magic act of yours can't be overlooked."

"That magic act saved your ass," I reminded Donaldson. I reached for my cold beer but remembered that it didn't taste quite right. I let it sit untouched between us on the Formica table. Condensation soaked into a cardboard coaster with the name of the bar imprinted in blue and red ink. *Leo's Roadhouse—Fish Fry Friday—Live Music Saturday.* I remembered the place. It burned down.

Donaldson looked the same as he always had. Buttoned down. Hard edged. Wearing a variation of the haircut a military barber gave him in Marine Corps boot camp that he never quite gave up on. It didn't matter whether he worked private security for a corrupt billionaire, or he served in the ranks of the FBI, Lee Donaldson always had that government-issue look about him. And more. Donaldson was the guy you didn't pick a fight with. The guy you wanted on your side.

"That was your wife," he shot back at me, but the smirk on his face told me he knew exactly who pulled him out of a burning roadhouse. He would have called it a joint operation. Andy drove the getaway car, a rented Nissan, that delivered Donaldson and his cracked skull to a hospital in time to keep him alive. Pidge dropped out of the sky and eliminated the threat chasing us. He owed her as much as he owed Andy and me.

Where is Pidge? I felt like she should be here with us.

"Pidge is dead," Donaldson answered matter-of-factly. "Or dying. Cardiovascular disturbances. Respiratory failure. Circulatory collapse. The usual."

Part of me wanted to scream. To leap from that booth and find Pidge. My muscles tried to lift me from the vinyl seat, but a fog of euphoria weighed me down like a lead blanket.

It was nice talking to Donaldson again, having a frank and comfortable conversation in—was this really a roadhouse? The place seemed dark. The furniture felt cheap. It smelled in here. Like old machinery. Like fuel and oil and wood and ancient leather. Noise thundered all around us, but at the same time Donaldson and I occupied a bubble of silence.

"I got a question," I said.

"Fire away, big boy," Lee tipped his brown bottle at me.

"How did you die?" I asked.

"Whadya mean, how did I die? You were there."

He was right. I was there. But I never saw him, and he never saw me that day at Siddley Mansion during Black Robe week.

"I meant *why* did you die you dumb sonofabitch? Why didn't you get out like Andy did?"

He shrugged. "I was busy. Got my ass blown to smithereens for my troubles, but at least it was quick. I can think of a lot worse ways to go. In fact, I thought I had already been dealt a much worse hand, remember?"

"What are you talking about?"

"You remember. C'mon, Will. Rub some neurons together. That's a hint by the way."

He leaned back in that red vinyl booth with his beer in his hand and a grin on his face. Like we were playing bar trivia, and he knew the correct answer was *Operation Mincemeat.*

The noise around us grew louder. Familiar old engine noise, throbbing, a little out of synch. Air moved against my face. Cold. Like somebody opened a window.

I raised my voice to be heard. "What are you talking about?"

"Living death, my friend." Donaldson leaned his elbows on the Formica. "You saw what I was like. I couldn't remember the word for cat. Or dish. Couldn't make my brain string together symbols or feelings or put one foot in front of the other without having to think about it so hard it made my brain hurt. After I took that hit to the head communicating was like shouting in a jar of molasses. That's a living death, Will. Remember?"

Rehab. Lee was in rehab after his brain injury. I flew to Omaha and found him because I needed to talk to him and there he was, struggling through physical therapy after his head injury turned the man who could handle any situation into a man who couldn't handle a salad fork.

Lee switched the beer to his left hand and raised his right hand.

"I, Lee Kenneth Donaldson, do solemnly swear that I will support and defend the Constitution of the United States against all enemies, foreign and domestic; that I will bear true faith and allegiance to the same; that I take this obligation freely, without any mental reservation or purpose of evasion; and that I will faithfully discharge the duties of the office on which I am about to enter. So help me GOD STEWART—WHAT THE FUCK?!"

I remembered.

Lee laughed. I could not hear him, but I could see him. Belly-laughing. The engine noise thundered. He shouted at me. *"Worst ice cream headache ever, pal. Felt like you rinsed the inside of my skull with gasoline, but it was worth it. That voodoo that you do."*

I remembered. I found him in a rehab hospital. I made him vanish. He went from barely able to string together a sentence to reciting his Marine Corps service oath without taking a breath.

"C'mon, man!"

What was he trying to tell me? And why was it so loud in here?

"Do the voodoo, Will."

Wind swirled around us. I worried about being blown out of the booth but Special Agent Lee Donaldson, cool as McQueen, just sat there with his beer in his hand and that knowing look on his face.

"DO IT!" he shouted. *"DO IT NOW!"*

FWOOOMP!

86

Air blasting through the open cargo door threw me against the bulkhead. I had no weight. No inertia. A feather in a typhoon. In a moment, I would be blown out the open cargo door. I jerked back the levers in my head.

The voodoo that I do.

Fwooomp!

I reappeared, dropped, and landed hard on the top of the row of wooden crates. Electric pain shot up my right forearm into my shoulder, but it was nothing compared to the worst ice cream headache I ever had.

I doubled over and heard myself making noise. Humming. Moaning. Biting down hard on a scream. The blade cutting through the middle of my skull had been dipped in liquid nitrogen. Cold and searing.

Desperate, I grabbed the levers in my head again.

Fwooomp!

I vanished and once more the wind swirling inside the Twin Beech tried to lift me off the crate. I threw one leg across the narrow cabin to apply pressure and brace my back against bare aluminum.

The pain vanished with me. A cool sensation not only wrapped my body, but it soothed the place in my head where moments ago an ice cream headache cut through my consciousness. Relief. Better than any drug. This felt so good, I was tempted to stay this way.

That's what Lee was trying to tell me.

Jesus…Lee Donaldson…

I ached to finish that beer with him.

Lee Donaldson was nowhere to be seen because he died almost a year ago in an explosion that left nothing but his DNA. And this wasn't *Leo's Roadhouse* because that burned to the ground. This was the interior of a Beechcraft D-18 almost a century old. Dual radial engines roared. The interior smelled of fuel and metal. This was a freighter that once carried auto parts coated in cosmoline and fertilizer packed in bags. Some smells never leave an airplane.

Roaring wind threatened to dislodge me. I could not stay this way.

Fwooomp!

I reappeared and settled once again on the wooden crates where I collected my bearings. I expected the floor to heave like waves rolling under anxious surfers. The expectation came from the last thing I remembered. Sitting in a hangar in a chair feeling dislodged and disoriented.

Drugged.

Stroud and his pals drugged me. GHB, I suspected. They put it in the beer. So, why was I clearheaded now? I lifted my hands and touched my skull. Why wasn't it spinning?

The other thing. Lillian Farris's autistic young charge put it simply. When I vanish, he said I became *matter in an altered state.* Reappear, and the matter returns to its original state, or more pointedly, the state it *should* be in. Lee Donaldson went from brain damaged to spitting out his Marine oath because I made him vanish. Lee's damaged neural paths didn't belong to his original design. Cancer cells don't belong to a child's birthright blueprint. I take those things out with me when I vanish. When I reappear, they don't come back.

The GHB didn't belong.

"Jesus," I said out loud, "I wonder if this works on a hangover?"

I lowered the hands that I'd been holding at my temples and realized they were free. No zip ties.

TJ, give Lou your kit and tell him to give 'em another dose before he takes off. Stroud gave the pilot instructions to dose us again. We were never meant to wake up. That sonofabitch—

What sonofabitch?

I looked at the front of the cabin. The pilot's seat was empty. The entire cockpit of the Twin Beech was empty. We were airborne, but whoever got us this far used the cargo door to leave. That accounted for the wind blowing around the cabin.

Pidge!

Donaldson told me she was dead or dying. His words came back to me with a hard jolt. GHB can be fatal. It can shut down the body. Respiratory failure. Circulatory collapse.

Pidge lay on the floor at my feet.

I shot one hand to the place on her neck where people on TV check for a pulse. I felt nothing. Desperate, I groped around and pressed harder. There it was. Weak and slow.

Thank God. Relief washed over me.

I jammed both legs against the opposite cabin wall, locking myself in position above her. I reached down and closed a firm grip on her upper arm.

I pushed hard.

FWOOOMP!

We both vanished. I wondered how quickly the effect—

"MOTHERFUCK! WHAT THE HOLY HELL?!"

She jerked her arm free and broke contact. An electric snap bit into my hand. She reappeared and dropped to the cabin floor. Both her hands flew to the sides of her head.

"Jesus H. Christ! What did you do to me?" She called out through clenched teeth. "My head!"

I grabbed her forearm.

Fwoomp!

She vanished.

Fwooomp!

We both reappeared. She froze, eyes like dual blue moons. She blinked.

"Okay. That's better." She looked at her hands which were no longer bound. "Jesus, Will. What the—?"

"I'll explain later. Check it out." I pointed at the cockpit. "Nobody home."

Still lying flat on the floor, she tipped back her head and surveyed the empty cockpit upside down. She jerked one thumb forward.

"After you."

I raised my legs. She sat up. After some close quarters maneuvering, I pulled myself forward to the partition behind the two front seats. I climbed over the throttle quadrant and into the pilot's seat. A moment later Pidge leaned through the partition with her hands on the seatbacks. She winced and rubbed one arm against her chest.

"Did that limp dick grab my tit?"

"Yup. But I think we have bigger problems." I tapped the yoke. It flopped back and forth. I pushed it forward, then pulled it back. Nothing happened.

Pidge leaned in. She ran her fingers down the back of the controls. With a little tugging, she pulled out the severed end of a cable. We checked the copilot's controls. Same thing.

"What the hell?" she asked. "Why bother? They had us drugged to shit back there."

"Insurance? In case we woke up? I dunno." I looked over the panel. "We got a G600. The autopilot servos are operating the controls."

"Okay. To where?"

We both examined the Garmin GTN750 navigation system. The moving map showed a series of waypoints. What looked like an approach. Something about the map wasn't right. The route segments were short. The waypoints were marked as latitude/longitude, not as established waypoints. The end had no identifier.

"Holy Mother of God," Pidge muttered. "Is that…?"

"Yeah. That's the Washington Flight Restricted Zone and we're about to fly right into it." The screen map showed a series of concentric airspace circles. The cobbled together flight route ended at the FRZ's center. I looked down at the aircraft transponder. "We're squawking VFR without clearance. That's gonna set off alarm bells."

Pidge looked out the front and side windows. Scattered clouds flowed by below us. A high overcast painted the day gray above us.

"If we stay on this path, they're gonna fucking shoot us outta the sky."

87

"See if you can find a headset." I searched my side of the cockpit. Pidge hopped into the copilot's seat. She dug through spaces at the side and behind both seats.

"I got nothing."

"A mic?"

She shook her head. Then froze.

"Uh…Will?" She touched her fingertip to glass on the instrument panel. A small white needle leaned all the way to the left in a set of gauges. "We got no gas."

"That can't be right." I looked for the airplane's fuel selectors. Maybe changing tanks was an option.

"That antique gauge may be next to useless, but I don't think it's lying. Check this out." She pointed again.

A digital fuel management instrument had been installed high on the panel. The time remaining feature reported bad news. The instrument showed eighteen minutes of fuel remaining.

"They have this programmed on some kind of approach," Pidge declared. "Those are step down legs with vertical descent programs."

"Zoom in on that and see where they have us landing, if you can call it that."

Pidge manipulated the screen on the navigation system. She pinched in closer, closer, keeping the white flight plan line centered.

"I don't see where this is taking us," she said. "There's no airport here."

We leaned until our shoulders touched. We looked at the display, then at each other. We both hit the same cold conclusion.

"Are you kidding me?" Some of the ice I felt in my brain earlier shivered down my spine.

"We are so screwed," she sat back in the seat.

Without an aerial image overlay, I couldn't be one hundred percent certain, but a guess was good enough for the location of the flight plan's final point in relation to the Potomac River.

Washington, D.C. The Capital. The White House. The Mall. One of America's landmarks rested under the terminal dot on the screen.

"We gotta turn this thing around. Turn off the autopilot."

"No. We can't." I tapped the floppy control wheel again. "We need to stay on autopilot. We got no control."

"Okay, okay. Decouple the autopilot and go to manual heading."

I pressed the button on the autopilot control panel. It would not move. I pressed harder. Nothing. Looking closer, I saw a trace of glossy residue at the corner of the button.

"Are you kidding me? That sonofabitch glued the button." I rapped the button with my knuckle. Nothing.

"Hold it, hold it," Pudge urged. "We'll delete the nav program and dial in a direct to—"

"I don't care—anywhere. Danville. Make it Danville."

Pidge swiped the touchscreen navigation system. Nothing happened. She tapped the screen. Nothing.

"Try manual. Use the knob."

She pinched the unit's control knob. It came off in her fingers.

"Are you shitting me?" She threw the severed knob over her shoulder.

"Hang on," I said. "We can pull the breaker. See if you can find the radio master breaker."

I've never been in a Beechcraft Model 18. I had no idea what to look for, but Pidge had an instinct for it. She found the breaker panel and ran her finger over the worn labels.

"Got it!"

"Pull it," I ordered.

She pinched the small round circuit breaker head and tugged. It snapped out a quarter of an inch.

The navigation screen went black. So did the fuel management system.

So did the autopilot.

Dammit! Dumb mistake.

The plane began a slow roll. I instinctively grabbed the yoke and tugged. The control wheel flopped in my fingers, useless.

"Okay, we gotta go. This thing is going to spiral." I pulled myself out of the pilot's seat and back into the cabin. "Come on!"

Pidge followed.

"What do you mean, go? You mean—like go?" She gestured at the door.

"Put your arms around my neck and hang on tight. I can't drop you because you'll be weightless, but I don't want the wind to pull us apart. Got it?"

This wasn't her first time. Nevertheless, fresh fear drained color from her features.

I moved to the door and waved at her to get in position. The airplane continued a slow roll to the left. The nose began to drop. This would become an accelerating spiral. As the wings tipped, their lift would pull us left instead of holding us level. With lift vectored left instead of up, the nose would drop. The spiral would tighten, steepening the bank, accelerating the dive. Speed would build up to a point where we could never get out. As it was, we were clocking at least 170 knots. I wished I had pulled back the power, but there was no going back.

"Hurry up!" I grabbed the side of the cargo door with one hand and threw my other arm around Pidge, who locked her arms around my neck. One pull and—

"*Hold it! HOLD IT! HOLD IT!*" she screamed in my ear.

"Dammit, Pidge, I got this."

"NO! LOOK!" She yanked her arms free and pushed herself away. The cabin leaned and she lost her footing and fell to the floor, but it didn't seem to matter. She pointed at the wooden crates.

At the black stencil in the upper left corner of the side of the wooden crate.

At the lettering.

HIGH EXPLOSIVE

As if it would make a difference, I looked from one crate to the next. Each one bore the same imprint, along with other numbers and letters.

Over my shoulder, in the open cargo door, the world rotated slowly. White fluff passed beneath us—a placid cloud oblivious to our peril. Beyond its ragged fringe, I saw the ground.

Patterns. Roads. Subdivisions. Homes. As far as I could see, the suburbs of

Washington, D.C. filled the landscape. Cookie-cutter homes on subdivision roads in curlicue patterns interspersed with soccer fields and schools and Kwik-Trip marts. Thousands of unsuspecting mothers and fathers and children.

This airplane potentially carried enough explosives to match the blast at Siddley Mansion that turned Lee Donaldson into vapor.

Pidge and I hit the same realization at the same instant. I leaped past her and scrambled to the cockpit. I thrust my arm forward and found the breaker she had pulled. I stabbed it back in.

Nothing happened. The airplane continued its slow roll to the left. The airspeed continued to rise.

"MOVE!" Pidge jerked my shoulder back. She jammed herself past me and wriggled into the pilot's seat. "Damned giants!" she cursed when she realized her feet wouldn't reach the pedals. She slouched deep into the seat. I felt the airplane jerk to the right when her foot found the right rudder pedal. She reached up for the power quadrant and pulled the right engine back slightly, adding asymmetrical thrust to the effort.

The airplane's nose stopped swinging left. The wings leveled and threatened to swing the turn in the opposite direction, but Pidge deftly corrected.

I fumbled around with her seat until I found a latch release. I pulled it and shoved the seat forward.

"Ow!" She banged one knee on the bottom of the instrument panel.

"Sorry."

She pulled herself upright and settled a grip on the throttles while her feet covered the pedals.

"I got rudder, and I got throttles. No pitch."

"Nav's coming back. Autopilot's coming back. Hit the test."

Pidge poked the HDG button on the autopilot. For a split second I feared that the Company W pilot glued all the buttons, but the autopilot executed its self-test. A moment later the device chimed readiness through the overhead speaker.

"We got autopilot." Pidge tapped the Level button. The airplane responded. The autopilot took command and squared the wings with gravity and the nose with the horizon.

I blew out a breath I felt like I'd been holding for the last ten minutes.

This wasn't so bad. Except maybe for the fact that we had spiraled through a full three hundred and sixty degrees and were heading back into the DC FIR airspace. I was about to comment on that—

Something black and violent filled the windscreen. Thunder broke through the cockpit. Turbulence rocked the airplane hard enough to make me lose my footing. I grabbed the seatback.

"What in holy hell was that?" Pidge hollered.

"We got company." I pushed the side of Pidge's head so that she would look out the left window at the menacing tail of a gray U.S. Air Force F-35 fighter that just buzzed our cockpit—then at the second one hanging on the lower limit of its speed envelope ten feet from our wingtip.

The pilot staring at us was not smiling.

88

—————

"They're probably trying to call us. Bring up Guard," Pidge said.

"How?" I pointed at the GTN750's non-functioning touchscreen and the missing manual control knob.

"Comm Two, dummy," Pidge said.

She had a point. The navigation stack included a second comm radio. It appeared to be on. I rolled the frequency knob to show 121.5, the universal emergency frequency and the line on which we could expect to be addressed by a very serious fighter pilot. I rolled the volume control.

Nothing.

I checked the audio panel. Comm One was selected. I punched the button for Comm Two.

"—immediately or you will be fired upon. Rock your wings to acknowledge." The voice coming through the overhead speaker belonged to a woman. There was no mistaking her seriousness.

Pidge kicked the rudder back and forth. It wasn't rocking the wings, but it came close. She turned her head and pointed at her ear and nodded, then pointed at her mouth and shook her head vigorously.

"What's that supposed to do?" I asked.

The Air Force pilot answered the question. "Confirm you can receive but are unable to transmit."

Pidge nodded vigorously.

"Begin your turn now," the pilot commanded.

"Jesus," I said abruptly. "I still have my phone." I jerked the device out

330

of the inside pocket of my flight jacket. From another pocket, I extracted the Bluetooth earpiece Andy makes me carry. I pushed it in my right ear and began thumbing the call screen.

"Hasn't anyone ever told you don't text and die?" Pidge looked around. "Where am I supposed to turn to? The autopilot is on Level. I can use the heading bug, but the AHRS won't come up." Pidge pointlessly tapped the primary flight display. A warning message blocked the screen saying that the instrument could not calibrate. The tiny electronics that replaced gyroscopic instruments and provided directional and attitude control were not up and running after we forced a system restart.

"Give it a minute to override," I said. "I'll be back."

"Where are you goi—?"

I didn't wait to answer. I scrambled back through the cabin, knocking my shin on the edge of one of the crates in the process. I reached the open cargo door and grabbed the frame with one hand. Wind tore at my clothes. Careful not to lose it, I held up my phone until the pilot glanced in my direction. I pointed at the phone and then made what I hoped was the universal signal for *Gimme a minute*. Then I pushed back and flopped onto the rearmost crate of explosives.

Pick up the damned phone Leslie!

"A little busy here, Will."

"Leslie! Remember Detroit? That business with the fighters? You gotta call Homeland Security and tell them not to shoot us down. I don't have time to explain. Get through to somebody NOW! We're in Louis Blaze's plane. It's full of explosives. We have no control and we're busting into DC airspace."

She said nothing. My heart sank. Lost connection, I thought. I was about to try dialing again when I heard beeps.

"Stay on the line, Will." Leslie, God bless her, was all business. She did not waste time with questions.

Pidge called to me from the cockpit. "Will! They want me to turn! What do I do?"

I struggled forward. The error message remained on the primary flight display screen.

"Try using rudder to override the autopilot. It's going to fight you to hold level, but you can override it."

She pressed the rudder. The nose swung left, then stabilized. Pidge uttered a curse. She pushed harder. The nose swung a few degrees, then the autopilot took control again and leveled us.

"Wait!" I pointed at the fuel management system. It had cycled through its startup and returned to full service. "Fuel management is back on."

"So?"

"We only have five minutes of fuel left."

"So?" Pidge asked.

"Will," Leslie spoke calmly into my ear. "I have Homeland Security on the line. They're connecting to the pilots. Stay with me."

"Tell them to hurry. Tell them we are not a threat, but we have a serious problem."

"They can hear you."

A new voice broke in, hollow and crisp, spoken through an aircraft mic. "This is Colonel Reilly. Pilot of the Twin Beech, go ahead."

"Colonel! This is the idiot in the Twin Beech who waved a cell phone at you! Do you copy?"

For a moment I could not separate the wind and engine noise of the airplane from noise on the line. I cupped my hand over the earpiece in my ear.

"What color is your jacket?" the woman's voice asked.

"It's an Air Force green flight jacket," I replied. "Listen up. My companion and I are not here voluntarily. We were kidnapped and placed on this airplane by the pilot who programmed a flight straight into DC. He's gone, but they loaded three crates of high explosives aboard. Copy that? Three crates of high explosives. If you blow us out of the sky, we're going to make a huge hole in whatever we hit."

"Turn around. Now. Do you copy?"

"We can't. The controls are cut. We're trying to get the autopilot heading function back online. But we have another problem."

"Of course you do," Leslie muttered. "Sorry."

"I don't care what your other problem is. You have thirty seconds before my wingman takes you down. Do you understand?"

"Colonel, your wingman doesn't need to take us down. They set us up to run out of fuel in about five minutes. We're coming down no matter what and we're going to make a loud noise if we don't do it under control. We need to steer this thing to where it's going to do the least damage. If you shoot us down, there's no telling what we will hit. Do you copy?"

Pidge turned and punched my shoulder. She pointed over the nose.

"The river! We put this thing in the river!"

I saw the thin, winding streak of the Potomac River ahead.

"Colonel, we're going in the Potomac. It's the only place where we can be sure we won't be killing hundreds."

No reply.

"Leslie, tell them!" I barked at the phone.

No reply.

I looked at the screen. Connection lost.

Water replaced the muscles in my arms and legs. My knees wanted to buckle. A knot in my throat formed when the fighter jet off our wing suddenly accelerated and rolled into a tight turn away from us. She wasn't pulling away. She was pulling in behind us for the kill.

I would later tell Andy that she kissed me at that moment. I felt her lips touch mine. I felt the imprint of her body against mine. I felt our child pressed between us.

For the last time, I thought.

"Sonofabitch!" Pidge wiggled in the seat. "Autopilot's back on. I got heading. I got rudder. I got throttle. And I have elevator trim." She reached down and wiggled the big wheel that eased pressure on the elevator in various regimes of flight. "I think I can line us up with the river."

"Do it. When we get close to the water, I'm going to see if I can get us both out before she hits. Set up a stabilized approach."

Pidge shook her head. "You should go. I'll take it into the water."

"No way."

"I'm serious, Will. I got this."

"Not a chance."

"Don't do this to me," she argued. "I don't want to be stuck in some level of Hell for eternity with you bitching about how you never got to see your daughter."

"Just keep your eye on the ball."

She heaved a sigh. "Alright, let's take this thing down before we run out of gas."

I looked back through the cargo door. No sign of the F-35s. Pidge wasn't wrong about me never seeing my son or daughter. She didn't know that any second now the fighter would be in position behind us, armed and asking for permission to fire. And I wasn't about to tell her.

Pidge eased the throttles back.

My phone vibrated.

Leslie.

"Jesus," I said.

The voice was distant and distilled. "No, sir. This is Colonel Reilly. Confirm for me that you are putting that piece of shit in the river."

"Affirmative, Colonel. I swear on my unborn child."

Leslie broke in. "This is the FBI. I can confirm his wife is pregnant."

"I don't give a shit," the Colonel snapped. "If you deviate in any direction but the water we will blow you into the next millennium. Copy?"

"Copy. But Colonel, give us the benefit of the doubt. All we have is rudder, elevator trim, autopilot heading function, and throttles. This won't be pretty. We'll do our best."

"Do better."

Pidge nudged my arm. "I'm going to line up on that bridge for a base leg. We'll approach it and turn upriver."

I gave her a thumbs up. "Colonel, we're lining up a left base on that bridge ahead. We'll make the turn upriver."

"Copy."

Pidge hunkered down in the seat like a kid at a video game console. Fingers on her left hand pinched the heading knob on the primary flight display. Her right hand shifted between the throttles and the big trim wheel. The power instruments confirmed what my ears told me; she had already set approach power. On either side of the cockpit, the radial engines rumbled at a reduced noise level. With the changes in power, Pidge rapidly adjusted the trim wheel. Elevator trim controlled the pressure on the elevator, which controlled the pitch of the airplane. As a result, our airspeed diminished. Pidge's actions resembled steering a car by changing tire pressure on the front wheels.

The altimeter reported passing through 1700 feet. My eye suggested we were about a thousand feet above the densely populated landscape below.

Pidge stared through the windshield, tweaking the controls, guiding the highly explosive missile strapped to her butt. She performed like a virtuoso playing an instrument she had never touched.

"You should sit down and put on a seat belt," she muttered.

"You should unstrap yours so I can pull you out of here when we're on final."

"Yeah, we'll discuss that. Meanwhile, remove all external apparel, place your head between your knees and kiss your ass goodbye."

Her hands moved deftly. The airplane sailed through light chop. She used rudder to compensate for a crosswind from the left, keeping the nose at a slight angle to the wide, low bridge across the Potomac. Directly ahead of the bridge, I saw the Lincoln Memorial, and beyond that more national landmarks, at least one of which Company W intended to obliterate with Pidge and me along for the ride.

I wondered about the fighters behind us. Our speed had dropped well below a point where they could remain in the air. Then I remembered they were F-35s, uniquely capable of vertical thrust vectoring. They could hover right up behind us and come to a full stop if they needed to.

"The autopilot's turn rate is three degrees per second," I reminded Pidge.

"No shit."

I meant it as a reminder for Pidge to allow for the turn. The autopilot wouldn't crank the airplane over quickly. I wanted to tell her she would have to start her turn around half a mile short of the bridge to roll out over the river. I wanted to tell her that at our current rate of descent, the turn should happen around five hundred feet.

I held my tongue. She knew.

At that instant everything changed.

"What the f—!"

Pidge grabbed the throttles. The nose heaved right.

"Right engine!" I called out. A glance at the fuel pressure confirmed it. The right engine surged, cut, surged, and cut again. "Feather the right!"

Pidge jerked the right engine pitch lever back through the feather detent. The props on the right side of the airplane swung to a stop aligned with the airflow to prevent windmilling and drag. Our airspeed sank toward the blue line on the indicator.

Pidge increased power on the good engine to maintain our descent rate. The asymmetrical thrust fought the autopilot. She compensated with rudder pressure, shoving her straight leg into the pedal.

"I got this," she said calmly, more to herself than me. The bridge remained aligned dead ahead, but my calculation for the turn was now off. We were low.

"You should start your turn," I said quietly.

"Not yet."

Four hundred fifty. Four hundred. Too low.

"Not yet."

The left engine shuddered, surged, and quit. Pidge said nothing. She pulled the prop control into Feather. The props on the left side swung to a stop. Stunning silence filled the cockpit. The bridge lay directly ahead. Our vertical speed plummeted along with our airspeed. Pidge automatically dropped the nose to sacrifice altitude for airspeed. There was no way to make the turn onto the river now.

"Twin Beech, start your turn!" Colonel Reilly commanded. "Turn or we fire."

"Tell 'em we're landing on the bridge," Pidge said. She worked the autopilot heading control in single-degree increments, augmenting with rudder, aligning the flight path with the bridge ahead. "Tell 'em." She repeated calmly.

"Colonel, we're dead stick. We can't make the water. We're putting it on the bridge."

"Put it in the water or we fire."

"Fire now and you will kill hundreds on the ground. *Dammit. We're out of gas and we're putting it on the bridge. We got this.*"

No reply. I held my breath.

"Sonofabitch," Pidge muttered. "Look at that."

I saw it. The bridge had four lanes. The right side, the side traveling east toward the capital, was choked with stopped traffic. Something about all that traffic looked strange but I had no time to figure out what. I could not stop staring at the left side.

The lanes traveling away from D.C. lay empty. I scrambled to check the seat pockets.

"What are you doing?" Pidge snapped.

"Looking for the POH so I can give you the numbers. Maybe not stall this thing."

"Leave it," she said calmly. "She'll tell me when she's done flying."

I stopped searching.

"Looks like around two thousand feet," I offered. "Hold off on the gear."

Dropping the landing gear would radically change our drag configuration, a change from which we might not recover. Pidge tweaked the trim control. The nose lifted slightly. Wind whistled past the cockpit and past the open cargo door behind us. Pidge maintained a shallow dive that would burrow into the center of a roundabout short of the bridge if unchecked.

Robert E. Lee's original home and thousands of sedate rows of grave markers passed under us.

"You might want to brace," Pidge said nonchalantly. She steadied her grip on the trim wheel. She tapped the rudder pedals. Both minutely and aggressively. She wiggled the nose to hold our track on the center line with a slight crab to the left to compensate for the crosswind.

Do it now.

She waited.

Do it NOW!

Pidge rolled the trim wheel. The airplane responded a second later—just in time. The nose swept up, arresting our descent.

A pine tree shot past the left wing. Sculpted eagles on top of pedestals at the bridge entrance all but ducked. We dropped below the line of light poles that ran down the center of the bridge. The backed-up traffic raced past our right wingtip. I saw flags on the vehicles.

The nose began to drift upward, lifted by Pidge's trim wheel input. In another second we would be too high.

"Gear!" she commanded.

I dropped the gear wheel. An electric motor whined. The airplane's wheels descended beneath the engine nacelles. Drag bit into the air. The airplane stopped rising. Pavement rose to meet the wheels.

Rubber squeaked on the pavement.

"Gear up!" she cried. I jerked the lever back up.

Instead of bouncing back into the air in an attitude from which we could not recover, the wheels folded. We dropped.

I shoved myself into the cabin and spun to put my back against the partition behind Pidge's seat.

A bone-jarring jolt transmitted through the floor and into my body. Screaming metal thunder erupted beneath us. The Twin Beech lurched and scraped down the open bridge lanes. The left wingtip gouged the wall at the edge of the bridge. The right wing ripped into SUV and pickup truck body panels and side doors, sending occupants and bystanders diving for cover. Chunks of something flew past the cargo door. Sparks flew into the twilight air behind us. I felt comforted that we had no fuel to burn.

Shudders and thumps and random snaps continued forever and ever until everything stopped. Silence erupted.

"Oh, Lord..." Pidge said softly. Reverently.

I dropped to the cabin floor next to a box labeled HIGH EXPLOSIVE wondering how close we had just come to setting off the contents.

Sound came from my earpiece. Still connected.

"We're down," I said to whoever was still on the line.

Colonel Reilly spoke. "Nice landing."

"Thanks for not shooting our asses out of the sky, Colonel."

"Any time. You're lucky you had a girl in the front seat."

"Leslie?" I asked. "You there?"

"Not now, Will. Got a bit of a problem here."

89

"Message from Leslie," Andy said over her shoulder. She pulled her carry-on at a furious pace through Reagan National Terminal 2. Arun jogged to keep up. Following her was easier than trying to move two abreast. "She says the intel was good and there's a car waiting for us outside baggage claim on Level 1, Exit 1."

"What did she mean by *good*?" Arun asked. "Is she patronizing us? Like, thank you for the completely mental idea, but we're busy with grown up things?"

"I don't think so, Arun."

Approaching the exit labeled number 1 on the baggage claim level, Arun asked, "How are we supposed to know what car is waiting for us?"

Andy pushed through the exit. A row of police cars with flashing lights occupied most of what otherwise would have been passenger pickup lanes. A large black SUV occupied the center of the apparent emergency.

"I have a feeling I know," Andy said.

The SUV door opened, and a distinguished man wearing a dark suit stepped out, momentarily causing concern for a second, younger man who jumped out of the front passenger seat.

"This way, Detective," FBI Director William Simmons waved for her to climb aboard.

Arun hesitated, or more to the point, froze. The young man from the front seat swept the carry-on from his grasp, then did the same for Andy's. He lifted both bags into the rear hatch of the big vehicle. He gestured for

Arun to come around to the other side. Simmons held the door for Andy. Arun boarded the land yacht and found himself beside Andy facing the director of the FBI. The agent who handled the bags hopped back in the front seat. Seconds later, they and the police escort roared off.

"I won't waste time, Detective. Special Agent Carson-Pel—Leslie—told me that the most expeditious way of understanding what we're dealing with would be to connect with you. Brief me as we go."

"Go where, sir?" Andy asked.

"The White House. There's a dinner there tonight that I have been diligently working to avoid. Now Leslie says it's imperative that I be there and that to be fully informed as to why, I need to talk to you." He started to settle in his seat, but then leaned forward and extended his hand to Arun. "Bill Simmons."

"A-Arun Dewar, sir," Arun stammered. He shook hands, mildly stunned.

"Did Leslie send you the map coordinates?" Andy asked.

"Yes. She's on her way there now."

"Then you assess it to be a credible threat?"

Simmons hesitated. "A few hours ago, Virginia state troopers tried to stop what they described as a caravan of vehicles. The occupants of the vehicles opened fire on the police, disabling their unit, injuring one of the officers. The vehicles were able to get away. Authorities believe they are entering D.C. Similar incidents have been reported in Indiana, Missouri, and North Carolina. In some cases, arrests were made. Weapons confiscated. Taken in connection with a nationwide pattern we have been seeing for several days, I am inclined to regard just about any weird-assed thing that happens as a credible threat. Your turn."

Andy cleared her throat.

"I should start with the night you cancelled my participation in the briefing on the Tiffany Vera Callum murder..."

90

Not now, Will. Got a bit of a problem here.

The woman had no idea.

"You okay?" I asked. My voice sounded loud in the bare metal cabin.

"Yeah. We should probably get out of this thing." Pidge climbed past me. She turned and gave me a hand to stand up. She tapped one of the crates lightly with one foot. "At least I didn't set these off. I wouldn't mind getting about a mile from here."

I looked down at the green wooden boxes. They looked military. Like Army ammunition cases.

"Yeah…" Padlocks secured each of the three boxes. Easy for me to open using *the other thing.*

"You coming?" Pidge held up at the cargo door.

I looked at the padlock. My curiosity stirred.

And what if you set the thing off by opening it?

I followed Pidge out the cargo door. The Twin Beech rested on its belly. I checked for smoke but didn't see anything, although the smell of hot metal infused the air. I felt bad seeing the old classic on her belly. Coming to rest on a major bridge in Washington, D.C. meant that clearing the road would take priority over conserving the airplane for restoration. I pictured a loader lifting it into the river or throwing torn-up chunks onto flatbed trucks.

Pidge climbed on the wing. She gazed back at the path we had scratched into the pavement. For someone anxious to get far away, she wasn't moving.

"Are you seeing this?"

I climbed onto the wing beside her.

Shreds of orange sunset clung to the western horizon. Twin rows of ornate lamps illuminated the pavement at intervals; the lights must have just turned on. I did not recall seeing them on our short final approach.

Four traffic lanes served the bridge, separated by a twin yellow line down the center. The empty westbound lanes had provided our landing strip. The eastbound lanes were choked with traffic, side by side, both lanes. I saw flags. Dozens. The picture grew clearer. I began to understand why we had been given the perfect landing strip at the perfect moment.

Eastbound traffic was blocked at the bridge's exit by stacked rows of police vehicles. I don't know how I missed them before, but the end of the bridge near the Lincoln Memorial was sealed off. Flashing blue and red lights winked, growing brighter as darkness descended.

The Twin Beech came to rest less than a hundred yards from the law enforcement perimeter.

"How did they have time to do that?" Pidge asked. "We didn't even know we were landing here."

I drew Pidge's attention to the stacked eastbound traffic off the airplane's right wing. Flags fluttered. Faces gaped at us. Men. Men stood beside their vehicles. Men stood in the beds of pickup trucks. Men wearing camouflage jackets and pants with a mixed bag of helmets and headgear.

Men brandishing weapons of every kind.

I spotted a familiar patch sewn on their cosplay soldier outfits.

"Oh, shit," she muttered.

91

—————

"**W**e gotta go," I said to Pidge. The men stared at us, still stunned that we'd dropped out of the sky onto their party. They wouldn't stay that way for long. I hopped off the wing and held out my hand. "C'mere."

"Go where?"

"Gimme your hand, Pidge, before they wake up. It's them. The whole freakin' army of them. We gotta go. *Now!*"

I heard shouts. Footsteps. People running. Someone called out, "Stop!"

Pidge reached. I grabbed her hand and pulled her off the wing.

"Hey!" The shout came from just off the leading edge of the wing behind us. More shouts came from behind the tail.

"Hang on to me," I told Pidge. We made the five-step dash to the low concrete wall lining the side of the bridge.

"Stop!"

Pidge muttered curses but she did not resist. We jumped the barrier like Olympic hurdlers. The dark waters of the Potomac raced up at us.

Fwooomp!

We vanished. Our trajectory took us straight down. Our feet broke the water. We sank to our thighs in twin splashes, but then bobbed back up and shot out of the river's surface toward the sky.

"*What the fuck was that?*" Pidge gasped.

"*Shhhhh!*"

I looked over my shoulder. Several armed men leaned on the concrete wall staring down at the spreading ripples on the surface of the river. While they waited and watched, we ascended. Our ripples spread into broad inter-locking circles, a Venn diagram of where Will Stewart and his pal Pidge met their end in the waters of the Potomac. Several of the men hurried around the airplane's tail and shouted to others to check the opposite side. Others poked their heads into the aircraft cabin.

They're going to like what they find, I thought.

"I need my hand," I told Pidge quietly. She gripped my right hand with both of hers, trying to crush the bones within.

"Don't you let go of me, Stewart. Goddammit."

"I'm not going to let go of you, but I need my hand." I found her with my left. "Here. Take my other hand." She did. "Now swap sides." We did. She pulled herself against the left side of my body and threw one arm around my back and the other around my chest. I put my arm around her thin waist to give her some degree of assurance that I was not going to dump her in the river.

With my now freed right hand I reached down and lifted my pants leg and probed my boot. The BLASTER and prop were just as I had left them. Stroud apparently felt that drugging us obviated a search.

Careful not to drop either, I extracted the parts from the boot and snapped them together. Both were wet. Water squelched in my boot. But the BLASTER worked.

"What's going on here?" Pidge asked.

A column of pickup trucks, SUVs, jeeps, and a smattering of what looked like military Humvees lined the eastbound lanes two abreast. American flags flew from many of the vehicles. Men inside leaned one arm out of open windows. Others stood in the open truck beds. Every one of them carried arms. Some wore heavy web belts with pouches. Some wore body armor.

"I think the revolution has arrived. Stroud said something about a rally point."

"Looks like they're not going very far."

The head of the column stopped at the eastern end of the bridge. A gap of roughly one hundred yards lay between the first two vehicles and a barrier of parked police vehicles staged between two stone pedestals on which golden statues stood. Dozens of cops in riot gear and body armor crouched behind their cars, some with long rifles of their own. Farther back, a police command truck sat crosswise where the lanes split off to send traffic about its business.

Halfway through the gap between the police and the head of the militia column a lone figure stood.

"Oh, crap."

She looked like the guy who faced down the tank in Tiananmen Square. Black blazer. Black pants.

Not now, Will. Got a bit of a problem here.

Leslie stood alone on the centerline between two lanes. Facing her, a group of seventy or one hundred men with rifles and pistols lined up across the road.

"Pidge, I'm dropping you off behind the police line. Get as far away from here as you can."

"Where are you going?"

"As if you need to ask."

92

I eased up to the side of the bridge and coasted over the low sidewall. The man facing Leslie shouted at her.

"We are a duly authorized force of American citizens empowered by the Second Amendment to bring Constitutionally guaranteed revolution for the good of this nation. Stand aside."

I drifted to a spot behind Leslie. Fifty yards away, police rifles trained on the men clustered at the head of their quasi-column. I pulsed the BLASTER and eased up close enough behind her to smell her shampoo.

"I feel like I can't leave you alone for five minutes," I said.

Her shoulders twitched with a chuckle.

"You probably don't want to be here, Will," she said without taking her eyes from the man who seemed to be the spokesperson. He had a rugged beard, bands of ammunition strung across his chest, and a mean-looking military rifle hooked and slung like they do in the real military and the movies.

"What's the deal here?" I asked. I hovered within reach of her. It would only take an instant for me to lunge, close an embrace, and make her vanish. If things went bad, I planned to grab her and kick off the surface of the bridge and get the hell out of there.

"These boys tell me that Texas is seceding from the union." Leslie said it to me and didn't care if Spokesman heard her.

"You dumb bitch, that's not what we said," the bearded man protested. "We are here to shut down the corrupt and criminal Congress, and to escort

345

the President, who backs us one thousand percent, to the new national capital in Austin, Texas. The State of Texas is not seceding from the union, you stupid—" he used the c-word which made me decide that after I carried Leslie free, I was coming back to dump this misogynist piece of dogshit in the river "—the union is forming a *more perfect* union around the Free State of Texas. Now stand aside."

"What was the part about the Second Amendment?" Leslie asked. I started wondering if I should just grab her and go.

"The Second Amendment guarantees our right to engage in insurrection if we can no longer abide the tyranny of an unjust government. Look it up, you stupid—" There it was again. This was starting to piss me off.

Unfazed, Leslie continued the debate.

"I'm not sure what version of The Constitution you're reading, but—"

Horns honked at the far end of the column. The police had not yet blocked the west end of the bridge. A tractor/trailer combination roared through low gears, pulling onto the bridge. It followed the line Pidge had used for landing the Twin Beech and now I understood the reason for the open lanes. The 18-wheeler pulled forward until it heaved to a stop at the head of the line. Airbrakes hissed. I recognized the vehicle from its stop at the airport.

They made good time, I thought, although I couldn't be certain how long I had been in GHB dreamland chatting with deceased Lee Donaldson.

The truck heaved to a halt short of the wrecked Twin Beech.

The bearded spokesman split a nasty grin at Leslie. The man had bad teeth. I couldn't stop looking at the stains.

"You folks best get out of our way. The Second Amendment just grew fangs." He shouted to his troops. "Unload her, boys!" He took several steps toward us, then stopped. Cranking up his sneer, he said, "You think we're a bunch of hicks with handguns. I got news for you. We got heavy weapons ready for action. There's two armored vehicles in there along with fifty-cals and twenty-millimeter cannons. We're coming through. Tell those cops back there they better join us or get the hell out of the way because this is happening."

Activity broke out near the back end of the big trailer. I heard latches thrown over and the big doors swung open on protesting hinges. I expected to hear ramps thrown down. The diesel engines of armored vehicles. The crash of crates of heavy weapons thrown to the ground.

I glanced at Leslie's nine-millimeter handgun.

This is not good.

93

———

ndy glanced through the heavily tinted side windows of the FBI Director's limousine-like SUV. She recognized the building Mark Twain once called the ugliest building in America, the office building eventually named for Dwight Eisenhower. Relentless stacks of polished granite reminded her of hundreds of egg cartons. The hurrying motorcade swept by as if passing a complex stone cloud.

The Eisenhower Office Building marked entry to the White House campus complex. A guarded gate stopped the first vehicle of the small motorcade, but only briefly. Simmons' SUV sailed past the military guards unchecked.

Arun, trying hard not to plaster himself against the glass like a child in a safari park, wore a look of growing wonder. The recognizable angles and dimensions of The West Wing peeked around a corner. Simmons' driver turned onto a secure access road and pulled up to an entrance covered by an awning.

Andy hesitated. "Sir…I…?"

"You're coming in with me," Simmons announced, eliminating any negotiation.

Andy glanced down at her attire. Jeans and calf-height boots. A light cashmere pullover. "This is a state dinner. I can't go in like this."

Simmons huffed. "Do you have something in your bag? It doesn't have to be formal. Something nice?"

Andy nodded.

"Ron, get Detective Stewart's bag from the back. And let's give the lady some privacy. Five minutes, Detective." Simmons gestured for Arun to precede him out the door. The driver hustled to the back of the SUV and produced Andy's bag for her. He snapped the door closed.

Andy unzipped the bag and dug through folded clothing. After a moment, she pulled out the dress she had worn for crashing Pedmann's party. She laid the gown across her knees and pressed away wrinkles with her hands.

"Oh, boy," she sighed, anticipating that the condition of the dress would not go unnoticed by…well, just about everyone. The good news was that the fabric where her knees pressed the pavement was in better shape than she remembered. The marks and scuffs were scarcely visible.

ANDY EMERGED from the vehicle in less than the allotted five minutes. She tucked and adjusted the dress as best she could. There had been no time for her hair, and only a moment to check her face in a compact mirror—mainly to apply a quick sheen of lip gloss. She wore no jewelry save the modest wedding diamond on her left hand.

Simmons paced the sidewalk in front of the West Wing awning with his phone pressed to his ear. Arun stood discreetly out of the way looking not at all certain of what he should do with himself. The question embossed on his face was not answered when Simmons waved at Andy to follow him into the building. Two FBI agents fell in behind Simmons and Andy. The entourage left Arun behind, for which Andy paid him a helpless shrug.

"Bob, Bill Simmons," the director said into his phone. One of the agents accompanying them opened dual doors and then hurried ahead to the next set. "Coming in. I've got Detective Andrea Stewart, Essex PD, with me. Have her cleared for me, okay? Oh, and is he here?"

Simmons nodded. Andy hurried to keep pace with his long strides. She listened to one side of the conversation.

"When?"

"Is Jake on that?"

"Estimates?"

"Jesus, Mary, and Joseph, do they think it's Blaze?"

"Unbelievable. What does this asshat want? Ruby Ridge out there on the Arlington?"

"Okay, we'll be inside in three."

He tucked away his phone.

"Did I hear you mention Louis Blaze?" Andy asked.

"Yeah," Simmons said without breaking stride. "The barbarian appears to be at the gate. He's got a caravan lined up on the Arlington Memorial Bridge. His revolution is royally screwing up traffic."

"That's the rally point. The coordinates I sent Leslie."

Simmons nodded. "Yup. The question now is whether this is some kind of tiki torch protest…or something more? First reports say they're armed. I may need to speak to the President."

"Sir, I don't think I'm the right person—"

"To get in his face. You got that right. You're not. If it comes to it, follow my lead."

Andy hardly had time to register the iconic sights of The West Wing as they scurried through narrow, red-carpeted hallways. She had trouble keeping her bearings thanks to turns in the cramped, maze-like layout—so much smaller than she expected. Eventually, a long corridor connected the working spaces of the administration to the ceremonial spaces beneath the second-floor residence. Almost without warning, an abrupt turn took Simmons and Andy into a large room filled with people mingling among beautifully set round tables attended by heavy, dark-wooded chairs. Tuxedos and evening dresses dominated, but a few business suits matched Simmons' attire, mostly on men standing near the doors. Andy marked them as Secret Service. The room bathed in a warm glow born of a multitude of electric candles mounted in clusters and on chandeliers.

She saw him at once. Pedmann attached himself to a cluster of men and women in a corner near what Andy guessed to be the head of the rectangular room where a large gold-framed mirror dominated the wall. Pedmann glanced at his reflection when he thought no one was looking. He adjusted his tie and touched what hair he had.

"He's with Senator Stapleton," Andy told Simmons, instantly wishing she hadn't blurted out the obvious.

"Where?" Simmons asked. Andy pointed out the target. Simmons nodded. "Who's the woman?"

"I don't know," Andy replied. "But this is the third time I've seen her in their company."

Simmons looked over the dark-haired woman on the Senator's arm. "That's about his speed." Simmons' comment suggested unspoken history that made Andy wonder if it was a compliment or insult. Senator Stapleton's relentless denigration of the FBI and its parent Department of Justice earned him no respect in Simmons' bureau or in Simmons' tone of voice.

A staff member in a White House uniform appeared in a doorway at the far end of the room. He stiffened to attention.

"Ladies, and gentlemen, the President of the United States."

The few people seated rose to their feet. Hands came together in applause. Beneath the applause, broadcast from hidden speakers, Andy heard the familiar strains of "Hail to the Chief" played through hidden speakers.

The President's entourage skirted but did not acknowledge the staff member who made his entrance announcement. No one in the small group paid heed to the crowd in the room or the applause except the President. He waved, clapped his hands, and gave thumbs-up gestures. He pointed at people he knew and nodded recognition in their direction. He stopped to admire the dress of a young woman, a dress Andy considered one step over the line separating good taste from overt sexual display. She suddenly felt self-conscious of her own plunging neckline and backless couture.

"With me," Simmons told Andy. He edged into the room, avoiding eye contact with lesser beings, tossing off small talk when he had no other choice, excusing himself to escape entanglements. Andy noticed that he navigated on a collision course with the path of the President.

"Sir, I'm not sure I should be doing this."

"Why? Because you tried to shoot the man?" The comment stopped Andy in her tracks. Simmons turned and winked. "If I really thought that, Detective, you wouldn't be here. Come."

Faces blurred. Conversation merged into white noise. The features of the room—the oak leaves woven into the carpet, the slim milled lines of wall panels—became randomly prominent in her mind or things she would later tell me she missed entirely. When I Googled a picture of the state dining room, she was amazed to see a full body portrait of Abraham Lincoln over a fireplace she never noticed.

Simmons clapped his hand on the shoulder of a man engaged in conversation with the woman Andy recognized as the Secretary of Commerce. She greeted the FBI Director, then made a polite excuse to turn a very cold shoulder and move to a new knot of conversation.

"She still hasn't forgiven you, Bill," the man, young by senior staff standards, said to Simmons.

"The day she does is the day I hang it up. Jake Rollins, Detective—"

"Andrea Stewart." The man extended his hand. To Andy's eye, he resembled FBI Assistant Director Mitchell Lindsey, whom we had briefly known. Handsome. A touch of gray in full, thick hair. Called from Central Casting to fit the part he played in a movie about the President. Rollins looked at Andy. "Are you here to punk POTUS, Bill? No, offense, Detective."

"Our phones are going to go off in about thirty seconds, Jake. Unless you already know."

"I heard. We're treating it like just another news cycle grab. My people say they're just taking over the bridge to mess up traffic long enough to get the camera crews out for the nine o-clock cable hour. Hannity is probably down there doing a remote."

"Your people are wrong. I want your permission to bring in a team." Simmons drilled a serious look into the man.

"Secret Service will never allow that, and you know it. And POTUS won't allow it, either. He pulls a lot of support from that end of the spectrum. Our people have this machine beyond well-oiled. If anything heats up, we'll be all over it."

"This is different, Jake."

Andy could feel the turf line sharpen between the two men.

"Mr. Rollins," Andy touched his arm, a female move she reserved for serious moments, "the threat to your principle is here. In the room."

Rollins glanced indifferently at Andy. He looked her up and down.

"Missy, if you're concealing something in that dress, you get my vote."

Andy smiled. "Well, dickhead, while you're voting on what's in my dress, your man is chumming it up with people who have ties to a known terrorist organization."

Simmons suppressed a smile. "I think the lady just called the director of the detail a dickhead, Jake. You best take her seriously. She's not wrong."

Rollins flashed a cold look at the FBI Director, then swiveled his head slowly to take in the scene two conversations away. The President glad-handed with Pedmann, Stapleton and his lady friend, paying his signature special attention to the woman among them. Andy watched the chief executive's eyes roam. It occurred to her that the First Lady was not present.

Andy switched her attention back to Rollins. She watched him make eye contact with men at the corners of the room. She saw him make almost imperceptible facial gestures that prompted the men to switch their focus and move in broken, nearly unobservable patterns, closer to the man they protected. She had to admit, she would have also described their subtle but practiced actions as well-oiled.

"You gonna read me in, Bill?" Rollins asked without bringing his gaze back to the trio.

"The people on the bridge are armed. And thanks to that man laughing at POTUS's joke, they may have arrived with thirty million dollars-worth of hardware from Alejandro Ruiz. Heavy military shit. Unconfirmed, but high probability. They're not tourist families, Jake. They're not sign-waving free speech protesters. They're militia. Whatever they're doing on the bridge isn't going to stay on the bridge."

"Jesus!" Rollins touched his ear. Andy thought the reaction a bit much, despite Simmons' concise and reasonably convincing description.

Rollins blanched.

"We have an unidentified aircraft inbound. We're going to lockdown."

94

Simmons reached into his coat for his phone.

Andy did not wait. She slipped past Rollins who had lifted a wrist mic to his lips to issue orders. She excused herself for pushing through a knot of people anxiously waiting their turn for the President's attention, ignoring their angry stares. She made eye contact with the Secret Service agent closest to the President and caught him in an instant of indecision as he watched a potentially threatening woman weave through the crowd while his boss barked fresh orders in his ear.

She reached the perimeter of a small circle where the President held the rapt attention of Pedmann and Stapleton. The woman with them leveled a steady gaze at Andy.

"You," the woman said under her breath.

"You," Pedmann said, startled.

"You," the President of the United States said to Andy. "You—how did you—? What are you—?"

"Doing here?" Andy finished for him. "Well, I'm not here to shoot at you, sir. Not that I ever have shot at you. The man you're speaking to here, Attorney General Pe—"

Rollins pushed Andy aside and closed a grip on the President's arm.

"Sir, we have a situation. We need to go."

Two more men closed in to back up Rollins. A murmur spread in the crowd. To enhance the confusion, a voice called out, "Ladies and gentlemen, if you would all please find your seats we are about to begin dinner service."

"Don't go with them, sir," Andy said sharply. "I can't be certain they're not in on it."

"In on what?" the President asked.

"Now, sir," Rollins countered.

"Tell him, Willis." Andy turned and faced Pedmann. "Tell him."

Rollins tugged at his charge, but the President pushed his hand free. "I'm the boss, here, Jake. Just—let go of me—I want to know what's going on. Willis? What's this about?"

Rollins touched his ear again. His face darkened.

"Sir," Rollins said, "we just got a tip that an aircraft loaded with explosives is entering the protected airspace. The Air Force is up. We need to move to the bunker."

"I'm not doing that again," the President snapped. "That gets all over the news and I look like an idiot. Tell the Air Force to shoot it down. Tell them those are my orders. Get the generals on the phone."

Andy felt her knees weaken. For reasons she could not pinpoint, she thought of me at that instant. Certain that I wouldn't—couldn't possibly be airborne in the D.C. airspace, she fought off the cold embrace of dark imagination. I was safe, she told herself. I would never.

"Sir," Willis Pedmann stepped in a direct line with the President's eyes, "this is your moment. That aircraft is no threat to you. I know what's happening. That aircraft is going to open a door to history. This is your moment, sir. True patriots, the blood and sinew of your core followers, are coming, right now. We're ready to make the move. The moment is now."

"What move?"

"Sir, we have to go," Rollins pulled.

"Get your damn hands off me. You're fired! Get away from me." He peeled away from Rollins' grasp. "What move, Willis? Who's coming?"

"Hundreds. Thousands loyal to you, sir. *Sworn to you.* They're not coming for you. They're going up to Capitol Hill to shut it down. All of it. The dirty lies. The useless bickering and committees sabotaging your agenda. The swamp. They're going up to Congress and they're putting an end to the travesty. America is rising up. All over America, true patriots loyal to you are rising up. *We can do this, sir.*"

A widening circle formed around the small group. Pedmann's voice grew strident. Simultaneously, conversation and the murmur of spreading news dropped to near silence.

"It's happening *right now,* sir," Pedmann urged. "The Great State of Texas stands with you. History stands with you. Shut it all down and start fresh. The people who are coming for you have risen to the challenge and begun the avalanche that you *must* command."

"Are you—are you talking secession?" someone asked.

"No!" Pedmann snapped at the gathering crowd. All eyes fell on him. "Texas is *not* seceding from the union; the union is joining Texas. The union is seceding from the corruption and deviance and liberal decay that oozes from this capital and has consumed our great nation. Texas stands ready to become the new capital of the new union. The new America." Pedmann, his face glistening, whirled back to face the President whose gaze locked on both the man speaking and the potential within his words. Andy saw the words seeping in, gaining a foothold.

"Is Governor Henry in on this?" someone who entered the room with the President asked.

"Governor Henry will join us," Pedmann insisted. "He just needs to be shown the way."

"Sir," Rollins tried one more time.

"You're fired. I said you're fired," he snarled. He stepped closer to Pedmann. "What are you saying?"

"I'm saying it's time for you to fill a new seat of government in America, Mr. President. With your leadership—*your permanent leadership*—we can put power in the righteous, iron fists of one man. You, sir. Our greatest leader. Lead us from Austin, sir. Make Texas the rightful first among fifty. We're prepared to anoint you, sir. You and your cabinet of ten, Senator Stapleton as the eleventh, and me, sir—there to guide you every step of the way as the twelfth at a round table, sir. Clear-eyed and powerful, like nothing seen in the world since Arthur."

Andy winced at the allusion. She looked around to see what Stapleton had to say but his face no longer hovered in the small circle. Nor was his companion present.

"Twelve knights? Like in the Bible…" the president mused.

Jaws in the circling crowd dropped.

"Sir, what he's talking about is insurrection. It's a threat to every principle this country was founded on," Simmons protested.

"Shut up, Bill," Rollins said. "Sir, my team will protect you under *any* circumstances, but right now there is a confirmed threat, *and we need to go.*"

Pedmann stepped beside Rollins.

"These people will protect you. Thousands are coming to protect you. There is no threat. It's rescue. It's redemption. It's a new birth and a glory that will last for a thou—"

Andy's fist found Pedmann's face dead center. Blood splashed from his instantly crushed nose. He dropped like a suit filled with sand.

No one spoke.

Andy didn't see it happen, but Simmons told her later that he had two men in the room with him and both stepped up behind her to form a barrier between her and the Secret Service agents closing in to take her down. Everyone froze.

"Willis Pedmann, you're under arrest for the murder of Tiffany Vera Callum," Andy snapped at the man on the floor.

A gasp burst from the crowd.

The President looked down at Pedmann who lay fully prone, moaning.

"Jake."

"Yes, sir."

"Grab a plate for me. Let's go to the bunker."

95

Spokesman fixed a menacing glare at Leslie for as long as he could. She waited.

"What's the holdup?" he shouted over his shoulder.

"You better come and look at this, Al," someone shouted back.

As if to freeze her where she stood, Spokesman cast one more searing look at Leslie, then whirled around and marched across the open pavement, past the forlorn Twin Beech, past the parked pickup trucks with their snapping flags. He marched past the idling Freightliner tractor and then the length of the trailer until he joined the group standing at the open rear tailgate.

"This is not going the way they thought it would," I said.

Leslie nodded.

"Do me a favor…" she uttered out of the side of her mouth.

"On it."

I tapped the concrete underfoot with my toes and launched. A short flight with the BLASTER at low power took me out over the water on the upriver side. I angled left and flew a wide curve back toward the bridge. I gained speed, then killed the BLASTER. In silence, I glided across the bridge rail fifteen feet above the pavement. My feet passed above the heads of the armed mob.

Spokesman joined a group I took to be his leadership clustered at the back of the trailer. Someone pointed. Spokesman grabbed a handle and used a step to haul himself up onto the trailer bed.

Two men stood inside the trailer pulling on a canvas curtain that had been hung across the back roughly ten feet in. Most of the curtain had already been pulled down. They ripped the fabric to bring down the rest.

Everyone stopped and stared.

"*What the—?*" Spokesman pushed one of the men aside.

Men muttered. Men snapped at each other and broke into an agitated discussion that skidded toward argument. Arms were waved. Heads shook.

Cruising past the open tailgate, I saw why.

The trailer was empty.

Spokesman spit curses at someone I assumed to be the driver—who pleaded ignorance. He recited his orders never to open the trailer—never to look past the canvas cover.

Spokesman kicked the canvas and jumped down from the trailer. He issued a rash of new commands. Men wearing fresh panic and uncertainty on their faces listened but hesitated. He cursed them. They darted back into the column. Word spread among the troops. Men jumped into their truck and SUV cabs, and into the pickup beds that conveyed them. More weapons appeared. Engines started.

Spokesman set off for the head of the column and Leslie.

I did not like the look on his face. Nor did I think much of the way the men behind him formed up with their motley collection of arms at the ready. I heard rifle bolts pulled and cocked, and handgun slides drawn back to chamber rounds.

Ignoring the risk of being heard, I cut a quick semi-circle through the air and swung back in for a landing behind Leslie. Passing over the ranks of police multiplied my unease. Their numbers had tripled. Officers in full combat gear crouched behind the parked units holding long rifles at the ready.

A strong shot of reverse BLASTER settled me directly behind Leslie.

"Something missing?" Leslie asked innocently.

"You knew?"

"A guess based on Dumbshit's expression."

Spokesman put on his war face and marched back to where Leslie stood. He towered over her and used height to his advantage.

"I'm giving you one minute to clear the road."

Leslie tipped her head to look past him. "Did you forget something?"

"Eat shit. We're coming through. Get your sorry ass out of our way and prepare for the new America. I told you. The President is with us a—"

"Thousand percent. Yeah. I heard you."

Spokesman leaned closer. "I gotta tell you, dykes like you are not gonna enjoy what's coming."

"Hold on one second," Leslie said. She held up one hand.

"Fuck you."

"No, seriously, just one sec." She pulled out her phone. "Can you just hold up the revolution for a minute? I have to take this." She turned sideways and put the phone to her ear. "Uh-huh. Yes. Yes, that would be lovely. About how long? No, that's fine. Thank you, Carol." She ended the call.

"You don't seem to understand, bitch. It's on. The President stands with us. There ain't gonna be no FBI or DOJ or corrupt tools of the Deep State anymore. People like you are gonna be in camps when it's all said and done, and you'll be lucky if you're one of the ones that gets deported. You best hightail your lesbo ass outta town and over a border, bitch. We're coming through." He turned his head. "Lock and load!"

"No," Leslie said calmly. "You're not."

"Says who?"

"Says me. Now, I'm going to give you forty seconds to go back and tell your merry men to drop every single weapon they have in that river. After that, my colleagues from the District of Columbia and Capital Police are going to peacefully escort you into custody."

He stepped closer, looking down at her. I prepared to grab her.

"Yeah?" he asked. His breath stunk. "You and what army?"

"Um...not Army. Air Force."

They came in hot from both sides. Two pairs of F-35s in full afterburner less than forty feet above the river. The roar was excruciating. One of each pair knifed over the bridge in opposite directions less than a wingspan from each other. Airshow perfect. Nearly everyone on the bridge dropped. As the two leads peeled off, the wingmen vectored their thrust and thundered into hover mode above the water. Tens of thousands of pounds of power blew down onto the surface spreading huge circles of foam and clouds of vapor.

Damn, Colonel Reilly...

I pressed my palms over my ears to save my hearing. Thundering jet engine noise rattled my bones. Gusts of disturbed air threw me backward until I had to use nearly full BLASTER power to pull back to within reach of Leslie. Clouds of exhaust and spray from the river rose and spiraled around the two fighters. Burned kerosene smell thickened the air.

The pilots positioned their armed fighters at angles facing the head of Company W's column. Weapons hot.

Spokesman looked up at Leslie from where he hugged the pavement. I had a second to smile at the meaning of the W in Company W. The bearded militiaman's face had drained of all color. He turned his white face up at the only person left standing erect on the bridge.

Leslie pointed her weapon at him. She mouthed words lost to the astonishing power backing her.

You're under arrest.

My phone rang.

Andy.

"Hi," I said. "Where are you?"

"Where are you?"

EPILOGUE I

"Don't answer it."

Andy ignored me. She rolled across the half acre of unused king-sized bed and plucked her phone from the hotel room nightstand. I punished her for the interruption by stroking one fingernail from the nape of her neck down her smooth back all the way to—

"Right now?" she asked the spawn of Satan that dared to call us during what I liked to think of as morning cardio. Andy looked over her shoulder. "Will, turn on the TV."

"I don't know where the remote is," I claimed. Andy detected the lie and made a face. "It's Leslie…she says they found Stroud…" Andy listened and relayed bits of play-by-play. "…a property in Virginia…near Richmond… really?…really? Both of them? A retired cadaver dog? That's amazing…Are you kidding? Wow… what about—okay…Okay. Okay. Yes, absolutely. Yes. Thanks." The call ended.

Andy rolled back across the bed, but not back to where we had left off. Instead, she pushed me onto my back and crawled partway over me.

"They found Stroud," I preempted her report. "Arrested him?"

"Nope." She smiled, her lips inches from mine. "Dead."

"Where?"

"A nice neighborhood in a Richmond suburb. A place owned by—one guess—too late. Louis Blaze."

"Was Blaze there? Was that woman there?"

"She was not. Not when Stroud's body was found. But someone else was. Guess who."

"Stapleton."

She touched her nose.

"Shot. Both of them. Want to know how they found them? A former firefighter who lives in the area rescued a dog last year. The man routinely walks the dog in this neighborhood."

I tried hard to listen, but honestly, the way she was resting herself on my chest…

"And guess what kind of dog it was?"

"A retired cadaver dog. You said so."

"Oh, right. Well, the guy walks the dog past this house where no one has been living and the dog goes nuts. The firefighter knows why, so he calls the cops. The cops show up and do a wellness check on the place and they find Ray Stroud shot dead inside the house along with the Senator from the great state of Oklahoma. But that's not all."

I stole glances at the smooth lines and fascinating contours of my wife.

"Woman, do you have any idea how hard it is for me to care right now?"

She smiled. "Oh, I think I do." She wiggled and made her point. "But you're going to want to hear this. They did a full search of the house. In the basement, sitting on what looked like a throne according to the first responders, they found the dried out, mummified body of none other than Louis Blaze."

She had my attention.

"Blaze?"

"Yeah. Dead for at least a year, they think. Maybe longer."

EPILOGUE II

Andy smiled—competition for the stunning sunset that touched the hills across the blue-green bay. The warm tropical breeze wiggled strands of hair draped across one eye like a veil guarding a mystery. The breeze carried her perfume to me. The sweet scent shamed the riot of tropical flowers lining the beachside deck on which we sat. She looked at home with the Caribbean Sea kicking highlights into her hair. The light caramel color of her skin hinted at a native affiliation with this British Virgin Island of Tortola. One shoulder of her silky frock hung down around her arm, revealing smooth skin that begged for my touch.

Nineteen weeks pregnant and she only grew more beautiful.

I lifted my condensation-coated Corona. She lifted her iced fruit juice.

"Us," we said together. We tapped glasses and sipped.

"Not bad duty," I said. "When Leslie offered it, I was skeptical. But then she reprieved the whole British Spy vibe. Works for me."

"I should hope so. We had to pay for not returning that tuxedo. Highway robbery. You will be expected to wear it often."

I rotated my beer bottle on its coaster and ventured carefully into the subject hanging over us. "I wasn't convinced you would do this. Are you sure you're okay with the whole thing? With Tom?"

Andy looked down at her hands.

"It was sooner than I planned to take leave, but I really put Tom in a bad spot with the city manager. Maternity leave avoids conflict. Yes, I'm okay with it. Besides, Tom says he'll hold my position open."

"Tom doesn't have to hold your position open. Any department would be lucky to have you. The Schultz brothers have firm offers on the table in Milwaukee and Chicago."

"I'm not ready for the big city. I like Essex. You do, too. Tom will come through. Despite the bluster, the manager's office doesn't want a war with Tom Ceeves. I'll miss it, of course. You know that."

"I do."

"This is a much longer leave than I intended. I thought I'd be out scratching rust off VINs on Al Raymond's lot until my water broke." She laughed. "That would scare the raccoons."

Her laughter put lipstick on the disappointment I knew she harbored. I tried to think of something to say that wasn't blatantly solicitous.

"We get a nice vacation out of it," I mustered. "Maybe Leslie will cook up more work like this."

Andy didn't comment.

I leaned back in the surprisingly comfortable white plastic chair. The last rays of sunlight warmed us before the night sky exploded with stars. The previous night, our first on the island, we stepped onto our balcony to marvel at the display.

Andy checked her watch. She looked across the deck at the bar that connected to the hotel. Her posture changed. Off duty to on duty.

"Right on time. Here she comes."

At a distance, the resemblance to Andy flickered briefly. Then the details separated them. The woman's black hair hung long and straight. Her hips were wider, her chest larger. She wore more makeup than Andy, though most women do. Her lips were ruby red. The light monochrome dress she wore draped her curves. Fabric rippled over the upper limits of legs not quite the length of Andy's.

She walked across the wooden deck with a rhythm few men at the bar could resist watching. From the table nearest to us, she lifted a spare chair and placed it at our table. She sat down between Andy and me, facing the beach.

"Hello," she said. "I'm Carmina Blaze. What have you done with my money?"

We got it on the first try. I would never have bet on that.

Breaking into her room at Sebastian's On The Beach posed no problem, although it proved more voyeuristic than I liked. I timed my break-in to when she returned from an afternoon on the town. She entered the room, undressed, and stepped into the shower as I lifted myself over the second-floor railing of her private balcony. An unlocked sliding screen door let me in. I was hesitant to report the shower part to Andy via my earpiece connection, but decided I would be in deeper trouble if I omitted the detail.

According to Leslie's briefing, the last FBI-monitored transfer of the money landed it in an account in the British Virgin Islands, a destination known for its banking security. The American government laid no claim to the funds, but the murder of a sitting Senator—despite his treasonous involvement in an attempted overthrow of the U.S. Government—sparked interest in the moving millions. A woman using the name Katherine Silby arrived on the island of Tortola around the same time as the cash. Leslie confirmed that Silby's photo matched Senator Stapleton's guest at the White House—a woman who had disappeared from the dinner along with the Senator shortly after Andy decked Willis Pedmann.

Leslie approached us with a simple request. Her timing was perfect. Andy's request for maternity leave had just been granted. I tried not to push, but every fiber of my being wanted Andy to agree to the job. She needed something more than gardening and nesting to occupy her mind and hands. Despite a new focus on her pregnancy, I worried about the vacuum left by Andy's temporary departure from law enforcement.

Plus, I was dying of curiosity.

Leslie handled the bookings, including a reservation at the seaside hotel where Katherine Silby reserved a room. The afternoon of our second day, I invaded the woman's suite. When the shower water shut off, I signaled Andy who placed a call using a phone provided by Leslie, a phone with a preset caller ID.

I heard the woman pick up the call in the bathroom.

"Miss Silby, this is Marie Delacroy at First BVI Bank International, good afternoon...yes, fine, thank you...I'm calling to confirm a transfer request, quite routine for accounts like yours...No? There's been no request?...No, I wouldn't worry. These things happen. It's likely just a clerical error. This is why we always ask for confirmation...In any event, you needn't be concerned. All transactions require your login and password...Yes, that's why we have them. Quite...You, too."

I heard none of that, but I knew the script. At the time Andy made the call I floated next to the ceiling fan in the main sitting room, directly above a slim laptop computer plugged in at the in-room desk.

During the brief conversation, I dropped down long enough to lay my phone on the desktop. It popped into sight as soon as I released my grasp. I selected the video camera and pressed the red record button. Assured that it was recording, I picked up the phone again, made it vanish in my hands, and reset myself above the laptop.

Silby hurried into the sitting room wearing a white terrycloth robe. Her long, wet hair lay plastered against her head. She sat down at the desk and opened her laptop, powered it up, and waited for the screens to settle. When the little wheel stopped spinning, she opened the First BVI Bank International online banking app.

I rotated and stretched out my arm. I held the camera directly above her hands on the keyboard.

She entered her login and password—a hunt and peck typist.

She confirmed that nothing had been disturbed in her account.

She closed the laptop and returned to the loo, in local parlance, and her personal grooming.

I maneuvered to the sliding door and eased out over the balcony. Closing the door behind me, I heaved myself over the railing and drifted down to the beach sand, anxious to see if my video recording effort paid off.

To my surprise, it had.

"First, you answer our questions," Andy replied to Carmina Blaze.

Blaze absorbed silence for a moment. I expected fury. I prepared for it, keeping one eye on the small purse she carried. A gun might fit inside. One of those tiny ones, for certain, but no less deadly.

I did not anticipate the smile that sprouted on her bright red lips. Or the light chuckle that followed.

"May I order? I'm dying for a marguerita."

Blaze signaled for a waiter who took her order and hurried off to the bar. Andy waited.

"What do you want to know, Detective Stewart? Ask me anything."

"You're Louis Blaze's daughter," I blurted. I'd been staring.

From the moment she said her name, I felt a flood of recognition. I don't know why I hadn't seen it before, but in my defense, she looked nothing like she had when I first saw her. Or the second time.

She cast me a questioning look.

"I—I've seen—uh—surveillance photos," I stammered.

Andy performed a rapid eye roll. *Smooth.*

Blaze let her gaze settle on the distant horizon. The smile waned.

"Yes," she said.

She stared at the sea and the sky. I wondered if her mind's eye repainted the moment when she waited patiently to be wed to Darryl Spellman, and the moment that followed when her wedding gown wore his blood and brains.

"You've changed."

She ignored me. I remained on alert. She seemed far too comfortable with having just lost millions of dollars. She turned to Andy.

"I'll tell you anything you want to know."

"Did you kill Ray Stroud?" Andy asked.

"Yes." She looked Andy in the eye. "Ray Stroud raped an innocent child and with the help of Pedmann's off-book investigators, burned her alive. They made a video of it. Ray thought it would galvanize Company W. Burning the girl who burned the flags, he said, was payback. Everybody loves payback. Yes. I killed him. If he were sitting in your chair, Detective Stewart, I would pick up a fork and drive it into his skull. As it happened, I put him down like the sick animal he was."

"After you used him," Andy said.

"Which only made killing him sweeter."

"And Senator Stapleton?"

She shrugged. "Equally guilty. If not of rape and murder, then guilty of insurrection, corruption, treason—you name it. I kept a significant cache of documents, videos, and photographs detailing the Senator's involvement. Copies have now been released to interested parties. His conviction will be postmortem, but the Senator would have certainly faced arrest and indictment. I saved the taxpayers millions in court costs and incarceration expenses—all for a twenty-nine-cent bullet. I would do the same for Willis Pedmann if I could, but he now belongs to the Department of Justice. Ironic, considering his disdain for the federal government. Do you intend to arrest me? Or have the authorities here arrest me?"

"Aren't you just as guilty?"

Her drink came. She thanked the server with a warm smile. I noticed that in smiling one side of her lips did not match the other.

She lifted her glass in a toast that Andy and I did not join. That distant look flashed again. She sipped, then quickly touched her fingers to the corner of her mouth.

"They make an amazing marguerita here, but you must call your tequila. Don Julio Añejo. I have a standing order." She heaved a long sigh. "Yes. Guilty as charged. I organized the whole thing. Ray would tell you it was his idea. Pedmann would say the plan was his, but men—really—they are so easily led by the—well, you know. I guided their hand. Would you like to know why?"

"I think your politics have been done to death on social media," I said. "I'm not up for another anti-government rant."

She laughed. "Oh, you're cute. I'm so glad those boneheads didn't kill you two last winter. That was a terrible, terrible idea."

"Why, then?" Andy asked.

"Why? Because the plan Ray Stroud and Willis Pedmann and Drew Stapleton thought they hatched to save White America by sending a small army of playtime soldiers to the Arlington Bridge on July 29th—that was the dumbest idea in the history of dumb ideas."

"You just said you organized it."

"Of course I did. Down to the last detail. My success was its massive failure. I worked a very long time under my father's name to guide the entire Company W organization to a titanic disaster."

"You meant for it to fail?" I asked.

"Certainly. What moron believes that point zero zero zero three percent of the population of this country should be ordained to dismantle the federal government, move it to Texas, and declare the president a supreme leader? Take that theory out of the inbred bubble where it festers and shine daylight on it, and it's laughable."

"Did you kill your father, too?"

"Over and over in my dreams, and then…" She closed her eyes. A look of ecstasy flooded her expression. "It was wonderful. It was liberating. Yes. I killed the great Louis Blaze. Yes. I placed him on his own throne in a dingy basement where he could rule over rats and roaches. And yes, for more than a year I pretended to be his voice. I delivered his messages. I stirred up his troops and true believers. I energized his cult. I sent tweets and posts for useful idiots to repost and fringe media sites to quote without question. I galvanized Company W and steered it to the revolution—or civil war, take your pick—they have been lusting for."

Blaze sipped her drink, touched her lip again, and leaned into her story.

"Detective, I hated my father since I was old enough to feel hate. I hated his lies. I hated his gross stories. I hated his racism and the pride he took in his stupidity. Him and every one of his followers. The militias. The weekend warriors and survivalists who make plans to reshape civilization after a good racial cleansing yet who can't hold down a job at Walmart. I hated the Ruby Ridge and Waco religion he preached. The anti-government oh-my-God-give-it-a-rest bullshit. My problem growing up was that I could read and think and form connective, critical thoughts. I *knew* his religion was raging nonsense. The cult of grievance he and those fools worshiped as a placebo for their ignorance and entitlement—it made me sick."

"You were going to marry Spellman," I challenged her.

"I don't think you would understand, but Darryl Spellman—hoo-boy, he had a—well, let's just say that all the girls that got a ride on that horse got the ride of their life. And for the girl I once was, becoming his bride made me *more* than every one of them for the first time. Or so I thought. I know now it was a delusional fantasy, but I genuinely wanted his child in me. I—well, I had my reasons. Silly me. All I got was his brains in my mouth. Gross."

"What happened in Louisiana?" Andy asked. "Your own people almost killed you on that boat."

She nodded.

"Indeed. That was Ray. He beat me to within an inch of my life. Here." She pointed at her jaw. "And here. And here." She pointed at her face, her cheekbones, her eyebrows. "All the right places where a good plastic surgeon can make a new person from broken parts. The doctor who did the work consulted with me beforehand. He told me what to break, how to be beaten. Ray did the work."

"What about the men who were killed?" Andy asked.

"They rejected the concept of moving the President to Texas and making him king. They wanted bombings. The killing of innocents. They pushed for a new style of mass shootings—military raid style without the suicide component at the end. School shootings, Detective, that would draw police into kill zones. *And they called my plan idiotic.* You can see why they had to be removed—for which I feel no shame. But that's not what you're asking, is it?"

Andy gave her silence to fill. She sighed and lowered her eyes.

"I swear," she said, "I didn't know about the undercover FBI agent. Truly. *I did not know.* I mean—why would I if he was any good at his trade? When Ray told me later, after the surgeries, after the healing, I was devastated. I almost gave up on everything and turned us both in."

"We're supposed to believe you had yourself beaten?" Andy gave her no slack.

"It really doesn't matter what you believe. I'm the one who paid the price." She pointed at the corner of her mouth she had touched earlier. "Here. I lost nerve function. I can't feel anything on this side. Most of my teeth and part of my jaw are prosthetic. I have constant pain. But it was worth it. I got a new face. New tits. New nose and cheekbones. I was one homely horseface before. That's what Darryl called me. He said he was willing to do me, you know, for the sake of the political marriage, but he told me he would not regularly screw such a homely horseface. I wish he could see me now. And, of course, I'm glad he can't."

"And this was all part of a scheme to destroy Company W?" Andy asked. "That's a lot to swallow."

"I think the results speak for themselves." Blaze pressed on, challenged by Andy's skepticism. "This was my childhood dream, Detective. Little girls dream of weddings and husbands and children. I dreamed of seeing everyone in my father's twisted orbit killed or in prison. I dreamed of getting them to do something stupid that would get them arrested or shot, but in my wildest imagination I never thought I would get eight hundred and sixty-eight of those dumbshits arrested for criminal armed insurrection in one stroke. One glorious stroke. Then that wonderful crazy Mrs. Palmer drove my father and his kind into hiding, and he made me his voice, his courier—and I realized I no longer needed Louis Blaze alive. *I became Louis Blaze.* My father's voice and this nice new body of mine gave me anything I wanted. An introduction to a lecherous U.S. Senator. A connection to a corrupt attorney general. I devised the GoFundMe scheme to launder money from Pedmann's rich donor friends and buy arms from Ruiz—the very criminal he's supposed to be investigating. Of course, I never purchased the weapons—and those boxes on the airplane were full of bricks. All I had to do was drop the Ruiz name and everyone believed me—or Louis Blaze—when he said the thirty million went for heavy weapons and high explosives. Stapleton and Pedmann licked up my every Louis Blaze word. I played Pedmann's obsession for Texas as the white capitol of America and his misogyny and his lawsuits. I played Stapleton's craving for power. Do you know that he sincerely thought the President would do it? That the President's ego could not resist a chance to destroy Congress, move the government to Austin, and be crowned king? Pure projection, of course. I think Drew planned to assassinate the President and take his 'rightful' place once the states rallied around Texas."

"That is the dumbest thing I ever heard," I said.

"*Precisely!*" Blaze clasped my arm. "It's so stupid it was guaranteed to fail—and so cloaked in lies and cultish belief that they *believed.* You need to understand that their extremist propaganda machine has been in high gear in this country for decades—on the radio, on television, exploding on the internet—unwittingly building a foundation for everything I needed to trigger a crowning moment of monumental idiocy."

I waved my empty bottle at the waiter. He set off for a fresh one.

Carmina Blaze looked from Andy to me and back again.

"How far along are you?" she asked as if the conversation had been about ice cream socials and soccer schedules.

"Nineteen weeks," Andy answered tersely, reluctant to share a private part of our lives with this woman.

Blaze sensed the barrier and did not press. Sadness flickered in her eyes.

"I can't have kids. How's that for irony? I was all set to show up all the girls by letting Darryl Spellman pump me full of his seed, and it turns out my plumbing is bad—even before the beating. Go figure."

"I'm sorry," Andy said. I knew she meant it regardless of any other feelings she had about the woman.

Blaze shrugged. "It gave me time to pursue my hobby."

My fresh drink came.

Andy drilled a hard look into Blaze.

"Your hobby? *They burned that girl alive.*"

Blaze said nothing for a moment. When she broke her silence, she spoke barely above a whisper.

"I didn't know that Ray enlisted Pedmann and his off-the-books investigators to go after that girl in Colorado and then Tiffany Vera Callum. Ray never told me—maybe because he knew I never, *never* would have let that happen. That girl. Those two girls…" She swallowed. *"I'm so sorry for that part of it. For those families.* I swore I would make him pay. Her name. Tiffany Vera Callum. That was the last thing I said to him. Her name. Right before I shot him."

Blaze drew a cleansing breath and chased it with tequila.

Andy said coldly, "I don't believe you. If Pedmann was involved, why did his office try to whitewash Company W's ownership of the murder? Why did they double down on the occult cover story when they tried to kill Mel Dalton?"

"I don't know who that is," Blaze said.

"Again, I don't believe you," Andy replied.

"Detective," Blaze said. "I have nothing to hide. Ray had his own agenda. What I *can* tell you is that Pedmann tried to whitewash the girl's murder because he was scared and I was furious. Willis Pedmann never anticipated the national media attention that exploded over killing that girl. The revulsion it generated. Here we were on the brink of rallying Company W patriots to save America—and suddenly America was watching unspeakable horror on *The Today Show* after Ray and Pedmann's hired help burned a girl at the stake and tried to make a propaganda movie out of it. Pedmann desperately tried to shift the narrative because, in his words, this was not good optics."

"Did you kill Thing One and Thing Two?" I asked. She blinked at me. "Those two off-book investigators."

"Oh. No. Ray again. Probably on Pedmann's orders. Cleanup."

"I thought Stroud was your puppet," Andy said.

"Ray swore his loyalty to my father and me when it was convenient. His only real loyalty was to himself. It's classic, really. One of the great risks of creating a monster is that the monster might develop a life of its own. I set Company W on a path to destruction. To do that, I created the monster. There was always a chance it might slip the leash."

"The airplane," I said. "What was the point?"

"Panic. Diversion. I convinced Pedmann that Louis Blaze had loyalists on the President's security detail. I told Pedmann that the airplane would trigger the detail to rush the President directly into the hands of the true patriots."

"That's ridiculous," Andy said.

Blaze raised her eyebrows. "You're catching on. I also said it would be the perfect moment for Pedmann to reveal himself. And the fool did exactly that. There were no explosives on the plane. The Air Force was supposed to bring it down. I never guessed someone would get on the plane and mess that up."

"Sheeesh," I muttered. "I repeat. This is the dumbest plot ever."

"Built on a foundation of ignorance and delusion," Andy added with just a hint of admiration.

"As I said, you're catching on." Blaze looked back and forth between us. "So, here we are. Are you turning me in to the authorities?"

I left the question in Andy's hands. She took a moment to examine the way the surface of the bay had changed color in the tropical twilight. She sighed.

"That's not our call. I suppose they could try to pin all the insurrection planning on you, but you can make a case that you did it to destroy a known terrorist organization. You have spectacularly discredited Company W and all its affiliated extremist groups. I assume you kept a record of your intent. A diary? A journal?"

"In detail."

"That throws intent into question. I don't know if a grand jury would indict."

Blaze let the shadow of a smile confirm Andy's uncertainty.

Andy continued. "Thanks to you the media is shining a harsh light on the lies politicians have been telling to stoke up support from these groups. There's a federal investigation into two of the less reputable online news networks for their roles in spreading disinformation. The FCC is taking a new look at its policies on talk radio. And our FBI contact said a huge cache of records, documents, lists, and other evidence got dumped on MSNBC. They're sharing it with DOJ. I presume that was you."

"My cache. I also cleaned out my father's files. Some upstanding citizens have a bit of explaining to do."

Andy absently rotated her iced juice on its coaster. She said, "The government might try to prosecute, but I think if the whole story is told, the people of the United States will end up giving you a medal and sending you on the talk show circuit. There's probably a book deal in it for you."

Blaze carefully eyed Andy. "That does not sit well with you, does it, Detective?"

"I don't like people who violate the law. Like murder. Or who are complicit in the deaths of innocents."

"Detective, I will not resist. I will abide by whatever decision is made. My work is done. It no longer matters what happens to me. But let me ask you a question. Is it better that I alone live with what I've done? Or will you deliver that burden to the collective consciousness of a country that is reeling from betrayal and armed insurrection? A country that must confront its tolerance for mass stupidity, mass delusion? Or worse, will you allow people like my father to build a fresh following based on new lies? Lies and conspiracy theories that spring from a prosecution—they would say persecution—of me? Because know this: They will try to make me a martyr." She leaned toward Andy. I kept an eye on her hands. "I won't be the hero of a new delusion. I will take my own life first."

"Which would only feed the delusion," Andy replied without flinching. "As I said, that's not our call."

"Yes, well, in that you are correct." Blaze sat back and nodded—it was more of a polite bow—at Andy. "Fate has a way of deciding things over which we have no control. May I ask about the money?"

"We transferred the funds to a foundation in the United States," Andy said. "From there, the twenty-five million dollars has already been donated to the American Cancer Society. It seems only fitting, given the GoFundMe legends."

Blaze nodded. She seemed surprisingly placid.

Andy said. "The original sum was thirty-one million. We only found twenty-five million in your account. Can I assume you have salted away the balance?"

"No. Six million was payment to Alejandro Ruiz for his part in the charade. Six million is a lot for an empty truck and three crates full of bricks, but that also bought the story that went with it."

She pushed her chair back and picked up her drink. The last glow of the sunset warmed her face. She lifted her head and reflected serenity back at the Caribbean sky. Or resignation.

"My mother named me Sally," she said distantly. "After she was gone, when I was old enough to understand my life, I changed it. Do you know the poem 'O Fortuna' from *Carmina Burana*? It's more famous in Carl Orff's musical form."

We shook our heads.

"*Since Fate strikes down the strong man, everyone weep with me.*" She raised her glass to us. "Goodbye, Stewarts."

We watched her weave a body she built herself between tables as men at the bar eyed her and radiated invitations. She did not join them.

I picked up my beer and drank to close her toast.

"She doesn't seem to protest about the money, Dee."

Andy said nothing for a moment. I searched my wife's gold-flecked green eyes for anger or resentment or a flicker of hate. I saw none.

"I don't think she cares."

EPILOGUE III

Two weeks before the last time Andy and I ever saw Carmina Blaze—three days after what became known as The Insurrection on the Arlington Bridge —Andy and I flew via commercial airline back to Wisconsin. From Austin Straubel International in Green Bay, we got a ride to Essex from Andy's sister Lydia. The next day, Pidge and Arun retrieved the Navajo and flew it from Danville, Virginia to Essex County Airport. They arrived late in the morning. I waited beneath the Foundation's open hangar door.

Pidge parked the airplane on the ramp where Andy, so long ago, had leaped from her Essex PD SUV. A few minutes after the props stopped, Pidge hopped down the airstair. It was the first time I'd seen her since I dropped her behind the police line near the Lincoln Memorial where Arun, who had been abandoned outside the West Wing of The White House that day, rode an Uber to her rescue. From there, Pidge and Arun disappeared to a D.C. hotel, stayed under the radar on orders from Leslie, then took a bus to Danville. To the media and public at large, the pilot of the crashed Twin Beech was never identified. It was fame Pidge gratefully shunned.

Andy and I spent two days at a different hotel, equally sequestered. Or I should say I was stuck in a hotel watching cable news report most of the details of the insurrection incorrectly. Andy spent long days at FBI head-quarters and at the Department of Justice answering questions.

On the third day, we gladly put D.C. in our jet exhaust wake and flew home.

"Thanks for retrieving my airplane," I told Pidge.

"You need to take better care of your things." She seemed lighter. Her gold blonde hair color had been restored, but that wasn't it. She no longer carried the weight that dropped on her in our kitchen the night Leslie broke the news about Tiffany Vera Callum.

For a jarring instant, as sunlight infused her natural hair color with highlights, I saw the girl in the photo that had been lovingly displayed in the Callum home. Shining eyes. A bright smile. The picture of possibility. This was all me, of course. Looking for a way to see a light that had been extinguished in one life illuminated in another.

"The Foundation's airplane," Arun said as he climbed out of the Navajo's cabin after Pidge. "It's the Foundation's airplane."

Pidge and Arun traded a gentle kiss. The swelling on her face had gone down, but she still carried a righteous purple and yellow bruise. The contusion took nothing away from the way she beamed at Arun. And in her light, he seemed different. I wanted to say older, but that wasn't precise. Stronger, perhaps.

"Later." She pecked him a second time and pranced away in the direction of the Essex County Air Service office.

"Hold up," I called after her.

"Can't! Earl's back and Rosemary II says he's eating babies and burning villages because he heard I was gone. She's got me booked out in twenty minutes and she thinks she can get me in the air without him seeing me."

"Hang on," I tried again. "You never told me how those asshats got hold of you in Danville."

"Gotta go!" She waved merrily.

"C'mon! Don't leave me hanging like this."

She flipped me the finger. Arun wandered over and stood at my side. We watched her until she disappeared into the Essex County Air Service office.

"Did she tell you?" I asked.

"Fuck no."

DIVISIBLE MAN – TWELFTH KNIGHT

September 9, 2023 to May 4, 2024

ABOUT THE AUTHOR

HOWARD SEABORNE is the author of the DIVISIBLE MAN[TM] series as well as a collection of short stories featuring the same cast of characters. He began writing novels in spiral notebooks at age ten. He began flying airplanes at age sixteen. He is a former flight instructor and commercial charter pilot licensed in single- and multi-engine airplanes as well as helicopters. Today he flies a twin-engine Beechcraft Baron, a single-engine Beechcraft Bonanza, and a Rotorway A-600 Talon experimental helicopter he built from a kit in his garage. He lives with his wife and writes and flies during all four seasons in Wisconsin, never far from Essex County Airport.

Visit www.HowardSeaborne.com to join the Email List
and get a FREE DOWNLOAD.

DIVISIBLE MAN

The media calls it a "miracle" when air charter pilot Will Stewart survives an aircraft in-flight breakup, but Will's miracle pales beside the stunning aftereffect of the crash. Barely on his feet again, Will and his police sergeant wife Andy race to rescue an innocent child from a heinous abduction. *Will's new ability might make the difference between life and death…if it doesn't kill him first.*

Available in print, digital, and audio.

Search: "DIVISIBLE MAN Howard Seaborne"

Join our Reader Email list at **HowardSeaborne.com**

DIVISIBLE MAN - THE SIXTH PAWN

A *BookLife from Publishers Weekly* Editor's Pick.

"A book of outstanding quality."

When the Essex County "Wedding of the Century" erupts in gunfire, Will and Andy Stewart confront a criminal element no one could have foreseen. Will tests the extraordinary after-effect of surviving a devastating airplane crash while Andy works a case obstructed by powerful people wielding the sinister influence of unlimited money in politics.

Available in print, digital, and audio.

Search: "DIVISIBLE MAN Howard Seaborne"

Join our Reader Email list at **HowardSeaborne.com**

DIVISIBLE MAN - THE SECOND GHOST

Tormented by a cyber stalker, Lane Franklin's best friend turns to suicide. Lane's frantic call launches Will and Andy Stewart on a desperate rescue mission. When it all goes bad, Will must adapt his extraordinary ability to survive the dangerous high steel and glass of Chicago as Andy and Pidge confront the edge of disaster. **Includes the short story, "Angel Flight," a bridge to the fourth DIVISIBLE MAN novel that follows.**

Available in print, digital, and audio.

Search: "DIVISIBLE MAN Howard Seaborne"

Join our Reader Email list at **HowardSeaborne.com**

DIVISIBLE MAN - THE SEVENTH STAR

A horrifying message turns a holiday gathering tragic. An unsolved murder hangs a death threat over Detective Andy Stewart's head. And internet-fueled hatred targets Will and Andy's friend Lane. Will and Andy struggle to keep the ones they love safe, while hunting a murderer who is supposed to be dead. As the tension tightens, Will confronts a troubling revelation about the extraordinary after-effect of his midair collision.

Available in print, digital, and audio.

Search: "DIVISIBLE MAN Howard Seaborne"

Join our Reader Email list at **HowardSeaborne.com**

DIVISIBLE MAN - TEN MAN CREW

An unexpected visit from the FBI threatens Will Stewart's secret and sends Detective
Andy Stewart on a collision course with her darkest impulses. A twisted road reveals
how a long-buried Cold War secret has been weaponized. And Pidge shows a daring
side of herself that could cost her dearly.

Available in print and digital.

Search: "DIVISIBLE MAN Howard Seaborne"

Join our Reader Email list at **HowardSeaborne.com**

DIVISIBLE MAN - THE THIRD LIE

Caught up in a series of hideous crimes that generate national headlines, Will faces the critical question of whether to reveal himself or allow innocent lives to be lost. The stakes go higher than ever when Andy uncovers the real reason behind a celebrity athlete's assault on an underaged girl. And Will discovers that the limits of his ability can lead to disaster.

A Kirkus Starred Review.

A Kirkus Star is awarded to "books of exceptional merit."

Available in print and digital.

Search: "DIVISIBLE MAN Howard Seaborne"

Join our Reader Email list at **HowardSeaborne.com**

DIVISIBLE MAN - THREE NINES FINE

A mysterious mission request from Earl Jackson sends Will into the sphere of a troubled celebrity. A meeting with the Deputy Director of the FBI that goes terribly wrong. Will and Andy find themselves on the run from Federal authorities, infiltrating a notorious cartel, and racing to prevent what might prove to be the crime of the century.

Available in print and digital.

Search: "DIVISIBLE MAN Howard Seaborne"

Join our Reader Email list at **HowardSeaborne.com**

DIVISIBLE MAN - EIGHT BALL

Will's encounter with a deadly sniper on a serial killing rampage sends him deeper into the FBI's hands with costly consequences for Andy. And when billionaire Spiro Lewko makes an appearance, Will and Andy's future takes a dark turn. The stakes could not be higher when the sniper's ultimate target is revealed.

Available in print and digital.

Search: "DIVISIBLE MAN Howard Seaborne"

Join our Reader Email list at **HowardSeaborne.com**

ENGINE OUT AND OTHER SHORT FLIGHTS

Things just have a way of happening around Will and Andy Stewart. In this collection of twelve tales from Essex County, boy meets girl, a mercy flight goes badly wrong, and Will crashes and burns when he tries dating again. Engines fail. Shots are fired. A rash of the unexpected breaks loose—from bank jobs to zombies.

Available in print and digital.

Search: "DIVISIBLE MAN Howard Seaborne"

Join our Reader Email list at **HowardSeaborne.com**

DIVISIBLE MAN - NINE LIVES LOST

A simple request from Earl Jackson sends Will on a cross-country chase. A threat to Andy's career takes a deadly turn. And a mystery literally lands at Will and Andy's mailbox. Before it all ends, Will confronts a deep, dark place he never imagined.

Available in print and digital.

Search: "DIVISIBLE MAN Howard Seaborne"

Join our Reader Email list at **HowardSeaborne.com**

DIVISIBLE MAN - TEN KEYS WEST

A terrifying incident lands Detective Andy Stewart in the grip of an indelible nightmare. A scheme to raise a fortune reveals that no life has value when billions are at stake. In this nail-biting adventure Will and Andy must enlist unlikely help to keep Will's secret from being exposed to the world.

Available in print and digital.

Search: "DIVISIBLE MAN Howard Seaborne"

Join our Reader Email list at **HowardSeaborne.com**

DIVISIBLE MAN - THE ELEVENTH HOURGLASS

A *BookLife from Publishers Weekly* Editor's Pick.

"A book of outstanding quality."

Will joins Pidge and Earl on a rescue mission that encounters a scene of unimaginable violence. The obvious explanation is impossible but grows equally impossible to ignore as the body count rises. Tensions spiral as billionaire Spiro Lewko, old secrets, and criminal lies push will to a breaking point.

Available in print and digital.

Search: "DIVISIBLE MAN Howard Seaborne"

Join our Reader Email list at **HowardSeaborne.com**